Beyond These Voices by Mary Elizabeth Braddon

Mary Elizabeth Braddon was born in London on 4th October 1835.

Braddon suffered early family trauma at age five, when her mother, Fanny, separated from her father, Henry, in 1840. When she was aged ten her brother Edward left England for India and later Australia.

However, after being befriended by Clara and Adelaide Biddle she was much taken by acting. For three years she took minor acting roles, which supported both her and her mother, However, her interest in acting began to wane as she began to write. It was to be her true vocation.

In 1860, Mary met John Maxwell, a publisher of periodicals. By the next year they were living together. The situation and the view from polite society was complicated by the fact that Maxwell was already married with five children, and his wife was under care in an Irish asylum. Until 1874 Mary was to act as stepmother to his children as well as to the six offspring their own relationship produced.

Braddon, with a large and growing family, still found time to produce a long and prolific writing career. Her most famous book was a sensational novel published in 1862, 'Lady Audley's Secret'. It won her both recognition and best-seller status.

Her works in the supernatural genre were equally prolific and brought new menace to the form. Her pact with the devil story 'Gerald, or the World, the Flesh and the Devil' (1891), and the ghost stories 'The Cold Embrace', 'The Face in the Glass' and 'At Chrighton Abbey' are regarded as classics.

In 1866 she founded the Belgravia magazine. This presented readers with serialised sensation novels, poems, travel narratives and biographies, as well as essays on fashion, history and science. The magazine was accompanied by lavish illustrations and offered readers an excellent source of literature at an affordable cost. She was also the editor of The Temple Bar magazine.

Maxwell's wife died in 1874 and the couple who had been together for so long were at last able to wed.

Mary Elizabeth Brandon died on 4th February 1915 in Richmond and is buried in Richmond Cemetery.

After her death her short story masterpieces would be regularly anthologised. But for the rest of her canon her reputation then went into decline. In the past decade her reputation and talent is once more being given the attention it so rightly deserves.

Index of Contents

CHAPTER I

Lady Felicia Disbrowe was supposed to condescend when she married Captain Cunningham of the first Life—since, although his people lived on their own land, and were handsomely recorded in Burke, there was no record of them before the Conquest, nor even on the muster-roll of those who fought and died for the Angevin Kings. Captain Cunningham was handsome and fashionable, but not rich; and when he had the bad luck to get himself killed in an Egyptian campaign, he left his widow with an only daughter seven years old, her pension, and a settlement that brought her about six hundred a year, half of which came from the Disbrowes, while the other half was the rental of three or four small farms in Somersetshire. It will be seen therefore that for a person who considered herself essentially grande dame, and to whom all degrading economies must be impossible, Lady Felicia's position was not enviable.

As the seven-year-old orphan grew in grace and beauty to sweet seventeen, Lady Felicia began to consider her daughter her chief asset. So lovely a creature must command the admiration of the richest bachelors in the marriage-market. She would have her choice of opulent lovers. There would be no cruel necessity for forcing a marriage with vulgar wealth or drivelling age. She would have her adorers among the best, the fortunate, the well-bred, the young and handsome. Nor was Lady Felicia mistaken in her forecast. When Cara came out under the auspices of her aunt, Lady Okehampton, she made a success that realised her mother's fondest dreams. Youth, rank, and wealth were at her feet. There was no question of riches raked out of the gutter. She had but to say the sweet little monosyllable "yes," and one of the best born and best-looking men in London, and town and country houses, yacht and opera box, would be hers; and her mother would cease to be "poor Lady Felicia."

Unhappily, before Lord Walford had time to offer her all these advantages, Cara had fallen in love with somebody else, and that somebody was no other than Lancelot Davis, the poet, just then the petted darling of dowagers, and of young married women whose daughters were in the nursery, and who had therefore no fear of his fascinating personality. Unfortunately for Lady Felicia, her head was too high in the air for her to take note of the literary stars who shone at luncheon parties, and even when her daughter praised the young poet, and tried to interest her mother in his latest book, Lady Felicia took no alarm. It was only in the beginning of their acquaintance that Cara talked of the poet to her unresponsive mother. By the time she had known him twenty days of that heavenly June, he was far too sacred to be talked about to an unsympathetic listener. It was only to her dearest and only bosom friend, who was also in love with the adorable Lancelot, that Cara liked to talk of him, and to her she discoursed romantic nonsense that would have covered reams of foolscap, had it been written.

"Lancelot!" she said in low, thrilling tones. "Even his name is a poem."

Everything about him was a poem for Cara. His boots, his tie, his cane, and especially his hair, which he took a poet's privilege of wearing longer than fashion justified.

Though educated at the Stationers' School, and unacquainted with either 'Varsity, nobody ever said of Mr. Davis that he was "not a gentleman." That scathing, irrevocable sentence, with the cruel emphasis upon the negative, had not been pronounced upon the man who wrote "The New Ariadne," a work of genius which scared the lowly-minded country vicar, his father, and set his pious mother praying, with trembling and tears, that the eyes of her beloved son might be opened, and that he might repent of using the talents God had given him in the service of Satan.

Lancelot Davis had made up for the lack of 'Varsity training by strenuous self-culture. He was passionate, exalted, transcendental, more Swinburne than Swinburne, steeped in Dante and Victor Hugo, stuffed almost to choking with Musset, Baudelaire, and Verlaine; he was young, handsome, or rather beautiful, too beautiful for a man—Paris, Leander, the Sun God—anything you like; and, at the time of his wooing, his pockets were full of the proceeds of a book that had made a sensation—and he was the rage.

Were not these things enough to fire the imagination and win the heart of a girl of eighteen, half-educated, undisciplined, the daughter of a shallow-brained mother, who had never taken the trouble to understand her, or taken account of the romantic yearnings in the mind of eighteen? If Lady Felicia had cultivated her daughter's mind half as strenuously as she had cultivated her person, the girl would have not been so ready to fall in love with her poet. But the girl's home life had been an arid waste, and the mother's conversation had been one long repining against the Fate that had made her "poor Lady Felicia," and had deprived her of all the things that are needed to make life worth living.

Lancelot Davis opened the gates of an enchanted land in which money counted for nothing, where there was no animosity against the ultra rich, no perpetual talk of debts and difficulties, no moaning over the hardship of doing without things that luckier people could enjoy in abundance. He let her into that lovely world where the imagination rules supreme. He introduced her to other poets, the gods of that enchanted land—Browning, Tennyson, Shelley, Byron. She bowed down before these mighty spirits, but thought Lancelot Davis greater than the greatest of them.

There was nothing mean or underhand about her poet's conduct. He lost no time in offering himself to Lady Felicia. He was not a pauper; he was not ill born; and he was thought to have a brilliant future before him. His suit was supported by some of "poor Felicia's" oldest and best friends; but Lady Felicia received his addresses with coldness and scarcely concealed contempt; and she told her daughter that while she had committed an unpardonable sin when she refused Lord Walford, were she to insist upon marrying Mr. Davis, it would be a heart-broken mother's duty to cast her off for ever.

"I never could forgive you, Cara," she said, and she never did.

Cara walked out of the Weymouth Street lodgings early one morning, before Lady Felicia had rung for her meagre breakfast of chocolate and toast. She carried her dressing-bag to the corner of the street, where Davis was waiting in a hansom. Her trunk, with all that was most needful of her wardrobe, had been despatched to the station over night, labelled for the Continental Express. There was plenty of time to be married before the registrar, and to be at Victoria, ready for the train that was to carry them on the first stage of that wonderful journey which begins in the smoke and grime of South London and ends under the Italian sky.

They went from the registrar's office straight to the Lake of Como, and lived between Bellagio and Venice for four years, years of ineffable bliss, at the end of which sweet summer-time of love and life—for it seemed never winter—the girl-wife died, leaving her young husband heart-broken, with an only child, a daughter three years old, an incarnation of romantic love and romantic beauty.

When he carried off Lady Felicia's daughter, the poet was at the top of his vogue, and his vogue lasted for just those four years of supreme happiness.

Nothing that he wrote after his wife's death had the old passion or the old music. His genius died with his wife. Heart-broken and disappointed, he became a consumptive, and died of an open-air cure, leaving piteous letters to Lady Felicia and his wife's other relations, imploring them to take care of his daughter. She would have the copyright of his five volumes of verse, and two successful tragedies, for her portion; so she was not altogether without means.

Lady Felicia's heart was not all stone; there was a vulnerable spot upon which the serpent's tooth had fastened. Obstinate, proud, and selfish, she had never faltered in her unforgiving attitude towards the runaway daughter; but when there came the sudden news of Cara's death, a blow for which the Spartan mother was utterly unprepared, an agony of remorse disturbed the self-satisfied calm of a mind which thought itself justified in resenting injury.

Perhaps she had pictured to herself a day upon which Cara would have come back to her and sued for pardon, and she would have softened, and taken the prodigal daughter to her heart. One of the girl's worst crimes had been that she had not knelt and wept and entreated to be forgiven, before she took that desperate, immodest, and even vulgar, step of a marriage before the registrar. She had shown herself heartless as a daughter, and how could she expect softness in her mother? But she was dead. She had passed beyond the possibility of pardon or love. That vague dream of reconciliation could never be realised. If there had been anything wrong in Lady Felicia's behaviour as a parent, that wrong could never be righted. Never more would she see the lovely face that was to have brought prosperity and happiness for them both; never more would she hear the sweet voice which the fashionable Italian master had trained to such perfection. The French ballads, and Jensen's setting of Heine, came out of the caverns of memory as Lady Felicia sat, poor and lonely, in a lodging-house drawing-room, on the borderland of West-End London, the last "possible" street, before W. became N.W.

"Ninon, que fait tu de la vie?" Memory brought back every tone of the fresh young voice. Lady Felicia could hardly believe that there was no one singing, that the room was empty of human life, except her own fatigued existence.

That last year of remorseful memories softened her, and she accepted the charge that Lancelot Davis left her. He lived just long enough in his bleak hospital on a Gloucestershire hill-top to read his mother-in-law's letter:

"Send the little girl to me. I will be kinder to her than I was to her mother."

Society, and especially Cara's other relations, said that poor Felicia had been quite admirable in taking the sole charge of the orphan. There was no attempt to foist the little girl upon aunts and cousins; and, considering poor Felicia's state of genteel pauperism, always in lodgings, her behaviour was worthy of all praise.

The grandchild brought back the memory of the daughter's childhood, and Lady Felicia almost felt as if she was again a young widow, full of care for her only child. So far as her narrow means permitted she made the little girl happy, and she found her own dreary existence brightened by that young life.

That calm and monotonous existence with Grannie was not the kind of life that childhood yearns for, and there were long stretches of time in which little Veronica had only her picture-books and fancy needlework to amuse her—after the cheap morning governess had departed, and the day's tasks were done. At least Grannie did not torture the orphan with over-education. A little French, a little easy music, a little English history, occupied the morning hours, and then Vera was free to read what books she liked to choose out of Grannie's blameless and meagre library. Lady Felicia's nomadic life had not allowed the accumulation of literature, but the few books she carried about with her were of the best, Scott, Thackeray, Dickens, Byron. Her trunks had room only for the Immortals, and as soon as Vera could read them, and long before she could understand them, those dear books were familiar to her. The pictures helped her to understand, and she was never tired of looking at them. Sometimes Grannie would read Shakespeare to her, the ghostly scenes in Hamlet, which thrilled her, or passages and scenes from the Tempest, or Midsummer Night's Dream, which Vera thought divine. She had no playfellows, and hardly knew how to play; but in her lonely life imagination filled the space that the frolics and gambols of exuberant spirits occupy in the life of the normal child. Those few great novels which she read over and over again peopled her world, a world of beautiful images that she had all to herself, and of which her fancy never wearied—Amy Robsart and Leicester, the Scottish Knight, the generous Saracen, the heroic dog, Paul Dombey and his devoted sister, David Copperfield and his child-wife. These were the companions of the long silent afternoons, when Grannie was taking her siesta in seclusion upstairs, and when Vera had the drawing-room to herself. No visitors intruded on those long afternoons; for Lady Felicia's card gave the world to know that the first and fifteenth of May, June, and July, were the only days on which she was accessible to the friends and acquaintances who had not utterly forgotten "poor Felicia's" existence.

It was a life of monotony against which an older girl would have revolted; but childhood is submissive, and accepts its environment as something inevitable, so Vera made no protest against Fate. But there was one golden season in her young life, one heavenly summer holiday in the West Country, when her aunt, Lady Okehampton, happening to call upon Lady Felicia, was moved to compassion at sight of the little girl, pale and languid, as she sat in the corner of the unlovely drawing-room, with an open book on her lap.

"This hot weather makes London odious," said Lady Okehampton. "We are all leaving much earlier than usual. I suppose you and the little girl are soon going into the country?"

"No, I shan't move till the end of October, when we go to Brighton, as usual. I have had invitations to nice places, the Helstons, the Heronmoors; but I can't take that child, and I can't leave her."

"Poor little girl. Does she never see gardens and meadows? Brighton is only London with a little less smoke, and a strip of grey water that one takes on trust for the sea. Wouldn't you like a country holiday, Veronica? What a name!"

"She is always called Vera. Her father was a poet—"

"Lancelot Davis, yes, I remember him!"

"And he gave her that absurd name because the Italian hills were purple and white with the flower when she was born."

"Rather a nice idea. Well, Vera, if Grannie likes, you shall come to Disbrowe with your cousins, and you shall have a real country holiday, and come back to Grannie in September with rosy cheeks and bright eyes."

Oh, never-to-be-forgotten golden days, in which the child of eleven found herself among a flock of young cousins in a rural paradise where she first knew the rapture of loving birds and beasts. She adored them all, from the gold and silver pheasants in the aviary to the great, slow wagon horses on the home farm, and the shooting dogs.

Among the children of the house, and more masterful in his behaviour than any of them, there was an Eton boy of sixteen, who was not a Disbrowe, although he claimed cousinship in a minor degree. He was a Disbrowe on the Distaff side, he told Vera, a distinction which he had to explain to her. He was Claude Rutherford, and he belonged to the Yorkshire Rutherfords, who had been Roman Catholic from the beginning of history, with which they claimed to be coeval. He was in the upper sixth at Eton, and was going to Oxford in a year or two, and from Oxford into the Army. He was a clever boy, old for his years, quoted Omar Khayyam in season and out of season, and was already tired of many things that boys are fond of.

But, superior as this young person might be, he behaved with something more than cousinly kindness to the little girl from London, whose pitiful story Lady Okehampton had expounded to him. He was familiar with the poetry of Lancelot Davis, whose lyrics had a flavour of Omar; and he was pleased to patronise the departed poet's daughter.

He took Vera about the home farm, and the stables, and introduced her to the assemblage of living creatures that made Disbrowe Park so enchanting. He taught her to ride the barb that had been his favourite mount four years earlier. He seemed ages older than Vera; and he condescended to her and protected her, and would not allow his cousins to tease her, although their vastly superior education tempted them to make fun of the little girl who had only two hours a day from a Miss Walker, and to whom the whole world of science was dark. What a change was that large life at Disbrowe, the picnics and excursions, the little dances after dinner, the run with the otter-hounds on dewy mornings, the rustic races and sports, the thrilling jaunts with Cousin Claude in his dinghy, over those blue-green West Country waves, a life so full of variety and delight that the pleasures of the day ran over into the dreams of night, and sleep was a round of adventure and excitement! What a change from the slow walk in Regent's Park, or along the sea-front at Brighton, beside Grannie's Bath chair, or the afternoon drive between Hove and Kemp Town, in a hired landau!

She thought of poor Grannie, who was not invited to Disbrowe, and was sorry to think of her lingering in the dull London lodging, when all her friends had gone off to their cures in Germany and Austria, and while it was still too early to migrate to the brighter rooms on the Marine Parade.

These happy days at Disbrowe were the first and last of their kind, for though Lady Okehampton promised to invite her the following year, there were hindrances to the keeping of that promise, and she saw Disbrowe Park no more. Life in London and Brighton continued with what the average girl would have called a ghastly monotony, till Vera was sixteen, when Lady Felicia, after a bronchial attack of unusual severity, was told that Brighton was no longer good enough for her winters, and if she wished to see any more Decembers, she must migrate to sunnier regions in the autumn. Cannes or Mentone were suggested. Grannie smiled a bitter smile at the mention of Cannes. She had stayed there with her husband at the beginning of their wedded life, when she was young and beautiful, and when Captain Cunningham was handsome and reckless. They had been among the gayest, and the best received, and had tasted all that Cannes could give of pleasure; but they had spent a year's income in five weeks, and had felt themselves paupers among the millionaire shipbuilders and exotic Hebrews.

Lady Felicia decided on San Marco, a picturesque little spot on the Italian Riviera, which had been only a fishing village till within the last ten years, when an English doctor had "discovered" it, and two or three hotels had been built to accommodate the patients he sent there. The sea-front was sheltered from every pernicious wind, and the sea was unpolluted by the drainage of a town. Peasant proprietors grew their carnations all along the shore, close to the sandy beach, and the olive woods that clothed the sheltering hill were carpeted with violets and narcissus.

Lady Felicia described San Marco as a paradise; but her friends told her that there was absolutely no society, and that she would be bored to death.

"You will meet nobody but invalids, dreadful people in Bath chairs!" one of her rich friends told her, a purse-proud matron who owned a villa at Cannes, and considered no other place "possible" from Spezzia to Marseilles.

"I shall be in a Bath chair myself," replied Lady Felicia. "I want quiet and economy, and not society. At Vera's age it is best that there should be no talk of dances and high jinks."

Mrs. Montagu Watson smiled, and shrugged her shoulders. "Girls have their own opinions about life nowadays," she said. "I don't think Theodora or Margaret would put up with San Marco, although they are still in the school-room. They want fine clothes and smart carriages to look at, when they trudge with their governess."

"Vera is more unsophisticated than your girls. She will be quite happy reading Scott or Dickens in a garden by the sea. I mean to keep her as fresh as I can till I hand her over to one of her aunts to be brought out."

"She is a sweet, dreamy child," said Mrs. Watson, who became deferential at the mere mention of countesses, "and I dare say she is going to be pretty."

"I have no doubt about that," said Lady Felicia.

They went to San Marco early in November, and found the hotel and the sea-front the abode of desolation, so far as people went. The habitual invalids had not yet arrived, and the weather was at its worst. The four cosmopolitan shops that spread their trivial wares to tempt the English visitor, and which gave a touch of colour and gaiety to the poor little street, were not to open till December. There were only the shabby little butcher, baker, and grocer, who supplied the wants of the natives.

Vera delighted in the scenery, but she found a sense of dulness creeping over her, in the midst of all that loveliness of mountain and shore.

Everything seemed deadly still, a calm that weighed upon the spirits. Her grandmother had caught cold on the journey, and the English doctor had to be summoned in the morning after their arrival.

He was their first acquaintance in San Marco, and was the most popular inhabitant in that quiet settlement. Old ladies talked of him as "chatty" and "so obliging"; but objected to him on the ground of too frequent visits, which made it perilous to call him in for any small ailment, whereby he was sometimes called in too late for an illness which was graver than the patient suspected.

Dr. Wilmot was essentially a snob, but the amiable kind of snob, fussy, obliging, benevolent, and with a childlike worship of rank for its own sake. He was delighted to find a Lady Felicia at the Hôtel des Anglais—where even a courtesy title was rare, and where for the most part a City Knight's widow took the pas of all the other inmates.

Dr. Wilmot told Lady Felicia that she had chosen the very best spot on the Riviera for her bronchial trouble, and that the longer she stayed at San Marco the better she would like the place.

The bronchial trouble was mitigated, but not conquered; and from this time Lady Felicia claimed all the indulgences of a confirmed invalid; while Vera's position became that of an assistant nurse, subordinate always to Grannie's devoted maid, a sturdy North Country woman of eight-and-forty, who had been in Lady Felicia's service from her eighteenth year, and who could talk to Vera of her mother, as she remembered her, in those long-ago days before the runaway marriage which was supposed to have broken Grannie's heart. Vera had no idea of shirking the duties imposed upon her. She walked to the market to buy flowers for Lady Felicia's sitting-room, and she cut and snipped them and petted them to keep them alive for a week; she dusted the books and photographs, and the priceless morsels of Chelsea and Dresden china, which Grannie carried about with her, and which gave a cachet to the shabby second-floor salon. She went on all Grannie's errands; she walked beside her Bath chair, and read her to sleep in the drowsy, windless afternoons, when the casements were wide open, and the sea looked like a stagnant pond. It was a dismal life for a girl on the edge of womanhood—a girl who had little to look back upon and nothing to look forward to. It seemed to Vera sometimes as if she had never lived, and as if she were never going to live.

Grannie talked of the same things day after day; indeed, her conversation suggested a talking-machine, for one always knew what was coming. The talk was for the most part a long lament over all the things that had gone amiss in Grannie's life. The follies and mistakes of other people: father, uncles and aunts, husband, daughter; the wrong-headedness and self-will of others that had meant shipwreck for Grannie. Vera listened meekly, and could not say much in excuse for the sins of these dead people, of whose lives and characters she knew only what Grannie had told her. For her mother she did plead, at the risk of offending Grannie. She knew the history of the girl's love for her poet-lover; for she had it all in her father's exquisite verse; a story poem in which every phase of that romantic love lived in colour and light. Vera could feel the young hearts beating, as she hung over pages that were to her as sacred as Holy Writ.

Grannie's bronchitis and Grannie's memories of past wrongs did not make for cheerfulness; and even the loveliness of that Italian shore in the celestial light of an Italian spring was not enough for the joy of life. There is a profound melancholy that comes down upon the soul in the monotony of a beautiful scene—where there is nothing besides that scenic beauty—a monotony that weighs heavier than ugliness. A dull street in Bloomsbury would have been hardly more oppressive than the afternoon stillness of San Marco, when Grannie had fallen asleep in her nest of silken cushions, and Vera had her one little walk alone—up and down, up and down the poor scrap of promenade with its scanty row of palms, tall and straggling, crowned with a spare tuft of leaves, and a bunch of dates that never came to maturity.

Companionless and hopeless, Vera paced the promenade, and looked over the tideless sea.

The only changes in the days were the alternations of Grannie's health, the days when she was better, and the days when she was worse, and when Dr. Wilmot came twice—dreary days, on which Vera had to go down to the table d'hôte alone, and to run the gauntlet of all the other visitors, who surrounded her in the hall, obtrusively sympathetic, and wanting to know the fullest particulars of Lady Felicia's bronchial trouble, and what Dr. Wilmot thought of it. They told her it must be very dull for her to be always with an invalid, and they tried to lure her into the public drawing-room, where she might join in a round game, or even make a fourth at bridge; or, if there were a conjuror that evening, the elderly widows and spinsters almost insisted upon her stopping to see the performance.

"No, thank you, I mustn't stay. Grannie wants me," she would answer quietly; and after she had run upstairs, there would be a chorus of disapproval of Lady Felicia's want of consideration in depriving the sweet child of every little pleasure within her reach.

Vera had no yearning for the gaieties of the hotel drawing-room, or the conjuror's entertainment; but she had a feeling of hopeless loneliness, which even her favourite books could not overcome. If she had been free to roam about the olive woods, to climb the hills, and get nearer the blue sky, she might have been almost happy; but Grannie was exacting, and Vera had never more than an hour's freedom at a time. The hills, and the rustic shrines that shone dazzling white against the soft blue heaven, were impossible for her. Exploration or adventure was out of the question. She might sit in the garden where the pepper trees and palms were dust-laden and shabby; or she might pace the promenade, where Grannie and Martha Lidcott, Grannie's maid, could see her from the salon windows on the second floor.

On the promenade she was safe and needed no chaperon. The hardiest and most audacious of prowling cads would not have dared to follow or address her under the glare of all those hotel windows, and within sound of shrill female voices and flying tennis balls. On the promenade she had all the hotel for her chaperon. Grannie asked her the same questions every evening when she came in to dress for the seven o'clock dinner. Had she enjoyed her walk? and was it not a delicious evening? And then Grannie would tell her what a privilege it was to be young, and able to walk, instead of being a helpless invalid in a Bath chair.

Vera wondered sometimes whether the privilege of youth, with the long blank vista of years lying in front of it, were an unmixed blessing.

CHAPTER II

It was the middle of February, and all the little gardens that lay like a fringe along the edge of the olive woods had become one vivid pink with peach blossoms, while the dull grey earth under the peach trees was spread with the purple and red of anemones. San Marco was looking its loveliest, blue sea and blue sky, cypresses rising up, like dark green obelisks, among the grey olives, and even the hotel garden was made beautiful by roses that hung in garlands from tree to tree, and daffodils that made a golden belt round the dusty grass.

Vera went to the dining-room alone at the luncheon hour on this heavenly morning, a loneliness to which she was now accustomed, as Grannie's delicate and scanty meal was now served to her habitually in her salon. Fortified by Dr. Wilmot, who was an authority at the "Anglais," Lady Felicia had interviewed the landlord, and had insisted upon this amenity without extra charge.

The hotel seemed in a strange commotion as Vera went downstairs. Chambermaids with brooms and dusters were running up and down the corridor on the first floor. Doors that were usually shut were all wide open to the soft spring breezes. Furniture was being carried from one room to another, and other furniture, that looked new, was being brought upstairs from the hall. Carpets and curtains were being shaken in the garden at the back of the hotel, and dust was being blown in through the open window on the landing.

Vera wondered, but had not to wonder long; for at the luncheon table everybody was talking about the upheaval, and its cause, and a torrent of rambling chatter, in which widows and spinsters were almost shrill with excitement, gradually resolved itself into these plain facts.

An Italian financier, Signor Mario Provana, the richest man in Rome, and one of the richest men in London, which, of course, meant a great deal more, was bringing his daughter to the hotel, a daughter in delicate health, sent by her doctors to the most eligible spot along the Western Ligura.

The poor dear girl was in a very bad way, the old ladies told each other, threatened with consumption. She had two nurses besides her governess and maid, and the whole of the first floor had been taken by Signor Provana, to the annoyance of Lady Sutherland Jones, quite the most important inmate of the hotel, who had been made to exchange her first-floor bedroom for an apartment on the second floor, which Signor Canincio, the landlord, declared to be superior in every particular, as well as one lire less per diem.

"I should have thought your husband would have hesitated before putting one of his best customers to inconvenience for a party who drops from the skies, and may never come here again," Lady Jones complained to the landlord's English wife, who was, if anything, more plausible than her Italian husband.

The Holloway builder's widow was uncertain in her aspirates, more especially when discomposed by a sense of injury.

Madame Canincio pleaded that they could not afford to turn away good fortune in the person of a Roman millionaire, who took a whole floor, and would have all his meals served in his private salle à manger, the extra charge for which indulgence would come to almost as much as her ladyship's "arrangement"; for Lady Sutherland Jones, albeit supposed to be wealthy, was not liberal. Her late husband had been knighted, after the opening by a Royal Princess of a vast pile of workmen's dwellings, paid for by an American philanthropist, and neither husband nor wife had achieved that shibboleth of gentility, the letter "h."

Vera heard all about Signor Provana, and his daughter, next morning from Dr. Wilmot, who was more elated at the letting of the first floor to that great man than she had ever seen him by any other circumstance in the quiet life of San Marco.

"I consider the place made from this hour," said the doctor, rubbing his well-shaped white hands in a prophetic rapture. "There will be paragraphs in all the Roman papers, and it will be my business to see that they get into the New York Herald. We must boom our pretty little San Marco, my dear Lady Felicia. Your coming here was good luck, for we want our English aristocracy to take us up—but all over the world Mario Provana's is a name to conjure with; and if his daughter can recover her health here, we shall make San Marco as big as San Remo before we are many years older. It was my wife's delicate chest that brought me here, and I have been rewarded by the beauty of the place and, I think I may venture to say, the influential position that I have obtained here."

He might have added that his villa and garden cost him about half the rent he would have had to pay in San Remo or Mentone, while a clever manager like Mrs. Wilmot could make a superior figure in San Marco on economical terms.

"How old is the girl?" Lady Felicia asked languidly.

"Between fifteen and sixteen, I believe. She will be a nice companion for Miss Davis."

"I do so hope we may be friends," Vera said eagerly. In a hotel where almost everybody was elderly, the idea of a girl friend was delightful.

Lady Felicia, who had been very severe in her warnings against hotel-acquaintance, answered blandly, though with a touch of condescension.

"If the girl is really nice, and has been well brought up, I should see no objections to Vera's knowing her."

"Thank you, Grannie," cried Vera. "She is sure to be nice!"

"Signor Provana's daughter cannot fail to be nice," protested the doctor.

Lady Felicia was dubious.

"An Italian!" she said. "She may be precocious—artful—of doubtful morality."

"Signor Provana's daughter! Impossible!"

Nothing happened to stir the stagnant pool of life at San Marco during the next day and the day after that. Vera asked Madame Canincio when Signor Provana and his daughter were expected, but could obtain no precise information. The rooms were ready. Madame Canincio showed Vera the salon, which she had seen in its spacious emptiness, with the shabby hotel furniture, but to which Signor Provana's additions had given an air of splendour. Sofas and easy chairs had been sent from Genoa, velvet curtains and portières, bronze lamps, and silver candlesticks, Persian carpets, everything that makes for comfort and luxury; and the bedroom for the young lady had been even more carefully prepared; but, beside her own graceful pillared bedstead, with its lace mosquito curtains, was the narrow bed for the night-nurse, which gave its sad indication of illness.

The flowers were ready in the vases, filling the salon with perfume.

"I believe they will be here before sunset," Madame Canincio told Vera. "We are waiting for a telegram to order dinner. The chef is in an agony of anxiety. First impressions go for so much, and no doubt Signor Provana is a gourmet."

Vera heard no more that day, but the maid who brought the early breakfast told her that the great man and his daughter had arrived at five o'clock on the previous afternoon. Vera went to the flower market in a fever of expectation, bought her cheap supply of red and purple anemones, her poor little bunch of Parma violets and branches of mimosa, thinking of the luxury of tuberoses and camellias in the Provana salon, but she thought much more of the sick girl, and the father's love, exemplified in all that forethought and preparation. For youth in vigorous health there is always a melancholy interest in youth that is doomed to die, and Vera's heart ached with sympathy for the consumptive girl, for whom a father's wealth might do everything except spin out the weak thread of life.

She heard voices in the hotel garden, as she went up the sloping carriage drive, with her flower basket on her arm; and at a bend in the avenue of pepper trees and palms she stopped with a start, surprised at the gaiety of the scene, which made the shabby hotel garden seem a new place.

The dusty expanse of scanty grass which passed for a lawn, where nothing gayer than aloes and orange trees had flourished, was now alive with colour. A girl in a smart white cloth frock and a large white hat was sitting in a blue and gold wicker chair, a girl all brightness and vitality, as it seemed to Vera; where she had expected to see a languid invalid reclining among a heap of pillows, a wasted hand drooping inertly, too feeble to hold a book.

This girl's aspect was of life, not of sickness and coming death. Her eyes were darkest brown, large and brilliant, with long black lashes that intensified their darkness, intensified also by the marked contrast of hair that was almost flaxen, parted on her forehead, and hanging in a single thick plait that fell below her waist, and was tied with a blue ribbon. Three spaniels, one King Charles, and two Blenheims, jumped and barked about her chair, and increased the colour and gaiety of her surroundings by their frivolous decorations of silver bells and blue ribbons; and, as if this were not enough of colour, gaudy draperies of Italian printed cotton were flung upon the unoccupied chairs, and covered a wicker table, while, as the highest note in this scale of colour, a superb crimson and green cockatoo, with a tail of majestic length, screamed and fluttered on his perch, and responded not too amiably to the attentions of Dr. Wilmot, who was trying to scratch himself into the bird's favour.

The doctor desisted from his "Pretty Pollyings" on perceiving Vera. "Ah, Miss Davis, that's lucky. Do stop a minute with Grannie's flowers. I want to introduce you to Mademoiselle di Provana."

The "di" was the embellishment of Dr. Wilmot, who could not imagine wealth and importance without nobility, but the financier called himself Provana tout court.

Vera murmured something about being "charmed," put down her basket on the nearest chair, and went eagerly towards the fair girl with the dark, lustrous eyes, who held out a dazzling white hand, smiling delightedly.

"I am so glad to find you here. Dr. Veelmot"—she stumbled a little over the name, otherwise her English was almost perfect; "Dr. Vilmot told me you were English, and about my own age, and that we ought to be good friends. I am so glad you are English. I have talked much English with my governess, but I want a companion of my own age. I have had no girl friend since I left the Convent three year ago. Dr Vilmot tell me your father was a poet. That is lovely, lovely. My father is a great man, but he is not a poet, though he loves Dante."

"My little girl is an enthusiast, and something of a dreamer," said a deep, grave voice, and a large, tall figure came into view suddenly from behind a four-leaved Japanese screen that had been placed at the back of the invalid's chair, to guard her from an occasional breath of cold wind that testified to the fact that, although all things had the glory of June, the month was February.

Vera was startled by a voice which seemed different from any other voice she had ever heard—so grave, so deep, with such a tone of solemn music; and yet voice and enunciation were quite natural; there was nothing to suggest pose or affectation.

The speaker stood by his daughter's chair, an almost alarming figure in that garden of ragged pepper trees, shabby palms, and sunshine—the sun dominating the picture. He was considerably over six feet, with broad shoulders, long arms, and large hands, very plainly clothed in his iron-grey tweed suit, which almost matched his iron-grey hair. He was not handsome, though he had a commanding brow and his head was splendidly poised on those splendid shoulders. Vera told herself that he was not aristocratic—indeed, she feared that there was something almost plebeian in his appearance that might offend Grannie, who, having had to do without money, was a fierce stickler for race.

While Vera was thinking about him, Signor Provana was talking to his daughter, and the voice that had so impressed her at the first hearing, became infinitely beautiful as it softened with infinite love.

What must it be to a girl to be loved so fondly by that great strong man? Vera had known no such love since her poet father's death.

She took up her basket of flowers, and then lingered shyly, not knowing whether she ought to go at once, or stay and make conversation; but Giulia settled the question.

"Oh, please don't run away," she said. "Don't go without making friends with my family. Let me introduce Miss Thompson," indicating a comfortable, light-haired person sitting near her, absorbed in Sudermann's last novel, "and look at my three spaniels, Jane Seymour, Anne Boleyn, and Catherine Parr. I called them after your wicked King Henry's wives. I hope you revel in history. It is my favourite study."

She stooped to pat the spaniels, who all wanted to clamber on her knees at once. Even under the full cloth skirt and silk petticoat Vera could not help seeing that the knees were sharp and bony. By this time she had discovered the too slender form under the pretty white frock, and the hectic bloom on the oval cheek. She knew the meaning of that settled melancholy in Signor Provana's dark grey eyes—eyes that seemed made rather for command than for softness.

She caressed the sparkling black-and-tan Anne Boleyn, and stroked the long silken ears of the Blenheims, Jane and Catherine, and allowed them to jump on her lap and explore her face with their affectionate tongues. Jane Seymour was the favourite, Giulia told her, the dearest dear, a most sensible person, and sensitive to a fault. Vera admired the cockatoo, and answered all Giulia's questions about San Marco, and the drives to old mountain towns and villages, old watch-towers and old churches—drives which Vera knew only from the talk of the widows and spinsters who had urged her to persuade Grannie to hire a carriage and take her to see all the interesting things to be seen in an afternoon's drive.

"Grannie is not strong enough for long drives," Vera had told them. They smiled significantly at each other when she had gone.

"Poor child! I'm afraid it's Grannie's purse that isn't strong enough," said the leading light in the little community.

"I believe they're reg'lar church mice for poverty, in spite of the airs my lady gives herself," said Lady Jones. "If it was me, and money was an objick, I wouldn't pretend to be exclusive, and waste ten lire a day on a salon. I don't mind poverty, and I don't mind pride—but pride and poverty together is more than I can stand."

The other ladies agreed. Pride was a vice that could only be allowed where there was wealth to sustain it. Only one timid spinster objected.

"Lady Felicia was a Disbrowe," she said meekly, "and the Disbrowes are one of the oldest families in England."

Vera had to promise to take tea with the Signorina at five o'clock that afternoon before Giulia would let her go.

"I am not allowed to put my nose out of doors after tea," Giulia said, not in a complaining tone, but with light laughter. "People are so absurd about me, especially this person," putting her hand in her father's and smiling up at him, "just because of my winter cough—as if almost everybody has not a winter cough. Promise! A riverderci, cara Signorina."

Vera promised, and this time she was allowed to go.

Mario Provana went with her, and carried her basket.

He did not say a word till they had passed beyond the belt of pepper trees that screened the lawn, and then he began to walk very slowly, and looked earnestly at Vera.

"I know you are going to be kind to my girl," he said, and his low, grave voice sounded mournful as a funeral bell. "Dr. Wilmot has told me of your devotion to your grandmother and how sweet and sympathetic you are. You can see how the case stands. You can see by how frail a thread I hold the creature who is dearer to me than all this world besides."

"Oh, but I hope the Signorina will gain health and strength at San Marco," Vera answered earnestly. "She does not look like an invalid! And she is so bright and gay."

"She has never known sorrow. She is never to know sorrow. She is to be happy till her last breath. That is my business in life. Sorrow is never to touch her. But I do not deceive myself. I have never cheated myself with a moment of hope since I saw Death's seal upon her forehead. In my dreams sometimes I have seen her saved; but in my waking hours, never. As I have watched her passing stage by stage through the phases of a mortal illness, I watched her mother ten years ago through the same stages of the same disease. Doctors said: Take her to this place or to that—to Sicily, to the Tyrol, to the Engadine, to India—to the Transvaal. For four years I was a wanderer upon this earth, a wanderer without hope then, as I am a wanderer without hope now. I have business interests that I dare not utterly neglect, because they involve the fortunes of other people. I brought my daughter here, because I am within easy reach of Rome. I ought to be in London."

He had walked with Vera beyond the door of the hotel. He stopped suddenly, and apologised.

"I would not have saddened you by talking of my grief, if I did not know that you are full of sympathy for my sweet girl. I want you to understand her, and to be kind to her, and above all to give no indication of fear or regret. You expected to find a self-conscious invalid, hopeless and helpless, with the shadow of death brooding over her—and you find a light-hearted girl, able to enjoy all that is lovely in a world where she looks forward to a long and happy life. That gaiety of heart, that high courage and unshaken hope, are symptomatic of the fatal malady which killed my wife, and which is killing her daughter."

"But is there really, really no hope of saving her?" cried Vera, with her eyes full of tears.

"There is none. All that science can do, all that the beauty of the world can do, has been done. I can do nothing but love her, and keep her happy. Help me to do that, Miss Davis, and you will have the heartfelt gratitude of a man to whom Fate has been cruel."

"My heart went out to your daughter the moment I saw her," Vera said, with a sob. "I was interested in her beforehand, from what Dr. Wilmot told us—but she is so amiable, so beautiful. One look made me love her. I will do all I can—all—all—but it is so little!"

"No, it is a great deal. Your youth, your sweetness, make you the companion she longs for. She has friends of her own age in Rome, but they are girls just entering Society, self-absorbed, frivolous, caring for nothing but gaiety. I doubt if they have ever added to her happiness. She wanted an English friend;

and if you will be that friend, she will give you love for love. Forgive me for detaining you so long. I will call upon Lady Felicia this afternoon, if she will allow me—or perhaps I had better wait until she has been so good as to call upon my daughter. I know that English ladies are particular about details!"

Vera dared not say that Grannie was not particular, since she had heard her discuss some trivial lapse of etiquette, involving depreciation of her own dignity, for the space of an afternoon. Clever girls who live with grandmothers have to bear these things.

Signor Provana carried her basket upstairs for her, and only left her on the second-floor landing, with a thoroughly British shake-hands. He was the most English foreigner Vera had ever met.

She had to give Grannie a minute account of all that had happened, and Grannie was particularly amiable, and warmly interested in Miss Provana's charm, and Mr. Provana's pathetic affection for his consumptive daughter.

"They are evidently nobodies, from a social point of view," Lady Felicia remarked, with the pride of a long line of Disbrowes in the turn of her head towards the open window, as if dismissing a subject too unimportant for her consideration; "but I dare say the man's wealth gives him a kind of position in Rome, and even in London."

Vera told her that Signor Provana wished to call upon her, but would not venture to do so till she had been so kind as to call upon his daughter. This was soothing.

"I see he has not lived in London for nothing!" she said. "I will call on Miss Provana this afternoon. You must help to dress me. Lidcott has no taste."

On this Vera was bold enough to say she had accepted an invitation to take tea with the invalid, without waiting to consult Grannie.

"You did quite right. Great indulgence must be given to a sick child. In that case I will defer my visit till tea-time, and we will go together. I want to be friendly, rather than ceremonious."

Vera was delighted to find Grannie unusually accommodating, and that none of those unreasonable objections and unforeseen scruples to which Grannie was subject were to interfere with her pleasure in Giulia's society.

Pleasure? Must it not be pleasure too closely allied with pain, now that she knew the girl she was so ready to love had the fatal sign of early death upon her beauty? But at Vera's age it is natural to hope—even in the face of doom.

"She may improve in this place. Her health may take a sudden turn for the better. God may spare her, after all, for the poor father's sake. At least I know what I have to do—to try with all my might to make her happy."

A footman in a sober but handsome livery was hovering in the corridor when lady Felicia arrived, supported by Vera's arm, and by a cane with a long tortoiseshell crook like the Baroness Bernstein's, an amount of support which was rather a matter of state than of necessity.

Lady Felicia had put on her favourite velvet gown and point-lace collar for the occasion. She had always two or three velvet gowns in her wardrobe, and declared that Genoa velvet was the only wear for high-bred poverty—as it looked expensive and never wore out.

The footman flung open the tall door of Signor Canincio's best salon, and announced the ladies.

The Provana salon was startling in its afternoon glory. The three long windows were open to the sunshine, which in most people's rooms would have been excluded at this hour. The balcony was full of choice flowers in turquoise and celadon vases from Vallauris. The luxury of satin pillows overflowing sofas and arm-chairs, the Dresden cups and saucers, and silver urn and tea-tray, the three dogs running about with their ribbons and bells, the gaudy cockatoo screaming on his perch, Giulia's blue silk tea-gown, and Miss Thompson's mauve cashmere, all lighted to splendour by the glory of the western sky, made a confusion of colour that almost blinded Lady Felicia.

Provana received her with grave courtesy, and led her to his daughter's sofa. She bent over Giulia with an affectionate greeting, and then, sinking into the arm-chair to which Provana led her, begged somewhat piteously that the sunshine might be moderated a little, a request that Provana hastened to obey, closing the heavy Venetian shutters with his own hands.

"Giulia and I are too fond of our sun-bath," he said, "and we are apt to forget that everybody does not like being dazzled."

"I came to San Marco for the sun, and it is seldom that I get enough; but your salon is just a little dazzling." "And your dogs are more than a little intrusive," Lady Felicia would have liked to add, the spaniels having taken a fancy to her tortoiseshell cane and velvet skirt. One had jumped upon her lap, and the other two were disputing possession of her cane. Serviceable Miss Thompson was quick to the rescue, carried off the dogs, and restored the cane to its place by the visitor's chair, while Provana brought an olive-wood table to Lady Felicia's elbow, and stood ready to bring her tea-cup.

"I hope you are pleased with San Marco," said Grannie, not soaring above the normal conversation in the hotel.

"We think it quite delightful so far," Provana replied, and Vera noticed that he never expressed an opinion without including his daughter. It was always "We," or "Giulia and I," and there was generally a glance in Giulia's direction which emphasised the reference to her.

"I love—love—love the place already," cried Giulia, who had beckoned Vera to her sofa, and was holding her hand. "Most of all because I have found this sweet friend here. You will let us be friends, won't you, cara Grannie?"

"Carissima mia!" murmured her father reprovingly.

"Please don't let us be ceremonious in this desert island of a place," said Lady Felicia, with a graciousness that was new to Vera. "I like to be called Grannie, and I can be Grannie to the Signorina as well as to this girl of my own flesh and blood. You can hardly doubt, Signor Provana, that it is pleasant for me to find that my poor Vera has now a sweet girl friend in this hotel, where we have lived three months and hardly made an acquaintance, much less a friend."

"But it has been your own fault, Grannie!" interposed Vera, who was essentially truthful. "People really tried to be kind to us when we were strangers."

"If you mean that some of the people were odiously pushing and officious, I cannot contradict you!" replied the descendant of the Disbrowes, with ineffable scorn.

But Grannie was not scornful in her demeanour towards the Roman financier. To him, and to Giulia, she was Grannie in her most urbane and sympathetic mood. She was charmed to find him so much of an Englishman.

"My mother was English to the core of her heart. She was the daughter of a colonial merchant, whose offices were in Mincing Lane, and his home in Lavender Sweep. I am told there is no such thing as Lavender Sweep now," Provana went on regretfully, "but when I was a boy, my grandfather's garden was in the country, and there were gardens all about it."

"And fields of lavender," said Giulia. "Oh, do say that there were fields of lavender!"

"No, the lavender fields had gone far away into Kent. Only the name was left; and now there are streets of shabby houses, and shops, and not a vestige of garden."

Encouraged by Lady Felicia's urbanity, Signor Provana went on to tell her that he was plebeian on both sides, and that all there was of nobility about him belonged to Giulia.

"My wife came of one of the noblest families in Italy," he said, "and when we want to tease Giulia, we call her Contessina, a title to which she has a right, but which always makes her angry."

"I don't want to be better than my father!" Giulia cried eagerly. "If he is not a noble, he comes of a line of good and gifted men. My grandfather's name is revered in Rome, and his charitable works remain behind him, to show that if he was one of the cleverest Roman citizens, he had a heart as fine as his brain. That is the noblest kind of nobility—non è vero, Grannie?"

Grannie smiled assent, and entertained a poor opinion of Giulia's intellect. A shallow creature, spoilt by overmuch indulgence, and inclined to presume. The two girls were sitting in the sun by an open window, a long way off. They had their own table, and Miss Thompson waited upon them with assiduity. Grannie had been warned that there was to be no doleful talk, no thinly-disguised pity for the consumptive girl. All was to be as bright as the room full of flowers and the untempered sunshine.

Provana told Lady Felicia that he had ordered a landau from Genoa, which had arrived that afternoon.

"The horses are strong, and used to hill work, and there is an extra pair for difficult roads," he said. "Giulia and I mean to see everything interesting that can be seen between breakfast and sundown. Of course we must be indoors before sunset. Everybody must in this treacherous climate. I hope Miss Davis may be allowed to go with us sometimes, indeed often!"

"Always, Padre mio, always!" cried Giulia from her distant sofa. She had begun to listen when her father talked of the carriage. "Vera is to come with us always. You will let her come, won't you, cara Grannie?"

"Please don't ask her," Vera said dutifully. "That would be deserting Grannie. She likes me to read to her in the afternoon."

"She shall enjoy your hospitality now and then, Signorina, and I will do without my afternoon novel. But you would soon tire of her if she were with you often."

"Tire of her! Impossible! Why, I don't even tire of Miss Thompson!" Giulia said naïvely.

"Please let Miss Davis come with us whenever you can spare her," Provana said, when he took leave of Lady Felicia at the foot of the stairs leading to her upper floor. "You see how charmed my daughter is at having found an English friend; and I think you must understand how anxious I am to make her happy."

Lady Felicia was all sympathy, and placed her granddaughter at the Signorina's disposal. If this man was of plebeian origin, he had a certain personal dignity that impressed her; nor was she unaffected by his importance in that mysterious world of which she knew so little, the world of boundless wealth.

When she arrived, somewhat breathless, in the shabby second-floor salon, she sank into her chair with an impatient movement, and breathed a fretful sigh.

"Think of this great coarse man, with his balcony of flowers, and four horses to his landau," she exclaimed disdainfully. "These Provanas absolutely exude gold!"

"Oh, Grannie, he is not the least bit purse-proud or vulgar," Vera protested. "You must see that he has only one desire in life, to make his daughter happy, and to prolong her life. I hope God will be good to that poor father, and spare that sweet girl."

"The girl is nice enough, and they will make this place pleasant for you. Extra horses for the hills! And I have not been able to afford a one-horse fly!"

"It is hard for you, Grannie dear; but we have been quite comfortable, and you have been better than you were at Brighton last year."

"Yes, I have been better, but it is the same story everywhere—the same pinching and watching lest the end of the quarter should find me penniless."

Lady Felicia resented narrow means, as a personal affront from Providence.

Signor Provana lost no time in returning Grannie's visit. He appeared at three o'clock on the following day, bringing his daughter, and a basket of flowers that had arrived that morning from Genoa, the resources of San Marco not going beyond carnations, roses and anemones.

"I fear you must have found the stairs rather tiring," Lady Felicia said, when she had welcomed Giulia.

"Not a bit. I rather like stairs. You see I came in my carriage," and it was explained that Giulia had an invalid chair on which her father and the footman carried her up and down stairs.

"Of course I could walk up and down just like other people," Giulia said lightly; "but this foolish father of mine won't let me. I feel as if I were the Princess Badroulbadore, coming from the bath in her palanquin; only there is no Aladdin to fall in love with me."

"Aladdin will come in good time," said Lady Felicia.

"I don't want him. I want no one but Papa. When I was three years old I used to think I should marry Papa as soon as I grew up; and now I know I can't, it makes no difference—I don't want anybody else."

An engagement was made for the next day. They were to start at eleven o'clock for the Roman Amphitheatre near Ventimiglia, looking at the old churches and palm groves of Bordighera on their way. It would be a long drive, but there were no alarming hills. Lady Felicia was invited, but was far too much an invalid to accept. There was no making a secret of Grannie's bad health. Her bronchial trouble was the staple of her conversation.

And now a new life began for Vera, a life that would have been all joy but for the shadow that went with them everywhere, like a cloud that follows the traveller through a smiling sky—that shadow of doom which the victim saw not, but which those who loved her could not forget. The shadow made a bond of sympathy between Mario Provana and Vera. The consciousness of that sad secret never left them, and many confidential words and looks drew them closer together in the course of those long days in lovely places—where Giulia was always the gayest of the little party, and eager in her enjoyment of everything that was beautiful or interesting, from a group of peasant children with whom she stopped to talk, to the remains of a Roman citadel that took her fancy back to the Cæsars. The chief care of father, governess, and friend, was to prevent her doing too much. Nothing in her own consciousness warned her how soon languor and fatigue followed on exertion and excitement.

Miss Thompson was always ready with a supporting arm, always tactful in cutting short any little bit of exploration that might tire her charge. She was one of those admirable women who seem born to teach and cherish fragile girlhood. People almost thought she must have been born middle-aged. It was unthinkable that she herself had been young, and had required to be taught and cared for. She was highly accomplished, and the things she knew were known so thoroughly, that one might suppose all those dates and dry historical details had been born with her, ready pigeon-holed in her brain.

Signor Provana treated her with unvarying respect, and always referred any doubtful question in history or science to Miss Thompson.

But her most valuable gift was a disposition of unvarying placidity. Nobody had ever seen Lucy Thompson out of temper. The most irritating of pupils had never been able to put her in a passion. She stood on one side, as it were, while a minx misbehaved herself. Her aloofness was her only reproof, and one that was almost always efficacious.

With Giulia Provana that placid temper had never been put to the proof. Giulia had a sweet nature, was quick to learn, and had a yearning for knowledge that was pathetic when one thought how brief must be her use for earthly wisdom; and, what was better, she loved her governess. Miss Thompson had a pleasant time in Signor Provana's household; moving from one lovely scene to another, or in Rome sharing all the pleasures that the most enchanting of cities could afford. Plays, operas, concerts, races, afternoon parties in noble houses.

From the day his daughter's health began to fail, and the appearance of lung trouble made the future full of fear, Signor Provana made up his mind that her life should never be the common lot of invalids. However few the years she had to live, however inevitable that she was to die in early youth—the years that were hers should not be treated as a long illness. The horrible monotony of sick rooms should never be hers. It should be the business of everybody about her to keep the dark secret of decay. Her trained nurses were not to be called nurses, but maids, and were to wear no hospital uniform. Everything about her was to be gay and fair to look upon—a luxury of colour and light. And she was to enjoy every amusement that was possible for her without actual risk. Into that brief life all the best things that earth can give were to be crowded. She was to know the cleverest and most agreeable people. She was to read the best books, to hear the most exquisite music, to see the finest pictures, the most gifted actors. Nothing famous or beautiful was to be kept from her. From the first note of warning this had been Giulia's education; and Miss Thompson's chief duty had been to read the best books of the best writers to an intelligent and sympathetic pupil. There had been no dull lessons, no long exercises in the grammar of various tongues—Giulia's education after her fifteenth birthday had been literature, in the best sense of that sometimes ill-used word. Signor Provana's system had been so far successful that his daughter had lived much longer than the specialists had expected, and her girlhood had been utterly happy. But the shadow was always in the background of their lives, and wherever he went with his idolised child there was always the fear that he might leave her among the flowers and the palm groves that filled her with joyous surprise on their arrival, and go back to his workaday life lonely and desolate.

Vera was astonished at the things Giulia knew, and was sorely ashamed of her own ignorance. For the first time in her life she had come into close association with cultivated minds—with people whose conversation, though without pedantry, was full of allusions to books that she had never read, and knowledge that she had never heard of. To know Giulia and her governess was a liberal education; and Vera showed a quickness in absorbing knowledge that interested her new friends, and made them eager to help her.

The world of poetry lay open and untrodden before this daughter of a poet.

The idea of her friend's parentage fascinated Giulia.

"Does she not look like a poet's daughter?" she asked her father, and Provana assented with smiling interest.

"All Giulia's geese are swans," he said; "but I believe she has found a real swan this time."

Vera's shyness wore off after two or three excursions in that ideal spring-time. The weather had been exceptionally mild this season, and there had been no unkind skies or cruel mistral to gainsay Dr. Wilmot's praise of San Marco. It might almost seem as if Provana had been able to buy sunshine as well as other luxuries. Day after day the friendly little company of four set out upon some new excursion, to spots whose very name seemed a poem. To Santa Croce, to Dolce Aqua, to Finalmarina, to Colla, the little white town among the mountains, where there were a church and a picture gallery, or by the Roman Road to the Tower of Mostaccini, on a high plateau crowned with fir trees, with its view over sea and shore, valley and wood, and far-off horizon; a place for a picnic luncheon, and an afternoon of delicious idleness. To Vera such days were unspeakably sweet. Could it be strange that she loved the girl who had begun by loving her, and who was her first girl friend? If she was not so impulsive as Giulia, she was as sensitive and as sympathetic, and Giulia's sad history had interested her before they met.

As friendship ripened in the familiarity of daily companionship, her interest in Giulia's father grew stronger day by day. His devotion to his daughter was the most beautiful thing she had ever known. He was the first man with whom she had ever lived in easy intimacy—for the uncles by blood or by marriage in whose houses she had been a visitor had always held her at arm's length, and her shyness had been increased by their coldness. The only creature of that superior sex with whom she had ever been at her ease was her young cousin, Claude Rutherford. He had been kind to her, and with him she had been happy; but that friendship was of a long time ago—ages and ages, it seemed to her, when she conjured up a vision of delicious days in the Park, hairbreadth escapes in Claude's dinghy, and thrilling rides on his Arabian pony.

Vera noticed that Signor Provana did not often join in the animated conversation which Giulia and her governess kept up untiringly during their morning drives. He was silent for the most part, and always meditative. His dark grey eyes seemed to be seeing things that were far away.

"You see Papa sitting opposite us, cara," said Giulia; "but you must not think he is really with us. He is in London, or in Paris, negotiating a loan that may mean war. He has to provide the sinews of war sometimes; and I tell him he is responsible for the lives of men. His thoughts are a thousand miles away, and he doesn't hear a word of our foolish talk. Non è vero, Padre?"

He looked at her with his fond parental smile. "I hear something like the songs of birds," he said; "and it helps me to think. Go on talking, anima mia. I like the sound, if I miss the sense."

"I have been telling Vera about Browning. She knows nothing of Browning, though she is a poet's daughter. Is not that dreadful?"

"I have had only Grannie's books, and she does not think there has been an English poet since Byron. We are birds of passage, and Grannie has only her poor little travelling library—but it has always seemed to me that Byron and my father were enough. I have never wearied of their poetry."

"Oh, but we shall widen your horizon," said Giulia; "You shall read all my books, and you must lend me your father's poems."

"I shall be very glad if you will read some of my favourites."

"All, all! When I admire I am insatiable."

Giulia was generally silent on their homeward journeys, wearied by the day's pleasure, in spite of the watchful care that had spared her every exertion. When the carriage had to stop at the foot of some grassy hill, at the top of which they were to take their picnic luncheon, or from which some vaunted view was to be seen, Provana would take his daughter in his arms and carry her up the slope—and once when Vera watched him coming slowly down such a hill with the tender form held by one strong arm, and the fair head nestling on his shoulder, she was reminded of that Divine Figure of the Shepherd carrying a lamb, the pathetic symbol of superhuman love. Her eyes filled with tears as she looked at him, holding the frail girl with such tender solicitude, walking with such care; and in the homeward drive, when Giulia was reclining among her pillows with closed eyes, Vera saw the profound melancholy in the father's face, and realised the effort and agony of every day in which he had to maintain an appearance of cheerfulness. These pilgrimages to exquisite scenes, under a smiling sky, were to him a kind of martyrdom, knowing all that lay before him, counting the hours that remained before the inevitable parting.

Vera knew what was coming. Dr. Wilmot had told her that the end could not be far off. The most famous physician in Rome had come to San Marco one afternoon. Passing through on his way to a patient at Nice, Provana had told his daughter, and coming casually to take his luncheon at the hotel—and the great man had confirmed Wilmot's worst augury. The end was near.

But even after this Giulia rallied, and the picnics in romantic places were gayer than ever, though Dr. Wilmot went with them, armed with restoratives for his patient, and pretending to be frivolous.

It was on the morning after a jaunt that had seamed especially delightful to Giulia that Lidcott came into Vera's room, with a dismal countenance, yet a sort of lugubrious satisfaction in being the first to impart melancholy news.

"I'm afraid it's all over with your poor young friend, Miss. She was taken suddenly bad at ten o'clock last night—with an hæmorrhage. Dr. Wilmot was here all night. I saw the day-nurse for a minute just now, as she was taking up her own breakfast tray—they're always short-handed in this house, Signor Canincio being that mean—and the nurse says her young lady's a little better this morning—but she'll never leave her bed again. She's quite sensible, and she doesn't think she's dangerously ill, even now, and all her thought is to prevent her father worrying about her. Worrying! Nurse says he sits near her bedroom door, with his face hidden in his hands, listening and waiting, as still as if he were made of stone."

"Would they let me see her?" Vera asked.

"I think not, Miss. She's to be kept very quiet, and not to be allowed to speak."

Vera went down to the corridor, directly she was dressed, and sat there, near the salon doors, waiting patiently, on the chance of seeing one of the nurses, or Miss Thompson. She would not thrust herself upon Signor Provana's sorrow even by so much as an inquiry or a message; but she liked to wait at his door—to be near if Giulia wanted her. They had been like sisters, in these few weeks that seemed so long a space in her life; and she felt as if she were losing a sister.

She had been sitting there nearly an hour when Signor Provana came out with a packet of letters for the post. He had been obliged to answer the business letters of the morning. The machinery of his life could not be stopped for an hour, for any reason, not even if his only child were dying. There was a look in his face that froze Vera's heart. What the nurse had said of him was true. He was like a man turned to stone.

He took no notice of Vera. He did not see her, though he passed close to her, as he went downstairs to post his letters—a matter too important to be trusted to a servant.

Vera was standing at the end of the corridor when he came back, and this time he saw her, and stopped to speak. "Ah, Miss Davis, the hour I have foreseen for a long time has come. I have thought of it every day of my life, and I have dreamt of it a hundred times; but the reality is worse than my worst dream."

He was passing her, and turned back.

"We dare not let her speak—every breath is precious. To-day she must see no one but her nurse—not even me; but if she should be a shade better to-morrow, will you come to her? I know she will want to see you."

"I will come at any hour, night or day. I hope you know how dearly I love her," Vera answered, and then broke down completely and sobbed aloud.

When she uncovered her face Provana was gone, and she went slowly back to the upper floor, where Grannie was waiting for her to sympathise with her indignation at certain offensive—or supposed to be offensive—remarks in the letters of a sister-in-law, a niece, and a dear friend.

"But indeed, dear Grannie, that could not be meant unkindly," urged Vera; for this offender was her favourite aunt, Lady Okehampton, who had been kind to her.

"Not meant? What could it mean but a sneer at my poverty?"

"I know Aunt Mildred wouldn't knowingly wound you."

"Don't contradict, Vera. I know my nephew's wife—a snob to the tip of her nails. She feels sure San Marco must be just the place for us—'so pretty and so quiet, and so inexpensive.' She dared not say cheap. And she does not wonder that I have stayed longer than I talked about staying when I left London."

Lady Felicia had remained in the dull Hôtel des Anglais six weeks beyond her original idea—six weeks longer than the London doctor had insisted upon; she had stayed into the celestial light of an Italian April, to the delight of Vera, who had thus enjoyed a new life with her new friend. She was not frivolous in her attachments, or ready to fall in love with new faces; but, in sober truth, she had never before had the chance of such a friendship—a girl of her own age, highly cultivated, attractive, and sympathetically eager to give her the affection of a sister. It would have been too cruel if Grannie's predetermination to leave Italy in the first week of March had cut short that lovely friendship.

Happily Grannie had found out that March in London might be more perilous for her bronchial tubes than December; and had made a good bargain with the rapacious Canincio, since several of his spinsters and widows were leaving him.

It was the third day after Giulia's fatal attack that Miss Thompson came to the upper floor to summon Vera to the sick room.

"The dear child has been pining to see you ever since yesterday morning, when she rallied a little. She has written your name on her slate again and again, but the doctor was afraid she would excite herself, and perhaps try to talk. She has promised to be quite calm, and not to speak—and you must be very, very quiet, dear, and make no fuss. You can just sit by her bedside for a little while and hold her hand; but above all you must not cry—any agitation might be fatal."

"Is there no hope—no hope?" Vera asked piteously.

"No, my dear. It is a question of hours."

Giulia's room was so full of flowers that it looked already like a chapelle ardente. Sinking slowly, surely, down into the darkness of the grave, she was still surrounded with brightness and beauty. Windows and shutters were open to the sky and the sun, and the blue plane of the sea showed far away melting into the purple horizon. Her three dogs were on the bed, Jane Seymour nestling against her arm, the other two lying at her feet. They were transformed creatures. No impetuous barking or restless jumping about. The wistful eyes gazed at the face they loved, the silken ears drooped over the silken coverlet, the fringed paws lay still. The dogs knew.

Giulia gazed at her friend with those too-brilliant eyes, and touched her lips with a pale and wasted hand, as a sign that she must not speak, and then she wrote on her slate eagerly:

"I have wanted to see you so long, so long, and now this may be the last time. I did not know I was so ill, but I know now. Oh, who will care take of my father when he is old; who will love him as I have done? I thought I should always be there, always his dearest friend. You must be his friend, Vera. He will be fond of you for my sake. You will find my place by and by."

"Never, darling. No one can fill your place," Vera said, in a quiet voice, full of calm tenderness.

A strange, suppressed sound, half sigh, half sob, startled her, and looking at the window she saw Signor Provana sitting on the balcony, motionless and watchful.

Again Giulia's tremulous hand wrote:

"Don't go till they send you away. Sit by me, and let me look at you. Oh, what happy days we have had—among the lovely hills. You will think of me in years to come, when you are in Italy."

"Always, always, I shall think of you and remember you, wherever I am. And now I won't talk any more, but I will stay till Miss Thompson takes me away."

Miss Thompson came very soon, and Vera bent over the dying girl and kissed the cold brow.

"A riverderci, Carissima; I shall come again when Miss Thompson fetches me."

She left the bedside with that word of hope, the luminous eyes following her to the door. The dogs did not stir, nor the figure in the balcony. Miss Thompson and the nurse sat silent and motionless. A stillness so intense seemed strange in a sunlit room, gay with flowers.

It was late next morning when Vera fell into a troubled sleep, filled with cruel dreams—dreams that mocked her with visions of Giulia well and joyous—in one of those romantic scenes where they had been happy together, in hours that were so bright that Vera had forgotten the shadow that followed them.

Lidcott came with the morning tea, and there was a letter on the tray.

"From the foreign gentleman," said Lidcott, who had never attempted Signor Provana's name.

Vera tore open the envelope, and looked wonderingly at the page, where nothing in the strong, stern penmanship indicated sorrow and agitation.

"My girl is at rest," he wrote. "She knew very little acute suffering, only three days and nights of weariness. She gave me her good-bye kiss after three o'clock this morning, and the light faded out of the eyes that have been my guiding stars. To make her happy is what I have lived for, since I knew that I was to lose her on this side of my grave. If prayer could reverse the Omnipotent's decree, mine would have been the mortal disease, and I should have gone down to death leaving her in this beautiful world, lovely and full of life.

"You have been very kind, and have helped me to make these last weeks happy for her. I shall never forget you, and never cease to feel grateful for your sweetness and sympathy. When she knew that she was dying she begged me to lay her at rest in this place where she had been so happy. Those were the words she wrote upon her slate when she was dying, her last words, the last effort of her ebbing life, and I shall obey her. You will go with us to the cemetery to-morrow morning, I hope, though you are not of our Church."

CHAPTER III

The sky over a funeral should be low and grey, with a soft, fine rain falling, and no ray of sunshine to mock the mourners' gloom; but over Giulia Provana's funeral train the sky was a vault of unclouded blue, reflected on the blue of the tideless sea, and olive woods and lemon groves were steeped in sunlight. It was one of those mornings such as Giulia had enjoyed with her utmost power of enjoyment, the kind of morning on which the pretty soprano voice had burst into song, from irrepressible gladness—brief song that ended in breathlessness.

The cemetery of San Marco was a white-walled garden between the sea and the hill-side, where the lemon trees and old, grey olives were broken here and there by a cypress that rose, a tall shaft of darkness, out of the silvery grey.

Never till to-day had those dark obelisks suggested anything to Vera but the beauty of contrast—a note that gave dignity to monotonous olive woods; but to-day the cypresses were symbols of parting and death. Their shadow would fall across Giulia's grave in the sunlight and in the moonlight. Vera would remember them, and visualise them when she was far away from the place where she had known and loved Signor Provana's daughter. She was thinking this, as she stood beside Grannie's chair by the gate of the cemetery—watching the funeral procession. There were no carriages. The priest and acolytes walked in front of the bier. The white velvet pall was covered with white flowers, and behind the coffin, with slow and steady step, followed Provana, an imposing figure, tall and massive, with head erect; calm, but deadly pale.

Miss Thompson, the two nurses, and Giulia's Italian maid followed, carrying baskets of violets; and Lady Felicia, who had left her chair as the priest and white-robed acolytes came in view, walked feebly behind them, with Vera by her side. They, too, had brought their tribute of flowers, roses white and red, roses which were now plentiful at San Marco.

It had been a surprise to Vera that Lady Felicia should insist upon getting up before nine o'clock to attend the funeral; she who had contrived to absent herself from all such ceremonies, even when an old friend was to be laid at rest, on the ground that her dear Jane, or her dear Lucy, could sleep no better at Highgate or Kensal Green because her friend risked rheumatism or bronchitis on her account.

"The poor dear herself would not have wished it," Lady Felicia always remarked on such occasions, as she wrote her apology to the nearest relation of the deceased. Yet for Signor Provana's daughter, almost a stranger, Grannie had put herself, or at least Lidcott, to infinite trouble in arranging a mourning toilette.

The Roman rites were simple and pathetic; and throughout the ceremony Signor Provana bore himself with the same pale dignity. He stood at the head of the open grave, and watched the rain of violets and roses, nor did his hand tremble when he dropped one perfect white rose upon the white coffin, the last of all the flowers, the symbol of the pure life that was ended in that cruel grave.

It was only when the earth began to fall thud after thud upon the flowers that his fortitude failed. He turned from the grave suddenly, and walked towards the gate before the priest had finished his office, and Vera did not see him again till she was walking beside Grannie's chair, on their way back to the hotel, when he overtook them.

"I want to say good-bye to you and your granddaughter, Lady Felicia," he said in his grave, calm voice, the voice that was so much more attractive than his person. "I shall leave San Marco by the afternoon train, and I shall go straight through to London."

"So soon?" exclaimed Grannie, with a look of disappointment. "Would it not be better to rest for a few days in this quiet place?"

"I could not rest at San Marco. It is the end of a journey that has lasted three years. I shall never lie down to rest in San Marco till I lie down yonder, beside my girl."

He looked towards the cemetery gate with a strange longing in his eyes, as if his heart were yearning for that last sleep in the shadow of the cypresses.

"Good-bye," he said, clasping Grannie's hand, and then Vena's. "I shall never forget," he said, earnestly. "Never, never." He walked away quickly towards the hotel, and Lidcott went on with her mistress's chair.

"A queer kind of man," said Lady Felicia. "I don't understand him. He ought to have shown a little more gratitude for your kindness to his daughter."

"There is no reason for gratitude. I have never had such happy days as those I spent with Giulia, while I could forget that she was to be taken from me."

"Oh, indeed," said Lady Felicia in an aggrieved voice. "You are vastly polite to me."

"Dear Grannie, of course I have been happy with you, and you have been very kind to me."

Grannie kept her offended air till they were in their sitting-room, when a sudden interest was awakened by the appearance of a sealed packet on her table. At the first glance it looked like a jeweller's parcel, but a nearer view showed that it was somewhat carelessly packed in writing-paper, and that the large red seal bore the monogram "M. P."

Grannie's taper fingers—bent a little with the suppressed gout that seems natural to the eighth decade—trembled with excitement, as she tore off the thin paper and discovered a red morocco jewel-case, heart-shaped.

While Lady Felicia was opening the case—a rather difficult matter, as the metal spring was strong and her fingers were weak—Vera picked up an open letter that had fallen out of the parcel.

"From Signor Provana," she said, and she read the brief note aloud, without waiting for Grannie's permission.

"DEAR LADY FELICIA,—I hope you will let your granddaughter wear this trinket in memory of my daughter. It was Giulia's own choice of a souvenir for a friend she loved. A friendship of two months may seem short to you and me; but it was long in that brief life.

"Yours faithfully,
"PROVANA."

The lid was open and the red light of diamonds flashed in the shaft of sunshine from the narrow slit in the Venetian shutters.

"You are a lucky girl, Vera," said Grannie approvingly, as she turned the heart-shaped locket about in the slanting sun-rays, unconsciously producing Newton's prism. "I know something about diamonds. That centre stone is splendid. Hunt and Roskell would not sell a diamond heart as good as this under three hundred pounds."

Vera's only comment was to burst out crying.

"For a commercial magnate, Signor Provana is a superior person," said Lady Felicia. "I hope we may see more of him. If he had given me time, I should have asked him to call upon me in London."

"Oh, Grannie, you could not! It would have been dreadful to talk about visiting to a man in such deep grief."

"I am not likely to do anything unseemly," Grannie replied with her accustomed dignity. "I ought to have asked the man to call."

Everybody was leaving the South, and San Marco had the dejected air that the loveliest place will assume when people are going away. For Vera San Marco seemed dead after the death of her friend; and, while she grieved incessantly for Giulia, she was surprised to find how much she missed Giulia's father. It seemed to her that some powerful sustaining presence had been taken out of her life. His strength had made her feel strong. He had been with them always, in those long Spring days that were warm and vivid as an English July. He had talked very little; but he had been interested in his daughter's talk, and even in Vera's. He had come to their assistance sometimes in their discussions, with grave philosophy or hard facts. He seemed to possess universal knowledge; but he was not romantic or poetical. He smiled at Giulia's flights of fancy, those voyages in cloud-land that charmed Vera. He was always interested, always sympathetic; and the grave, beautiful voice and the calm, slow smile were not to be forgotten by Vera, now that he had gone out of her life.

"It is all like a long dream, beautiful, but oh, so sad," Vera said to Grannie, who was more sympathetic than usual upon this subject.

"It has been an interesting experience for you, which one could never have hoped for in such an hotel as this," she said. "Dr. Wilmot tells me that Signor Provana has a house in Portland Place—the largest in the street, where he used to entertain the best people in his wife's time. Her rank and beauty gave distinction to his money; so I can believe Wilmot that he was by way of being a personage in London."

Lidcott was packing the trunks, and the Bath chair, while Grannie talked. The luggage, except the trunk with Grannie's best velvet gown, and a frock or two for Vera, and the absolute needs of daily life, was to go by Petite Vitesse, which meant being so long without it, that old familiar things would seem new and strange when the trunks came to be unpacked.

The long journey was dull—Grannie and Lidcott having a curious capacity for creating dullness. It was their atmosphere, and went with them everywhere. The change from summer sunshine to the grey sky and drizzling rain of an English April was a sad surprise; and the lodging-house in the street off Portland Place seemed the abode of gloom. It was the London season, and carriages and motor-cars were rolling up and down the handsome street in which Signor Provana's house had been described as the largest. Vera looked at all the houses as the cab drove past them, trying to find the superlative in size; but there was no time for counting windows or calculating space.

The lodging-house drawing-room, albeit better furnished than Canincio's second-floor salon, looked unutterably dreary; for the miniatures and books, and old china, that were wont to redeem the commonness of things, were creeping along the shores of the Rhone or mewed up in an obscure station, and though flowers were cheap in the street-sellers' baskets, not a blossom brightened the dingy drawing-room.

"How odious this house looks," said Lady Felicia, while she scanned the cards in a cheap china dish, and read the pencilled messages upon some of them. "I see your Aunt Mildred and your Aunt Olivia have called, surprised not to find us. But not a word from Lady Helstone, though I know she is in town. She was always heartless and selfish—but as she is the one I rely on for taking you about, we shall have to be civil to her."

"Poor dear Grannie, I really don't want to be taken out. I don't care a scrap about Society—and, above all, I don't want to cost you money for clothes, and I couldn't go to parties without all sorts of expensive things."

"Don't talk nonsense, Vera. I am used to scraping and pinching. It will only mean pinching a little harder. But there's time enough to settle all that before you are eighteen. Of course, you will have to be launched, if you are ever to marry—unless you want to sneak off to a registry office with the first scribbler you meet."

"Oh, Grannie," cried Vera, and walked out of the room in a sad silence, which made Grannie rather sorry for herself—as a poor old woman who was being trampled upon by everybody.

The long hot journey had tired her limbs and her nerves, and this damp, grey London, this shabby lodging-house had been too irritating for placid endurance. Somebody must suffer; and Lidcott, that sturdy child of the West Riding, was apt to retaliate.

Vera was perfectly sincere in her indifference to that grand event of "coming out," which had always been held before her by Grannie as the crown of girlhood, the crisis upon which all a young person's future depended, the opening of a gate into the paradise of youth, the paradise of dances and dinners, treats of every kind, where beauty was to be surrounded with a circle of admirers, among whom there would be at least one—the eligible, the rich, the inexpressive he—who could lift her at once to the summum bonum, whether in Carlton House Terrace, or Park Lane, whether titled or untitled—-but rich—rich—ricconaccio.

No, Vera had no eager desire for crowds of well-dressed people—for music and lights and dancing, and those things that she had heard the young cousins, still in the school-room, talk about with rapture and longing. The joys she longed for, while the slow spring and the fierce hot summer went by in the dull side street and the lodging-house drawing-room, were woods and streams, and rural joys of all kinds, such as she had known in that one happy summer of her childhood, for slow rides in leafy glades, in and out of sunshine and shadow, for the sound of a waterfall on moonlit nights, for young companions like the cousin who was once so kind—for many more books, and spacious rooms, and portraits of historic people—beautiful women—valiant soldiers—looking at her from a panelled wall. These were the things she wanted, and the want of which made life dreary.

In that long summer and autumn she often thought of the girl who was lying between the olive woods and the tideless sea; and, meditating on that short life, she could but compare it with her own, and wonder at the difference.

Is was not the difference that wealth made—but the difference that love made, that filled her with wonder as she recalled all that Giulia had told her of her childhood and girlhood.

She looked back at her own fatherless years—remembering but as a dream the father whom she had last seen on her birthday, when she was three years old—and when a woman in whose rustic cottage she had been living for what seemed a long time, took her to the nursing home where the fading poet was lying on a sofa in a garden. It was to be her birthday treat to visit "poor Papa, who would be sure to have something pretty for her." But the poet had no birthday gift for his only child. He had been too ill to think much about anything but his own weakness and pain. He had not remembered his little girl's third anniversary. He could only give her kisses, and sighs and tears; and she clung to him fondly, and said again and again: "Poor Papa, poor Papa!"

Kind Mrs. Humphries, of the pretty rose-covered cottage, had told her that Papa was ill, and had taught her to pray for him.

"Please God, bless poor Papa, and make him well again."

The prayer was not answered, and that spectral face, beautiful even on the brink of the grave, was all she could remember of a father.

And then had come the long, slow years with Grannie, who had been kind after her lights, but who required the subjugation of almost all childish impulses and inclinations. Long years in which Vera had to amuse herself in silence, and play no games that involved running about a room, or disturbing things. She had been surrounded by things that she must not touch; and her rare toys, the occasional gifts of aunts and cousins, were objects of reprobation if they were ever left on a chair or a table where they could offend Grannie's eye. The winter season, when there was only one habitable room, was terrible; for then Grannie was always there, and to play was impossible. She could only sit on a hassock in her favourite corner and look at old story books, too painfully familiar; and if she began to sing or to talk to herself, there came a reproachful murmur from Grannie's sofa: "My dear child, do you think I have no nerves?"

The summer was better, for she could play in the second-floor bedroom, which she shared with Lidcott, a room with three windows upon which the sun beat fiercely, but where she could talk to her dolls, and sing them to sleep, and do anything except run about, as she had always to remember that every step would beat like a hammer upon poor Grannie's head.

And in these years Giulia, who was within a few months of her own age, was being indulged with everything that could make the bliss of childhood, in the loveliest country in the world, and then, as she grew into a thinking, reasonable being, she had been her father's dearest companion, his distraction after the dull round of business, his choicest recreation, his unfailing delight. It was worth while to die young after such a childhood, Vera thought.

Grannie's winter in Italy had been a success, and she had a summer unspoiled by bronchial trouble. She wore her velvet gowns and her diamond earrings very often, and had her hair dressed in the latest fashion, with diamond combs gleaming amidst the silvery white, and was quite a splendid Lady Felicia at the friendly dinners and small and early parties to which she accepted invitations from her nieces and very old friends. She had been reproached with burying herself alive, but this year her health was better, and she was going out a little more; chiefly on Vera's account, who was now seventeen, and must really make her début next season. Her nieces told her that Vera was pretty enough to make a sensation, or at any rate to have offers.

"If she does, I suppose she will refuse the best of them, as her mother did," Lady Felicia said bitterly; "but whatever happens I shall not interfere. If she chooses to fall in love with the first detrimental who proposes to her, I won't forbid the banns."

Perhaps there was more of the serpent than the dove in this protest from Lady Felicia. In long hours of brooding over an irrevocable past it may have been borne in upon her that if she had not harped so much, and so severely, upon the necessity of marrying for money, her daughter might not have been so determined to marry for love.

The aunts who praised Vera did not forget to add that she would never be as handsome as her mother.

"She may 'furnish,' as the grooms call it," said Lady Helstone, who rode to hounds and bred her hunters; "but she will never be a striking beauty. She won't take away the men's breath when she comes into a ballroom. I'm afraid it may be the detrimentals, the poets, and æsthetes, and impressionist painters, who will rave about her. She is ethereal—she is poetical—and in spite of the man Davis she looks thoroughbred to the points of her shoes. After all, she may make a really good match, and make things much more comfortable for you by and by, poor dear Auntie."

"I shall never be a dependent upon my granddaughter's husband," Grannie retorted, with an offended blush. "The pittance which has sufficed for me since my own husband's death, and which has enabled me to keep out of debt, will last me to the end. I require nobody's assistance—and as I have never found blood-relations eager to help me, I should certainly expect nothing from a grandson-in-law; if there is such a thing."

Vera felt a sudden thrill when Lady Felicia told her that they were to winter at San Marco. She hardly knew whether the thrill was of pleasure or of pain. The place would be full of melancholy thoughts. Giulia's grave would be the one significant point in the landscape; but the long parade, with its shabby date palms and ragged pepper trees, could never again be as dull and grey and heartbreakingly monotonous as it had been a year ago; for now San Marco was peopled with the shadows of things that had once been lovely and dear. Now all that beauty which had once been far away and unknown had been made familiar in the long drives in the big, luxurious carriage drawn by gay and eager horses, whose work seemed joy—and the al fresco luncheons on the summit of romantic hills, with all the glory of the Western Ligura laid out below them like an enchanter's carpet, and the semi-Moorish cities, and Roman ruins of circus and citadel, the white cathedrals—remote among the mountains, yet alive with priests and nuns and picturesque villagers, and the sound of bells and swinging of censers—San Marco no longer meant only that level walk above the sluggish sea. It meant historical Italy. Her feelings about the place had altered utterly after the coming of the Provanas, and her mind was full of her lost friend when she alighted at the door of the Hôtel des Anglais, where Madame Canincio was waiting to receive honoured guests.

Inmates who stopped till the very end of the season, and who came again next year, were worthy of highest honour (albeit they paid the minimum second-floor pension; and though Canincio had audaciously declared that he lost money by the arrangement). Lady Felicia was a distinct asset, were it only for keeping the Cit's wife, Lady Jones, in her place.

Vera looked sadly along the spacious corridor, that had been so bright with flowers during the Provana occupation.

"Have you nice people on your first floor, Madame Canincio?" she asked.

"Alas, no, Mademoiselle. Our noble floor is empty. If we had six third floors and ten fourth floors, we could let every room—but for the first floor there is no one. Rich people do not come to San Marco. They want gambling-tables and pigeon-shooting, or the vulgarity of Nice."

"I suppose you have heard nothing of Signor Provana since he left?"

"Nothing, Mademoiselle, except that he is in Rome, and one of the greatest men there. And he was so simple and plain in his ways, and always so kind and courteous. He wanted so little for himself, and never once found fault with our chef, who, good as he is, must have been inferior to his own."

"I hope your chef did not give him risotto or chopped-up liver, or macaroni three times a week for luncheon," Lady Felicia said, sourly.

It was not till Grannie had been read to sleep that Vera was free to go where she liked. She had done her morning's work in the flower market, and at the so-called circulating library, where the Tauchnitz novels of the year before last were to be found by the explorer, stagnating on dusty shelves. This morning duty had to be done hurriedly, as Grannie liked to see the flower-vases filled, and a novel on her sofa-table when she emerged from her bedroom, ready to begin her monotonous day. Vera was secretary as well as reader, and had to write long letters to her aunts, at Grannie's dictation; letters which were not pleasant to her to write on account of the sense of injury and general discontent which was the Leit-Motiv running through them. In the beginning of her secretaryship she had sometimes ventured a mild remonstrance, such as, "Oh, Grannie, I don't think you ought to say that. I know Aunt Olivia is very fond of you," or "Aunt Mildred is very affectionate, and would be the last to neglect you." Whereupon Lady Felicia had told her that if she presumed to express an opinion, the letters should be written by Lidcott.

"Her spelling is as eccentric as the Paston letters; but I would rather put up with that than with your impertinence."

It was rather late in the afternoon before the drowsy Tauchnitz novel produced its soporific effect upon Grannie, though Vera had been reading in a semi-slumber; but at last the withered eyelids fell, and the grey head lay back upon the down pillow, and Vera might beckon to Lidcott, who crept in from the bedroom, with her work-basket, and seated herself by the open window most remote from Grannie, leaving Vera free to go out for her afternoon walk; only till five o'clock, when she must be at home to pour out Grannie's tea.

A church clock struck as she left the hotel garden, the garden where she had often sat with Giulia, who used to breakfast on the lawn, and only leave the garden to go to the carriage—spending as much of her life as possible under the blue sky.

All show of brightness had vanished from the stretch of thin grass and the ragged pepper trees—no pretty chairs or bright Italian draperies, no gaudy-plumaged cockatoo, or be-ribboned Blenheims. All was desolate, and tears clouded Vera's eyes, as she paused to look at the place where she had been happy.

"How could I ever forget that she was going to die?" she wondered.

"It was she herself who made me forget. She was so full of joy—so much alive—that I never really believed she was dying. I could not believe; I never did believe, till she was lying speechless, with death in her face."

She was going to the cemetery, to her friend's grave. It was almost as if she were going to Giulia. She could not believe the bright spirit was quenched, although the lovely form had passed into everlasting darkness. Somewhere between earth and heaven that happy soul was conscious of the beauty of the world she had loved, and of the love that had been given to her—somewhere, not utterly beyond the reach of those who loved her, that sweet spirit was floating—not dead, but emancipated.

Miss Thompson had told her of the heroic fortitude behind that light-hearted gaiety which had been Giulia's special charm. Although she was sustained by the unconsciousness of her doom, which goes so often with pulmonary disease, she had not been exempt from suffering. The sleepless night, the wearying cough, breathlessness, pain, exhaustion, fever, had all been borne with a sublime patience; and her only thought when the tardy morning stole at last upon the seeming endless night—had been of her father. He was never to be told she had slept badly—or had not slept at all—and it was her own cheerful voice that answered his inquiry as he stood at the half-open door: "Pretty well, Padre mio, si, si; not a bad night—a pretty good night—very good, upon the whole." No hint of the weariness, the suffering, of those long hours—and the nurse, though unwilling, had to indulge her, and allow the anxious father to be deceived. After all, as Miss Thompson said, a detail like that could not matter. He knew.

Remembering this, it seemed to Vera that Giulia's death meant emancipation—a blessed escape from the mortal frame that was fraught with suffering, to the freedom of the immortal spirit, winged for its flight to higher horizons, a being with new capacities, new joys—yet not unremembering those beloved on earth, nay, with a higher power to love the clay-bound creatures it had loved when it was clay.

In Vera's reverence for her father's genius, there had been much of the child's unquestioning faith in something it has been told to admire, for a considerable part of Lancelet Davis's poetry, and that which his review book showed to have been most appreciated by his critics, soared far beyond the limits of Vera's understanding. There were verses which she recited to herself again and again, with a delight in their music—verses where the words followed each other with an entrancing melodiousness—but for whose meaning she sought in vain. A Runic rhyme would have been as clear. She had repeated them dumbly in the dead hours of the night. Mellifluous lines that had a soothing charm. Lines that rose and fell like the waves of the sea; and lines drawn out in a slow monotony like the long, level stretch of wind-swept marshes—visions of white temples and strange goddesses; but they were shapeless as dreams to Vera—a confusion of lovely images without one distinct idea.

There were others of his poems that she understood and loved; the poems that the critics had mourned over as a disappointment, a falling away from the promise of a splendid career. There was his story of his courtship and wedded life, which Vera thought better than "Maud," written during his three happy years; and there was a poem called "Afterwards," written after her mother's death, which she thought better than "In Memoriam," a poem in which, after descending to the darkness of the grave, the poet soared to the gate of heaven, and told how where there is great love there is no such thing as death. The bond of love is also the bond of the dead and the living. Those who love with intensity cannot be parted. The spirit returns from behind the veil, and soul meets soul. Not in the crowded city—not within the sound of foolish voices, not amidst people or things that are of the earth earthy—but in the quiet graveyard, in the shadowy gloom of the forest, in lonely places by the starlit sea, or in the silence of sleepless nights, that other half of the soul is near, and, though there is neither voice nor touch, the beloved presence is felt, and the message of consolation is heard.

It was with her father's poem in her hand that Vera went to the white-walled enclosure under the hill, where the silver-grey of the olive woods shivered in the faint wind that could not stir a fibre of the cypress.

She had no trouble in finding Giulia's resting-place, for the picture of the spring morning when she had stood beside the open grave was in her mind, as if the funeral had been yesterday. It was at the farther end of the cemetery, in a little solitude guarded by a triangle of cypresses that marked the end of the enclosure, a spot where the ground rose considerably above the level of the larger space. Upon this higher level the massive marble tomb—so severely simple, so dazzling in its whiteness—dominated the lower plane, where memorial devices of every shape and form, Gothic cross, and broken column, winged angel, inverted torch, and Grecian urn, seemed poor and trivial by comparison.

It was a massive, oblong tomb without device or symbol, and only an artist would have been conscious of the delicate workmanship with which every member of the unobtrusive mouldings had been executed. There was no elaborate ornament, only a Doric simplicity, and the perfection of finely finished work.

The same simplicity marked the brief inscription on the level slab.

"Giulia, the only child of Mario Provana." This—with the date of birth and death—-was all. No record of parental love, nothing for the world to know, except that a father's one ewe lamb had lived and died.

A yew hedge, breast high, made a quadrangular enclosure which isolated Giulia's resting-place—a cemetery within a cemetery—and, at the end facing Genoa and the morning sun, there was a broad marble bench, and here Vera sat for nearly an hour, reading her father's poem, the work of his last year, written after the hand of death had touched him.

It was an hour of pensive thought, and as she pondered over pages where every line was familiar, it seemed to her that Giulia's spirit could not be remote from the friend whose sudden tears fell on the page, where some deeper melancholy in the verse brought last year's sorrow back with the force of a new grief.

The sun was low when she left the cemetery, and the shiver that comes with sundown chilled her as she hurried back to the hotel, more than five minutes late for Grannie's tea. But the following afternoon, and the day after that, she went back to the Roman bench, and sat there till sunset, with the green cloth volume that had grown shabby with much use, and her memory of Giulia, for her only companions. After this she went there every afternoon, sometimes with "Afterwards," sometimes with a volume of Byron or Shelley. The sense of dullness and monotony that had depressed her in her walk up and down the parade under the palm trees seldom came upon her in this silent enclosure, where the yew hedge— that only wealth could have attained in so brief a time—screened her from observation. She sometimes heard the voices of tourists admiring the monuments, or reading the epitaphs, in the cemetery; but it was rarely that anyone looked in at the opening in the green quadrangle where she sat.

It was more than a fortnight after her first visit to this mournful solitude when for the first time Vera was startled by the sound of approaching footsteps, and looking up she saw the tall form of Mario Provana, standing in the golden sunset. She rose as he came towards her, and gave him her hand, a hand so slender that it seemed to disappear in the broad palm and strong fingers that clasped it.

"I was told that you were in San Marco," he said; "but I never thought I should find you here. Then you have not forgotten?"

"I shall never forget. I come here every afternoon with my father's book—the poem he wrote when he knew that he was dying."

"May I sit by your side for a few minutes? I should like to see your father's book. I have not forgotten that he was a poet. Since you told me that, it has seemed as if I ought to have known beforehand. You look like a poet's child. I suppose everybody who saw Miranda for the first time, without having seen Prospero, ought to have known that her father was a magician."

His tone was grave and thoughtful, and his speech hardly sounded like a compliment. There was no air of gallantry to alarm her.

He took the shabby little volume from her hand, and turned the pages slowly, pausing to read a few lines, here and there.

"'Part the first, Thanatos, Part the second, Eros.' From darkness to light," he said, in the deep, grave voice which was her most distinctive impression of Mario Provana. "He believed in the victory of spirit over flesh. He was a poet; and faith is easy where the imagination is strong. Tennyson knew that all religion, all peace of mind, hung upon that one vital question—the Afterwards—the other world that is to give us back lost love, lost youth, lost genius, lost joy. I am not a religious man, Vera; indeed, to the Church of Rome I count as an infidel, because I cannot subject my mind to the outward forms and conventions which seem to me no more than the dry husks of spiritual things. But I am more of a Pantheist than an infidel—my gospel is the gospel of Christ—my faith is the faith of Spinoza."

And then, after a silence, he said:

"I called you Vera just now. Do you mind? My daughter loved you as if you had been her sister. May I call you by your pretty Christian name?"

"Pray do. I'm sure Grannie won't mind," Vera answered naïvely.

"We will ask Grannie's permission," he said, with a grave smile. "If you will allow me to walk back to the 'Anglais' with you, I will call on Lady Felicia this afternoon, and we can get that small matter settled."

He talked to her as if she had been a child; and the difference between his forty years and her seventeen made the fatherly tone seem natural.

He walked slowly round the tomb, lingering beside it now and then, and leaning his hand on the marble slab while he stood with bent head looking at the inscription, in a pause that seemed long; and then he rejoined Vera, and they left the cemetery together.

"You are not out yet, I think," he said, when they had walked a little way. "I read a paragraph in a London paper to the effect that Lady Felicia Cunningham's granddaughter, Miss Veronica Davis, the daughter of the poet whose early death had been a loss to literature, was to be presented next season."

"It is so foolish of them to write like that, as if I were a person of importance; when Grannie is so poor that it will be cruel to let her spend a quarter's income upon a Court dress and party frocks—and I don't care a scrap about parties or the Court."

"What a singular young lady you must be. I doubt if I could find your parallel in London or Rome. If you don't care for society, what are the things that make your idea of happiness?"

"Beautiful places, and the sea, books and music, and Shakespeare's plays," she answered quite simply. "I saw Henry Irving in 'Hamlet,' when I was twelve years old. It was my birthday, and my kindest aunt took me to her box at the Lyceum. I have never forgotten that night."

"You admired the actor?"

"I admired Hamlet. I never remembered that he was an actor," she answered, while her eyes brightened, and her cheek flushed with enthusiasm. "But when someone told me suddenly that Sir

Henry Irving was dead, I felt as if one great joy had gone out of the world. I saw Browning once—at an afternoon party at my aunt's; and she took me to him as he stood among a group of young people, talking and laughing, and told him who my father was; and he was too kind for words, and patted my head, and stooped and asked me to kiss him. I knew nothing about poetry then, not even about my father's, but now when I read Browning, I always recall the noble face and the silvery hair, and I am heart-broken when I think that he is dead, and that I shall never see him again."

She stopped, blushing at her own audacity, and surprised at finding herself talking as she had never talked to Grannie, but as she had often talked to Provana's daughter.

Lady Felicia received the unexpected visitor with exceeding graciousness, and showed a friendly interest in Signor Provana's doings. She hoped he was going to spend some time at San Marco.

"I have a selfish interest in the question," she said, with her urbane smile, "for at present Dr. Wilmot is the only person in the place who has intelligence enough to make conversation possible. This poor child and I come back to the 'Anglais' to find the same obese widow, the same pinched spinsters with wisps of faded hair scraped over their poor heads, too conscientious to put their trust in Lichtenstein. There is one poor creature who would be almost pretty if she knew how to put on her clothes and would treat herself to a wig."

Lady Felicia prattled gaily, not considering it her duty to put on a mournful air and remind Provana of his bereavement. It was half a year ago—and it was better taste to ignore the melancholy past. Vera busied herself at the tea-table, providing for all Grannie's wants before she gave the guest his tea. He looked colossal as he stood beside the small wicker tea-table, and the fragile figure of the girl sitting there, in her dark blue serge frock, a frock two years old, from a cheap tailor.

Lady Felicia had a convenient theory, that the intrinsic value of clothes hardly mattered. It was the putting on that was the consequence; and this philosophy, severely instilled into Vera's growing mind, had certainly resulted in an exquisite neatness that went some way to prove the truth of the theory.

In answer to friendly inquiries, Signor Provana told Lady Felicia that he was staying at the "Metropole," and might possibly take another week of quiet rest before he went back to Rome, where he was to spend the winter.

"Rome and London are my two counting-houses," he said; "and I have to divide my life between the two cities, with an occasional fortnight in New York, where I have offices, and an American partner."

"How you must hate London after Rome," said Vera.

"You know Rome?"

"Only in books—Byron—and Corinne."

"Corinne sounds very old-fashioned," Grannie apologised, "but Vera has been brought up by an old woman, and has had to put up with an old woman's books. Vera and I can just afford to live, but we can't afford to buy things we don't want."

Vera blushed hotly at this remark. She thought Grannie talked too much about her poverty. It seemed quite as bad form as if Signor Provana had expatiated upon his wealth.

Nothing could exceed Grannie's graciousness. Yes, of course, Provana was to call the child Vera. "Miss Davis" would be absurdly formal.

"Even if Davis were not such a horribly commonplace name," added Grannie, at which Vera protested that she had never been ashamed of her father's name.

"An utterly ridiculous name for a poet!" And then Grannie went on to lament that Signor Provana should think of going back to Rome in a week. "But in that case I hope you will be charitable, and take tea with me every afternoon."

She said "with me," not "with us"—ignoring the child.

Her hours were so long and so dull, she complained, and she loved conversation; to hear about, and talk about, everything that was going on in the world; the political and the social, the scientific and the literary world. Art, letters, everything interested her; and she had only such driblets of news as Dr. Wilmot could bring her.

"The man is fairly intelligent, but oh, so narrow," she complained.

"It will be an act of real benevolence if you will drop in at tea-time," urged Grannie, when Provana was taking leave.

He promised to be benevolent, to take tea with Grannie every afternoon, if so dull a person's company could give her any pleasure. He knew no one at San Marco, wanted to know no one. He had come there only to be near his daughter for a little while, just a short spell of thought and rest.

"If I had been a good Catholic, I should have gone into retreat at the nearest monastery," he said; "but my religion is too vague and shadowy for such discipline; so I just wander about among the woods and hills, and think, and remember."

The profound melancholy with which those words were spoken convinced Grannie that, although his sorrow was half a year old, it was still an absorbing grief, and that she must be prepared to take him seriously.

Vera felt a certain shyness about going to the spot where so many of her afternoons had been spent. Signor Provana might be there before her, and she would seem to intrude upon his sorrow. He had told them why he had come to San Marco. He must want to be alone with sad thoughts and cherished memories.

She took last year's dull walk on the parade, and met several of her hotel acquaintances, one of whom, no less a personage than Lady Jones, stopped to talk.

"I hear you had a visitor yesterday afternoon," she said; "the Italian millionaire. Miss Mason saw him leave the hotel after dark. He must have stopped with her ladyship quite a long time."

Lady Jones always talked of Grannie as her ladyship.

"I hope he has got over the loss of his daughter."

"In six months!" cried Vera. "How could you suppose such a thing!"

"Men's grief never lasts very long, not even a widower's," said Lady Jones; "and I've always noticed that the more a widower wants to throw himself into his wife's grave at the funeral, the sooner he begins to think about marrying again. And from the fuss Signor Provana made over his daughter, I should have expected six months would have been long enough to make him forget her."

"I don't think he is that kind of man," Vera said gravely, trying to move away; but Lady Jones detained her.

"What's your hurry?" she asked. "You must find it awfully dull walking alone every afternoon."

"I rather like being alone—if I can have a book," Vera answered, glancing at the little volume under her arm, and thinking how far the charm of solitude surpassed Lady Jones's conversation.

"Well, I'll walk a little way with you," said that lady, with exasperating patronage. "I don't like to see a young girl leading such a dull life. Why don't you never come down to the drawing-room of an evening?"

"I don't want to leave Grannie."

"You'd find us quite gay after your solitary salong. Two bridge tables, and besique, and sometimes even games, How, when, and where, and Consequences."

"I hate cards, and I like books better than society," Vera answered frankly.

"Well, you are an oddity. But you seem to have a high opinion of this Italian gentleman."

"No one could help liking Signor Provana after seeing him with his daughter—and I was a good deal with them."

"Yes, driving out with them on all the most expensive excursions. They quite took you up, didn't they? And it must have been very nice for you to go about in such a luxurious way after being cooped up with Gran'ma."

"They were very kind."

"He's a fine-looking man," said Lady Jones thoughtfully. "Not what anyone could call handsome; but a fine figure, and carries himself well. I suppose he has been in the Army. Most of these foreigners have to do a bit of soldiering in their young days."

They were at the end of the parade, and Vera stopped, and held out her hand to her insistent companion.

"Aren't you coming back?" asked Lady Jones.

"Not yet. I shall sit here and read for a little while."

"Don't you go and get a chill and make her ladyship angry with you. She won't like Dr. Wilmot's coming every day, or twice a day if he can find an excuse for it—as he did when I had my influenzer. But, of course, he knew I could afford to pay him. Well, O revore, dear," and the portly form that had been blocking out the western glow over the promontory of Bordighera slowly removed itself.

Vera was not destined to be alone that afternoon. She had not read three pages when a tall figure came between her and the light, and she rose hastily to acknowledge Signor Provana's greeting.

"It is too near sunset for you to be sitting there," he said. "Will you walk a little way with me—until five o'clock?"

Vera shut her book, and they walked on slowly and in silence to the gate of the cemetery, and still in silence till they stood by the white tomb.

There were flowers lying upon the slab, choice flowers, in their first freshness; and Vera thought that Provana had laid them there that afternoon.

They stood beside the tomb for some minutes, till the chapel clock struck the quarter before five, and no word was spoken till they were going back to the gate. Then Provana began to talk of his daughter, opening his heart to the girl she had loved.

He talked of her childhood, of her education, the bright, eager mind that made learning a delight, the keen interest in all that was most worthy to be admired, the innate appreciation of all that was best in literature and art, her love of music, and of the beautiful in all things. He was sure of Vera's sympathy, and that certainty made it easy to talk of his girl, whose name had rarely passed his lips in the long half-year of mourning.

"I have never talked of her since Miss Thompson left me," he said; "there was no one who would understand or care. There were friends who were kind and would have pitied me; but I could not endure their pity. It was easier to stand alone, and keep an iron wall between my heart and the world. But you were her companion in those last weeks; you are of her own age; you seem a part of herself, as if you were really her sister, left behind to mourn her, almost as I do."

After this confidence he made no more apologies for the sad note in all his conversation, as he and Vera loitered in the place of graves, or walked in the lemon orchards and olive woods on the hill-side above the cemetery. It became a settled thing for them to walk together every afternoon in the half-hour before Lady Felicia's tea-time; and as the week that Provana had talked of drew near its close, their rambles took a wider range, always with Grannie's approval, and they visited the white towns on the hills where they had been with Giulia and her governess in the golden spring-time. It was rapture to Vera to tread the narrow mule-paths, winding through wood and orchard, to walk with light, quick feet through scenes where everything was beautiful and romantic; to visit wayside shrines, and humble chapels hidden in the silver grey of the century-old trees, or to talk to the country women tramping homeward, carrying their baskets of the ripe black fruit. Provana helped her in her talk with the women, and contrived that they should understand her shy little discourse, the broken words and stumbling sentences.

Lady Felicia, usually so severe a stickler for etiquette, was curiously lax at San Marco, and could see nothing strange or unseemly in these unchaperoned rambles with the Roman financier, who, as she observed to Dr. Wilmot, was so obviously correct in all his ideas, to say nothing of his being almost old enough to be Vera's grandfather.

"Say father," said the doctor, smiling. "But you are perfectly right in your appreciation of Provana. He is a man of the highest character, and you may very well waive all conventionality where he is concerned."

Signor Provana did not leave San Marco at the end of the week. He stayed from day to day; but he was always going to-morrow.

As time went by he and Vera found a world of ideas and experiences to talk about. In the confidence that grew with every hill-side ramble, with every half-hour spent among ruined convents or Roman remains, they became licensed egotists, and talked of themselves and their own feelings with unconscious self-absorption.

Led on from trifles to speak of vital things, Provana told Vera the story of his unloved youth, motherless before his sixth birthday, and soon under the subjection of a stepmother who disliked him.

"I was an ugly boy," he said, "and her only child was as beautiful as the Belvedere Apollo, a creature to be worshipped, and I was made to feel the contrast. I had inherited my English mother's plain features and plain ways. I had none of the graces that make children adorable. My father was not unkind, but he was indifferent, and left me to servants, or later to my tutor, a German, middle-aged, learned, and severely practical, a man to whom affection and emotion were unknown quantities. It was always kept before me that I was to succeed to a great business, to the certainty of wealth, and the paramount purpose of my education was to make me a money-spinning machine.

"My brother's death in the flower of boyhood hardened my father's heart against me; and the indifference to which I had resigned myself became undisguised dislike. I lived in a frozen atmosphere; and of sheer necessity had to devote all my energies to the barren ambition of the man whose task in life is to sustain and augment the fortune that others have created. That is where the emptiness of my career comes in, Vera. A fortune inherited from those who have gone before him can give no dignity to a man's life. He is no better than a clerk, succeeding to a stool in a counting-house. For a man who has laboured and invented, who has lived through long, slow years of hardship and self-denial, who has endured the world's contempt, and persevered in the teeth of disappointment, over such a man's career success may shed a golden glory. He is a conqueror who has fought and won, and may be proud even of a triumph that brings him nothing but money. But I could have no pride in a career that was mapped out for me before I was born. All I can ever be proud of is that personally caring nothing for riches, I have been a conscientious worker, and have done what I was expected to do."

He told Vera how his own unloved childhood had been in his mind when his wife died, and he took his motherless girl to his heart, and, while she sobbed against his breast, swore dumbly that she should never know the need of a mother's love; and that which had begun as a duty became afterwards the dominating purpose of his life—the thing for which he lived.

"There had been a time after her mother's death when my heart was frozen, and that sweet child's presence was something that called for fortitude rather than affection, but that lovely nature soon prevailed even over grief, and my daughter crept into my desolate heart, my consolation and my joy."

In those quiet walks these two mortals, so far apart in age, in experiences, and in mental tendencies, became curiously intimate, telling each other almost everything that could be told about two dissimilar existences, each interested in vivid pictures of an unknown world, the child's monotonous life with an old woman, her glimpses of more joyous houses, the young cousin, the Arab pony and family of dogs— the old English garden, steeped in the August sunshine; and again of the dull upstairs-room in London, and the solitary hours of silent play, in which childish fancies had to serve instead of playfellows, the doll that was almost alive, the toy train that travelled to fairyland, the old, old stories in the ragged books, "Cinderella" and the "Forty Thieves." Provana listened to these naïve revelations as if they had been the childish experiences of a Newton or a Shakespeare, while Vera hung enthralled upon his memories of the liberation of Italy, the tempestuous years of revolt and battle, Victor Emanuel, Garibaldi, Cavour, the giant of thought and will-power, whose bold policy had made a great kingdom.

Afternoon tea in Lady Felicia's salon had become an institution in that week which spun itself out to fifteen days, and tea-time generally lasted for an hour and a half, since Grannie wanted to hear everything that Signor Provana had heard or read of the world of action since yesterday. As a dweller in London for nearly half his life, he was as keenly interested and as instructed in English politics, literature, science, and art as any Englishman Grannie had ever known; and she seemed to feel an inexhaustible interest in his conversation. She was intelligent, and often said good things; so this appreciation must needs be flattering, and Provana was naturally gratified. Flowers and Tauchnitz novels were almost daily tributes to Grannie; but no tribute was offered to Vera, no tribute except the tender watchfulness of dark grey eyes, eyes that followed the fragile figure as she moved about the room, or went in and out through the window in the desultory half-hour when her duties at the tea-table were finished. She left him to devote himself to Grannie in this half-hour, and showed how much milder was her interest in the talk of the political world, and people of importance in London, than in Provana's personal reminiscences. It was his life that had interested her, not the lives of other people.

They had come to the evening before his last day at San Marco. He must be on his way to Rome the day after to-morrow—that was inevitable.

"I should like to take Vera a little farther afield to-morrow, Lady Felicia," Provana said, as he took up his hat to go. "She has never seen the Chocolate Mills, though the way to them is one of the most picturesque within range. One must ride or walk. There is no carriage road; but if you will let Vera come with me to-morrow afternoon, I will bring the surest-footed donkey in San Marco, and his owner for our guide. I shall go on foot. The walk will be nothing for me; but it would be too tiring for your granddaughter."

Lady Felicia hesitated, but only enough to make her consent seem the more gracious.

"The poor child has been pining to see the Chocolate Mills; but for me it was impossible," she concluded.

"We must start soon after your luncheon; and if you can give me time for a little conversation before we go, I shall be greatly obliged," Signor Provana said, with a curious gravity.

Vera wondered what he could have to say to Grannie that needed to be arranged for beforehand. She felt a thrill of horror at the idea that Lady Felicia's frequent reference to her small means might have given him a wrong impression, and that he was going to offer to lend her money.

"You must allow that I have not let les convenances stand in the way of your enjoyment of Signor Provana's society," Lady Felicia said, with her kindest smile, when the visitor had gone. "There are very few men—even of his age—whom I could permit you to walk about with, even in such a half-civilised place as San Marco; but Provana is an exceptional man, a person whom scandal could never touch."

"And I think you like being with him," Grannie said, after a long pause, in which she had reclined in her most reposeful attitude, smiling at the after-glow above Bordighera.

It was not that fine promontory only, but all life and the world that Lady Felicia saw before her bathed in golden light.

Certainly Grannie had been curiously indulgent, curiously heedless of conventionalities, and curiously forgetful of the ways of the world in which she had lived from youth upward, when she thought that because San Marco was a quiet little place that had never basked in the sunlight of fashion, there would be no ill-natured talk about her granddaughter's tête-à-tête rambles with the Roman millionaire.

To say that people had talked—the season visitors at the "Anglais," the spinsters and widows, the invalid parsons and their wives, who were mostly languishing for something to talk about—to say that these had talked about Vera and her millionaire would not have described the situation. They had talked of nothing else; and the talk had grown more and more animated and exciting with every day that witnessed another audacious sauntering to the cemetery, or ascent of a mule-path through the wood. Spinsters, whose thin legs had seldom carried them beyond the parade, adipose widows, whose scantness of breath made the gentlest ascent labour and trouble, took a sudden interest in the little white chapels and shrines among the olives, and happened to meet Provana and Vera returning from the hill, which made something to whisper about with one's next neighbour at dinner, and was at least an agreeable change from the daily grumbling about the bill of fare.

"Veal again! and as stringy as ever.—Yes, I came face to face with them. He stalked past me in his gloomy way; and she did not even blush, but just said, good afternoon, as bold as brass."

"How Lady Felicia can be so utterly regardless of etiquette!"

"Oh, it's just like the rest of the smart set. They think they can defy the universe; and it's a surprise to them when they find themselves in the divorce court!"

"I don't believe Lady Felicia was ever in the smart set. You have to be rich for that. I put her down as poor and proud, and those sort are generally ultra-particular."

"I believe she's playing a deep game," said the spinster, and then the two friends looked down the long, narrow table to the corner where Vera sat, silent and thoughtful, pale in her black evening frock.

"Do you think her so remarkably pretty?" asked the spinster, following on a discussion in the drawing-room after luncheon, when the parsons had expressed their admiration of Vera's delicate beauty.

"Far from it," answered the plethoric widow. "You may call her ethereal," which one of the parsons had done; "I call her half-starved. She has no complexion and no figure, and looks as if she had never had enough to eat."

It mattered little to Lady Felicia next day—after a quarter of an hour's grave conversation with Signor Provana, or to Vera, putting on her hat in the sunny little front room, and hearing the donkey's bells jingling in the garden below; it mattered really nothing to either grandmother or granddaughter what the world, as represented by the table d'hôte of the "Anglais," might think of them. Lady Felicia lay back among her pillows, smiling at the sea and the far-off hills as she had never smiled before; for, indeed, that lovely coast had taken a new colour under a new light—not the light that never was on sea or land, but the more mundane light of prosperity, a smiling future in which there should be no more the year in year out effort to keep up appearances upon inadequate means.

And yet that smiling future depended upon a girl's whim, and at a word from Vera that cloud-built castle might vanish into thin air.

"She could never be such an idiot as to refuse him," mused Grannie, disposed to be sanguine; "and, what is better, I believe she is really in love with him. After all, he is her first admirer, and that goes for a good deal. I was in love with an archbishop of seventy when I was fifteen; and I remember him now as quite the most delightful man I ever met."

Provana was walking about the garden, while the surest-footed donkey in San Marco shook his bells and pawed up the loose gravel with the forefoot of impatience, lazily watched by his owner, a sun-baked lad of nineteen.

There were several pairs of eyes on the watch at various windows when Vera came tripping out in her neat blue riding-skirt and sailor hat. It was her kit for the riding-school near Bryanston Square, where Grannie had given her a season's lessons, lest she should grow up without the young lady's indispensable accomplishment of sitting straight on a horse, and going over a fence without swinging out of her saddle.

She had brought a handful of sugar for the donkey, and he had to be fed and patted and talked about before Signor Provana was allowed to take the slender foot in his broad hand while she sprang lightly to the saddle; and then the little company moved away, Vera on her great grey donkey, bells jingling, red and blue tassels flying, Provana walking beside her, and the sunburnt youth at the donkey's head, ready to hold the bridle when they came to the narrow hill-tracks.

"Do they take that lad with them to play propriety?" asked the sourest of all the spinsters, with a malevolent giggle—a question which nobody answered—while the two parsons agreed that little Miss Davis looked prettier than ever in her riding clothes.

Provana walked for a long time in absolute silence, while Vera prattled with the donkey-driver, exchanging scraps of Italian and insisting upon the donkey's biography.

"How did he call himself?" "Sancho." "Was he called after Don Quixote's Sancho?" "Perdona, Signorina— Non so." "How old was he? Was he always good? Was he always kindly treated?" His driver assured her that the beast lived in a land of milk and honey, and seldom felt the sting of a whip, to emphasise which assurance his driver gave a sounding whack on Sancho's broad back. The only comfort was that the back was broad and the animal seemed well fed.

"I would not have let you ride a starveling," Provana said; "but these people to whom God has given the loveliest land on earth have waited for the sons of the North to teach them common humanity."

After this he walked on in silence till they were far away from the "Anglais," slowly climbing a stony ascent that called upon all Sancho's sure-footedness and the guide's care.

Suddenly, in the silence of the wood, where the light fell like golden rain between the silver-grey leaves, Provana laid his hand on Vera's, and said in a low voice:

"I feel as if you and I were going to the end of the world together; but in half an hour we shall be at the mill, and after that there will be the short down-hill journey home, and Grannie's tea-table, and the glory of my last day will be over."

Vera looked at him wonderingly in a shy silence. The words seemed to mean more than anything he had ever said before. His tone had an underlying seriousness that was melancholy, and almost intense.

They did not give much time to the mill and the processes of chocolate-making. The picturesque gorge, the waterfall leaping from crag to crag, the blue plane of sunlit sea, and the pale grey glimmer on the purple horizon that was said to be Corsica—these were the things they had come to look at, and they looked in silence, as if spell-bound.

"Let us sit here and talk of ourselves, while Tomaso gives Sancho a rest and a mouthful of oats," Provana said; and he and Vera seated themselves on a stony bank above the waterfall, while Tomaso and Sancho retired to a distance of twenty yards, where a bend in the path hid donkey and driver.

It was not usual for Provana to be silent when they two were alone together. There always seemed too much that he wanted to say in the short space of time; but now the minutes went by, seeming long to Vera In the unusual silence, which she broke at last by asking him, "Were you ever in Corsica?"

"Often; but we won't talk of that, Vera," taking her hand suddenly. "I have a question to ask you, and the longer I think about it, the more difficult it will seem—a question that means my future existence. I can't wait for eloquent speech. I have no words to-day. Vera, will you be my wife?"

She looked at him as if she thought he was joking.

"Yes, it has come to that. My happiness depends upon a girl of eighteen, who thinks that such an offer must be a jest—something to laugh at when she tells Grannie how foolish Signor Provana was this afternoon. For me it is life or death. In all those days that we were together last year never a thought of love came into my mind. I watched the two faces side by side, and wondered which was the lovelier, but my mind was too full of sorrow for any other feeling than gratitude to the girl who helped to make those last days happy for my dearest. She was my dearest, the only creature I had cared for since her mother's death. There was no room in my heart for anything but the father's despairing affection for the child he was soon to lose. It was when I met you by my darling's grave that your face came back to me with a strange flash of joy, unexpected, incomprehensible. I had thought of you seldom in the half year that had parted us; yet in that moment it seemed to me that I had been longing for you all the time. And the next day, and the next, with every hour that we were together, with every time I looked into your sweet face, the more I realised that the happiness of all my days to come depended upon you. My love did not expand like a flower creeping slowly through dull earth into beauty and light. It rose like a flame, instantaneous, unquenchable.

"Will you make me happy, Vera? Will you trust your life to me? Answer, love, can you trust me?"

Her murmured "Yes" was the nearest thing to silence; but he heard it, and she was folded in his arms, and felt with a sudden thrill what it was to be loved with all the strength of a man's passionate heart.

CHAPTER IV

Shadows of a November twilight are gathering in the two great drawing-rooms of the largest house in Portland Place, rooms that have the grandeur of space, and a certain gloomy splendour that has nothing in common with the caprices and elegances of a modern London drawing-room. The furniture is large and massive. There are tables in Florentine mosaic; cabinets of ebony inlaid with ivory; dower-chests painted by Paul Veronese or his pupils; the richness of arts that are dead; walls hung with Italian tapestry, the work of cloistered nuns whose fingers have been lying in the dust for three centuries; silver lamps suggestive of mortuary chapels.

"I love the Provana drawing-rooms because they are romantic, and I hate them because they give me the horrors," little Lady Susan Amphlett told people.

Romantic was one of her pet words. Her vocabulary was made up of pet words, a jargon of divers tongues, and she used them without mercy. She was very small, very whimsical and pretty, as neat and dainty as a Dresden shepherdess; but she got upon some people's nerves, and was occasionally accused of posing, though she was actually as spontaneous as a tropical parasite in a South American forest, a little egotist, who thought, spoke, and acted only on the impulse of the moment, and whose mind had no room for the idea of an external world, except as its people and scenery were of consequence to herself. The people she did not know or care about were non-existent. Romantic was her word for Madame Provana. She adored Madame Provana, with whom she had some thin thread of affinity, the kind of distant connection that pervades the peerage, and makes it perilous for an outsider to talk of any recent scandal in high life, lest he should fall upon a cousin of the delinquent's.

"Vera and I are connections. Her grandmother was a Disbrowe," Lady Susan told people. "But it is not on that account I adore her. I love her because she is romantic; and so few of the people one knows are romantic."

If asked where the romance came in, Susan was ready with her reasons.

"Can there be anything more romantic than the idea of a lovely, ethereal creature, who looks as if a zephyr might blow her off her feet, married to an ugly giant whose sole thought and business in this life is to heap up riches, a man who cares for nothing but money, whose brain is a ledger, and whose heart is a cheque-book? Can anything be more romantic, when one considers the woman she is and the man he is, and that they absolutely dote upon each other?"

"Provana may dote," someone would say; "but I question the lady's feelings. That an impassioned Italian should be fond of a pretty woman, young enough to be his daughter, and whom he married without a penny for the sake of her sweet looks, all the world can understand. But that Madame Provana worships her money-merchant is another story."

"Did not Desdemona dote upon Othello?" cried Susan. "At least Provana is not black, and adoration such as his would melt a statue. To be worshipped by a case-hardened money-dealer, a man who trades in millions, and holds the sinews of war when nations are spoiling for a fight, a man who is a greater master of finance than half the Chancellors of the Exchequer who have helped to make history! To see how he worships that child-wife of his! It is absolutely pathetic."

"Pathetic" was the pretty Susie's word for Mario Provana. She used the adjective at the slightest provocation. "You are absolute pathetic," she said, when he brought his wife a necklet of priceless cat's eyes set with brilliants, and handed her the velvet case across the tea-table as carelessly as if it had been a box of bonbons.

He was pathetic, impayable, stupendo, all the big adjectives in little Lady Susie's vocabulary.

Susan Amphlett was Susie, or Lady Susie, for everybody who knew her socially; and for a good many people who had never seen her little minois chiffoné nearer than in a photograph. People who spelled over the society papers in their snug suburban drawing-rooms, and loved to follow the flight of those migratory birds, the Mr. and Mrs. Willies and Jimmies, and Lady Bettys and Lord Tommys, who were always flitting from branch to branch, in the only world that seemed worth living in, when one read the Society papers—those shining-surfaced, richly-illustrated sixpennies, which brought the flavour of that other world across the muffin dishes and savoury sandwiches of suburban tea-tables.

Mr. Amphlett was something in the City! Or that was his description when people wanted to describe him. He was briefly described as "rolling," and yet a pauper, if you weighed him against that mountain of gold, Mario Provana, the international money-dealer.

"If ever Provana goes under, half Europe will have to go under with him," Susie's cousin, Claude Rutherford, ex-guardsman, ex-traveller, ex-artist, ex-lion-shooter, said, when he discussed the great financier with inquisitive outsiders.

Claude was in the Portland Place drawing-room this afternoon, lounging against the mantelpiece, near the lamp-lit tea-tables, at one of which Madame Provana presided, his tall, slender figure half lost in a deepening gloom, above that island of bright light made by the lamps on the tea-table.

It was easy for Claude to be lost in shadow, since there was so little of him to lose. Euclid's definition of a line, length without breadth, was his description; but his slender figure was a line that showed race in every inch. His scientific acquaintance called him a crystallisation. "Everything that was ever in the Disbrowes and the Rutherfords, good or bad, he has in its quintessence," the poet Eustace Lyon said of him. "Whatever the worst of the Rutherfords or the Disbrowes, from King Stephen downwards, ever did, Claude is capable of doing. Whatever the best of them ever accomplished he could do, if he had a mind to."

Unhappily, Claude had a mind to do nothing more with his life than lounge through it in placid idleness. He had done so much with life, that it seemed to him that the inconsiderable remnant at his disposal was not enough for action, and so nothing mattered. He had been a soldier, and had seen active service, not without a certain distinction. He had hunted lions and shot harmless elephants, with still more distinction; indeed, in the exploring, lion-annihilating line he had made himself almost a celebrity. He had painted and exhibited pictures that had pleased the public and the critics, and had been told that he might excel in the world of art; but though he loved art, he had not tried to excel. The success of a season satisfied him. Nothing pleased or interested him long. He had no staying power. He painted occasionally to distract himself, but in an amateurish way, and he no longer exhibited. His pictures had not work enough in them to be shown; and, indeed, rarely went beyond the impression of an hour; but the impression was vivid and vigorous, and always suggested how much the painter might have done, if he had cared. He had not long passed the third milestone on the road of life; but he had left off caring for things before his thirtieth birthday. Languor, light sarcasm, and unfailing good temper, were among the qualities that had made him everybody's favourite young man, the very first a smart hostess thought of when she was counting heads for a dinner-party. One incentive that has helped some indolent young men to success was wanting in this case. He was not obliged to earn his daily bread. The Rutherfords had coal-mines on the Scottish border, and were rich enough to provide for indolent scions of the family tree.

Six or seven years ago, before he left the Army, Claude Rutherford had been an arbiter of fashion among the men of his age. In those days he had taken the business of his outer clothing more seriously than the cultivation of a mind in which fancy had ever predominated over thought; and in those days that element of fancy had entered even into his transactions with tailor and bootmaker, and he had allowed himself some flights of imagination in form and colour. Of all the names given to golden youth the old-fashioned name of "exquisite" was the one that fitted Captain Rutherford. It seemed to have been invented for him. He was exquisite in everything, in his habiliments and his surroundings, in speech, and manner, in every detail of his butterfly life. But when he left the Grenadiers—to the infinite regret of his brother officers, who were all his fast friends—he flung foppery from him as it were a cast-off garment; and from the time he worked seriously at his easel, and began to exhibit his pictures, he had become remarkable for the careless grace of clothes that were scrupulously unoriginal, and in the rear rather than in the van of fashion, the sleeves and coat-tails and checks and stripes of the year before last. But he was still exquisite. The grace and the charm were in his own slender form, and not in the stuff that clothed him.

He was not handsome. He was not like David, ruddy and fair to see. He had very little colour, and his pale grey eyes were only brilliant in moments of mirth or strong feeling. He had a long, thin nose, and thin, flexible lips, and his mouth, which was supposed to be the Disbrowe mouth, and a speciality of that ancient race, was strong in character and expressiveness. His hair was light brown, with a natural wave in that small portion which modern barbers allow to remain on the masculine head. A rippling line above his brow indicated that Claude Rutherford might have been as curly as Absalom if he had let his hair grow.

In the afternoon shadows that small head and slim form contrasted curiously with the spacious brow of the tall and commanding figure at the other end of the mantelpiece, the imposing presence of Father Cyprian Hammond, at that time a famous personage in London society, the morals and manners whereof he had of late made it his chief business to satirise and denounce. But the people of pleasure and leisure, the butterflies and humming-birds of the world, the creatures of light and colour, have a keen relish for reproof and denunciation, though they may wince under the lash of irony. For them anything is better than not being talked about.

It had been asked of Father Cyprian why he, who was so scathing a critic of the follies and general worthlessness of the idle rich, was yet not infrequently to be met in their houses.

"If I did not go among my flock, I could not put my finger upon the festering spot," he said. "I am a student of humanity. If Lord Avebury could devote his days to watching bees and wasps, do you wonder that I am interested in watching my fellow-creatures? A professional beauty affords a nobler scope for observation than a queen bee; a gambler on the stock exchange offers more points of interest than the industrious ant. If insects are wonderful, is not the man or the woman who hazards eternal bliss for the trivial pleasures of a London season a creature infinitely more incomprehensible? And if, while I watch and listen, I can discover where these creatures are assailable, if I can find some penetrable spot in their armour of pride, I may be able to preach to them with better chance of being heard."

Father Cyprian was a conspicuous figure in that crowd of pretty women and "nice boys." Tall, even among guardsmen, he held himself like a soldier. He had a fair complexion, light brown hair, and blue eyes. A Saxon of the finest Saxon type, and coming of a family whose genealogical tree had put forth its earliest branches before the Heptarchy. It was the consciousness of superior race, perhaps, that made his fashionable flock tolerant of his stinging denunciation and unmeasured scorn of vice and folly in high places. Everything relating to him was superior. His vestments were superb, his chapel was a thing of beauty. The genius of a Bossuet would hardly have persuaded that world of the successful rich to listen to a withering analysis of its vices and pettinesses from the lips of some little Irish priest, reared in a hovel and nourished on potatoes and potheen; but it bowed the neck before Father Cyprian's good birth and grand manner.

Anglicans who met him in society, mostly in the houses of the powerful or the rich, talked of him as a worldling; but his own flock knew better. They knew that wherever the brilliant Jesuit might be seen, however light his manner or trivial his conversation, one deeply-seated purpose was at the back of his mind, the making of proselytes, the aggrandisement of his Church, that Invincible, Indestructible, Incomparable, Supreme, and Unquestionable Power, to which he had given the service and the devotion of his whole being. If he went much among statesmen and rulers it was because his Church wanted influence; if he cultivated the friendship of millionaires it was because his Church wanted money. For himself he wanted nothing, for he had been born to independence; and though he had given much of his fortune to the necessities of his Order, his income was still ample for the only scheme of life that was possible for him. He was not a man who could have lived in sordid surroundings, though he could go down into the nethermost depths of East-End poverty, and give his days and nights to carrying the lamp of Faith into dark places. He had a refinement of sense that would have made squalor, or even shabby-genteel ugliness, unbearable; and he had an ardent and artistic imagination which made some touch of beauty in his surroundings as needful to him as fresh air and cold water.

The attention of both these men, the priest and the man-about-town, was concentrated upon the lady of the house, who, just at this moment, was taking very little notice of either of them. She was surrounded by the smartest and prettiest women in the room, chief amongst them Lady Susan Amphlett, who was always to be found near Vera at these friendly tea-parties.

Vera let Lady Susan and the other women do almost all the talking. She sat looking straight before her, dreamily silent, amidst the animated chatter about trivialities that had ceased to interest her.

She was still as delicately slender as she had been six years ago at San Marco, when the parsons had called her ethereal, and the spinsters had called her half-starved; but those six years had made a transformation, and she was not the same Vera.

She had tasted of the Tree of Knowledge. She had enjoyed all the amusements and excitements that great cities can give to rich and beautiful women. She had been flattered and followed in Rome and Paris and London, had been written about in the New York Herald, and had been the fashion everywhere; a person whom not to know was to confess oneself as knowing nobody and going nowhere. Indeed, it was a kind of confession of outsiderism not to be able to talk of Madame Provana as "Vera."

She had accepted the position with a kind of languid acquiescence, taking all things for granted, after the first year, when everything amused her. In this sixth year of marriage, and wealth without limit, she was tired of everything, except the society of authors and painters and actors and musicians—the people who appealed to her imagination. She had inherited from her father the yearning for things that earth cannot give—the au delà, the light that never was on sea or land. "The glory and the dream."

She admired and respected Father Cyprian Hammond, and she liked him to talk to her, though she could divine that steadfast purpose at the back of his head, the determination to bring her into the Papal fold. She argued with him from her Anglican standpoint, and pleaded for that via media that might reconcile old things with new; and she felt the weakness of her struggle against that skilled dialectician; but she refused to be converted. Half the pleasure of her intimacy with this Eagle of Monk Street would be lost if she surrendered, and had to exchange the struggle for the attitude of passive submission.

His arguments sometimes went near to convincing her; but the Faith he offered did not satisfy those vague longings for the something beyond. It was too simple, too matter-of-fact to arrest her imagination. It offered little more than she had already in the ritual of her own Church. The change did not seem worth while.

She looked up suddenly in the midst of the silvery treble talk about theatres and frocks.

"Claude, do you ever keep a promise?" she asked.

"Always, I hope."

"You promised to bring Mr. Symeon to see me."

"Did I?"

"Indeed you did. Ages ago."

"Ages?"

"Well, nearly three weeks. It was at the Helstones' dinner."

"Three weeks. Mr. Symeon is not at the call of the first comer."

There was a little cry from the women, who had left off talking in order to listen.

"He calls Madame Provana the first comer!" exclaimed the youngest and pertest of the circle.

"I call myself the first comer where Symeon is concerned. I am not one of his initiated. I belong to the outer herd of wretches who eat butcher's meat and attach importance to dinner. Mr. Symeon condescends when he gives me half an hour of a life that is spent mostly in the clouds."

"I would give worlds to know him," said Lady Susan. "I have taken his quarterly, The Unseen, from the beginning, His articles upon the spiritual life are adorable, but I am not conceited enough to pretend to understand him."

"If people understood him, he would be less admired," said Rutherford.

"What does he do?" asked the youngest and flippantest. "I am always hearing of Mr. Symeon and his spook magazine; but what does he do? Is it thought-reading, slate-writing, materialisation? Does he float up to the ceiling, as Home did? My Grannie swears she saw him, yes, positively floating, in that large house by the Marble Arch."

"Mr. Symeon does nothing," replied Claude. "He is the high priest of the Transcendental. He talks."

"How disappointing!"

"Most people find that enough."

"They are bored?"

"No; they are fascinated. Mr. Symeon is more magnetic than Gladstone was. He must have stolen those green eyes of his from a mermaid. His disciples get nothing but his eyes and his talk; and they believe in him as Orientals believe in Buddha. I have heard people say he is Buddha—Gautama's latest incarnation."

"That's rather lovely!" exclaimed Miss Flippant. "I would give worlds to see him."

"We'll excuse you the worlds, even if you owned them," said Claude in his lazy voice. "You may see him within the next ten minutes, unless he is a promise-breaker. I had not forgotten your commands, Vera. I spent half a day in hunting Symeon, and did not leave him till he promised to come to tea with you. I believe tea is the most material refreshment he takes."

"You are ever so much better than I thought you," said Vera, with one look up at Rutherford, before she turned to gaze at the distant door, heedless of the talk that went on round her, until after some minutes a servant announced "Mr. Symeon."

Claude Rutherford left his station by the mantelpiece and went to meet the visitor.

The spacious rooms were mostly in shadow by this time, all the lamps being so tempered by artistic shades in sea-green silk that they gave faint patches of colour rather than light, and some people started at the sound of Mr. Symeon's name, almost as if they had seen a ghost.

It was a name that all cultured people knew, even when they did not know the man. Francis Symeon was a leader in the spiritual world, and there were no depths in the mysteries of occultism, from ancient Egypt to modern India, that he had not sounded. He was the editor and proprietor of The Unseen, a quarterly magazine, to which only the most advanced thinkers were allowed to contribute—a magazine which the subscriber opened with a thrill of anticipation, wondering what new revelation of the "life beyond" he was to find in those shining, hot-pressed pages, where the matter was often more dazzling than the gloss on the paper.

Vera watched with eager interest and a faint flush of pleasure as Rutherford and Symeon came through the shadows towards her.

"You see I have kept my promise, and here is Mr. Symeon, to answer some of those far-reaching questions with which you often bewilder my poor brain."

Vera left her table, where there had come a sudden lull in the soprano voices as Mr. Symeon drew near—a pause in the discussion of frocks and hats in the new comedy at the St. James's. She stood up to talk to Mr. Symeon, telling him how she had been reading the last number of The Unseen, and more especially his own contribution, an essay on the other life, as understood by Tennyson and Browning.

In that half-light which makes all beautiful things more beautiful, she had a spirit look, and might have seemed the materialisation of Mr. Symeon's thought, as she stood before him, fragile and slender, with glimmering lamplight on her cloud of brown hair, and on the simple white gown, of some transparent fabric, loosely draped over satin that flashed through its fleecy whiteness. Her only ornament was a necklace of aqua marina in a Tiffany setting.

"She wears that thing when she wants to look like a mermaid," Miss Pert whispered to her pal.

"No; she wears it to remind us that she has some of the finest jewels in London, and that she despises them," said the pal, who had reached that critical age which is described as "getting on," and was inclined to take a sour view of a young woman who had married millions.

Symeon and Vera talked for some time, she with a suppressed eagerness—earnest, almost impassioned; Symeon grave and reserved, yet obviously interested.

"We cannot talk of these things in a crowd," he said. "If I had known you had a party—"

"It is not a party. People come every afternoon in the winter, when there is not much for them to do; but if you will be so kind as to come early some day, at three o'clock, for instance, I will not be at home to anybody, unless it were Claude, who loves to hear you talk."

"I will come to-morrow," said Symeon; and then, with briefest adieu, he walked slowly through the crowd, acknowledging the greetings of a few intimates with a distant bend of his iron-grey head, and walking amongst the pretty faces and smart frocks as he might have done through so many sparrows pecking on a lawn.

Lady Susan came to Vera, excited and eager.

"Why didn't you keep him? I wanted you to introduce him to me. I have been pining to know him. I read every line of his Review. He is wonderful! I believe he has secrets that ward off age. You must ask me to meet him—at luncheon—a party of four, with Claude. Claude has been horrid about him."

"I value his friendship too much to introduce him to Tom, Dick, and Harry," said Claude. "Vera and he are elective affinities."

Father Cyprian and Claude Rutherford left the house together.

"May I walk with you as far as your lodgings?" Claude asked.

"By all means, and come in with me, if you can. It is early yet, and I have long wanted a talk with you."

"Serious?"

"Yes, even serious. When one cares as much for a young man as I do for you, there is always room for seriousness. You look alarmed, but there is no occasion. I don't preach long sermons, especially not to young men."

They walked to the end of the street in silence. They were old friends; and though Claude was the most lax among Papists, Cyprian Hammond had never lost hope of bringing him back to the fold. He was emotional and imaginative, and he had a heart. Sooner or later there would come a day when he would want the utmost the Church could do for him.

"You can't wonder if I am a little afraid," Claude said presently. "There has been some hard hitting from your pulpit within the last year."

"You have heard my moralities—I won't call them sermons?"

"Yes, I have heard; but I doubt if I have enjoyed your diatribes as much as the other sinners, especially the women of your flock. They love to be told they are a shade worse than Semiramis, if you will only imply that they are as fascinating as Cleopatra."

"Poor worms," said the priest with a long-drawn sigh. "They are such very poor creatures. Even their sins are petty."

"Would you prefer them if they were poisoners, like the Borgia?"

"No; but I might despise them less. And I should have more hope of their repentance. These creatures don't know they are sinners. They gamble, they squander their husbands' fortunes, shipwreck their sons' inheritance; and when the domestic ship goes down they are injured innocents, surprised to find that 'things are so expensive.' I have talked with them—not in the confessional—and I have sounded the shallows of their silly minds—there are no depths, unless it were a depth of self-love. They come to Mass, and sit fanning themselves and sniffing eau-de-Cologne, while I expostulate with them and try to turn their thoughts into new channels. And then they get tired of the creed in which they were brought up; tired of hearing hard things, and of tasting wormwood instead of honey."

"Is modern London so like Babylon?"

"I doubt if the city with a hundred gates was much worse. And your substitutes for the Church you have deserted—your Christian Science, Pragmatism, Humanism, your letters from the dead, your philanthropy—expressed in oranges and buns for workhouse children, and in fashionable bazaars; charities that overlap each other and pauperise more than they relieve; and all for want of that one tremendous Central Power that could harmonise every effort, bring every man and woman's work into line and rule. In the history of God's chosen people, the one unpardonable sin was the worship of strange gods. Their Creator knew that religion was the only basis of conduct, and that the worshippers of evil gods must themselves become infamous. But this is the age of strange gods. You all have your groves and high places, your Baal and Astarte, your Kali or your Siva, your shrines upon mountain tops and under green trees, your Buddha, your Nietzsche, your Spinoza, your Comte. You run after the teachers of fantastic things, the high priests of materialism. You worship anywhere but in your church; you believe anything but the faith of your forefathers."

They were at Father Cyprian's door by this time, in one of those wide streets west of Portland Place, and north of the world of fashion. Streets that may still be described as quiet, save for the ceaseless roar of traffic in the Marylebone Road, a sound diminished by distance, the ebb and flow of life in an artery of the great city. It was in a street parallel with this that the great Cardinal who defied the law of England had lived and died half a century before.

They had been walking slowly through the thickening mist of a fine November evening, a grey vapour, across which street lamps and lighted windows glimmered in faint flashes of gold, an atmosphere that Claude Rutherford loved, all the more, perhaps, because he had never been able to satisfy himself in painting it.

"What is the good of trying, when one must always fall short of Turner?" he had said to himself in those younger and more eager days when he still tried to do things.

Father Cyprian had talked with a kind of suppressed passion as they walked through solitary streets, and now he laughed lightly, as he turned the key in his door.

"You have had the sermon after all," he said.

"It didn't touch me. I am not an extravagant, bridge-playing woman, and I worship no strange god."

"I shall touch you presently; your withers are not unwrung."

"Suppose I say good night and give you the slip."

"You won't do that. I was your father's friend."

That was enough. Claude bent his head a little, as if at a sacred name, and followed the priest up the uncarpeted stone staircase to a large room on the first floor—the conventional London drawing-room, with its three long windows and chilling white linen blinds.

But, except the shape of the room and the white blinds, there was nothing to offend the eye that looked for beauty. The floor was cheaply covered with sea-blue felt, which echoed the colouring of the sea-blue walls, and the central space was occupied by a massive knee-hole desk of ebony, inlaid with ivory, evidently of Italian workmanship, and picturesque enough to please without being a chef d'oeuvre. There were only two objects of art in the spacious room, but each was supreme after its kind. A carved ivory crucifix of considerable size, mounted on black velvet, was centred on the wall facing the windows; and over the marble mantelpiece there hung a Holy Family by Fra Angelico. These, which were exquisite, were the only ornaments that Father Cyprian had given himself, in his ten years' residence in this house, where this spacious sitting-room, with a large bedroom for himself and a small room for his servant, comprised all his accommodation.

Six high-backed arm-chairs, covered with old stamped leather, and a massive gate-legged table, black with age, on which he dined, completed his furniture. To some visitors the sparsely-furnished room might have seemed cold and cheerless; but there was an air of repose in its simplicity that satisfied the artistic mind. It looked like a room designed for prayer and meditation; not a room for study, for the one bookcase, with its neat range of theological works, would not have sufficed for the poorest student. It looked like a room meant for solitude and thought, and for only the most serious, the most confidential conversation.

"I have always a sense of rest when I come into this room," Rutherford said, while Father Cyprian was lighting the candles in a bronze candelabrum on his desk.

"You should come here oftener, Claude. You might make a retreat here once or twice a week. Sit on the bank for a few hours, and let that tumultuous river of modern life go by you, while you think of the land where there is no tumult, only a divine repose, or an agony of regret. When did you make your last confession, Claude?"

"I have a bad memory, Father. Don't tax it too severely."

The priest was not to be satisfied by a flippant answer. He pressed the question with authority.

"What have I to confess? An empty, dissatisfied soul, a useless life; no positive wickedness, only negative worthlessness. I am not an infidel," Claude added eagerly. "If I were an unbeliever, I would not presume to claim your friendship. I should think it an insolence to cross your threshold. I have been slack, I have fallen into a languid acceptance of my own shortcomings."

"You have fallen in love with another man's wife," said the priest gravely. "That is the name of your sin."

The thin face paled ever so slightly, but there was no indignant protest; indeed, the head drooped a little, as if the sinner had whispered mea culpa.

"I have never made love to her," he said in a low voice. "But I am human, and can't help loving her."

"You can help going to her house. You can help hanging over her as she sits among her friends. When it comes to making love the Rubicon is passed, and the chances of retreat are as one in fifty. You are on the downward slope, Claude. Every time you enter that house you go there at the hazard of your soul."

"She has so few real friends. She is alone among a crowd. She and I were friends as children, or at least when she was a child. I should be a cur if I kept away from her, when she needs my friendship, just because of the risk to myself. I am too fond of her ever to hazard a situation that would mean danger for her. I know how much a woman in her position has to lose. She is not the kind of woman who could pass through the furnace of the divorce court, and hold up her head and be happy afterwards. She is a creature of spirit, not of flesh. Passion would never make amends to her for shame."

"Yet, knowing this, you make yourself her intimate companion!"

"I shall never betray myself. She will never know what you know. For her I am a feather-brained amateur of life; interested in many things, caring for nothing, a saunterer through the world, without much heart, and without any serious purpose. She often scolds me for my frivolity."

"I admit that she has a certain childlike innocence which might keep her unconscious of your feelings, till the fatal moment in which you will fling principle, prudence, honour to the winds and declare yourself her lover—"

"That moment will never come. The day I feel myself in danger I shall leave her for ever. In the meantime, if I am essential to her happiness, I shall stop."

"How can you be essential? She has crowds of friends, and a husband who adores her."

"A husband of fifty years of age, grave, silent, with his mind concentrated upon international finance; a man who is thinking of another Turkish loan while he sits opposite her, with his stony eyes fixed upon space—a man whose brain is a calculating machine and his heart a handful of ashes."

"Has she complained of him?"

"Never; but things have leaked out. She was not eighteen—little more than a child—when she married him. She gave herself to him in a romantic impulse, admiring his force of character, her heart touched by his affection for a dying daughter. To be so loved by that strong nature seemed to her enough for happiness. But that was six years ago, and she has lived six years in the world. The romance has gone out of her love. What can she have in common with such a man?"

"The bond of marriage—his love, and her sense of duty," answered the priest.

"She has a keen sense of a wife's duty: she preaches sermons upon her husband's goodness of heart, his fine character; and she ends with a sigh, and regrets that for some mysterious reason she has not been able to make him happy."

"She is too rich and too much indulged, and she is without a saving creed. Poor child, I would give much to save her from herself and from you."

"Don't be afraid of me, Father. Men of my stamp may be trusted. We are too feather-brained to be intense, even in sin. Good night. I hear the jingle of glass and silver, and I think it must be near your dinner-time. Good night!"

The priest gave him his hand, but not his blessing. That was withheld for a better moment.

CHAPTER V

When a woman's imagination, still young and ardent, begins to find the things of earth as Hamlet found them, "weary, flat, stale, and unprofitable," it is only natural that she should turn with a longing mind to the life that earth cannot give, the something unseen and mysterious that certain gifted individuals have attributed to themselves the power of seeing. Vera, after six years of marriage, six years of unlimited wealth and unconscious self-indulgence, had begun to discover that most things were stale, and some things weary, and all things unprofitable; and then, to a mind steeped in modern poetry and modern romance, and the modern music that always means something more than mere combinations of harmonious sounds, there had come a yearning for the higher life, the transcendental life that only the elect can realise, and only the earth-weary can ardently desire.

Francis Symeon was the philosopher to whom she turned with unquestioning faith; for even those who had spoken lightly of his creed and of his reasoning faculty had admitted that the man was essentially sincere, and that the faith he offered his followers was for him as impregnable as the rock of Holy Scripture.

He was announced on the following day as the clock in Vera's morning-room struck three, a punctuality so exceptional as to seem almost uncanny, when compared with the vague sense of time in the rest of her acquaintance. She received him in a room where there was no fear of interruption—her sanctuary, more library than boudoir, where the books she loved, her poets and novelists and philosophers, in the bindings she had herself invented, filled her book-cases, alternating with black-and-white portraits of the gods of her idolatry—Browning, Tennyson, Byron, Scott, de Musset, Heine, Henry Irving, Gounod. Only the dead had place there—the dead musician, the dead poet, the dead actor. It was death that made them beloved and longed for. They had gone from her reach for ever; and it was this sense of something for ever lost that made them adorable.

Mr. Symeon looked round the walls with evident admiration.

"I see you prefer the faces of the noble dead to water-colour sketches and majolica plates," he said. "Divine books, divine faces, those are the best companions a woman can have."

"I spend a good deal of my life in this room," Vera answered. "I have no children. I suppose if I had I should spend most of my time with them. I should not have to choose my companions among the dead."

"You have chosen them among the living," Mr. Symeon answered in a voice that thrilled her. "Do you think that Tennyson is dead? He who knew that the whole question of religion hinges upon the after life: immortality or a godless universe. Or Browning, who has gone to the very core of religion, whose magnificent mind grasped the highest and deepest in Divine love and Divine power? Such spirits are unquenchable. This rag of mortality upon which they hang must lie in the dust, but for the elect death is only the release of the immaterial from the material, the escape of the butterfly from the worm. You have the assurance from the lips of Christ: God is the God of the living; and for those whose existence on earth is only the apprenticeship to immortality, there is no such thing as death."

This was the chief article in Mr. Symeon's creed; hinted at, but not formally stated in his contributions to the magazine which he edited. He claimed immortality only for the elect—for those in whom the spirit predominated over the flesh. To Vera there was no new idea in his exposition of faith. She had a feeling that she had always known this, from the time she stood beside Shelley's grave in the shadow of the

Roman Cenotaph, and that other grave under the hill, the resting-place of Shelley's Adonais. The thought of corruption had been far from her mind, albeit she knew that the heart of one poet and the wasted form of the other were lying in the darkness below those spring flowers on which her tears were falling, and it was no surprise to her to hear a serious man of sixty years of age declare his faith in the unbroken chain of life.

"I saw that you were not one of those who scoff at transcendental truths," Mr. Symeon said, after a few moments' silence. "I read in your eyes last night that you are one of us in spirit, though you may know nothing of our creed. You must join our society."

"Your society?"

"Yes, Madame Provana. We are a company of friends in the world of sense and in the world of spirit. The majority of us have crossed the river. As corporal substance they have ceased to be; their dwelling is in the starlit spaces beyond Acheron. For the common herd they are dead; but for us they are as vividly alive as they were when they walked among the vulgar living, and wore life's vesture of clay. They are nearer to us since they have passed the gulf, and we understand them as we never could while they wore the livery of earth. They are our close companions. The veil that parted us is rent, and we see them face to face."

Vera listened in silence, and the grave, slow speech went on without a break.

"We have our meetings. We discuss the great problems, the everlasting mysteries; we press forward to the higher life. We are not afraid of being foolish, romantic, illogical. We are prepared for contempt and incredulity from the outside world; but for us, whose minds have received the light from those other minds, who have been consoled in our sorrows, strengthened in our faith by those influencing souls, there is nothing more difficult in our creed than in that of Newman, who saw behind each form of material beauty the light, the flower, the living presence of an angel. The spirits of the illustrious dead are our angels; and our communion with them is the joy of our lives. We call ourselves simply Us. Our chosen poets, philosophers, painters, musicians, even the great actors of the past, those ardent spirits in whom genius was unquenchable by death, men and women whose minds were fire, and their corporal existence of no account in the forces of their being: those who have lived by the spirit and not by the flesh—all these are of our company. These are the influencing souls who are our companions in the silence and seclusion of our lives. Not by the trumpery expedient of an alphabet rapped out upon a table, or by the writing of an unguided pencil; but by the communion of spirit with spirit, we feel those other minds in converse with our own. They teach, they exhort, they uplift us to their spirit world, sometimes in hours of meditation, and sometimes in the closer communion of dreams."

"Are their voices heard—do they speak to you?" Vera asked, deeply moved, her own voice trembling a little.

"Only in dreams. Speech is material, and belongs to the earthly machine. It is not from lip to ear, but from mind to mind that the message comes."

"And do they appear to you? Do you see them as they were on earth?" Vera asked.

The November twilight had filled the room with shadow, and the face of the spiritualist, the sharply-cut features, and hollow cheeks, and luminous grey-green eyes, looked like the face of a ghost.

"Only in dreams is it given to us to look upon the disembodied great. We feel, and we know! That is enough. But in some rare cases—where the earthly vesture has worn to its thinnest tissue—where death has set its seal upon the living, to one so divested of mortal attributes, so marked for the spirit world, the vision may be granted. Such an one may see."

"You have known...?" faltered Vera.

"Yes, I knew such a case. In the final hour of an ebbing life the chain of wedded love that death had broken was reunited, and the wife died with her last long gaze turned to the vision of her husband. Her last word was 'reunited!'"

Vera was strangely impressed. It was not easy for the unbelieving to make a mock of Mr. Symeon's creed. The force of his convictions, the ideas that he had cultivated and brooded upon for the larger part of his life, had so possessed the man, that even scoffers were sometimes moved by his absolute sincerity, and found themselves, as it were unawares, treating his theories almost seriously. For Vera, in whom imagination was the greater part of mind, there was no inclination to scoff, but rather a most earnest desire that the spiritualist's creed might be justified by her own experience, that it might be granted to her to sit in the melancholy solitude of that room, with a volume of Browning on her lap, and to feel that the poet was near her, that an invisible spirit was breathing enlightenment into her mind, as she read the dying words of the beloved apostle in "A Death in the Desert," which had been to her as a new gospel—and to know that when she raised her eyes to the portrait on the wall, it was not the dead, but the living upon whom she looked.

This was involved in the creed of her Church—the Communion of Saints.

Were not the gifted, who had lived free from all the grossness of clay, from the taint of earthly sin, worthy to be numbered among the saints, and like them gifted with perpetual life, perpetual fellowship with the faithful who adored them?

When he left the great, silent house Mr. Symeon knew that he had made a proselyte. Though Vera had said little, it was impossible to mistake the fervour with which she had welcomed his revelation of the spirit world. Here was a mind in want of new interests, a heart yearning for something that the world could not give.

She sat by the dying fire, in the gathering darkness, long after her visitor had left her. Yes, this had been her need of late—something to think of, something to wish for. Her life—so over full of the things that women desire, pomp and luxury, troops of friends, jewels and fine clothes, the "too much" that money always brings with it—had vacant spaces, and hours of vague depression, in which the sense of loneliness became an aching pain.

CHAPTER VI

Mario Provana's wife was the fashion. The prestige for which some women strive and labour for years, spending themselves and their husband's fortunes in the strenuous endeavour, and having to confess themselves failures at last, had been won by Vera without an effort. Her husband's wealth had done much; her youth, and the something rare and exceptional in her beauty, had done more; but the Disbrowes had done the most of all. With such material—a triple millionaire's wife in the first bloom of her loveliness—the work had been easy; but no one could deny that the Disbrowes had worked, and might fairly congratulate themselves, as well as their fair young cousin, (first, second, or third, as the case might be) upon the result of their tactful efforts. All Disbrowes were supposed to have tact, just as they had arched insteps, and long, lean hands. It was as much a mark of their race.

From the day of Vera's return from her long Italian honeymoon she found herself walled round and protected by her mother's kindred. They came from all the points of the compass. Lord Okehampton from his park in North Devon, Lady Balgowrie from her castle in Aberdeenshire, Lady Helstone from the Land's End. They came unbidden, and overflowing with affection, but much too tactful to be vulgarly demonstrative.

"Poor Lady Felicia's foolish pride kept us all at a distance," they told Vera; "but now that you are emancipated, and your own mistress, I hope you will let us be useful."

From countesses down to hard-up spinsters, they all said the same thing, and no one could accuse them of "gush." They all announced themselves as worldlings, pure and simple, and they made no professions.

"You have made a great match, my dear," said Lady Helstone, "and you have a great career before you, if you are careful in the choice of your friends. That is the essential point. One black sheep among your flock might spoil all your chances. There are men about town that my husband calls 'oilers'—they were called tigers when my mother was young—and one of those in a new woman's visiting list can wreck her. The creatures are intolerably pushing, and don't rest till they can pose as cavaliere servente or at least as l'ami de la maison."

Vera welcomed this army of blood relations with amiability, but without enthusiasm. She was ready to love that one kind lady who had given her the only happy holiday of her childhood, under whose hospitable roof she had known Claude Rutherford; but the countesses who had been unaware of her existence while she was a dependant upon "poor Lady Felicia," could have no claim upon her affection. Yet they and their belongings were all pleasant people; and in that large and splendid house which was to be her home in London, she found that people were wanted.

The emptiness of those spacious rooms, during the long hours when her husband was at his offices in the City, soon became appalling; and she was glad of the lively aunts and cousins, and their following, who transformed her drawing-rooms into a parrot house, both for noise and brilliant colour, to say nothing of the aquiline beaks that prevailed among the dowagers and elderly bachelors. Once established as her relations—the distance of some of the cousinship being ignored—they came as often as Vera cared to ask them, and they brought all the people whom Vera ought to know, the poets, and novelists, and playwrights, who were all dying to know the daughter of Lancelot Davis, that delightful poet whom everybody loved and nobody envied. His fame had increased since he had gone into the ground; and his shade was now crowned with that belated fame which is the aureole of the dead. They brought the newest painting people, and the fashionable actors and actresses, English or American, as well as that useful following of "nice boys," who are as necessary in every drawing-room as occasional chairs, or tables to hold tea-cups.

Instigated by the Disbrowes, and with Mario Provana's approval, Vera soon began that grand business of entertaining, to which a triple millionaire's wife should indubitably devote the greater part of her time, talent, and energy. Countesses and countess-dowagers gave their mornings to her, advising whom she should invite, and how she should entertain. They instructed her in the table of precedence as solemnly as if it had been the Church Catechism, showed her how, in some rare concatenation, a rule might be broken, as a past master of harmony might, on occasion, allow himself the use of consecutive fifths.

They were never tired of extending Madame Provana's knowledge of life as it is lived in the London that is bounded on the south by Queen Anne's Gate and by Portland Place on the north. They called it opening her mind—and praised her for the intelligence with which she mastered the social problems.

Her husband was pleased to see her admired and cherished, above all to see her happy; yet he could not but feel some touch of disappointment when he looked back upon those quiet afternoons in the olive woods at San Marco, and the tea-parties of three in Lady Felicia's sitting-room, and remembered how he had thought he was marrying a friendless and unappreciated girl, who would be all the world to him, and for whom he must be all the world, in a long future of wedded love.

He thought he was marrying a friendless orphan, whose divine inheritance was poetry and beauty; and he found that he had married the Disbrowes.

They were all terribly friendly. They never hinted at his inferior social status, his vulgar level as a tradesman, only trading in money instead of goods. They behaved as if, by marrying their cousin, he had become a Disbrowe. Lady Helstone, Lady Balgowrie, Lord and Lady Okehampton treated him with affection without arrière pensée. The most that Okehampton, as a man of the world, wanted from the great financier was his advice about the investment of his paltry surplus, so trifling an amount that he blushed to allude to the desire in such exalted company.

But now a time had come when Vera needed no counsel from the Disbrowes, and when she was beginning to treat those social obligations about which she, as a tyro, had laboured diligently, with a royal carelessness. Her aunts complained that she had grown casual, and that she had even gone very near offending some of their particular friends, people whom to have on her visiting list ought to have been the crown of her life.

Vera apologised.

"I know far too many people," she said; "my house is becoming a caravanserai."

She said "my house" unconsciously—with the deep-seated knowledge that all those splendid rooms and the splendid crowds that filled them meant very little in her husband's life.

Six years of the "too much" had changed Lady Felicia's granddaughter. The things that money can buy had ceased to charm; the people whom in her first season she had thought it a privilege to know had sunk into the dismal category of bores. Almost everybody was a bore; except a few men of letters, who had known her father, or who loved his verses. For those she had always a welcome; and she was proud when they told her that she was her father's daughter. Her eyes, her voice were his, these enthusiasts told her. She was a creature of fire and light, as he was.

After three or four years of pleasure in trivial things, she had grown disdainful of all delights, except those of the mind and the imagination. The opera, or the theatre when Shakespeare was acted, always charmed her, but for the olla podrida of music and nonsense that most people cared for she had nothing but scorn. She never missed a fine concert or a picture show, but she broke half her engagements to evening parties, or appeared for a quarter of an hour and vanished before her hostess had time to introduce the new arrivals, American or continental, who were dying to know her.

The general impression was that she gave herself airs: but they were airs that harmonised with her fragile beauty, the something ethereal that distinguished her from other women.

"If any stout, florid creature were to behave like Madame Provana, she would be cut dead," people told Vera's familiar friend, Lady Susan Amphlett.

Lady Susan pleaded her friend's frail constitution as an excuse for casual behaviour.

"She is all nerves, and suffers agonies from ennui. Her father was consumptive, and her mother was a fragile creature who faded away after three years of a happy married life. It was a marriage of romance and beauty. Davis and his wife were both lovely; but they had no stamina. Vera has no stamina."

Lady Felicia had been lying more than a year in the family vault in Warwickshire. Her last years had been the most prosperous and comfortable years of her life, and the vision of the future that had smiled upon her in the golden light above the jutting cliff of Bordighera had been amply realised by the unmeasured liberality of her granddaughter's husband. Before Vera's honeymoon was over, the shabby lodgings in the dull, unlovely street had been exchanged for a spacious flat in a red brick sky-scraper overlooking Regent's Park. Large windows, lofty ceilings, a southern aspect, and the very newest note in decoration and upholstery had replaced the sunless drawing-room and the Philistine walnut furniture, and for those last years the Disbrowe clan ceased to talk of Captain Cunningham's widow as poor Lady Felicia. What more could any woman want of wealth, than to be able to draw upon the purse of a triple millionaire? As everything in Lady Felicia's former surroundings, her shifting camp of nearly twenty years, had been marked with the broad arrow of poverty, every detail of this richly feathered nest of her old age bore the stamp of riches; and the Disbrowes, who knew the price of things, could see that Mario Provana had treated his wife's relation with princely generosity.

Once more Lady Felicia's diamonds, those last relics of her youth, to which she had held through all her necessitous years, were to be met in the houses of the fashionable and the great; and Lady Felicia herself, in a sumptuous velvet gown, silvery hair dressed by a fashionable artist, emerged from retirement in a perfect state of preservation, having the advantage by a decade of giddy dowagers who had never missed a season.

The giddy dowagers looked at her through their face à main, and laughed about Lady Felicia's "resurrection."

"She looks as if she had been kept in cotton-wool and put to bed at ten o'clock every night," they said.

Grannie enjoyed that Indian summer of her life, and was grateful.

"You have married a prince," she told Vera, "and if you ever slight him or behave badly, you will deserve to come to a bad end."

Vera protested that she knew her husband's value, and was not ungrateful.

"I want to make him happy," she said.

"That is easy enough," retorted Grannie. "You have only to love him as he deserves to be loved."

"Was that so easy?" Vera wondered sadly.

It seemed to her that, by no fault of hers, there had come a difference in her relations with her husband. He was always kind to her, but he was farther from her than in the first year—the Italian year—which, to look back upon, was still the happiest of her married life. He was absorbed in a business that needed strenuous labour and unflagging care. He had told her that it was not his own interests alone that he had to guard; but the interests of other people. There were thousands of helpless people who would suffer by his loss of fortune, or his loss of prestige. The pinnacle upon which the house of Provana stood was the strong rock of a multitude. A certain anxiety was therefore inevitable throughout his business life. He could never be the holiday husband, sharing all a wife's trivial pleasures, interested in all the nothings that make the sum of an idle woman's existence.

Vera accepted the inevitable, and it was only when she began to think the best people rather boring, that she discovered how the distance had widened between herself and her husband. Without a dissentient word, without a single angry look, they had come to be one of those essentially modern couples whose loveless unions Father Cyprian deplored.

She thought the blame was with Mario Provana. He had ceased to care for her. Just as she had grown weary of her troops of friends, her husband had wearied of the wife he had chosen after a week's courtship.

"He thought he was in love, but he could not really have cared for me," she told herself. "His heart was empty and desolate after the loss of his daughter, and he took me because I was young and had been Giulia's friend."

This was how Vera reasoned, sitting in her lonely sanctuary, while on the other side of the wall there was a man of mature age, a man with a proud temper and a passionate heart, a man who had endured slights in his youth, whose first marriage had ended in disappointment, the crushing discovery that the beautiful girl who had been given to him by a noble and needy father had sacrificed her inclinations for the sake of her family, and had never loved him. She had been faithful, and she had endured his love. That was all. And in those last years, when disease had laid a withering hand upon her beauty, and when the world seemed far off, and when only her husband's love stood between her and death, she had learnt the value of a good man's devotion, and had loved him a little in return. He had suffered the disillusions of that first union. Yet again, after many years, he had staked his happiness upon a single chance, and had taken a girl of eighteen to his heart, in a state of exaltation that was more like a dream than sober reality. He had lavished upon this unsophisticated girl all the force of strong feelings long held in check. At last, at last, in the maturity of manhood, the love that had been denied to his youth was being given to him in full measure. He could not doubt that she loved him. That innocent, unconscious love, trusting as the love of children, revealed itself in tones and looks that he could not mistake. Before he asked her to be his wife he was sure that she loved him; but after six years of marriage he was no longer sure of anything, except that his wife was the fashion, and that her Disbrowe relations were innumerable. He was sure of nothing about this girl whom he had clasped to his breast in a rapture of triumphant love, on the hill above the Mediterranean. Year after year of their married life had carried her farther away from him. Who could say precisely what made the separation? He only knew that the years which should have tightened the bond had loosened it; and that he could no longer recognise his child-wife of their Roman honeymoon in the fragile ennuyée whom Society had chosen to adore.

CHAPTER VII

"Well, now your whim has been gratified, I should like to know what you think of Francis Symeon?" Claude Rutherford asked, as he put down his hat in Vera's sanctum, the day after her conference with the high priest of occultism.

The question was his only greeting. He slipped into the low and spacious chair by the hearth, and seemed to lose himself in it, while he waited for a reply. He had the air of being perfectly at home in the room, with no idea that he could possibly be unwelcome. He came and went in Madame Provana's house with a lazy insouciance that many people would have taken for indifference. Only the skilled reader of men would have detected the hidden fire under that outward serenity of the attractive man, who flirts with any attractive woman of his acquaintance, and cares for none.

"I think he is wonderful."

"And you believe in him?"

"Yes, I believe in him, because his ideas only give form and substance to the thoughts that have haunted me ever since I began to think."

"Grisly thoughts?"

"No, Claude; happy thoughts. When I first read my father's poetry and began to think about him—in my dull grey room in Grannie's lodgings—I had a feeling that he was near me. He was there; but behind the veil. When I read 'In Memoriam' the feeling grew stronger, and I knew that death is not the end of love. There was nothing that shocked or startled me in what Mr. Symeon told me yesterday."

"About 'Us,' the spiritual club, in which the dead and the living are members on the same footing? The club that elects, or selects, Confucius or Browning one day, and Lady Fanny Ransom—mad Lady Fanny as they call her—the next?"

"I saw nothing to ridicule in a companionship of lofty minds. But you know more about the society than I do. Perhaps you are a member?"

Claude answered first with a light gay laugh, and then in his most languid voice.

"Not I! I am of the earth earthy, sensual, sinful. If I went to one of their meetings I should have to go disguised as a poodle. Lady Fanny owns a fine Russian, that has a look of Mephisto, though I believe he is purely canine."

"Tell me all you know about their meetings."

"Imagine a Quakers' meeting, with the female members in Parisian frocks and hats—a large room at the back of Symeon's chambers in the 'Albany.' It was once a fashionable editor's library, smelling of Russia leather, and gay with Zansdorf's bindings—but it is now the abode of shadow, 'where glowing embers through the room, teach light to counterfeit a gloom.' And there the congregation sits in melancholy silence, till somebody, Lady Fanny or another, begins to say things that have been borne in upon her from Shakespeare or Browning, or Marlowe or Schopenhauer; or her favourite bishop, if she is pious. They wait for inspiration as the Quakers do. I am told Lady F. is tremendous. She is strong upon politics, and is frankly socialistic; she has communications from Karl Marx and Fourier, George Eliot and Comte. Her inspiration takes the widest range, and moves her to the wildest speech; but she is greatly admired. They never have a blank day when she is there."

"I should like to hear her. I know she is eccentric; but she is immensely clever, and she seems to have read everything worth reading, in half a dozen languages."

"She crams her expansive brain with the best books; but I am told she occasionally puts them in upside down, and the author's views came out topsy-turvy. You are of imagination all compact, Vera; but I should be sorry to see you lapsing into Fannytude."

"You scoff at everything. There is nothing serious for you in this world or the next."

"Which next world? There are so many. Symeon's for instance, and Father Hammond's. What could be more diverse than those? I have thought very little about the undiscovered country. But you must not say I am not serious about something in this world."

"I cannot imagine what that something is."

"I hope you will never know. If fact, you are never to know."

His earnestness startled her. When a man's dominant note is persiflage any touch of grave feeling is impressive. Vera was silent—and they sat opposite each other for a few moments, she watching the rise and fall of a blue flame in the heap of logs, he watching her face as the blue light flashed upon it for an instant and then left it dark.

It was a face worth watching. She had her mermaid look this evening, and her eyes—ordinarily dark grey—looked as green as her sea-water necklace.

"How is Provana?" he asked at last; an automatic question, indicating faintest interest in the answer.

"Oh, he is very well; but I am afraid he is worried. He stays longer in the City than he used to stay, and he is very grave and silent when we dine alone."

"What would you do if the great house of Provana were to go down like a scuttled ship? Would you stick to a bankrupt husband—renounce London and all its pomps and vanities—give up this wilderness of a house and all the splendid things in it?"

"Can you suppose the loss of money would change my feeling for him? If you can think that you must think I married him because he was rich."

"And didn't you?"

"I hate you for the question. When Mario asked me to be his wife I had not a thought of his wealth. I knew that he was a good man, and I was proud of his love."

"But you were not in love with him?"

"I don't know what you mean. I loved him for his noble character. I was proud of his love."

"That is not being in love, Vera. A woman who is in love does not care a jot for her lover's character. She loves him all the better, perhaps, because he is a scoundrel—the last of the last—the off-scouring. There were women in Rome who doted upon Cæsar Borgia; women who knew that he was a poisoner—take my word for it. You liked Provana because he was your first lover, and you were tired of a year in year out tête-à-tête with Grannie."

"You know nothing about it. If he were to lose his fortune to-morrow I think I should be rather glad. We could live in Italy. Poverty would bring us nearer together—as we were in our honeymoon year. We should have plenty to live upon with my settlement."

She rose and moved towards the door.

"It is nearly five, and there will be people coming," she said.

The door opened as she spoke, and Lady Susan Amphlett looked in.

"Aren't you coming, Vera? There is a mob already, and people want their tea. What are you two talking about, entre chien et loup? You look as weird as Mr. Symeon, Claude."

"We were talking of Symeon, when Vera began to worry about the people downstairs, who are not half so interesting."

"I should think not. Mr. Symeon is thrilling. To know him is like what it must have been to be intimate with Simon Forman or Dr. Dee. I would give worlds to belong to his society. It is quite the smart thing to do. The members give themselves no end of airs in a quiet way."

Lady Susan would have stood in the doorway talking in her crisp and rapid way for a quarter of an hour, oblivious of the people in the drawing-room; but Vera slipped a hand through her arm, and they went downstairs together, Susan talking all the way.

"Fanny Ransom has just come in, with her girl—not out yet, but ages old in knowing what she oughtn't to know. How can a woman like Fanny, eaten up with spiritualism, look after a daughter? They say she went to Paris last winter on purpose to attend a Black Mass."

"The not-out daughter?" asked Claude.

"No, the mother; but she told the girl all about it, and the minx raves about the devil—and says she would rather be initiated than presented next year."

"Lady Fanny had better take care, or she will be expelled from Us. I don't think Symeon would approve of the Black Mass. His philosophy is all light. Light and darkness are his good and evil."

Claude spoke in an undertone, as they were in the room by this time, but he ran small risk of being overheard in a place where everybody seemed to be talking and nobody listening.

Lady Fanny was the centre of a group, her large brown eyes flashing, her voice the loudest, a tall, commanding figure in a black and gold gown, and a black beaver hat with long ostrich feathers and a diamond buckle, a hat that suggested Rupert of the Rhine rather than a modern matron.

Her girl stood a little way off, with three other not-outs, listening to her mother's "balderdash" with unsuppressed mockery.

"Isn't she too killing?" this dutiful child exclaimed, in a rapture of contemptuous amusement, and then she and her satellites bounced down upon the most luxurious ottoman within reach, and employed themselves in disparaging criticism of the company generally—their dress, demeanour, and social status, with much whispering and giggling—happily unobserved by grown-ups, who all had their own interesting subjects to talk about.

Lady Fanny was deserted in favour of Vera, who, at the tea-table, became the focus of everybody's attention. At the beginning she had taken a childish pleasure in pouring out tea for her friends, rejoicing in the exquisite china, the old-world silver, glittering in the blue light of the spirit lamps, the flowers, and beauteous surroundings; so different from the scanty treasures of shabby-gentility—the dinted silver, worn thin with long use, the relics of a Swansea tea-service with many a crack and rivet—to which her youth had been restricted. She performed the office automatically nowadays, oppressed with the languor that hangs over those who are tired of everything, most especially the luxury and beauty they once longed for. One can understand that in the reign of our Hanoverian kings it was just this state of mind which made the wits and beauties eager for a window over against Newgate—to see a row of murdering pirates hanging against the morning sky. Nothing could be too ghastly or grim for exhausted souls in want of a sensation.

The afternoon droppers-in had long become a weariness to Madame Provana, yet as her fashion had depended much upon her accessibility, she could not shut her door upon people who considered themselves obliging when they used her drawing-room as a rather superior club.

Claude Rutherford slipped out of the room imperceptibly, eluding the people who wanted to talk to him with the agility of a vanishing harlequin. He had another visit to pay before his evening engagements, an almost daily visit.

There was just one person in the world for whom he, who had left off caring for people or things, was known to care very much. In expatiating upon the blemishes in an agreeable young man's character, people often concluded with:

"But he is a model son. He adores that old woman in Palace Place."

It was to the old woman in Palace Place that Claude was going this November afternoon, and walking briskly through the clear, cold grey, he knew as well what the old woman was doing as if he had been gifted with second sight.

She was sitting in her large, low chair, with her table and exquisite little tea-service—his gift—at her elbow, and with her eyes fixed on the dial of the Sèvres clock on the mantelpiece, while her heart beat in time to the ticking of the seconds, and he knew that if he were but ten minutes later than usual those minutes were long enough for the maternal mind to visualise every form of accident that can happen to a young man about town.

Nobody talked of "poor Mrs. Rutherford," or pitied her widowed solitude, as they had pitied Lady Felicia. The fact that she had her own house in a fashionable quarter, and a handsome income, made all the difference.

The house was not spacious, but it was old—an Adams house—and one of the prettiest in London, for whatever had been done to it, after Adams, had been done with taste and discretion. Much of the furniture was of the same date as the house, and all that was more recent was precious after its kind, and had been bought when precious things were easier to buy than they are now. And Mrs. Rutherford was as perfect as her surroundings—a slim, pale woman, dressed in black, and wearing the same widow's cap which she had put on in sorrow and anguish fifteen years before—and which harmonised well with the long oval face and banded brown hair, lightly streaked with grey. She was a quiet person, and entertained few visitors except those of her own blood, or connections by marriage; but the name of those being legion, nobody called her inhospitable. Altogether she was a mother whom no well-bred son need be ashamed of loving.

Once, upon his friend saying something to this effect, Claude had turned upon the man fiercely:

"I should have loved her as well if she had been a beggar in the streets, and had hung about the doors of public-houses with me in her arms. To me she is not Mrs. Rutherford, but just the sweetest, tenderest mother on this earth—and she would have been the same if Fate had made her a beggar."

"You believe that in your fantastic fits—but you know it ain't true," said his friend.

Mrs. Rutherford looked up with a radiant face when her son entered the room. She had heard his light step on the stair. He had a latchkey, and there was no other sound to announce his coming.

"Am I late, mother?"

"It is eight minutes past five."

"And you have been watching the clock instead of taking your tea."

The butler entered with the tea-pot as he spoke, having made the tea immediately upon hearing the hall door open.

"What have you been doing with yourself this afternoon, dearest?" Mrs. Rutherford asked, looking up at him fondly, as he stood with his back to the mantelpiece, looking down at her.

"Loafing as usual. I looked in at the New Gallery—their winter show began to-day—half a dozen grand things—the rest croûtes."

"And then?" she asked gently, seeming sure there would be something else.

"Then I walked up Regent Street—it was a fine bracing afternoon—from the Gallery to the 'Langham,' and along Portland Place."

"And you had tea with Vera Provana?"

"No—not tea. There is no tea worth tasting out of this room. There was a mob as usual at the Provanas'—and I slipped away."

"Was Signor Provana there?"

"Not he. He was last heard of in Vienna. But I believe he is coming home next week."

"An unsatisfactory husband for a young thing like Vera," said Mrs. Rutherford, with a faint cloud on her thoughtful face.

Claude knew that look of vague trouble. It was often on his mother's forehead when she spoke of Vera.

"I don't think women ought to call him unsatisfactory. He is the most indulgent husband I know. He adores his wife, and she reigns like a queen in that great house of his—and in their Roman villa."

"That kind of indulgence is a dangerous thing for a young woman—especially if she is capricious and full of strange fancies."

"Poor little Vera. You don't seem to have a high opinion of her."

"I don't want to be unkind. She has passed through an ordeal that only a woman of high principles and strong brain can pass without deterioration. A girlhood of poverty and deprivation, under close surveillance, and a married life of inordinate luxury and liberty. She was married at eighteen, remember, Claude—before her character could be formed. Nor was Lady Felicia the person to lay the foundation of a fine character. One ought not to speak ill of the dead—but poor Felicia was sadly trivial and worldly-minded."

"Madre mia, what a sermon. If you think poor little Vera is in danger, why don't you contrive to see a little more of her? She would love to have you for a real friend. She has a host of acquaintances, but not too many friends. Susan Amphlett is devoted to her; but Lady Susie is not a tower of strength."

"I believe they suit each other. They are both feather-headed, and both poseuses."

At this Claude fired, and was almost fierce.

"Vera is no poseuse," he said. "She is utterly without self-consciousness. I don't think she knows that she is lovely, in spite of the Society papers. Fortunately she has no time to read them. She is too absorbed in her poets—Browning, Shakespeare, Dante. I doubt if she reads a page of prose in a day."

"And is not that a pose? Her idea is to be different from other women—a creature of imagination—in the world, but not of it. That is what people say of Madame Provana.—So charming! So different!

"She can't help what people say, any more than she can help looking more like Undine than a woman whose clothes come from the Rue de la Paix."

Mrs. Rutherford let the subject drop. She did not want to bring unhappiness into the sweetest hour of her life, the hour her son gave her; and she knew she could not talk of Vera without the risk of unhappiness. He who was the joy of her life was also the cause of much sorrow; but from the day he left the Army, under some kind of cloud, never fully understood, but divined, by his mother, she had never let him know what a disappointment his broken career had been to her. She was a soldier's daughter, and a soldier's widow; and to be distinguished as a leader of men was to her mind almost the only way to greatness.

Yet she had smiled when this cherished son had made light of military fame, and told her he would rather be another Millais than another Arthur Wellesley. She had expressed no regret, a few years later, when he told her that art was of all professions the most hateful—and that he did not mean to follow up the flashy success of his early pictures.

"They might make me an Associate next year, if my work was a little better," he told her; "but I am not good enough to hit the public taste two years running. It was the subject or the devilry in my picture that caught on. I might never catch on again—and I'm sick of it all—the critics, the dealers, and the whole brotherhood of art."

There again his road in life came to a dead stop; but this time it was not a wicked woman's form that barred the vista, and shut out the Temple of Fame. As he had missed being a great soldier, he was to miss being a famous painter, though the men who knew, the men who had already arrived, had told his mother that a brilliant career might have been his, if he had chosen to work for it; to work, not by fits and starts, like a fine gentleman in a picturesque painting-room, but as Reynolds had worked, and Etty, and Wilkie, when he sat on the floor painting, with his own legs for his subject.

Again, after trying her powers of persuasion, and trying to fire his ambition, Mrs. Rutherford had resigned herself to disappointment, and had been neither reproachful nor lugubrious.

She was an ambitious woman, and her son had disappointed her ambition. She was a deeply religious woman, and she saw her son indifferent to his religion, if not an unbeliever; and she never persecuted him with tears and remonstrances, only on rare occasions, and with the utmost delicacy, pleading the urgency of a strong faith in the midst of a faithless generation, and the deadly risk the man runs who neglects the sacraments of his Church.

Although she did not often approach this subject in her talk with Claude, it was not the less a subject of anxious thought; and she relied on the influence of her old and devoted friend, Father Cyprian Hammond, rather than her own, for the saving of her son's soul.

If a good woman's prayers could have guarded his path and kept him from temptation, Claude Rutherford would have walked between guardian angels.

CHAPTER VIII

While Claude Rutherford's peril was a subject of troubled thought for his mother and her friend and father confessor, Cyprian Hammond, no friendly voice had breathed words of warning into Vera's ear; nor had she any consciousness that warning was needed, or that danger threatened.

Claude was a part of her life. From the day when she had met him for the first time after her marriage, at a luncheon party at Lady Okehampton's, and they two had sat talking in the embrasure of a window, recalling delicious memories of her childhood's one happy holiday—the ponies, the dogs, the gardens, the woods, the beach and sea—all the joy his kindness had created for her in that verdant paradise, upon that summer sea—from that happy hour when they had sat, talking, talking, talking, while Lady Okehampton waited with growing displeasure for an unpunctual dowager duchess, she had felt that this kinsman of hers belonged to her, that to him she might look as the guide, philosopher, and friend, indispensable to the happiness of every woman whose husband is occupied with serious interests and has a mind above trivialities.

There was nothing too trivial for Claude to understand and discuss with interest. The merest nothing would command his serious thought, if it were something that interested Vera; nor was any flight of her fancy too wild or too high for him. From the colour of a frock or the shape of a hat, to the most oracular utterance of Zarathustra, she could command his attention and counsel. He came and went in her house like the idle wind; and his entrances and exits were no more considered than the wind. When her particular friends asked her whether she had seen Mr. Rutherford lately, she would shrug her shoulders and smile.

"My cousin Claude? Yes, he was here yesterday. I see him almost every day. If he has nothing better to do he comes in after his morning ride, and sometimes stays for luncheon."

People were not unkind; but as years went on the situation was taken for granted, and there were quiet smiles, gently significant, when Madame Provana and her cousin were talked about. Their relations were accepted as one of those open secrets, not to know which is not to be in Society.

Lady Susan did her best to establish the scandal by telling people that Vera and Claude had been brought up together, or almost, and that their attachment was the most innocent and prettiest thing imaginable—"like Paul and Virginia"—a classic which Lady Susan had never read. The "almost" was necessary, as most people knew that Vera had been brought up with Lady Felicia, in furnished lodgings, and had hardly had a second frock to her back, to say nothing of being underfed, which early privation was the cause of the pale slenderness that some people called "ethereal."

Lady Susan's friends, furthermore, being well up in Burke, were satirical about the link of kindred between third or fifth cousins.

Yet on the whole there was indulgence; and when Vera went on a week-end visit to the seats of the mighty she generally found Mr. Rutherford one of the party; which was hardly a cause for wonder, since he was of the stuff of which week-end parties are made.

Vera was more than innocent. She was unconscious of anything particular in her friendship for this friend of her childhood. What could be more natural than that she should love to talk of that one blissful interval in her dull existence—the solitary oasis in the desert of genteel poverty? Only then had she known the beauty of woods and gardens; only then had she known what summer could mean to the emancipated child: the rapture of riding over dancing waves in a cockle-shell of a boat, with the warm wind blowing her hair and the sea-gulls flashing their white wings overhead, the adorable birds whose name was legion. To talk of those young days, and to feel again as she had felt then, was a delight which only Claude could give her; and the more hollow and unsatisfying the things that money could buy became to her, the more she loved to sit with her locked hands upon her knee and talk of that unforgotten holiday.

"Do you remember that evening I asked you to row me out to the setting sun, right into the great golden ball, and you said you would, and you went too far, and we were out till after dark, and everybody was first frightened and then angry?"

All their talk began with "Do you remember?" His memory was better than hers, and he recalled adventures and moments that she had forgotten. One day he brought her a little sketch on thick cardboard, roughly painted in oils, one of his early bits of impressionism before he had studied art, a little girl in a short white frock, with hair flying about her head, cheeks like roses, and the blue of the sea in her eyes.

"What a funny child. You didn't mean that for me?"

"For no one else. I have dozens of such daubs. You remember how I used to sit on a rock and paint while you were looking for shells or worrying the jelly-fish."

"Poor things. I wanted to see them move. I hope they have no feelings. Yes, you used to sit and paint; and I thought you disagreeable because you would not play with me."

Beyond these pictures of the past they had inexhaustible subjects for talk. There was a whole world of literature, the literature of decadence, in which Vera had to be initiated, and Claude was a past master in that particular phase of intellectual life. Baudelaire, Verlaine, Nietzsche, the literature of pessimism, and the literature of despair, that rebellion against law, human and divine, which Shelley began, and which had been a dominant note among young poets since the "Revolt of Islam" filled romantic minds with wonder and a vague delight.

Imperceptibly, naturally, and in no manner wrongfully, as it seemed to Vera, Claude Rutherford's society had become essential to her happiness. She accepted the fact as placidly, and with as complete confidence in him and in herself, as if such a friendship between an idle young man and an imaginative young woman had never been known to end in shame and sorrow. She had lived in the world half a dozen years, and had known of many social tragedies; but as these had not touched any friend she valued, and as she was not a scandal-lover, those dark stories of husbands betrayed and nurseries abandoned had never deeply impressed her, and had been speedily forgotten. Nobody, not even Lady Susie, who was a mauvaise langue, had ever hinted at impropriety in her association with her cousin. Signor Provana saw him come and go, and asked no questions. That stern and lofty nature was of the kind that is not easily jealous. Had there been no Iago, Cassio might have come and gone freely in the noble Moor's household, and no shadow of fear would have darkened that great love. Vera's husband was a disappointed man. His dream of a young and loving wife who would make up to him for all that he had missed in boyhood and youth had melted into thin air. He was sensitive and proud, and the memory of his unloved childhood and of his first wife's indifference was never absent from his mind when he considered his relations with his second wife. He thought of his age, he saw his stern, rough features in the glass, and a faint touch of coldness, the fretful weariness of an over-indulged girl, was taken for aversion, and all his pride and all his force of character rose up against the creature he loved too well to judge wisely. It was he who built the wall that parted them; it was his gloomy distrust of himself rather than of Vera that made the gulf between them.

Let her be happy in her own way. He had sworn to make her happy: and if it was her nature to delight in trivial things, if the aimless existence of a rich man's sultana was her idea of bliss, she should reign sole mistress of a harem which he would never enter while he believed himself unwelcome there. Vera accepted this gradual drifting apart as something inevitable, for which she was not to blame. The strong man's impassioned love, which had appealed to the romantic side of her character, had languished and died with the passing years. She brooded on the change with sorrowful wonder before she became accustomed to the idea that the lover who had taken her to his heart with a cry of ineffable rapture had ceased to exist in the grave man of business, whose preoccupied manner and absent gaze, as of one looking at things far away, chilled her when she sat opposite him on those rare occasions when they dined tête-à-tête—occasions when the dinner-table was only a glittering spot in the dark spaciousness of the room, a world of shadows, where the footmen moved like ghosts in the area between the table and the far-off sideboard. They had been married six years; but Vera thought sadly that her husband looked twenty years older than the companion by whose side she had climbed the mule-paths, through the lemon orchards and olive woods of San Marco, the man whose conversation had always interested her, her first friend, her first lover.

She accepted the change as inevitable, having been taught by the wives of her acquaintance to believe that marriage was the death of love, and as gradually as she learned to dispense with her husband's society, so guiltlessly, because unconsciously, she came to depend upon Claude Rutherford for sympathy and companionship.

She did not know that she loved him, though she knew that the day when they did not meet seemed a long-drawn-out weariness, and that when the evening shadows came, they brought a sense of desolation and a strange lassitude, as of one weighed down by intolerable burdens.

All occupations and all amusements were burdens if Claude was not sharing them—Society the heaviest of all. Far easier to endure the dreary day in the solitude of her den, with the faces of her beloved dead looking at her, than among empty-headed people, who could only talk of what other empty-headed people were doing, or were going to do, with that light spice of malice which makes other people's mistakes and misfortunes so piquant and interesting.

Claude Rutherford had become a part of her life, and life was meaningless without him: a fatal stage in the downhill path, but it was a long time before her awakened conscience gave the first note of warning.

Then—waking in the first faint flush of a summer dawn, after a night of troubled sleep and feverish dreams—a night succeeding one of those dismal days that she had been obliged to endure without the sight of the familiar face, the glad, gay call of the familiar voice, the sound of the light footstep on the stairs—she told herself for the first time, with unutterable horror, that this man was dearer to her than he ought to be—dearer than her husband, dearer than her peace of mind, dearer than all this world held for her and all the next world promised. Oh, the wickedness of it! the shame, the horror! To be false to him—the man who had put his strong arms round her and lifted her out of the dismal swamp of shabby gentility and taken her to his generous heart; the man who trusted her with unquestioning faith, who had never by word or look betrayed the faintest doubt of her truth and purity.

No lovers' word had been spoken, no lovers' lips had met; yet as she rose from that uneasy bed, and paced the spacious room in fever and agitation, a ghostly figure, with bare feet and streaming hair, and long white draperies, she felt as if she were steeped to the lips in dishonour—a monster of ingratitude and treachery.

And then she began the struggle that most women make—even the weaker souls—when they feel the downward path sloping under their feet, and know that the pit of shame lies at the bottom of it, though they cannot see it yet—the impotent struggle in which all the odds are against them, their environment, every circumstance of their lives, their friends, the nearest and dearest even, to whom they cannot cry aloud and say: "Don't you see that I am fighting the tempter, don't you see that I am half way down the hill and am trying to make a stand, that I am over the edge of the cliff, and am hanging to the bushes with bleeding, lacerated hands in the desperate endeavour to keep myself from falling? Have you neither eyes nor understanding that you don't try to help me?" Rarely is any friendly hand stretched out to help the woman who sees her danger and tries to escape her doom. Acquaintances look on and smile. These open secrets are accepted as a part of the scheme of the universe, a particular phase of existence that doesn't matter as long as the chief actors are happy. The wife, her familiar friend, her complaisant or indifferent husband, are smiled upon by a society of men and women who know their world and take it for what it is worth. Only when the actors begin to play their parts badly, and when the open secret becomes an open scandal, does Society cease to be kind.

Vera did not think of Society in that tragic hour of an awakened conscience. That which would have been the first thought with most women had no place in her mind. It was of her sin that she thought—the sin of inconstancy, of ingratitude, of faithlessness. Had she crossed the border line, and qualified herself for the Divorce Court, she could not have thought of herself with deeper contrition.

To love this other man better than she loved her husband; to long for his coming; to be happy when he was with her, and miserable when he was away; there was the sin.

But no word of love had been spoken. There was time for repentance. He did not know that she loved him. Although, looking back, and recalling words and tones of his, she could not doubt that he loved her, she could hope that no word of hers had revealed the passion whose development had been gradual and imperceptible as the growth of the leaf buds in early spring, which no eye marks till they flash into life in the first warmth of April.

Her friendship with this man, who was of her kindred, the companion of the only happy days of her childhood, had seemed as natural as it would have been to attach herself to a brother from whom she had long been separated. She had welcomed him with a childish eagerness, she had trusted him with a childish belief in the perfection of the creature who is kind. She had admired him—comparing him with all the other young men she knew, and finding him infinitely above them. His very weakness had appealed to her. All that was wanting in his character made him more likable, since compassion and regret mingled with her liking. To be so clever, so gifted by nature, and to have done nothing with nature's gifts—to be doomed to go down to death leaving his name written in water—to die, having finished nothing but his beaux jours: people who liked him best talked of him as a young man with a beau passé. Shoulders were shrugged, and smiles were sad, when his painter friends discussed him.

"We thought he was going to do great things in art, and he has done nothing."

Soldiers who remembered him before he left the Army lamented the loss of a man who was made for a soldier.

There had been trouble—trouble about a woman that had made him exchange to a line regiment—and then the war being over, and the chance of active service remote, disgust had come upon him, and he had done with soldiering.

Vera had seen the shoulders shrugged, and had heard the deprecating criticism of this kinsman of hers, and had been all the kinder to him because Fate had been cruel.

She had tried to fire him with new hope; she had been ambitious for him; had steeped herself in art books, and spent her mornings in picture galleries, in order that she might be able to talk to him. She had implored him to go back to his work, to paint better pictures than he had painted when critics prophesied a future from his work.

"I am too old," he said.

"Nonsense. You have wasted a few years, but you will have to work harder and buy back your lost time. Quentin Matsys did not begin to paint till he was older than you."

"There were giants in those days. Compared with such men I am an invertebrate pigmy."

"Oh, if you loved art you would not be content to live without the joy of it."

"Yes, that's what people who look at pictures think—the joy of painting a thing like that. The man who paints knows when the disgust comes in and the joy goes out. He knows the sense of failure, the disappointment, the longing to fling his half-finished picture on the floor and perform the devil's dance upon it, as Müller used to do."

And then, one day, as they were going round a picture gallery together, he said:

"Well, Vera, I have been meditating on your lecture; and I am going to paint another picture—the last, perhaps."

"No, it won't be the last."

"I am going to paint your portrait. After all that sermonising you can't refuse to sit to me."

"I won't refuse—unless Mario should object."

"How should he object? He will be in New York, or Madrid, or Constantinople, most likely, while I am painting you. I am nothing if not an impressionist, so it mustn't be a long business."

"I shall love sitting to you. To see you at work—"

"Yes, to see me earning my bread in the sweat of my brow, like the day-labourer, will be a novelty. I shouldn't want to be paid for the picture, but I dare say Provana would insist upon my taking a fee, and as he counts in thousands, it would be a handsome one. No, Vera, don't blush! I won't take money for my daub. You shall give it to the Canine Defence League. It shall be a labour of love; a concession to a sermonising cousin. I shall paint your portrait, just to convince you that I can't paint, and that the life I am wasting is worth nothing."

Thus in light talk and laughter the plan was made that brought them into a closer intimacy than they had known before, and although Claude Rutherford was an impressionist, that portrait was three months upon the easel which he had rigged up in Vera's morning-room.

"I want to paint you in the room where you live; not with a marble pillar and a crimson curtain for a background."

The sittings went on at irregular intervals, in a style that was at once sauntering and spasmodic, all through that season. Signor Provana looked in now and then, stood watching the painter at work for five or ten minutes, criticised, and made a sudden exit, driven away by Lady Susan's shrill chatter.

But Lady Susan was not always there; and there were more tranquil hours, when Vera sat in her half-reclining attitude on a low sofa spread with a tiger skin, fanning herself with a great fan of peacock's feathers, and gazing at the pictures on the wall with dreaming eyes: hours in which the painter and his subject talked by fits and starts—with silent pauses.

After all the pains that had been taken, the picture was a failure. The painter hated it, Provana frankly disapproved; and in the haggard, large-eyed siren smiling over the edge of the fan, Vera could not recognise the face she saw in the glass.

"I have been much too long over the thing," Claude told Provana, with slow and languid speech, half indifference, half disgust; "and it is a dismal failure. But I shall do better next time, if Vera will let me make a rapid sketch of her, when the daffodils are in bloom, and we shall be week-ending at Marlow Chase. I could make a picture of her on the hill above the house, in the yellow afternoon light, and among the yellow flowers. I am an open-air painter if I am anything; but I had almost forgotten how to set a palette. I shall work in a friend's studio in the autumn, and I may do better next year."

Vera urged him to persevere in this good intention, and not to mind his failure.

"I mind nothing," he said. "I have had three happy months. I mind nothing while you are kind, and forgive me for having put you to a lot of trouble, with this atrocious daub for the outcome of it all."

Privileged people only were allowed to see the daub; but those, although supposed to be few, in the end proved to be many. Critics were among them, and Mr. Rutherford was too shrewd not to discover that every connoisseur had a little hole to pick in the portrait, and that when all the little holes were put together there was nothing left.

And this picture, so poor a thing as it was, made the beginning of that open secret, which everybody knew long before the awakening of Vera's conscience, and while Mario Provana saw nothing to suspect or to fear in his wife's intimacy with her cousin.

But now, with the awakening of conscience, began the fight against Fate, the fight of the weak against the strong, the woman against the man, innocent youth against an experienced lover. She was single-hearted and pure in intention, counting happiness as thistledown against gold, when weighed against her honour as a wife; but she entered the lists without knowing the strength of her opponent, the passive force of a weak man's selfishness. The main purpose of her life was henceforward to release herself from the web that had been woven so easily, so imperceptibly; first a careless association between two people whose likings and ideas were in harmony; then friendship, confidence, sympathy; and then unavowed love; love that made the days desolate when the lovers were not together. He had been too frequent and too dear a companion. He had become the master of her life, and it was for her to release herself from that unholy bondage. She had to learn to live without him.

It needed more than common cleverness and tact to bring about a change in their manner of life, without making a direct appeal to Rutherford's honour and telling him that their friendship had become a danger. To do this would be to tell him that she loved him, to confess her weakness, before he had passed the border line that divides the friend from the lover. No, she could make no appeal to the man whose smouldering fires she feared to kindle into flame. She knew that he loved her, and that he had made her love him. She had to escape from the web that he had woven round her; and she had, if possible, to set herself free without his knowing the strength of her purpose, or the desperate nature of the struggle.

All the chances were against her. She could not forbid him the house without an open scandal. As he had come and gone in the last four years, he must still be free to come and go. She could only avoid those familiar hours—hours that had been so dear—by living in a perpetual restlessness, always finding some engagement away from home.

It was weary work, but she persevered, and enlisted all the Disbrowes in her cause, unconscious that they were being made use of. She accepted every invitation, lent herself to everybody's fads, philanthropic or otherwise; listened to the same fiddlers and singers day after day, in drawing-rooms and among people that she knew by heart; or stood with aching head under a ten-guinea hat, selling programmes at amateur theatricals.

She contracted a closer alliance with Lady Susan Amphlett, and planned excursions: a day at Windsor, a day at Dorking, at Guildford, to rummage in furniture shops, at Greenwich to see the Nelson relics, to Richmond and Hampton, even to Kew Gardens. Lady Susan was almost worn out by these simple pleasures; but as she professed, and sincerely, an absolute culte for Vera Provana, she held out bravely.

These excursions were fairly successful, and as Vera took care that no one should know where she and her friend were going—not even Susan herself till they were on the road—it was not possible for Claude to follow her. It was otherwise in the houses of her friends, where she was always meeting him, and where it was essential that she should not seem to avoid him, least of all to let him see that she was so doing.

She greeted him always with the old friendliness—a little more cousinly than it had been of late; and she showed a matronly interest in his health and occupations, as if she had been an aunt rather than a cousin.

"It is quite delightful to meet you here this afternoon," he told her, in a ducal house where guinea tickets for a charity concert seemed cheap to the outside public. "You are to be met anywhere and everywhere except in your own house. I have called so often that I have taken a disgust for your knockers. When I am dead I believe those lions' heads will be found engraven on my heart, like Queen Mary's Calais."

It was only natural that, with the awakening of conscience, there should come the thought of those two first years of her married life, when her husband's love had made an atmosphere of happiness around her, when she had cared for no other companion, needed no other friend; those blessed years before Claude Rutherford's pale, clear-cut face, and low, seductive voice had become a part of her life, essential to her peace. The change of feeling, the growing regard for this man, had come about so gradually, with a growth so slow and imperceptible, that she tried in vain to analyse her feelings in those four years of careless intimacy, and to trace the process by which an innocent friendship had changed to a guilty love. When had the fatal change begun? She could not tell. It was only when she felt the misery of one long day of parting that she knew her sin. The husband had become a stranger, the friend had become the other half of her soul. He had called her by that sweet name sometimes, but with so playful a tone that the impassioned phrase had not scared her. It was one of many lightly spoken phrases that she had heard as carelessly as they were uttered.

And now, looking back at the last two years, she told herself that it was her husband's fault that she had leant on Claude for sympathy, her husband's fault that they had been too much together. For some reason that she had never fathomed, Mario Provana had held himself aloof from the old domestic intimacy. It was not only that his business engagements necessitated his absence from home several times in the course of the year, and on occasion for a considerable period. He had business in Russia, and in Austria, and he had crossed the Atlantic twice in the last year, the affairs of his New York house calling for special attention in a disturbed state of American finance. These frequent absences alone were sufficient to weaken the marriage bond; but in the last year he had given his wife very little of his society when they were under the same roof.

"You have hosts of friends," he said one day when she reproached him for keeping aloof, "people who share your tastes and can be amused by the things that amuse you. I bring back a tired brain after my continental journeys, and am still more tired after New York. I should make a wretched companion for a young wife, a beautiful butterfly who was born to shine among all the other butterflies."

"I am nearly as tired as you are after your business journeys, Mario," she said. "I shall be very glad when we can go back to Rome."

"But you will have other butterflies there, and a good many of the same that flutter about you here," he answered.

"We will shut our doors upon them and live quietly."

"Like Darby and Joan—old Darby and young Joan. No, Vera, we won't try that. You weren't made for the part."

She had been too proud to say more. If he was tired of her—if he had ceased to care for her, she would not ask him why.

But now, in her desperate need, sick to death of those aimless excursions and unamusing amusements with Lady Susan, and of the dire necessity of keeping away from her own house, to flutter from party to party, almost sure of meeting Claude wherever she went, she turned in her extremity to her natural protector, and tried to find shelter in the love that ought to be her strong rock.

Her husband had been on the Continent, moving from city to city, for the greater part of the June month in which she had been making her poor little fight against Fate—trying to cure herself of Claude Rutherford, as if he had been a bad habit, like drink or drugs. And then one morning, when she was beginning the day dejectedly, tired of yesterday, hopeless of to-morrow, a telegram from Paris told her to expect her husband at seven o'clock that evening.

Her heart beat gladly, as at the coming of a deliverer.

She was not afraid of meeting him. She longed for his coming, as the one friend who might save her from an influence that she feared.

The face she saw in the glass while her maid was dressing her hair almost startled her. There were dark marks under the eyes, and the cheeks were hollow and deadly pale. The black gauze dinner-gown she had chosen would accentuate her pallor; but it was nearly seven o'clock, and there was no time for any change in her toilet. She paced the great empty rooms in sun and shadow, listening to every sound in the street, and wondering if her husband would see the sickening change that sickening thoughts had made in her face, and question her too closely.

She heard the hall door open, and then the familiar footstep, rapid, strong, and yet light, very different from the footfall of obese middle age; the step of a man whose active life and energetic temperament had kept him young.

She met him on the threshold of the drawing-room.

"I am so glad you have come home," she said, holding up her face for his kiss.

He kissed her, but without enthusiasm.

"I am glad you are glad," he said, "but can that mean that you have missed me? From your letters I thought you and Lady Susan were having rather a gay time."

"I was rushing about with her and going to parties, partly because I missed you."

"Partly, and the other part of it was because you like parties and are dull at home, I suppose, unless you have your house full."

"Oh, I am sick of it all, Mario," she said, with a sort of passionate energy that made him believe her, "and I would live quite a different life if you were not away so often, and if I were not thrown too much on my own resources."

"My dear Vera, this is a new development," he said gravely, sitting down beside her, and looking at her with eyes that troubled her, as if they could see too much of the mind behind her face. "You are looking thin and white. Has anything happened while I have been away, anything to make you unhappy?"

"No!" she exclaimed with tremendous emphasis, for she felt as if he were going to wrest her secret from her. "What could happen? But I suppose there must come a time in every woman's life when she has had enough of what the world calls pleasure, when the charm goes out of amusements that repeat themselves year after year; and when one begins to understand the emptiness of a life, occupied only with futilities, when one begins to tire of running after every new thing, actors, dancers, singers, and all the rest of them. I have had enough of that life, Mario; and I want you to help me to do something better with the liberty and the wealth you have given me."

"Do you want a mission?" he asked with a faint smile. "That is what women seem to want nowadays."

"No, Mario. I want to be happy with you. Your business engagements take you so much away from home, that our lives must be sometimes divided; but not always—we need not be always living a divided life, as we have been in the last three years."

A crimson flush swept across her face as she spoke, remembering that these were the years in which Claude Rutherford's influence had grown from a careless comradeship to an absorbing intimacy.

Her husband looked at her in silence for a few moments; and his grave smile had now a touch of irony.

"Has it dawned upon you at last?" he asked. "Have you discovered that we have been living apart; that we have been man and wife only in name?"

"It was not my fault, Mario. It was you who kept aloof."

"Not till I saw repulsion—not till I saw aversion."

"No, no—never, never, never! I have never forgotten your goodness—never forgotten all I owe you."

They had been sitting side by side on the spacious Louis Quatorze sofa, his hand upon her shoulder; but at her last words he started to his feet with a cry of pain.

"Yes, that is it—you recognise an obligation. I have given you a fine house, fine clothes, fine friends—and you think you ought to repay me for them by pretending to love me. Vera, that is all over. There must be no more pretending. I can bear a good deal, but I could not bear that. I told you something of my past life before we were married; but I doubt if I told you all its bitterness—all the blind egotism of my marriage, the cruel awakening from a dream of mutual love—to discover that my wife had married me because I could give her the things she wanted, and that love was out of the question. I compared myself with other men, and saw the difference; and as I had missed the love of a mother, so I had to do without the love of a wife. I was not made to win a woman's love—no, not even a mother's. This was why my affection for my daughter was something more than the common love of fathers. She was the first who loved me—and she will be the last."

"Mario, you are too cruel! Have I not loved you?"

"Yes—perhaps for a little while. You gave me a year of infinite happiness—our honeymoon year. That ought to be enough. I have no right to ask for more—but let there be no talk of gratitude—if I cannot have love I will have nothing."

"You have been so cold, so silent and reserved, so changed. I thought you were tired of me."

"Tired of you? Poor child! How should you know the measureless love in the heart of a man of my life-history? When I took you in my arms in the evening sunshine, I gave you all that was best and strongest in my nature—boundless love and boundless trust. All my life-history went for nothing in that hour. I did not ask myself if I was the kind of man to win the heart of a girl. I did not think of my five-and-forty years or my forbidding face. I gave myself up to that delicious dream. I had found the girl who could love me, the divine girl, youth and innocence incarnate. Think what it was after a year of happiness to be awakened by a look, and to know that I had again been fooled, and that if in the first surprise of my passionate love you had almost loved me, that love was dead."

"No, no," she sobbed; and then she hid her streaming eyes upon his breast, and wound her arms about his neck, clinging to the husband in whom she found her only shelter.

Was it some curious instinct of the flesh, or some power of telepathy, that told him not to take these tears and wild embrace for tokens of a wife's love?

"My dearest girl," he said with infinite gentleness, as he loosened the clinging arms and lifted the hidden face, "if this distress means sorrow for having unwittingly deceived me, for having taken a man's heart and not been able to give him love for love, there need be no more tears. The fault was mine, the mistake was mine. You must not suffer for it. To me you will always be unspeakably sweet and dear—whether I think of you as a wife, or as the girl my daughter loved—and whom I learned to love in those sad days when the shadow of death went with us in the spring sunshine. Yes, Vera, you will always be dear—my dearest on this earth. But there must be no pretending, nothing false. Think of me as your friend and protector, the one friend whom you can always trust, your rock of defence against all the dangers and delusions of a wicked world. Trust me, dearest, and never keep a secret from me. Be true to yourself, keep your honour stainless, your purity of mind unclouded by evil associations. Let no breath of calumny soil your name. Rise superior to the ruck of your friends, and have no dealings with the lost women whose guilt Society chooses to ignore. I ask no more than this, my beloved girl, in return for measureless love and implicit faith."

He was holding both her hands, looking at her with searching eyes; those clear grey eyes under a brow of power.

"Can you promise as much as this, Vera?"

"Yes."

"With heart and mind?"

"With heart and mind."

"And you will never take the liberty I give you for a letter of license?"

"No, no, no. But I don't ask for liberty. I want to belong to you, to be sheltered by you."

"You shall have the shelter, if you need it; but be true to yourself, and you will need no defender. A woman's safest armour is her own purity. And again, my love," with a return of the slightly ironical smile, "never was a woman better guarded than you are while you are fringed round by Disbrowes, protected at every point by your mother's clan, people at once well born and well bred, with no taint of Bohemianism, unless indeed it may lurk in your poco curante cousin, the young painter who made such a lamentable failure of your portrait."

She felt as if every vestige of colour was fading out of her face, and that even her lips must be deadly white. They were so parched that when she tried to shape some trivial reply the power of speech seemed gone. She felt the dry lips moving; but no sound came.

This was the end of her appeal to the husband whose love might have saved her. Their relations were changed from that hour. He was not again the lover-husband of their honeymoon years; but he was no longer cold and reserved, he no longer held her at a distance. He was kind and sympathetic.

He interested himself in her occupations and amusements, the books she read and the people she saw. He was with her at the opera, where Claude Rutherford sometimes came to them and sat through an act or two in the darkness at the back of the box. He was infinitely kind and tender; but it was the tenderness of a father, or a benevolent uncle, rather than of a husband. He held rigidly to that which he had told her. There was to be no make-believe in their relations.

If she was not happy, she was at peace for some time after her husband's home-coming—a period in which they were more together than they had ever been since those first years of their married life. She tried to be happy, tried to forget the time in which Claude Rutherford had been her daily companion, the time when she planned no pleasure that he was not to share, and had no opinions about people or places, or books or art, that she did not take from him: loving the things he loved, hating the things he hated; as if they had been two bodies moved by one mind. She tried not to feel an aching void for want of him; she tried not to think him cruel for coming to her house so seldom, and tried to be sorry that they met so often in the houses of her friends.

The time came when the awakened conscience was lulled to sleep, and when her husband's society began to jar upon her strained nerves. She had invoked him as a defence against the enemy; and now she longed for the enemy, and had ceased to be grateful to the defender.

The rampart of defence was soon to fall. A financial crisis was threatened, and Signor Provana was wanted at his office in New York. He told his wife that he might be able to come back to London in a fortnight, allowing ten days for the double passage, and four for his business; but if things were troublesome in America he might be a good deal longer.

"I shall try to be home in time to take you to Marienbad," he told her. "But if I am not here, Lady Okehampton will take you, and you can get Lady Susan to go with you and keep you in good spirits. I had a talk with your aunt last night, and she promised to take you under her wing."

"I don't want to be under anybody's wing; and Aunt Mildred will bore me to death if I see much of her at Marienbad."

"Oh, you will have your favourite Susie for amusement, and your aunt to see that she doesn't lead you into mischief. Lady Susan is a shade too adventurous for my taste."

This idea of Marienbad was a new thing. A certain nervous irritability had been growing upon Vera of late, and her husband had been puzzled and uneasy, and had called in a nerve specialist recommended by Lady Okehampton, one of those new lights whom everybody believe in for a few seasons. After a quiet talk with Vera, that grave authority had suggested a rest cure, the living death of six weeks in a nursing home; and on this being vehemently protested against by the patient, had offered Marienbad as an alternative.

Provana had been startled by this sudden change in his wife's temper, from extreme gentleness and an evident desire to please him, to a kind of febrile impatience and irritability; and remembering her curious agitation on the evening of his home-coming, her pallid cheeks and passionate tears, he had an uneasy feeling that these strange moods had a common source, and that there was something mysterious and unhappy that it was his business to discover before he left her.

He came to her room early on the day of his departure, so early that she had only just left her bedroom, and was still wearing the loose white muslin gown in which she had breakfasted.

She was sitting on her low sofa in a listless attitude, looking at the faces on the wall—Browning, Shelley, Byron—the faces of the inspired dead who were more alive than the uninspired living; but at her husband's entrance she started to her feet and went to meet him.

"You are not going yet," she exclaimed. "I thought the boat-train did not leave till the afternoon."

"It does not; but I must give the interval to business. I have come to bid you good-bye."

"I am very sorry you are obliged to go," she said.

"For God's sake do not lie to me. For pity's sake let there be no pretending."

He took both her hands and drew her to him, looking at her with an imploring earnestness.

"I have trusted you as men seldom trust their wives," he said. "I thought I had done you a great wrong when I took you in the first bloom of your young beauty and made you my own; cutting you off for ever from the love of a young lover, and all the passion and romance of youth. Considering this, I tried to make amends by giving you perfect freedom, freedom to live your own life among your own friends, freedom for everything that could make a woman happy, except that romantic love which you renounced when you accepted me as your husband. I believed in you, Vera, I believed in your truth and purity as I believe in God. I could never have reconciled myself to the life we have led in this house if it were not for my invincible faith in your truth. But within this month that faith has been shaken. Your eyes have lost the old look—the lovely look through which truth shone like a light. There is something unhappy, something mysterious. There is a secret—and I must know that secret before I leave you."

Her face changed to a look of stone as he watched her.

It was no time for tears. It was time for a superhuman effort at repression, to hold every feeling in check, to make her nerves iron.

There was defiance in her tone when she spoke, after a silence that seemed long.

"There is no secret."

"Then why are you unhappy?"

"I am not unhappy. I have a fit of low spirits now and then, a feeling of physical depression, for which there is no reason; or perhaps my idle, useless life, and the luxury in which I live, may be the reason."

"It is something more than low spirits. You are nervous and irritable and you have a frightened look sometimes, a look that frightens me. Oh, Vera, for God's sake be frank with me. Trust me half as much as I have trusted you. Trust me as a daughter might trust her father, knowing his measureless love, and knowing that with that love there would be measureless pity. Trust me, my beloved girl, throw your burden upon me, and you shall find the strength of a man's love, and the self-abnegation that goes with it."

"I have no secret, no mystery; I mean to be worthy of your trust. I mean to be true to myself. If you doubt me let me go to America with you. Keep me with you."

His face lighted as she spoke, and then he looked thoughtfully at the fragile form, the delicate features, the ethereal beauty that seemed to have so frail a hold on life.

"No, you are not the stuff for sea voyages, and the storm and stress of New York. If we went there together I should have to leave you too much alone among strangers. I shall have an anxious time there; but it shall not be a long time. If possible, I shall be here to take you to Marienbad, and in the meantime you must live quietly, and do what your doctor tells you. He is to see you next week, remember."

He held her to his heart, with stronger feeling than he had shown for a long time, and gave her his good-bye kiss. She flung herself on her knees as the door closed behind him.

"God help me to be true to him in heart and mind."

That was the prayer she breathed mutely, while her tears fell thick and fast upon her clasped hands.

He was gone, the unloved husband, and she had to face the peril of the undeclared lover. She felt helpless and forsaken, and she sat for a long time in listless misery; and then, looking up at the pictures on the wall, she tried to realise that silent companionship, the souls of the illustrious dead—tried to believe that she was not alone in her dejection, that in the silence of her lonely room there was the sympathy and understanding of souls over whom death has no more dominion, and whose pity was more profound than any earth-bound creature could give her.

She thought of Francis Symeon, and of those meetings of which he had told her. Nothing had come of her interview with him. Claude Rutherford's light laughter had blown away her belief in the high-priest of the spiritual world; and she had thought no more of the creed that had appealed so strongly to her imagination.

Now, when life seemed a barren waste, her thoughts turned to the philosophic visionary who had so gravely expounded his dream. Everything in her material world harassed and distressed her, and she turned to the spiritual life to escape from reality.

She wrote urgently to Mr. Symeon, telling him that she was unhappy, and asking to be admitted to the society of which he had told her. She had not to wait long for an answer. Symeon called upon her that afternoon, and was with her for more than an hour, full of kindness and sympathy; sympathy that scared her, for it seemed as if those strange eyes must be reading the depths of her inner consciousness, and all the disgust of life and vague longing that were interwoven with her thoughts of Claude Rutherford.

It was to escape those thoughts—to dissever herself from that haunting image, that she pleaded for admission to the shadow world.

"Bring me in communion with the great minds that are above earthly passions," would be her prayer, could she have spoken freely; but she sat in a thoughtful silence, soothed by the spiritualist's exposition of that dream-world, which was to him more real than the solid earth upon which he had to live—a reluctant participator in the life of the vulgar herd.

"The mass of mankind, who have no joys that are not sensual, and who live only in the present moment, have nothing but ridicule and disbelief for the faith that makes even this sordid material world beautiful for us, who see in earthly things the image of things supernal," he said, with that accent of sincerity, that intense conviction, which had made scoffers cease from scoffing under the influence of his personality, however they might ridicule him in his absence.

Everyone had to admit that, though the creed might be absurd, the man was wonderful.

There was to be a meeting of "Us" at his chambers on the following afternoon, and Symeon begged Vera to come.

"You may find only thought and silence," he said, "a company of friends absorbed in meditation, but without any message from the other world; or you may hear words that burn, the voices of disembodied genius. In any case, while you are with us you will be away from the dust and traffic of the material world."

Yes, she would go, she was only too glad to be allowed to be among his disciples.

"I want to escape," she told him. "I am tired of my futile life—so tired."

"I thought you would have joined us long ago," he said, as he took leave, "but I think I know the influence that held you back."

The hot blood rushed into her face, the red fire of conscious guilt that always came at the thought of Claude Rutherford. She had never minimised her sin. It was sin to have made him essential to her happiness, to have lost interest in all the rest of her life, to have given him her heart and mind.

"I think the psychological moment has come," continued Symeon's slow, grave voice, "and that you should now become one of us. You have drained the cup of this trivial life, and have found its bitterness. Our religion is our faith in the After-life. We have the faith that looks through death. The orthodox Christian talks of the life beyond; and we must give him credit for sometimes thinking of it—but does he realise it? Is it near him? Does he look through death to the Spirit-world beyond? Does he realise the After-life as Christ realised it when He talked with His disciples?"

CHAPTER IX

The meeting in Mr. Symeon's library lasted all through the summer afternoon, till the edge of evening. The large and gloomy room was darkened by Venetian shutters, nearly closed over open windows. There was air, and the ceaseless sound of traffic; but the summer sun was excluded, and figures were seen dimly, as if they belonged to the shadow world.

Among those indistinct forms Vera recognised people she knew, people she would never have expected to find in a society of mystics: a statesman, a poet, three popular novelists, and half a dozen of the idlest women of her acquaintance, two of whom were the heroines of romantic stories, women over whose future friends watched and prophesied with the keen interest that centres in a domestic situation where catastrophe seems imminent.

Vera wondered, seeing these two. Had they come, like her, for a refuge from the tragedy of life? They had not come for an escape from sin; for, if their friends were to be believed, the border line had been passed long ago.

An hour of silence, broken now and then by deep breathing, as of agitation, and sometimes by a stifled sob, and then a flood of words, speech that was eloquent enough to seem inspired, speech that might have come from him who wrote "Christmas Eve," and "Easter Day," and "A Death in the Desert," the speech of a believer in all that is most divine in the promise of a future life. And after that burst of impassioned utterance there were other speakers, men and women, the men strong in faith, strong in the gift of tongues, possessed by the higher mind that spoke through organs of common clay; the women semi-hysterical, romantic, eloquent with remembered poetry. But in men and women alike there was sincerity, an intense belief in that close contact of disembodied mind, sincerity that carried conviction to an imaginative neophyte like Vera Provana.

Suddenly from the stillness there came a voice more thrilling than any Vera had heard in that long séance, a voice that was not altogether unfamiliar, but with a note more intense, more poignant than she knew. Gleaming through the shadows, she saw eyes that flashed green light, and a long, thin face of marble pallor, in which she knew the face of Lady Fanny Ransom.

And now came the most startling speech that had been heard that afternoon—the passionate advocacy of Free Love—love released from the dominion of law, the bonds of custom, the fear of the world; love as in Shelley's wildest dreams, but more transcendental than in the dreams of poets; the love of spirit for spirit, soul for soul, "pure to pure"—as Milton imagined the love of angels. All the grossness of earth was eliminated from that rarefied atmosphere in which Francis Symeon's disciples had their being. Their first and indispensable qualification was to have liberated thought and feeling from the dominion of the senses. While still wearing the husk of the flesh, they were to be spirits; and not till they had become spirits were they capable of communion with those radiant beings whose earthly vesture had been annihilated by death.

To Vera there was an awful beauty in those echoes of great minds; and her faith was strong in the belief that among this little company of aspiring mortals there hovered the spirits of the illustrious dead. She left Mr. Symeon's room with those others, who dispersed in absolute silence, as good people leave a church, with no recognition of each other, stealing away as from a service of unusual solemnity. They did not even look at each other, nor did they take leave of Mr. Symeon, who stood by one of the shuttered windows, gravely watching as his guests departed.

It was past seven, and the sun was low, as Vera went to her carriage, which was waiting for her in Burlington Gardens. She was stepping into it, when a too familiar voice startled her. She had been too deep in thought to see Claude Rutherford waiting for her at the gate of the "Albany."

"Send your carriage home, Vera, and walk through the Green Park with me. You must want fresh air after the gloom of Symeon's Egyptian temple."

"No, no. I am going straight home."

"Indeed you are not," and without further argument he took upon himself to give the order to the footman.

"Your mistress will walk home."

She would have resisted; but it was not easy to dispute with a man who had a way of taking things for granted, especially those things he wanted. It would have been easier to contend against energy, or even brute force, than against that nonchalant self-assurance of an amiable idler, who sauntered through life, getting his own way by a passive resistance of all opposing circumstances.

"I have been waiting nearly two hours," he said. "It would be hard if you couldn't give me half an hour before your dinner. I know you never dine before half-past eight."

"But I have to be punctual. Aunt Mildred is coming to dinner, and Susie Amphlett."

"It has only just struck seven. You shall be home before eight, and I suppose you can dress in half an hour."

"I won't risk not being in the drawing-room when Aunt Mildred comes."

"Lady Okehampton is a terror, I admit. You shall be home in good time, child. But I must have something for my two hours."

"How absurd of you to wait," she said lightly. "And how did you know I was at Mr. Symeon's?"

They were going through the "Albany" to Piccadilly. She had recovered from the shock of his appearance, and was able to speak with the old trivial air, the tone of comradeship, an easy friendliness, without the possibility of deeper feeling. It had seemed so natural before the consciousness of sin; and it had been so sweet. This evening, as she walked by his side, she began to think that they might still be comrades and friends, without the shadow of fear; that her agony of awakened conscience had been foolish and hysterical, imaginary sin, like the self-accusation of some demented nun.

"How did I know? Well, after calling at your house repeatedly, only to be told you were not at home, I lost my temper, and determined to find out where you were—at least for this one afternoon, when I knew of no high jinks in the houses of your friends; and so, having asked an impertinent question or two of your butler, I found that Symeon had been with you yesterday, and guessed that you might be at his occult assembly this afternoon. I had heard a whisper of such an assembly more than a week ago—so you see the process of discovery was not difficult."

"But why take so much trouble?"

"Why? Because you have treated me very badly, and I don't mean to put up with that kind of treatment. If it comes to why, I have my own 'why' to ask—a why that I must have answered. What ignorant sin have I committed that it should be 'Darwaza band' when I call in Portland Place? What has become of our cousinship; our memory of childish pleasures, the sea, the woods, the heather; the pony that ran away with you, while I stood with my blood frozen, telling myself, 'If he kills her I shall throw myself over the cliff'? What has become of our past, Vera? Is blood to be no thicker than water? Is the bond of our childish affection to go for nothing? Is it because I am a failure that you have cut me?"

"I have not cut you, Claude. How can you say such a thing?"

"Have you not? Then I know nothing of the cutting process. To be always out when I call—to take infinite trouble to avoid me when we meet in other people's houses! The cut direct was never more stony-hearted and remorseless."

"You must not fancy things," she said lightly.

They were in the Green Park by this time, the quiet Green Park, whence nursemaids and children had vanished, and where even loafers were few at this hour between afternoon and evening.

She spoke lightly, and there was a lightness at her heart that was new. It was sweet to be with him—sweet to be walking at his side on the old familiar terms, friends, companions, comrades, as of old. His careless speech, his supreme ease of manner, seemed to have broken a spell. She looked back and thought of her troubled conscience, and all the scheming and distress of the last two months, and she felt as if she had awakened from a fever dream, from a dreary interval of delirium and hysteria. What danger could there be in such a friendship? What had tragedy to do with Claude Rutherford? This airy trifler, this saunterer through life, was not of the stuff of which lovers are made. He was a man whom all women liked; but he was not the man whom a woman calls her Fate, and who cannot be her friend without being her destroyer. How could she ever have feared him? He was of her own blood. His respect for her race—the race to which he belonged—would hold him in check, even if there were no other restraining influences. The burden of fear was lifted; and her spirits rose to a girlish lightness, as she walked by her cousin's side with swift footsteps, listening to his playful reproaches, his facetious bewailing of his worthlessness. From this time forward she would treat him as a brother. She would never again think it possible that words of love, unholy words, could fall from his lips. No such word had ever been spoken; and was it not shameful in her to have feared him—to imagine him a lover while he had always shown himself her loyal kinsman? In this new and happy hour she forgot that it was her own heart that had sounded the alarm—that it was because she loved him, not because he loved her, that she had resolved upon ruling him out of her life.

Perhaps this evening, after the glamour of Mr. Symeon's assembly, she was "fey." This sudden rush of gladness, this ecstasy of reunion with the friend from whom she had compassed heaven and earth to hold herself aloof, seemed more than the gladness of common day. She trod on air; and when they pulled up suddenly at Hyde Park Comer, it was a surprise to find that they had not been walking towards Portland Place.

"We must make for Stanhope Gate and cross Grosvenor Square and Bond Street," Claude said gaily. "We have come a long way round, but a walk is a walk, and I have no doubt we both wanted one. Perhaps you would prefer a cab."

"No, I like walking, if there is time."

"Plenty of time. You walk like Atalanta, if that young person ever condescended to anything but a run."

"Do you remember our walks in the woods, and the afternoon we lost our way and could not get home for the nursery tea?"

"You mean when I lost my way, and you had to tramp the shoes off your dear little feet. Brave little minx, I shall never forget how plucky you were, and how you kept back the tears when your lips quivered with pain."

Once launched upon reminiscences of that golden summer there was no gap in their talk till the lions' heads were frowning at them on the threshold of Vera's home.

She was flushed with her walk, and the colour in cheeks that were generally pale gave a new brightness to her eyes. That long talk of her childish days had taken her out of her present life. She was a child again, happy in the present moment, without the wisdom that looks before and after.

"Good-bye," said Claude; and then, pausing, with his hand on the moody lion, "if you had some vague idea of asking me to dinner, it would be a kindness to give shape to the notion, for I shan't get a dinner anywhere else. My mother is in the country, and a solitary meal at a restaurant is worse than a funeral."

Vera hesitated, with a faint blush, not being able utterly to forget her determination to keep Claude Rutherford out of her daily life.

"Lady Okehampton expects to find me alone," she said.

"But you have Susie Amphlett?"

"Susie invited herself."

"As I am doing. Three women! What a funereal feast; as bad as Domitian's black banquet. Your aunt dotes upon me, and so does Susan. You will score by having secured me. You can say I threw over a long engagement for the sake of meeting them. I dare say there is some solemn dinner invitation stuck in my chimney glass. I often forget such things."

The doors were flung open, and the suave man in black and his liveried lieutenants awaited their mistress's entrance.

"A ce soir," said Claude, as he hailed a prowling hansom; and he was seated in it, smiling at her with lifted hat, before Vera had time to answer him.

"Mr. Rutherford will dine here this evening," she told the butler.

CHAPTER X

Vera was walking up and down her drawing-room at twenty minutes past eight, dressed in one of those filmy white evening gowns with which her wardrobe was always supplied, one of her mermaid frocks, as Lady Susan called them. This one was all gauzy whiteness, with something green and glittering that flashed out of the whiteness now and then, to match the emerald circlet in her cloudy hair.

The tender carnation that had come from her walk was still in her cheeks, still giving unusual brightness to her eyes.

She had been happy; she had put away dark thoughts. Life was gay and glad once again, glad and gay as it had always been when she and Claude were together. A load had been lifted from her heart, the vulgar terror of the conventional wife, who could not imagine friendship without sin. The things that she had heard that afternoon had given a new meaning to life, had lifted her thoughts and feelings from the commonplace to the transcendental; to the sphere in which there was no such thing as sin, where there were only darkness and light, where the senses had no power over the soul that dwelt in communion with souls released from earth. She no longer feared a lover in the friend she had chosen out of the common herd.

Lady Okehampton sailed into the drawing-room as the silvery chime of an Italian clock told the half-hour. Her expansive person, clad in amber satin, glowed like the setting sun, and her smiling face radiated good nature.

She put up her long glass to look at Vera, being somewhat short-sighted physically as well as morally.

"My dear child, you are looking worlds better than when I last saw you. You were such a wreck at Lady Mohun's ball; looked as if you ought to have been in bed, doing a rest cure—a ghost in a diamond tiara. I find that when a woman is looking ill diamonds always make her look worse; but to-night you are charming. That emerald bandeau suits you better than the thing you wore at the ball. You haven't the aquiline profile that can carry off an all-round crown."

Claude and Lady Susan came in together.

"My car nearly collided with his taxi," said Lady Susie, when she had embraced her friend; "but I was very glad to see a man at your door. From what you said this morning, I expected a hen-party. Now a big hen-party is capital fun; but for three women to sit at meat alone! The idea opens an immeasurable vista of boredom. I always feel as if I must draw the butler into the conversation, and bandy an occasional joke with the footmen. No doubt they could be immensely funny if one would let them."

"It was an after-thought," said Claude. "Vera took fright at the eleventh hour, and admitted the serpent into her paradise."

"No doubt Adam and Eve were dull—a perpetual tête-à-tête, tempered by tame lions, must soon have palled; but at least it was better than three women, yawning in each other's faces, after exhausting the latest scandal."

"I think the early dinner in 'Paradise Lost' quite the dullest meal on record," said Claude. "To begin with, it was vegetarian and non-alcoholic. A man and his wife—the wife waiting at table—and one prosy guest monologuing from the eggs to the apples."

"There is no mention of eggs. I don't think they had anything so comfortable as a poultry yard in Eden; no buff Orpingtons, or white Wyandottes, only eagles and nightingales," said Susie, and at this moment the butler announced dinner in a confidential murmur, as if it were a State secret. He was neither stout nor elderly; but in his tall slimness and grave countenance there was a dignity that would have reduced the most emancipated of matrons to good behaviour.

"I should never dare to draw him into the conversation," whispered Susie, as Claude offered his arm to Lady Okehampton. "Nothing would tempt that perfect creature to a breach of etiquette."

The hen-dinner, relieved by one man, was charming. Not too long a dinner; for one of the discoveries of this easy-going century is that people don't want to sit for an hour and a half steeping themselves in the savour of expensive food, while solemn men in plush and silk stockings stalk behind their back in an endless procession, carrying dishes whose contents are coldly glanced at and coldly refused. The dinner was short, but perfect: too short for the talk, which was gay and animated from start to finish.

Lady Susan and Mr. Rutherford were the talkers, Vera and her aunt only coming in occasionally: Lady Okehampton with a comfortable common-sense that was meant to keep the rodomontade within bounds.

Claude was an omnivorous reader, and had always a new set of anecdotes and epigrams with which to keep the talk alive, anecdotes so brief and sparkling that he seemed to flash them across the table like pistol shots. French, German, or Italian, his accent was faultless, and his enunciation clear as that of the most finished comedian; while in the give and take of friendly chaff with such an interlocutor as Lady Susan, he was a past master.

Vera did not talk much, but she looked radiant, the lovely embodiment of youth and gladness. Her light laughter rang clear above Susan's, after Claude's most successful stories. Once only during that gay repast was a graver note sounded, and it came from the most frivolous of the party, from Susie Amphlett, who had one particular aversion, which she sometimes enlarged upon with a morbid interest.

Age was Susan's bugbear.

"I think of it when I wake in the night, like Camilla, in 'Great Expectations,'" she said, looking round the table with frightened eyes, as if she were seeing ghosts.

The grapes and peaches had been handed, and it was the confidential quarter of an hour after the servants had gone.

"I don't like to give myself away before a butler," Susie said, as the door closed on the last of the silk stockings. "Footmen are non-existent: one doesn't stop to consider whether they are matter, or only electricity; but a butler is a person and can think—perhaps a socialistic satirist, seething with silent scorn for his mistress and her friends."

"And no doubt an esteemed contributor to one of the Society Papers," said Claude.

"I am not afraid of Democracy, nor the English adaptation of the French Revolution, though I feel sure it is coming," continued Lady Susan, planting her elbow on the table in an expansive mood. "I am afraid of nothing except growing old. That one terror swallows up all trivial fears. They might take my money, they might steep me in poverty to the lips, and if I could keep youth and good looks, I should hardly mind."

Again she looked at the others appealingly, like a child that is afraid of Red Riding-hood's wolf.

"Age is such a hideous disease—the one incurable malady. And we must all have it. We are all growing old; even you, Vera, though you have not begun to think about it. I didn't till I was thirty. As we sit at this table and laugh and amuse ourselves, the sands are falling, falling, falling—they never stop! Glad or sorry, that horrible disease goes on, till the symptoms suddenly become acute—grey hair, wrinkles, gout."

"But are there not some mild pleasures left in the years that bring the philosophic mind?" asked Claude.

"Does that mean when one is eighty? At eighty one might easily be philosophic. Everything would be over and done with. One would be like old Lord Tyrawly, who said he was dead, though people did not know it."

"Some of the most delightful people I have known were old, and even very old," said Claude, "but they didn't mind. That's the secret of eternal youth, my dear Susie—not to mind: to wear the best wig you can buy, and not to pretend it is your own hair: to wear pretty clothes, especially suited to your years, sumptuous velvet and more sumptuous fur, like a portrait of an old lady by Velasquez: never to brag of your age, but never to be ashamed of it. The last phase may be the best phase, if one has the philosophic mind."

"Oh, you," exclaimed Susan scornfully, "you are like Chesterfield. You will have your good manners till your last death-bed visitor has been given a chair. A fine manner is the only thing that time can't touch."

Vera saw her aunt looking bored, and smiled the signal for moving.

"Half a cigarette, and I shall follow," said Claude, as he opened the door for the trio, "unless I am distinctly forbidden."

"Why should we forbid you? You are an artist, and you know more about frocks and hats than we do, after years of laborious study," said Lady Susan, and then, with her arm through Vera's as they went slowly up the broad staircase, with steps so shallow that people accustomed to small houses were in danger of falling over them, "Isn't he incomparable?" she exclaimed. "There never was such a delightful failure."

"Poor Claude," sighed Lady Okehampton. "I suppose it is only the men who fail in everything who have time to be agreeable. If a young man has a great ambition, and is thinking of his career, he is generally a bear. Claude has wasted all his chances in life, and can afford to waste his time."

"It was a pity he left the Army," said Susan. "He looked lovely in his uniform. I remember him as he flashed past me in a hansom, one summer morning after a levée, a vision of beauty."

"It was a pity he got himself entrapped by a bad woman," said Lady Okehampton with a sigh.

"His Colonel's second wife," put in Lady Susan. "Isn't it always the elderly Colonel's second wife?"

Lady Okehampton gave another sigh.

"It was a disgraceful story," she murmured. "Let us try to forget all about it."

Vera had flushed and paled while they were talking.

"But tell me about it, Aunt Mildred," she said, with a kind of angry eagerness. "Where was the disgrace, more than in all such cases? A wicked woman, a foolish young man—very young, wasn't he?"

"Not five and twenty."

"Where was the disgrace?"

"Don't excite yourself, child. Duplicity—an old man's heart broken—Isn't that enough? An elopement or not an elopement; something horrid that happened after a regimental ball. I know nothing of the details, for it all took place while the regiment was in India, which only shows that Kipling's stories are true to life. The husband would not divorce her—which was a blessing—or Claude would have had to marry her. He spoilt his career by the intrigue; but marriage would have been worse."

Vera's heart was beating violently when Claude sauntered into the room presently, and made his leisurely way to the sofa where she was sitting aloof from the other two, who had just entered upon an animated discussion of the last fashionable nerve-specialist and his methods.

"What has made you so pale?" Claude asked, as he seated himself by Vera's side. "Was our walk through the streets too much for you? I should never forgive myself if—"

"You have nothing to be sorry for. The walk was delightful. My aunt and Susie have been talking of unpleasant things."

"What kind of things?"

"Of your leaving the Army. You have never told me why you threw up your career."

"My career! There was not much to lose. The Boer War was over; my regiment was in India all the time, and I never had a look in. Oh, they have been telling you an ugly story about your poor friend; and it will be 'The door is shut' again, I suppose."

"Why did not you tell me of your past life? I have told you everything about mine."

"Because you had only nice innocent things to tell. My story would not bear telling—and why should you want to know?"

"There should not be a wall between friends—such friends as we have been—like brother and sister."

"Do brothers tell old love stories? Stale, barren stories of loves that are dead?"

"Perhaps not. I oughtn't to have spoken about it. Come and talk to Aunt Mildred. Her carriage has been announced, and she'll be huffed if we don't go to her."

Claude followed meekly, and in five minutes Lady Okehampton had forgotten that it was eleven o'clock, and that her horses had been waiting half an hour. He had a curious power of making women pleased with themselves, and with him. He always flattered them; but his flattery was so discreet and subtle as to be imperceptible. It was rather his evident delight in being with them and talking to them that pleased, than anything that he said.

"Come to River Mead for next Sunday. It will be my last week-end party before we go to Scotland," Lady Okehampton said to him before she bade good night. "Vera and Susan are coming. We shall be a small party, and there will be plenty of bridge."

Claude accepted the invitation as he took Lady Okehampton to her carriage.

"I wish Provana were not so much away from his wife," she said. "It is a very difficult position for Vera."

"Vera is not la première venue. She knows how to take care of herself."

"That's what they always say about women; but is it true in her case? She is very young, and rather simple, and knows very little of the world."

"Not after six years as the wife of a financial Croesus?" murmured Claude, while he arranged the matron's voluminous mantle over her shoulders as carefully as if the outside atmosphere had been arctic.

He knew that the drift of her speech had been by way of warning for him. Dear, inconsistent soul! It was so like her to invite him to spend three days with her niece in the sans gêne of a riverside villa, and five minutes afterwards to sound a note of warning.

He walked along the lamp-lit streets with the light foot of triumphant love. Vera's pale distress and unwise questioning had set his heart beating with the presage of victory. Poor child! For his acute perceptions, the heart of a woman had seldom been a mystery, and this woman's heart was easier to read than most. Poor child! She had been trying to live without him. She had fought her poor little battle, with more of resolution and of courage than he would have expected from a creature so tender. She had kept him out of her life for a long time—time that had seemed an eternity for him, in his longing for her; and then, at a word, at a smile, at the touch of his hand, she had yielded, and had let him see that to be with him was to be happy, and that nothing else mattered. Light love had been his portion in the light years of youth; but this was no light love. He had sacrificed his career for the sake of a woman; but the sacrifice had been forced upon him, and it had killed his love. But now he was prepared for any sacrifice—for the sacrifice of life-long exile, and strained means. He thought of a home in a summer isle of the great southern ocean, like Stevenson's; or, if gaiety were better, in some romantic city of Spanish America. There were paradises enough in the world, there would be no one to point the finger of scorn, where "Society" was a word of no meaning.

He would carry his love to the world's end, beyond the reach of shame. Nothing mattered but Vera. Yes, there was one who mattered. His mother! But to-night he could not even think of her, or if he thought of her it was to tell himself that if Provana divorced his wife, and he and Vera were married, his mother would be reconciled to the inevitable. Her religion would be a stumbling block. To her mind such a marriage would be no marriage. To-night he could not reason, he would not see obstacles in his path. Vera's pale looks and anxious questions had been a confession of love, a forecast of surrender; and in the tumult of his thoughts there was no room for hesitation or for fear.

He thought of his love now as duty. It was his duty to rescue this dear girl from a loveless union with a hard man of business, old enough to be her father, from splendours and luxuries that had become as dust and ashes. He had known for a long time that she cared for him; but he had never reckoned the strength of her attachment. Only this afternoon, in her radiant happiness, as they walked through the unromantic streets; only in her pale distress to-night, as she questioned him, had he discovered his power: and now there seemed to be but one possible issue—a new life for them both.

His mother's absence from London was an inexpressible relief to him. How could he have met the tender questioning of the eyes that watched over his life, and had learned how to read his mind from the time when thought began? How could he have hidden the leaping, passionate thoughts, the sense of a crisis in his fate, the ardent expectation, the dream of joy, the fever and excitement in the mind of a man who is making his plan of a new life, a life of exquisite happiness?

CHAPTER XI

It was Saturday, and they were at River Mead—one of those ideal places that seem to have been raised along the upper Thames by an enchanter's wand rather than by the vulgar arts of architect and builder, so exquisitely do they harmonise with the landscape that enshrines them.

No hideous chimney, no mammoth reservoir, no thriving metropolitan High Street, defiled the neighbourhood of River Mead. All around was rustic peace. Green meadows and blue waters, amidst which there lay gardens that had taken a century to make—grass walks between yew hedges, and labyrinths of roses; and in the distance purple woods that melted into a purple horizon. It was a place that people always thought of as steeped in golden sunlight; but not even in the glory of a midsummer afternoon was River Mead quite as lovely as on such a night as this, when Claude and Vera strolled slowly along the river path, in the silver light of a great round moon, hung in the blue deep of a sky without a cloud.

The magic of night and moonshine was upon everything; the mystery of light and shadow gave a charm to things that were commonplace by day—to the white balustrade in front of the drawing-rooms, to the flight of steps and the marble vases, above which the lighted windows shone golden, the gaudy yellow light of indoor lamps shamed by the white glory of the moon.

The windows were all open, and the voices of the card-players travelled far in the clear air—they could even hear the light sound of their cards, manipulated by a dexterous hand. Everybody was playing bridge, everybody was absorbed in the game, winning or losing, happy or unhappy, but absorbed— except these two. Everybody except these two, who had been missing since ten o'clock; and the great stable clock had sounded its twelve slow, sonorous strokes half an hour ago. They had not been wanted.

The tables were all full. Two or three of the players had looked round the room once or twice, and, noting their absence, had exchanged the quiet smile, the almost imperceptible elevation of arched eyebrows, with which, in a highly civilised community, characters can be killed. For Lady Okehampton— she who had more than once sounded the note of warning, and who should have been on the alert to see danger signals—from the moment the tables were opened and the players seated, the world of men and women outside that charmed space—where cards fluttered lightly upon smooth green cloth, four eager faces watching them as they fell—had ceased to exist. She was not a stupid woman; but she had a mind that moved slowly, and she could not think of two serious things at once. For her bridge was a serious thing; and from tea-time on Saturday till this Sunday midnight bridge had occupied all her thoughts, to the exclusion of every other consideration. Smiles might be exchanged and eyebrows raised when, on Sunday morning, Claude Rutherford carried off her niece two miles up the river to a village church, which by his account was a gem in early Gothic that was worth more than the two miles' sculling a light skiff against the current; but Lady Okehampton was too absorbed even to wonder whether there was anything not quite correct in the excursion. Why should not people want to see the old church at Allersley? It was one of the lions of the neighbourhood, and counted among the attractions of River Mead.

Lady Okehampton's cards on Saturday night had seemed to be dealt to her by a malignant fiend, an invisible devil guiding the smooth white hands of human dealers. She had lain awake till the Sunday morning bells were ringing for the early service to which good people were going, fresh and light of foot, with minds at ease. She had tossed and turned in her sumptuous bed in a feverish unrest, playing her miserable hands over and over again, with the restless blood in her brain going round and round like a mill wheel, or plunging backwards and forwards like a piston rod. There had been no time to think of Vera and Claude. She could think only of Sunday evening, and of her chance of revenge. It was not that she minded her money losses, which were despicable when reckoned against the price of Okehampton's autumn sport. Two thousand pounds for a grouse moor and a salmon river—an outlay of which he talked as lightly as if it were a new hat. The money was nothing. He would give as much for an Irish setter as she lost in an evening. But the vexation and humiliation of a long evening's bad luck were too much for nerves that had been strained to snapping point by many seasons of experimental treatment, all over Europe; and the mistress of River Mead had left her visitors to amuse themselves at their own sweet will, until dinner-time on Sunday evening, while their hostess slept in her easy-chair by the open window of her morning-room, soothed by the lullaby of the stream running down the weir, and sweet airs from a garden of roses, such roses as only grow in a riverside garden.

The choice of amusements or occupations after luncheon on this Sunday afternoon was somewhat limited. Two girls and their youthful admirers played a four-handed game of croquet. A middle-aged spinster, who had been suspected of tricky play on Saturday, trudged a mile and a quarter to the little town where there was a church so old-fashioned as to provide a substantial afternoon service for adult worshippers. Most of the masculine guests wrote letters, or read Sunday papers in the billiard-room, or slumbered in basket chairs on the river lawn. Vera and Claude did nothing out of the common in strolling up the hill to the wood, where they lost themselves during the lazy two hours between the end of a leisurely luncheon and the appearance of tea-tables in the shady drawing-room. Coming back a little tired after her idle afternoon, Vera sat on a sofa in the darkest corner of the spacious room, by the side of a comfortable matron, an old friend of her aunt's, with whom she exchanged amiable truisms, and mild opinions upon books, plays and sermons—a kind of talk that demanded neither thought nor effort, while Claude sat among a distant group, bored to death, but smiling and courteous.

After tea there was the garden till dressing time. Everybody was in the garden, so it was only natural that these two should be sauntering in lanes of roses, exchanging light talk with other saunterers, and lingering a little at the crossing of the ways, where the slow drip of a fountain made a coolness in the sultry evening, or stopping at an opening in the flowery rampart, to look across the blue water towards the grey old tower, and listen to the pensive music of church bells.

These two had been alone all day, without interference or espial from chaperon Aunt, unconscious of observation, if they were observed, alone in this little world of summer verdure and sunlit water; as much alone as in a pathless wilderness. All that long summer day they had been alone, talking, talking, talking, as only lovers talk; and now, at midnight, they were still alone in the garden that was changed in the moonlight, changed from the warm glow of colour to the silvery paleness and mysterious shadow, in which the prolific clusters of the Félicité pérpétuelle looked like the ghosts of roses.

If it were sin to love, the sin had been sinned; from the hour in which he had drawn the confession of her love from the lips that he kissed for the first time.

She had tried to hold him off—tried to keep those lips unprofaned by the kiss of guilt. They were alone in the wood on the hill that fatal Sunday afternoon, safe only for the moment, since the woodland path was a favourite walk with visitors at River Mead. But he had drawn her from the footpath into the shade of great beech trees, and they were alone. He had kissed her, and she had submitted to the guilty kiss, and she knew that she was lost.

Did she love him? She whispered yes. With all her heart and soul? Yes. Could she be happy if he left her for ever? No, no, no. Could she give up all the world for him, as he would for her? The lips that he had kissed were too tremulous for speech. She hid her face upon his breast, and was dumb.

"The die is cast," he said in a low, grave voice, "and now we have only to think of our future."

"Our future?" Henceforth they were one; united by a bond as strong as if they had been married before the high altar in Westminster Abbey, with all the best people in London looking on and approving the bond. Nothing else could matter now. They belonged to each other. He was to command, and she was to obey. It was almost as if, in the moment of her confession, her personal entity had ceased. In all those hours of delicious intimacy, in fond imaginings of their future life, the thought of her husband had never come between her and her lover—and to-night, when she thought of Mario Provana, it was only to tell herself that he had long ceased to care for her, and that it would not hurt him if she were to vanish out of his life.

Provana had been gone more than fourteen days, and his cabled messages told her of delays and difficulties. The financial crisis was more serious than he had anticipated, and he would have to see it out. He had sent her several messages, but only one letter—a kind letter, such as an uncle might have written to a niece; but it seemed to her there was no love in it, not even such love as he had lavished on his daughter. There was nothing left of the love that had wrapped her round like summer sunlight, the strong man's love that had made her so proud of having been chosen by him, so tranquil in the assurance of a happiness that nothing could change.

The change had come before they had lived a year in that great, gloomy London house, when she had been less than two years a wife.

It was after parting with Claude in the garden, and creeping quietly up to her room in the second hour of the new day, while doors were beginning to open and voices to sound as the card-players bade good-night; it was in the stillness of the pretty guest-chamber that Vera began to think of Mario Provana, and the impassioned love that had ended in a frozen aloofness.

He had said, "Let there be no pretending." Could he have told her more absolutely that his love was dead, and that no charm of sweetness in her could make it live again? She had made her poor little attempt to win him back; and it had failed. What more was left but to be happy in her own way?

CHAPTER XII

The season was dying hard. Lady Leominster's ball, at the great old house at Fulham, was the last flash of an expiring fire. The Houses of Parliament had closed their historic doors. The walls of the Royal Academy had been stripped of their masterpieces, and empty themselves, looked down upon dusty emptiness. All the best theatres were shut; London was practically empty. The few thousand lingerers in a wilderness of deserted streets bewailed the inanity of the daily Press. There was nothing in the morning papers; and the evening papers were worse, since they were obliged to echo the morning nothingness.

The people who never read books were longing for something startling in those indispensable papers, were it even a declaration of war. Suddenly their longing was satisfied. The morning papers were devoured with eagerness. The evening paper was waited for with feverish expectancy. All of a sudden the great army of the brainless found themselves with something to think about, something to talk about, something upon which to build up hypotheses, to which, once built, they adhered with a fierce persistency.

There had been a murder. A murder in the heart of London, in one of the fine houses of the West End; not one of the finest, for, after all, spacious and splendid as the house might be, it was not like Berkeley or Devonshire, Lansdowne or Stafford. It was only one in a row of spacious houses, the house of a foreign financier, a man who dealt in millions, and who was himself the owner of millions.

Mario Provana had been murdered in his own house—shot through the heart by an unknown assassin, who had done his work well enough to leave no clue to his identity. Speculation might rove at will, theory and hypothesis might run riot. Here was endless talk for dinner-tables—inexhaustible copy for the newspaper.

A man of great wealth, of exalted position in the world of finance—finance, not commerce. Here was no dealer in commodities, no manufacturer of cocoa, or sugar, or reels of cotton, but a man who dealt in the world's wealth, and could make peace or war by opening or closing his money-bags.

People who had never seen the great man's face in the flesh were just as keenly interested in the circumstances of his death as the people who had dined at his table and had known him as intimately as such men ever are known. A rough print of his photograph was in every halfpenny paper, and the likeness of his beautiful young wife was travestied in some of them. Pictures of the house in Portland Place, front and back view, were in all the papers. Columns of picturesque reporting described the man and the house, the beautiful young wife, the sumptuous furniture, the numerous household, the splendid entertainments which had made the house famous for the last six or seven years.

And for the murdered man himself, no details were omitted. Interviews were invented, in which, during the last year, Signor Provana had expounded his opinions and views of that sphere of life in which he exercised so vast an influence—his ideas political, his tastes in art and literature, music, and the drama. Minute descriptions of his person were given in the same glowing style. The picturesque reporter made the dead man alive again for the million readers who were panting for details that would help them to strengthen their own pet theory or to crush an opponent.

Thousands of sensation-hunters went to Portland Place to look at the house that held that dreadful mystery of a life untimely cut short by the hand of a murderer. Loafers stood on the pavement and gazed and gazed, as if their hungry eyes would have pierced dead walls and darkened windows. The loafers knew that the house was in charge of the police, and that a vigilant watch was being kept there. They wondered whether the lovely young wife was in the house. They pictured her weeping alone in one of those darkened rooms; yet were inclined to think that her friends would have insisted on her leaving that house of gloom, and would have carried her off to some less terrible place for rest and comfort.

The first idea was the correct one. Vera was lying in that spacious bed-chamber behind three windows on the second floor, where ivy-leaved geraniums were falling in showers of pale pink blossom from the flower-boxes. She was lying on the vast Italian bed, lying like a stone figure, while Susan Amphlett sat by the bed, and wept and sighed, with intervals of vague, consoling speech, till, finding that speech elicited no reply, and indeed seemed unheard, she had at last, in sheer vacuity of mind, to take refuge in the first book within reach of her hand.

It was one among many small volumes on a table by the bed—Omar Kháyyam.

"Oh, what a dreary book," thought Susie, who was beginning to feel her office of consoler something of a burden.

She had hated entering that dreadful house, as she always called it in her thoughts, since she had heard of the murder; and now to be sitting there in that deadly silence, in that grey light from shrouded windows, to be sitting there with the knowledge that only a little way off, in another darkened room at the back of the dreadful house, there lay death in its most appalling form, was a kind of martyrdom for which Susie was unprepared, and which she was not constituted to suffer calmly or lightly. As she had hated old age, so, with a deeper hate, she hated death. To hear of it, to be forced to think of it, was agonising; and to visualise the horror lying so near her, a murdered man in his bloodstained shroud, made her start up from her easy chair and begin to roam about the room in restlessness and fear.

She lifted the edge of a blind and peered into the street.

The sight of the people staring up at the house was comforting. They were alive. There were people standing in the road, looking up with widened eyes, so absorbed in what they saw, or wanted to see, that they ran a risk of sudden annihilation from a motor-car, and skipped off to the opposite pavement, there to content themselves with a more distant view.

"There never was such a murder," Susie said to herself. "I think every soul in town must have come to look at this horrid house since eleven o'clock this morning."

It was now past three, in a dull, sultry afternoon. Susie spent all the intervening hours in the silent room in the dreadful house. She was sorry for her friend; but she was still more sorry for herself. All those hours of silent horror, without any luncheon, and no good done! What was the use of sitting by the bed where a woman lay dumb and motionless, unconsoled by affectionate murmurs from a bosom friend, apparently unconscious that the friend was there.

Lady Susan called in Hanover Square on her way home, and ordered a black frock, lustreless silk that would stand alone, with a shimmer of sequins flashing through crêpe: not this week's fashion, nor last week's, but the fashion of the week after next. The style that was coming; not the style that had come. This was her one agreeable half-hour in all that dismal day.

"I may be dining with Vera next week, and it will be only kind to wear mourning," Susan told herself, as she ordered the gown.

CHAPTER XIII

Mrs. Provana's French maid was the first witness at the coroner's inquest. The first question she had to answer was as to when she had last seen Mr. Provana alive; and the same question was put to all succeeding witnesses. The answer in each case was the same. Neither any member of the household, nor the confidential clerk from the City, had seen the deceased after he left London on his journey to New York. It was Louison Dupuis, Mrs. Provana's maid, who had discovered the dead man lying on the floor of his dressing-room, close against the door of communication with her mistress's bedroom. Hers had been the first foot on the principal staircase that morning. No other servant was licensed to tread those stairs in the routine of their servitude. The rooms they slept in, and the stairs by which they went up and down, were at the back of the house, remote from the principal staircase.

Mademoiselle Louison looked scared, and trembled a little as she told her dreadful story. It was her duty to carry Madame her tea at seven o'clock. Madame desired to be called at that hour, even when she had come home from a party after midnight. The witness stated that the still-room maid had the tray ready for her at ten minutes to seven, and that she went up the staircase of service with it to the second floor, and through the palier outside Madame's room, and thence through the open doorway of Monsieur's cabinet de toilette. She saw a figure lying with the face downward. She had reason to believe that Monsieur Provana was in America. Nothing had been said in the household of his expected return: yet she knew at the first glance that the man lying there was her master. He was a man of imposing figure, not easily mistaken. The horror of it had unnerved her, and she had rushed down the great staircase to the hall, where two of the footmen were opening windows and arranging the furniture. She told them what she had seen, and one of them went to fetch Mr. Sedgewick, the butler.

Her evidence was given in a semi-hysterical and somewhat disjointed manner, with occasional use of French words for familiar things; but the coroner had been patient with her—as an important witness, being the first who had cognisance that murder had been done in the night silence.

Alfred Sedgewick, the butler, was a very different witness—self-possessed and ready, eager to express his opinion, and having to be held with a tight hand.

He described, with studious particularity, how on leaving his room on that morning, having just finished dressing, and having been kept waiting for his shaving water, he had run against Ma'mselle, who was rushing along the passage in a frantic manner, pale as death, and with eyes starting out of her head. A young person who was apt to excite herself about trifles, and who on this occasion seemed absolutely demented.

On hearing Ma'mselle's statement, given in so distracted a manner that only a person of superior intelligence could find out what she meant, he had immediately sent one of the footmen to the police office, to fetch a capable officer. It was no case for the first constable called in from the street.

He, Sedgewick, had then gone upstairs with another of the men, and had found the dead body lying, as Ma'mselle had stated, against the door of communication with Mrs. Provana's bedroom. The face was hidden, but he had not an instant's doubt as to the dead man's identity, for, apart from the commanding figure, the left hand was visible, on which the witness observed an old Italian ring that his master always wore. He had touched the hand, and found it was the hand of death; yet, in the circumstances, he had considered it his duty to telephone for the doctor. The room in which the body lay was used by his master as a dressing-room; but it was also used by him as a study, and there was a large office desk in front of one of the windows, at which Mr. Provana sometimes sat writing late into the night. There was also a safe in which his master was supposed to keep important papers, and possibly cash. It was not a large safe, but it was of exceptional strength, and of the most modern and costly make. This safe was open when the police took possession of the room, after the removal of the body under the doctor's superintendence. There were no signs of disorder in the room, except that the pistol case on the desk was open, and both pistols were lying on the floor, one near the hand of the deceased, the other near the desk. The safe had not been forced open. The key was in the door, one of three small keys on a steel ring engraved with Signor Provana's name and address. His master always carried these keys in one of his pockets.

"When was Madame Provana informed of her husband's death?"

"Not until half-past eight o'clock, when Lady Okehampton came. Mrs. Manby, the housekeeper, went in a cab to Berkeley Square to tell her ladyship what had happened, and Lady Okehampton came to the house in the cab with Mrs. Manby."

"Had not Mrs. Provana been awakened by the sounds of voices and footsteps on the landing?"

"No. Everything had been done with the utmost quiet. There had been no talking above a whisper. His mistress had been at the ball at Fulham Park, and had not come home till three o'clock, and she was still sleeping when Lady Okehampton went into her room."

The doctor was the next witness.

The medical evidence did not take long. In answer to the coroner, the doctor stated that he was in the habit of attending the household, and had been summoned by telephone immediately on the discovery of the tragedy. The body was lying facing the door between the two rooms, and at no great distance from it. It was semi-prone on its left side, the arms extended from the body, but flexed. A loaded pistol lay close to the fingers of the right hand. Life was extinct. Blood had trickled from a wound in the back of the head and formed a pool on the floor. The direction of the trickle from wound to floor was vertical. There were no other blood-stains.

A further examination demonstrated that the wound was due to a bullet; that the bullet had entered the head horizontally and penetrated the brain. The bullet was found to fit a pistol lying in the room, recently discharged, evidently companion to the one already mentioned. Both fitted a case found on a table in front of the window.

The witness was of opinion,

1. That death was due to shock from bullet wound.

2. That death had been almost instantaneous, and had taken place within three hours of the time when the witness examined the body.

3. That the wound was not self-inflicted nor accidental; but that the shot had been deliberately fired and at no great distance. The person who fired the shot was probably somewhat taller than the deceased.

Upon this Sedgewick, the butler, was recalled, and there followed an exhaustive interrogation as to the arrangements on the ground floor of the house. A plan had been made of the doors and passages on this floor, the great double doors of ceremony opening into the hall, the tradesmen's door, and another door communicating with the stables, which were almost as spacious in that old London house as in a country mansion of some importance. At the back of the hall there was a wide stone corridor leading to the door opening on the stable-yard, and other passages to pantry, plate room, lamp room, and the menservants' bedrooms, which were all on the ground floor.

He valeted his master when he was at home, but he did not travel with him. Mr. Provana required very little personal attendance. He had always been aware that his master kept loaded pistols in the case on his desk. He understood that there was a large amount of valuable property in that room, where the deceased used often to sit writing late at night, with open windows in summer-time, when Mrs. Provana was at evening parties.

The pistols were in charge of the police on a table in court, old-fashioned duelling pistols, choice specimens of Italian workmanship.

The door at the end of the corridor was often used by Mr. Provana, and one of the keys on the ring before mentioned was the latch-key belonging to this door. He was in the habit of walking to the City, and he used this door every morning, passing the stables on his way. He was very fond of his horses, and he often went into the stables, or had the horses brought out, to look at them. The stable-yard opened into Chilton Street. This door, communicating with the well-guarded stable-yard, was fastened with a latch lock and heavy bolts; but the bolts were not often used, and Sedgewick said that it was by this door his master must have entered the house on the night of the murder, as the doors in Portland Place had been bolted and chained at ten minutes past three o'clock, after Mrs. Provana came home.

The coroner, with the plan of the rooms before him, pointed to that occupied by Sedgewick.

"Was it possible for a stranger to have entered the house after or before your master without your hearing the opening of the door or his footsteps in the passage?"

Sedgewick concluded that it was possible, since the thing must have happened. He was ordinarily a particularly light sleeper. Was there ever a servant who confessed to being anything else? He had been to a theatre that evening, and may have slept sounder than usual.

"Did none of the other men hear anything?"

John, footman, had heard the dog bark.

John was duly sworn, and stated that he had been awakened by hearing the dog, an Irish terrier, and he had sat up in bed and listened; but the dog had given only that one bark, by which he, John, concluded that the animal, which slept on a mat outside his room, had been dreaming. Interrogated as to time, he had heard the hall clock strike five not very long after the dog barked. It might be a quarter of an hour, or it might be half an hour.

On this followed the interrogation of stable servants, as to the gates opening into Chilton Street, the result of which showed that the stable gates had not been locked that morning. It was broad daylight when the grooms finished their work and turned in for a morning sleep. The last of the stable servants to retire had heard the clocks strike four as he went to his bedroom.

Mrs. Provana was there to answer all further questions concerning herself.

She stood up by the table, facing the coroner. She stood there, an exquisite figure, slender and erect, her countenance and her attitude sublime in composure, grace and refinement in every line.

The few of her friends who had found their way into the court, and who were standing discreetly in the background, Mr. Symeon, Mr. Amphlett and Lady Susan, Father Cyprian Hammond, Claude Rutherford, Eustace Lyon, the poet—these admired and wondered.

With no vestige of colour in cheek or lip, with eyes that had grown larger in the new horror of her life, yet unutterably calm, with not one passing tremor in the low voice, and with not one instant of hesitation, she answered the coroner's questions.

"At what time had she fallen asleep after her return from Fulham Park?"

"It must have been past four o'clock."

"Was your maid in attendance upon you when you went to bed?"

"No, I have never allowed my maid to sit up for me after a late party."

"Are you a heavy sleeper?"

"Not usually; but I was very tired that night."

Eustace Lyon noticed that she spoke of "that night," the night before last, as if it had been ages ago. The fact appealed to his imagination as a poet. He remarked afterwards that it is only poets who perceive such subtle indications.

"Did you hear nothing between six and half-past eight o'clock?"

"Nothing."

A plan of the upper floor was lying in front of the coroner, and he was studying the position of the rooms.

"The room in which the shot was fired has a door communicating with your bedroom?"

"Yes."

"Was that door shut?"

"It is always shut."

"Shut, but not locked?"

"No, it was not locked."

The poet and Mr. Symeon looked at each other as she made this answer, with unalterable composure.

The coroner was an elderly man, a doctor—grave always, but especially so on this occasion, for this was an exceptional case, and appealed to him in an exceptional manner. The murder was even more mysterious than terrible; and he was at once touched and mystified by the unshaken composure of this young woman, who had been awakened from her morning sleep to be told that her husband had been murdered within a few yards of the room where she had been sleeping, full of happy dreams, perhaps, after the pleasant excitement of a dance.

Except for a strained look in the large grey eyes, there was nothing in her aspect to indicate the ordeal through which she had passed within the last two days.

"Isn't she simply wonderful?" murmured Susan Amphlett in the ear of Mr. Symeon, who was standing by her chair. "She has been like that ever since." There was no need to say since what. "I was with her all yesterday; but it was not a bit of use. She has turned to stone. Not a tear, not a cry; only that dreadful look in her eyes, as if she were seeing him murdered. It would have been a relief to hear her scream, or burst into a flood of tears."

"That kind of woman does neither," said Symeon. "She is a grand soul, not a bundle of nerves. She has force and courage; and she knows that death does not matter."

The coroner treated this witness with the utmost respect, but he did not spare her. A crime so extraordinary demanded a severe investigation, and searching questions had to be asked.

Had Mr. Provana a quarrel with anybody, either in his social or business relations? Did the witness know of any incident in her husband's life—in England or in Italy—which might suggest a motive for the crime?

The answer to both questions was a negative.

"But he might have had a secret enemy without your knowledge?"

"It is possible. He would not have told me anything that would have made me anxious or unhappy."

For the first time there was a faint tremor in her voice as she said this; and the poet whispered three words in Lady Susan's ear—"She loved him!"

Asked whether she expected her husband's return, she replied that she had received no cablegram naming the steamer by which he was to return. She had received letters and cablegrams, but none within the last six days before his death. Asked whether they were on good terms when he left England, she replied that there had never been a difference of any kind between them.

She refused to be seated during this ordeal, and stood facing her questioner till he had asked his last question; and when Lady Okehampton came to her, wanting to lead her away, she insisted upon remaining near the end of the table, where the witnesses came one after another to give their evidence.

The coroner heard those low, distinct words, "I want to hear everything," and he noted how she stood there, watching and listening to the end of the inquiry, regardless of her aunt's endeavour to get her away from the spot.

A confidential clerk from Mr. Provana's office in Lombard Street was able to give an account of the safe in his principal's dressing-room, as he had often been in the room, occupied in examining documents with his employer, and in taking shorthand notes for letters to be written in Lombard Street. He had examined the contents of this safe after the murder. The door had been opened with Mr. Provana's private key, which he always carried about him. Certain securities were missing, but the valuables abstracted were of a much less amount than might have been taken by anyone acquainted with the nature of the papers the safe contained, and able to use his knowledge to advantage. Two parcels of foreign bonds were missing, the present value of which would be about six thousand pounds. The witness had an inventory of everything in this safe, and he had found all other parcels intact, although the contents of the drawers and shelves had been greatly disturbed, and the papers thrown about, as if by some person in haste.

"Would these bonds be easily convertible into cash?"

"They are bonds to bearer, and there would be no difficulty of disposing of them at their value."

The inquiry was adjourned. Vera was surrounded by her friends, Lady Okehampton, Lady Susan, Mr. Symeon, and Claude Rutherford. Even Eustace Lyon ventured to approach her.

"Forgive me for intruding at such a moment," he said, almost breathless with excitement. "I feel that I must speak. You were sublime! Symeon is right. You are spirit and not clay. It needs something more than flesh and blood to go through what you have endured to-day."

She looked at him with the same strained look in her eyes with which she had looked at the coroner; a look of surprise, as if, in the midst of a dream, she had been startled by a living voice.

CHAPTER XIV

Vera insisted on going back to the house of death, although her aunt and Susan Amphlett were equally urgent in trying to take her home with them.

"Why should you make a martyr of yourself?" Susie urged in her vehement way. "You can do him no good. He will not know. All the dead want is silence and darkness, and to be mourned by those they love. You will mourn for him just as sincerely in my dainty spare room in Green Street as in that wilderness of empty rooms where he lies."

"Yes, I shall mourn for him," said Vera in low, measured tones. "I shall mourn for him all my life."

"No, no, chérie," murmured Susan confidentially, as they moved towards the door. "You will always be sorry for his quite too dreadful death, and you will remember all his goodness and absolute devotion to you. But you have your own life before you. You are not like some poor old thing, who feels that life is done with when she is left a widow; nothing to look forward to but charity bazaars and pug dogs. Remember how young you are, child! Almost on the threshold of life. You don't know how I envy you when I think I am such ages older. You are going to be immensely rich; and by and by you will marry someone you can adore, as poor Provana adored you: and whatever you do, Vera, don't wait till you are fat and elderly, and then marry a boy, as I've known a widow do—out of respect for a first husband."

Susan felt that she had now hit upon the right note, and was really a consoler; but nothing she could say had any effect upon her friend.

"I am going home," she said. "The house is dreadful; but I would rather be there than anywhere else."

She had only the same answer for her aunt, when urged to stay at Berkeley Square, "at least until all this troublesome business of the inquest is over."

"I can't think why the coroner could not have finished to-day," Lady Okehampton said to her husband at dinner that evening. "They had the doctor's evidence, and the servants', and the clerk's; all the circumstances were made clear, every detail of the poor thing's death was gone into. What more could be wanted?"

"Only one detail. To find the murderer. If ever I were to be murdered I hope the inquiry would address itself more to the man who did it than to the way in which it was done; and that the coroner would stick to his work till he found the fellow who killed me. If he didn't, I believe I should walk at midnight, like Hamlet's father."

Claude Rutherford was among the friends who surrounded Vera as she left the court. His mother was with him, an unexpected figure in such a scene; and while her son said no word, Mrs. Rutherford murmured the gentle assurance of her sympathy. She had held herself aloof from Vera for a long time, disapproving of an intimacy in which she saw danger for her son, and discredit for Mario Provana's wife; but she came to this dismal court to-day moved by divine compassion for the fragile creature who had become the central figure in so awful a tragedy.

For the first time since she had entered the court, Vera's strained eyeballs clouded with tears, and the hand which Mrs. Rutherford held with a friendly pressure trembled violently. That unnatural calm of the last two hours had given way in the surprise of this meeting. Her carriage was waiting for her, and she stepped into it too quickly for Claude to help her; he could only stand among the others to see her driven away.

"It was more than good of you to come to this dreadful place," he told his mother, as they walked towards Piccadilly.

"I would do anything to help her, if it were possible. She has not made the best use of her life, so far. Perhaps she has only gone with the stream, like the herd of modern women, who seem to have neither heart nor conscience. But this tragedy was a terrible awakening, and no one can help being sorry for her."

"The ruck of her friends will not be sorry. They will only chatter about her husband's death, and discuss the amount of her fortune as his widow. You are right, mother. They have neither heart nor conscience. They care for nothing, hope for nothing, except to be better dressed and dine out oftener than other women."

He spoke with unusual bitterness, and his mother looked at him anxiously. All the marks of a too feverish life showed upon his delicate countenance in the clear light of summer. He had never counted among handsome men; but a face so sensitive was more interesting than the beauty of line and colour, and people who knew Claude Rutherford knew that the sensitive face was the outward evidence of a highly emotional nature.

"You are looking so tired and worn, Claude," his mother said anxiously.

"Oh, this ghastly business has been a shock for me as well as for her. I was with her at the Fulham House ball the night before. We were waltzing in a mob of dancers, sitting out among tropical flowers, laughing together in the noise and laughter and foolish talk in the supper-room. Such diamonds; such bare shoulders and enamelled faces. It was half-past two when I took her to her carriage, and a blackbird was whistling in the avenue. Everybody was pretending to be happy; and she went alone to that great, gloomy house, to be awakened a few hours later to be told that her husband had been murdered."

"What could have been the motive for such a murder?"

"Plunder. What else? Of course, it was known that he kept valuables in that safe."

"How was it that he came home so unexpectedly?"

"Heaven knows. Perhaps he wanted to give his wife a surprise—a grim joke in such a husband; and the result was grimmer than he could have anticipated." There was a savage bitterness in his tone that shocked the tender-hearted woman.

"Don't speak of it like that, Claude. It is too dreadful to think of. He was a devoted husband, from all that I have heard; only too blindly indulgent, letting his wife lead the wretched, empty-headed existence that can spoil even a good woman."

They were at Mrs. Rutherford's door by this time, and she asked her son to give her a few minutes more before he went away.

"As long as you like," he said. "I am at a loose end. My usual diversions are out of the question; and all manner of work is impossible."

"You must go away, Claude. You are too sensitive, too warm-hearted to get over this business easily. You ought to leave London for a long time."

And then, with her hand on his shoulder, looking up at him with tearful solicitude, she enlarged upon that source of consolation to which a woman of deep religious convictions turns instinctively in the time of trouble. She reminded him of his happy and innocent boyhood, the unquestioning faith of those early years, before the leaven of doubt had entered his mind, before the Christian youth had become the trifler and cynic.

He listened in silence, with downcast eyes, and then, tenderly kissing her, he said gently:

"Yes, perhaps there lies the cure. I must go back to those tranquil days. I must leave this hateful town. Yes, mother, I mean to go away—for a long time. I shall take your advice. If you see Father Hammond I should like you to tell him about this talk of ours."

"Why not go to him at once and make your confession? You would feel happier afterwards."

"I have not come to that yet. I mean to have a talk with him later. A riverdervi, Madre mia."

"Where are you going?"

"I don't know. To my rooms, most likely. I have letters to write."

He was gone before she could question him further. That business of letter-writing was the most arduous work he knew. Since he had "chucked" art, his days had no more strenuous employment; his life was the over-occupied existence of a man of pleasure.

CHAPTER XV

Lord Okehampton, discussing the financier's fate in a tête-à-tête dinner with his wife, was only one among a multitude who were thinking of the Provana murder. There is nothing that English men and women enjoy more than the crime which they call "a really good murder." They will import sensation cases from America or the colonies, and will try to feel as keenly interested in a murder in New York or Melbourne as in a London tragedy. But the keen relish is lacking where the crime has been done afar off. It is impossible to realise the scene in unfamiliar surroundings. The sense of nearness, of the street or the countryside we know, is a strong factor in the interest of the story. To the man who knows his Paris thoroughly a Parisian crime may appeal; but to the woman who buys frocks in the Rue de la Paix, and hats on the Boulevard des Italiens, the most diabolical murder in the Marais, or on the heights of Belleville, seems tame.

Thus the murder of a millionaire in the midst of the rich man's London was a crime that set every sensation-seeker theorising and arguing. Every man is at heart a Sherlock Holmes, while every woman thinks herself a criminal investigator by instinct; and the theories worked out and expounded over tea-tables, and maintained with a red-hot intensity, were various and startling. The most sanguinary murder is a poor thing if people know how and by whom it was done. Mystery is essential in a crime that is to occupy the mind of the public. The murder in the great house in Portland Place had all the elements of enduring success—wealth, beauty, secrecy, and that Italian flavour which offered poignant possibilities of jealousy or revenge, or perhaps a life-long vendetta, as the motive of the crime.

The inquiry in the coroner's court dragged slowly towards an indeterminate and unsatisfactory close, being adjourned at long intervals to give the police time to make discoveries.

So far the police had made no discoveries, and the daily Press was beginning to be angry with the Criminal Investigation Department; and to make uncivil comparisons between the home article and the same thing in France and Germany. In the meantime the newspapers found subject for occasional paragraphs, though they had no new facts to communicate. So long as the inquest went on, picturesque reporters found a spacious field for their pen in the descriptions of witnesses and spectators in the coroner's court; the spectators being mostly women of some fashion, and more or less famous in the world of art and letters. The stage, also, had been represented among that morbidly curious crowd; popular actresses coming to study the appearance and demeanour of the young widow, whose marble calm in the witness box had been written and talked about. But in spite of searching and patient inquiry, the murder in Portland Place remained an insoluble mystery, a standing reproach against Scotland Yard.

While the man in the street and the daily papers he battens upon were expatiating upon the supineness and incompetency of the Criminal Investigation Department, the chief of that department was not idle. Scotland Yard is not greatly in favour of the offering of rewards for the apprehension of criminals. Scotland Yard has an idea that such offers do more harm than good, and prefers to rely upon the intelligence of its officials; and on that spontaneous and disinterested help which is often afforded by outsiders.

But after the man in the street had expended much wonder and indignation upon the fact that no reward had as yet been offered by the murdered man's widow or family, the Disbrowes had taken upon themselves to arouse Vera to a proper sense of her position and responsibilities. Among Provana's friends and allies in the City—the great semi-oriental banking house of Messrs. Zeba and Zalmunna, with whom he had been closely associated, and other firms almost as distinguished—there was also a feeling that strong measures were required, and some wonderment that the widow had as yet done nothing.

Lady Okehampton, who had been in Portland Place nearly every day—although not always allowed to see her niece—took the matter in hand, as spokeswoman for the Disbrowes, and told Vera that she must offer a reward for the apprehension of her husband's murderer.

"It ought to have been done before how," she said, "but you have been so lost in grief, that I have been afraid to talk of poor Provana; however, as time goes on people must think it extraordinary that you can let things slide; especially after that splendid will which makes you the richest woman in London."

The splendid will, executed in the first year of her marriage, left Vera residuary legatee, after a long list of legacies, which although generous, did not absorb more than a sixth of Mario Provana's estate. If not actually the richest woman in London—a fact not easily to be ascertained—Vera was at least rich enough to support that reputation.

She gave a little moan of anguish when her aunt spoke of the will, and replied, with averted face, that her uncle was to do whatever he thought right.

Before darkness came down the police stations of London exhibited bills, offering a thousand pounds for information leading to the discovery of the murderer, and the man in the street was a little easier in his mind.

In the meantime Scotland Yard was pursuing its own course, and one of the most experienced and intelligent members of the force had the Provana affair in hand, and was actually established in Portland Place, where he was explained to the household as a picture-restorer, who had been engaged by Mr. Provana shortly before he left England, to examine and restore certain pictures among those somewhat depressing examples of the early Italian school which gave gloom to the too spacious dining-room.

It might seem strange that work of this kind, ordered by the dead man, should be carried out at such a time; but Mr. James Japp, of the Criminal Investigation Department, had a power of impersonation which rarely failed him in the most critical circumstances; and having assumed the role of artistic man-of-all-work, he omitted no detail that could impress and convince the house servants, among whom he hoped to put his hand upon the murderer. Plausible, friendly, and altogether an acquisition in that low-spirited household, Mr. Japp, alias Johnson, was soon upon terms of cordial friendship with butler and housekeeper, while he was genially patronising to the four stalwart footmen, and by no means stand-offish to the coachman and his underlings, who sometimes crept into the servants' hall in the gloaming to talk over the last paragraph upon the mystery in Portland Place. For them the mystery was meat and drink. They hung upon it with a morbid tenacity, never tired of re-stating the same facts, and going over the same arguments, and doing battle, each for his own solution of the ghastly problem. For these Mr. Johnson, artist and picture-restorer, was a godsend.

The man was so delightfully innocent in the ways and workings of criminals. He showed the simple faith of a child when listening with avidity to Mr. Sedgewick's views, and allowed himself to be browbeaten by the coachman. He would turn the drift of the talk aside at a most interesting point to relate his early aspirations as a student, and his dismal failure as an artist, and how he had been driven from the painting of colossal historical pictures to the humbler art of the varnisher and restorer, working for a daily wage. He would tell stories of his early struggles that evolved laughter and good-natured scorn.

He had a room allotted to him for his work, one of those rooms opening out of the long passage that led to Mr. Provana's private door, that door by which he and his murderer must have entered the house on the fatal night. Mr. Johnson had examined the door with studious attention, confessing to a morbid interest in the details of crime, co-existent with a curious ignorance of the law of the land. The nature and methods of a coroner's court had to be explained to him, condescendingly, by Mr. Sedgewick, when the Provana murder was under discussion.

He had his room for his artistic work, where he installed himself with three of the largest pictures from the dining-room, his bottles of oil and varnish, and his stock of brushes, and where he insisted upon being undisturbed. He was of a nervous temperament, and could not bear to have his work looked at. He talked of his progress from day to day, expatiating upon the dangers of blue mould, the horrors of asphaltum and other pernicious mediums, and the superiority of the old painters, who ground their own colours; but no one, not even Mr. Sedgewick, was allowed to see him at work.

He was altogether a superior person, yet it was something of a surprise to the household that he should be admitted every evening to an interview with Mrs. Provana, who received him in the great, lonely drawing-room, where he remained with her for about a quarter of an hour, giving an account of his day's work.

This privilege was explained by Mr. Johnson as a natural result of the lady's interest in art, and the value she set upon pictures which it appeared were especial favourites with her husband.

"At the rate he goes at it, I don't fancy he can have much progress to report," remarked Mr. Sedgewick, "for I don't believe he works a solid hour a day at those pictures. He takes things a bit too easily, to my mind. He knows he's got a soft job, and he means to make it last as long as the missus will let him. He's got his head pretty well screwed on, has our friend Johnson; and he knows when he's in for a good thing. And he's got a tongue that would talk over a special commissioner of income tax; so no doubt he makes Mrs. Provana believe that he works heavens hard at fetching up the colour in the Frau Angelicas."

"I shall think something of his work if he can do anything to brighten up those Salvini Roses, which are about the dismallest pictures I ever saw in a gentleman's dining-room," the housekeeper remarked with conviction.

Mr. Johnson was a desultory worker. He told his friends in the household that he worked like a tiger while he was at it, but your real artist was ever fitful in his toil. It was in the artistic temperament to be desultory. He would emerge from his den after an hour or so, in a canvas apron so stained with oil, and so sticky with varnish, that none could doubt his industry. He was eminently sociable. He couldn't get on without company and conversation. The four young footmen afforded him inexhaustible amusement.

"The oldest of 'em ain't over twenty-five," he said, "but every one of 'em is a character in his way. Now I love studying character. There's no book, no, nor no illustrated magazine, you can give me that I enjoy as I do human nature. Give me the human document, and leave your mouldy old books for mouldy old scholars. Every one of those four lads is a romance, if you know how to read him."

This taste, which Mr. Sedgewick and Mrs. Manby thought low, led Mr. Johnson to consort in the friendliest way with the four youths in question. He had not been in the house a fortnight before he knew all about them; their sweethearts; their ambitions; their tastes for pleasure, and their craving for gain. Even the odd man, a creature whom the élite of the household esteemed as hardly human—a savage without a livery, by whom it was a hardship to be waited on at one's meals—was not without interest for Johnson. While he delighted in Mr. Sedgewick's company, and was proud to spend an evening with him at his club, he shocked everybody by taking the old man to a music hall, and giving him supper after the entertainment.

"I think you're all too hard upon Andrew," he said. "I find him distinctly human."

With the ladies of the household he was at once friendly and gallant. He aired his little stock of French with Ma'mselle, and took her for evening walks in Regent's Park, which to dwellers north of Langham

Place is "the Park." He bought her little gifts, and took her to the theatre. He played dummy whist with Mrs. Manby, who was sadly behind the age, and could not abide bridge; and the result of all this friendly intercourse, which had kept the establishment in good spirits during a period of gloom, culminated one evening, when he told Mrs. Provana that his residence under her roof had only a negative result, and that he had exhausted all the means in his power without arriving at any clue to the murderer of her husband.

"It has been a great disappointment to me, Madam," said Mr. Japp, standing before Vera, with his hat in his hand, serious and subdued in manner and bearing. The change from the sociable and trivial Johnson to the business-like and thoughtful Japp showed a remarkable power in the assumption of character.

"It has been the most disappointing case I have been engaged in for a long time. I came into this house assured that I should put my hand upon the guilty party under this roof. Every circumstance indicated that the crime had been committed by someone inside the house. The idea of an outsider seemed incredible. That a house with such a staff of servants—with five men and an Irish terrier sleeping on the ground floor—could have been entered by a burglar seemed out of the question. Mr. Provana being known to keep large sums of money in one shape and another in the safe in his private room, and no doubt being also known to carry the keys of that safe upon his person, there was a sufficient inducement for robbery; while it is our common experience that any man bold enough to attempt robbery on a large scale is not the man to shrink from murder, when his own skin is in danger. My theory was that one of your men servants had been waiting for his opportunity during Mr. Provana's absence in America; that he had provided himself with implements for forcing the lock of the safe, perhaps with the aid of an outside accomplice, and that, by a strange coincidence, he had stumbled upon the night of his master's unexpected return, and had been surprised at the beginning of his work. There are scratches on the polished steel about the lock of the safe that might be made by one of those graduated wedges which burglars use. I thought that, being surprised by Mr. Provana's entrance, he snatched up one of the pistols from the case on the table—which he might have examined previously— and fired within narrow range, as Mr. Provana was about to open the door of your room, without having seen him; that he took the keys from Mr. Provana's pocket after he fell, unlocked the safe, and abstracted the two parcels of bonds which are missing. The disordered state of the safe, and the keys left in the lock, indicate that everything was done in extreme haste. This was my theory before I came into your house, Madam; but after nearly five weeks' careful study of every individual under this roof, I have reluctantly arrived at the conclusion that nobody in your household is in it, either as principal or accomplice, before or after the fact. I think it is in an old play that the remark has been made that 'Murder will out,' also that 'Blood will have blood.' Both remarks are perfectly correct; but there is another remark that might have been made with even greater truth, and that is 'Money will out.' You can't hide money—at least the average criminal can't. That's where he gives himself away. He can't keep his plunder to himself—the money burns—it burns—he must spend it. Some spend it on drink; some, begging your pardon, Madam—spend it on ladies; some, the weakest of the lot, spend it on clothes and hansom cabs; but spend they must. There's not one of those four young men that could keep five or six thou' in his pocket and not give himself away—somehow or somewhere. Nor yet Mr. Sedgewick, fine gentleman and philosopher as he is—nor yet even the odd man. Being a poor creature, he'd have melted those securities with the first low fence he could hear of, and would have been on the drink night after night, till he got the horrors and gave himself up to the police. I've been looking for the money, Madam, and finding no trace of that, I know I've not come within range of the party we want. We must look outside, Madam, and we may have to look a long way off. If the possessor of those bonds is an old hand, he is not likely to turn them into money anywhere in this City; for though they are bonds to bearer, a transaction of that kind must leave some trace. I feel the humiliation of my failure, Madam, and I have no doubt you are disappointed."

Vera looked up at him with melancholy eyes, pale, hollow-cheeked, a sombre figure in the severest mourning that the Maison de Deuil near the Madeleine could supply, and French mourning knows no compromise.

"Disappointed," she repeated slowly in a low, tired voice, and then, to Mr. Japp's surprise and almost horror, she said, "I don't think it much matters whether the wretched creature who killed him is discovered or not. It can make no difference to him lying at rest, beyond all pain and sorrow, that his murderer is hidden somewhere out of reach of the law, and may escape the agony of a shameful death."

The horror in her widening eyes as she said these words showed that her imagination could realise the horror of the scaffold. "However he may escape human law," she went on, in the same slow, dull tones, "he must carry his punishment with him to the grave. He can never know one peaceful hour. He can never know the comfort of dreamless sleep. He will be a haunted man."

"Excuse me for differing with you, Madam, but you don't know what stuff the criminal classes are made of. They don't mind. One more or less sent to kingdom come don't prey upon their nerves. Where are they found, as a rule, when they do get nicked? Why at a theatre or in a music-hall, or at the Derby—and generally in ladies' society. The things you read of in novels, conscience, remorse, Banquo's ghost, don't trouble them."

Mr. Japp apologised for having expressed himself so freely, and stood for a few minutes fingering the brim of his hat, waiting for Mrs. Provana to speak. Her speech just now had been a surprise to him, for never had he met with so silent a lady. Night after night she had listened hungrily to his statement of his day's progress, his suspicions, his glimpses of light, now seeming full of promise, and anon delusive. She had listened with keen attention; but she had expressed no opinion, and had asked no questions. And now for him—the accomplished Criminal Investigator, the man who had worked at the science of detection as superior persons work at the higher mathematics—to hear this lady say that the discovery of her husband's murderer did not matter, that, for her part, he might go about the world a free man, with nothing worse than a mind full of scorpions and a sleepless bed, seemed too monstrous for comprehension. She, to whom the murdered man had left millions, not to hunger for the ignominious death of his murderer!

"It must be Christian Science," thought Mr. Japp, as he packed his portmanteau. "Nothing less can account for it."

CHAPTER XVI

Everybody in the Red Book had left London. The West End was a desert, and the shrill summons of the telephone was heard no more in Mayfair. Nobody, unless it were the caretaker, was being asked to luncheon or dinner, and the only tea-parties were in the basement, where the late lettuce had not yet given place to the early muffin. Only people with urgent and onerous business were to be found in London. Lord Okehampton was shooting grouse, and Lady Okehampton ought to have been doing an after-cure in Switzerland; but "the sad state of my poor niece after her husband's ghastly death, and the legal business connected with her colossal inheritance, make it impossible for me to leave town. Much as I need a complete change, I must stay here, while that poor child wants me."

This was what Lady Okehampton wrote from her deserted house in Berkeley Square, to numerous friends, with more or less variation of phrase.

Vera's health was now the most pressing question. She had taken her bereavement with a dumb, self-contained grief, that is the most morbid and the most perilous kind of sorrow; the sorrow that kills. When questioned, pressingly but tenderly, by her aunt, she always replied in the same unresponsive manner. There was nothing the matter with her. Of course, as Aunt Mildred said, the shock had been terrible; but no doubt she would get over it in time. People always get over things. She only wanted to be left to herself. She was quite strong enough to bear her burden. No, she was not eating her heart out in solitude. It was best for her to be alone.

"You are more than kind, Aunt Mildred, and so is Susan Amphlett; but I am better sitting quietly and thinking out my life."

"But, my poor child, you are perishing visibly—just wasting away. I would rather see you in floods of tears, hysterical even, than in this hopeless state."

"What is the use of making a fuss? If tears could bring my husband back and make life what it was before his death, I would drown myself in tears. But nothing can change the past. That is what makes life terrible. The things we have done are done for ever."

Lady Okehampton trembled, first for her niece's life, and next for her sanity. And here was this stupendous fortune left to Vera for her life, and to her children after her—her children by the husband who was dead—but, in default of such children, to be divided among a horde of Italian relations—third and fourth cousins, people for whom Mario Provana might not have cared twopence—and among Roman charitable institutions—sure to be badly managed, Lady Okehampton thought.

It seemed to her that if Vera were to die, that stupendous wealth, which while she possessed it must be a factor in the position of the Disbrowes, would be absolutely thrown to the dogs. To divide that mass of riches into eights, and twelfths, and sixteenths, was in a manner to murder it. All its power and prestige would be gone, frittered away among insignificant people, who might be better off without it, as it would put a stop to laudable ambition and enterprise, and might ultimately be the cause of unmitigated harm.

"It is so sad to think there were no children," sighed Lady Okehampton into the ears of various confidential friends. "The dear man made this will shortly after his marriage, and evidently built upon having an heir—he was so absolutely devoted to my niece. I know it was a bitter disappointment for him," concluded the chieftainess of the Disbrowes, to whom Mario Provana had said no word of his inmost feelings upon that or any other subject.

Strange indeed would it have been for that strong hand to lift the curtain from that proud heart. Courteous, generous, chivalrous, he might be to the whole clan of Disbrowes. He might scatter his gold among them with a careless hand; but to scatter the secrets of his lonely life among that frivolous herd was impossible to the man who had endured a mother's dislike, a father's neglect, and the disillusions of a mariage de convenance, without one hour of self-betrayal.

Vera was childless, and on her frail thread of life hung Mario Provana's millions.

Lady Okehampton told herself this in the watches of the night, and told herself that something must be done. It was all very well for Vera to declare that there was nothing the matter with her, while it was visible to the naked eye that the poor child was fading away, in an atrophy of mind and body.

"She will either die or go mad," said Lady Okehampton, and the alternative offered visions of a conseil de famille, doctors' certificates, and that rabble of fourth and fifth cousins tearing their prey.

Long and confidential talks with Mrs. Manby, the housekeeper, and Louison, the maid, had revealed the desperate state of their mistress's health.

"No, my lady, she doesn't complain," asserted Mrs Manby. "I'm afraid it's all the worse because she won't complain. But she can't sleep, and she can't eat. Sedgewick knows what her meals are like: just pretending, that's all; and Louison says that, go into her mistress's room when she will, in the middle of the night or in the early morning, she's always lying awake, sometimes reading, sometimes staring at the sky above the window sash, but asleep—never! And it isn't for want of taking things, for she has tried every drug you can put a name to."

"Does the doctor prescribe them?"

"He used to send her things, in the first few weeks after—the funeral. But she made him believe that she was quite well, and was sleeping and eating as usual, and he left off coming. And then Lady Susan Amphlett brought her tabloids—always the newest thing out. But they've never done her any good. It's the mind that's wrong, my lady."

"She was absolutely devoted to Mr. Provana," sighed Lady Okehampton.

"No doubt, my lady."

"And she can't get over her loss."

"No, my lady."

Susan Amphlett was of Aunt Mildred's opinion. Something must be done, and it must be done quickly, before any of those Roman cousins could appear upon the scene, prying and questioning, and hinting at a commission of lunacy. Things had come to a perilous pass, when Mrs. Manby, the housekeeper, could talk of her mistress's mind as the seat of the mischief. People who go out of their minds seldom take a long time about it, Lady Susan urged. "It's generally touch and go."

Lady Okehampton waited for no permission, but marched into her niece's room one dark September afternoon with the fashionable nerve specialist at her heels, the bland elderly physician from Cavendish Square, whom nobody in Mayfair had even heard of till he had entered upon his seventh decade, and who had languished at the wrong end of Harley Street for a quarter of a century, before the great world had made the remarkable discovery that he was the one man in London who could cure one of everything.

He was kind and sensible, and really clever; but the great world loved him most because he had all the new names for old diseases at the tip of his tongue, and had the delightful manner which implied that the patient to whom he was talking was the one patient whose life he considered worth saving.

"He really does think about you when he's feeling your pulse," said a dowager. "He ain't totting up last night's winnings at bridge all the time. He does really think, don't you know."

Dr. Selwyn Tower, as he held Vera's wasted wrist in his broad, soft hand, looked as serious as if the fate of a nation were at stake. Indeed, he had been told that millions were in jeopardy, and in the modern mind the destinies of big fortunes are as serious as the rise and fall of peoples.

The physician asked no troublesome questions; but he contrived to keep Vera in conversation—on indifferent subjects—for about a quarter of an hour, her aunt joining in occasionally with sympathetic nothings; and by the end of that time he had made up his mind about the case, or at least about his immediate treatment of the case. He might have thoughts that went deeper and farther—but those could be held in abeyance. The thing to be done was to save this fragile form, which was obviously perishing.

A rest cure—nothing else would be of any use—an uncompromising rest cure. Six weeks of solitary confinement in the care of a resident doctor and a couple of highly trained nurses.

Lady Okehampton anticipated a struggle, remembering how resolutely Vera had resisted this line of treatment three months before; but her niece surprised her by offering no vehement opposition.

"There is absolutely nothing the matter with me," she said, "but if it will please you, Aunt Mildred, I will do as Dr. Tower advises."

"Nothing the matter! And you neither eat nor sleep! Is that nothing?"

"Who told you that I can't sleep?"

"My dear lady, your eyes tell us only too plainly. Insomnia has unmistakable symptoms," said the doctor.

"Yes, it is true," Vera answered wearily. "I seem to have lost the faculty of sleep. It is a habit one soon loses. I lie staring at the daylight, and wondering what it is like to lose count of time."

And then, after a little more doctor's talk, soothing, and rather meaningless, she asked abruptly:

"What time of year is it?"

"Dear child," exclaimed Lady Okehampton, "can you ask?"

"Oh, I have left off writing letters and reading newspapers, and I forget dates. I know the days are getting shorter, because the dawn is so long coming when I lie awake."

"We are in the middle of September," said the doctor, "a charming month for country air—neither too hot nor too cold—the golden mean."

"And in six weeks it will be the end of October, and I can go to Rome for the winter!"

"You could not do better. We shall build up your constitution in those six weeks. You will be another woman when you leave Sussex."

"But, my dearest Vera," protested her aunt, "you can never think of a winter alone in that enormous villa. You will die of ennui."

"No, no, Aunt Mildred, I love Rome. The very atmosphere of the place is life to me. I am not afraid of being alone."

Dr. Tower shot a significant look at her ladyship, which silenced remonstrance, and no more was said.

Two days later Vera found herself on a windy hill in Sussex, under the dominion of the house-doctor and two nurses, and almost as much exposed to the elements as King Lear on the heights near Dover. An eider-down coverlet and a hot-water bottle made the only difference. Lady Okehampton, having sacrificed her own cure to her niece's, went with a mind at ease to join her husband in Yorkshire; an arrangement almost without precedent in their domestic annals.

CHAPTER XVII

Father Cyprian Hammond returned to his comfortable rooms in the north-west region one rainy autumn evening after a long day in the dreariest abodes of East London. He was almost worn out by the bodily fatigue of tramping those dismal streets with one of his friends and allies, a priest from the Cathedral at Moorfields; and by the mental strain that comes from facing the inscrutable problem of human suffering—the mystery of sorrow and pain, inevitable, unceasing, beyond man's power to help or cure.

He had visited the poor in great hospitals where every detail testified to the beneficence of the rich; yet he knew that the comfort and cleanliness of the hospital must needs accentuate the dirt and squalor of the slum to which the patient must return.

He sank into his armchair, with a sigh of relief, and was sorry to hear of a visitor, who had called twice that afternoon and would call again after nine o'clock.

"Did he leave his card?"

Yes, the card was there on the table.

"Mr. Claude Rutherford."

Father Cyprian had not seen Claude since the opening day of that inquest which had been so often adjourned, only to close in an open verdict, and a mystery still unsolved. He had not seen Claude; but he had seen Mrs. Rutherford more than once in that quiet month when life in West End London seems to come to a stand-still. She had talked about her son as she talked only to him, opening her heart to the friend who knew all its secrets, the best and the worst of her. Hitherto she had never failed to find him interested and sympathetic; but in those recent interviews it had seemed to her as if the close friend of long years had changed; as if he was talking to her from a distance; as if some mysterious barrier had arisen between them.

She had told him of that conversation with her son, in which he had promised to confide in this old and trusted friend. That had happened more than a month ago, and the confidence had not yet come. Perhaps it was coming to-night.

"I will see Mr. Rutherford at whatever time he calls," Father Cyprian told his servant.

His dinner was short and temperate, but not ill-cooked or ill-served. He drank barley water, but the jug that held it was of old cut-glass, picked up at a broker's shop in a back street for seven shillings, and worth as many pounds. His silver was old family plate, his napery of the finest.

It was past nine when Claude Rutherford appeared, and the first thing Father Cyprian observed was that he was physically exhausted. He dropped into a chair with a long sigh of fatigue, and it was three or four minutes before he was able to speak.

"I knew you would have finished your Spartan dinner by this time," he said, "but I hope I am not spoiling your evening."

"You ought to know that I have nothing better to do with my evening than to talk with anybody who wants me," answered the priest in the low, grave voice that was like the sound of Hollmann's bow in an adagio passage, "and I think you must want me, or you would not come to this house a third time. What have you been doing since six o'clock? You look horribly fagged."

"I have been to Hampstead. It is a fine night, and I wanted a walk."

"You have walked too far. You are ill, Claude."

"A little under the weather. The modern complaint, neuritis, and its concomitant, insomnia."

"You ought to go to one of my neighbours in Harley Street."

"No. I want you—the physician of souls. This corporal frame of mine will mend itself when I get out of London; a thousand miles or so. Do you remember the night we walked home together from Portland Place? You pressed me very hard that evening. You tried to bring me back to the fold—but the time had not come."

"And now the time has come?" questioned the priest, pushing aside the book that he had been reading, and bending forward to look into a page of human life, bringing his searching eyes nearer to the haggard face in front of him.

"Yes, the time has come."

"What is the matter?"

"Oh, only the old disease—in a more acute phase. The disgust of life—satiety, weariness of the world outside me, loathing of the world inside; the old disease in a virulent form. I want you to help me to the cure. It must be heroic treatment. Half measures will be no use. I want you to help me to enter one of the orders that mean death to the world. Dominicans, Benedictines, La Trappe, anything you like; the harder the rule the better it may be for my soul."

"This is strangely sudden."

"Perhaps it is an inspiration. But no, my dear friend, it is not sudden. The complaint is chronic, and has been growing upon me for the last ten years, ever since I found that I was a failure. That discovery is a crisis in a man's life. He looks inside himself one day, and finds that the fire has gone out. It must all come to that. Life, mind, heart, all are contained in that central fire which is the soul of a man. While the fire burns he has hope, he has ambitions, he has a future; when the fire goes out, he has nothing but the past; the memory of things that were sweet and things that were bitter; nothing but memory to live upon in all the years that are to come: and he may live to be ninety, a haunted man! I have done with the world, Father Cyprian. Am I to walk about like a dead man for ten or twenty or thirty years? I have done with the world. I want to give the rest of my life to the God you and my mother believe in."

"You would not want to do that if you were not a believer."

"I was reared in the true faith. Yes, I believe. Help thou mine unbelief."

"I will help you with all my heart; but I do not think you are of the stuff that Benedictine monks are made of; and it is a foolish thing to put your hand to the plough, unless you have the force of mind to finish your furrow."

"I will finish my furrow."

"And break your mother's heart, perhaps. Your love is all she has in this life, except her religion."

"Her religion is no less a force than her love. My neglect of my duties has been a grief to her. She has never ceased to remonstrate with me, to remind me of my boyish ardour, my days of implicit faith."

"She wants to see you return to the faith, and the obedience, of those days; but it would distress her if you took a step that would mean separation from her."

"That would be inconsistent, after all her sermons."

"Women are apt to be inconsistent—even the best of them."

"In any case, even if my mother should object, which I think unlikely, I have made up my mind. I had time to commune with my soul in that three hours' walk through the darkness. I came to you this night fully resolved not to ask your advice as to the step, but your help in taking it. Where can I go? To whom can I submit myself?"

"Frankly, Claude, I am too much in the dark to help you. Come to me at my church to-morrow morning after mass, with your mind more at rest, and make your confession. Let me see into the bottom of your heart. I cannot talk to a man behind a mask. I can say nothing till I know all."

"No, I cannot do that. I must have time. I want solitude and a cell. I want to shake off the husk of the world I have lived in too long. I want to be done with earthly desires. I shall have a new mind when I am in my woollen gown."

"Alas, Claude, I doubt, I doubt. Do you remember all we talked about when you were last in this room—a long time ago?"

"Yes, I remember."

"You remember how I tried to awaken you to the danger of your relations with Mario Provana's wife."

"Those are things a man does not forget."

"You denied the danger; but you did not deny your love. You gave me your assurance, not as to a priest, but between man and man, that no evil should ever come of that love."

"Yes, I remember. I was not afraid of myself. I belong to the great army of triflers and dilettanti—I am not of the stuff that passionate lovers are made of."

"But now Death has intervened, and the situation is changed. Two years hence you might marry your cousin without shame to either, without disrespect to the dead. Are you capable of renouncing that hope by burying yourself in a cloister? Are you equal to the sacrifice? Would there be no looking back, no repentance?"

"I shall never marry my cousin Vera."

"Because she does not love you? Is that the reason?"

"No need to enter into details, or to count the cost. I have made up my mind. For once in my life I have a purpose and a will."

"You seem in earnest."

The words came slowly, like a spoken doubt, and the priest's searching eyes were on the pale face in front of him. The countenance where the refinement of race—a long line of well-born men and women, showed in every lineament.

"This sudden resolve of yours is inexplicable," the priest continued in a troubled voice, after a silence that seemed long. "It is not in your temperament or your manner of life, since you came into a man's inheritance, to cut yourself off from all that makes life pleasant to a young man with talent, attractiveness, and independence. I would give much to know your reason for such a step."

"Haven't I told you, my dear friend? Welt Schmerz. Isn't that enough?"

"No, it is not enough. Welt Schmerz is the chronic disease of a decadent age. If every sufferer from Welt Schmerz were to turn monk, this world would be a monastery. It is a phase in every man's life—or a pose. I know it is not that with you. There is something behind, Claude—something at the back of your mind. Something that you must tell me, before I can be of any real help to you. But you are your mother's son, and were you steeped in sin, I would do my uttermost to help you. Come to me the day after to-morrow. I shall have had time to think over your case, and you will be in a better mood for considering the situation: to surrender this worldly life and all it holds is not a light thing that a man should do in a fit of the blues, a man still on the sunward side of forty. I, who have entered my seventh decade, have no yearnings for a woollen gown."

"I have made up my mind," Claude repeated, in a dull, dead voice, the voice of an obstinate man. "Good night."

CHAPTER XVIII

The six weeks' captivity on the hill in Sussex had been a success, and Vera was able to leave England before the first November fog descended upon Portland Place. She was in Rome, in the city where she had spent the happiest period of her life—the time in which she had first known what it meant for a woman to be adored, and lovely, and immeasurably rich. There she had first known the power of wealth and the influence of beauty; for her husband's position and her own attractions had assured her an immediate social success, and had made her a star in Roman society during her first season, while, over and above all other graces, she had the charm of novelty. But it was not the memory of social triumphs or of gratified vanity that was with her as she sat alone in the too spacious saloon, or roamed with languid step through other rooms as spacious and as lonely.

Sympathy had flowed in upon her from all her Roman acquaintances, and acquaintances of divers nationalities, the birds of passage, American, French, Spanish, German. Cards and little notes had descended upon the villa like a summer hailstorm; and she had responded with civility, but with no uncertain tone. Her mourning was to be a long mourning; and her seclusion was to be absolute. She had come to live a solitary life in her villa and gardens, to wander among ruins and steep herself in the poetry of the city. She had come not to the Rome of the present, but to the Rome of the past. This was how she explained her life to the officious people who wanted to force distractions upon her; and who in secret were already hatching matrimonial schemes by which the Provana millions might be made to infuse new life into princely races that were perishing in financial atrophy.

The Villa Provana was on high ground, beyond the Porta del Popolo, and the view from the gardens commanded the roofs and towers and cupolas of the city, and the dominating mass of the great basilica, which dwarfs all other monuments, and reduces papal Rome, with its heterogeneous roofs and turrets, steeples and obelisks, to a mere foreground for that one stupendous dome.

Day after day, in those short winter afternoons, Vera stood on the terrace in front of the villa, leaning languidly against the marble balustrade, and watching the evening mists rising slowly over the city, and the grey of the great dome gradually deepening to purple, while the golden light in the west grew more intense, and orange changed to crimson.

She was never tired of gazing at that incomparable prospect. How often in her honeymoon year she had stood there, with Mario Provana at her side, questioning him with a childish delight, and making him point out and explain every tower and every cupola, the classic, the papal, the old and the new; churches, palaces, public buildings, municipal and royal, picture-galleries, museums, fountains! It was there, as an idolised young wife, with her husband's strong arm supporting her, as she leant against him, in the pleasant fatigue after a day of pleasure, that she had learnt to know Rome, and that she had discovered how dearly the hard man of business loved the city of his birth. It was there he had told her what Victor Emanuel and Cavour—the soldier and the statesman—had done for Italy; and how that which had been but a geographical expression, a patchwork of petty states—for the most part under foreign rulers—had become the name of a great nation in the van of progress.

She thought of him now, evening after evening, in the unbroken silence and solitude of the long terrace on the crown of the hill, and only a little lower than the terrace on the Pincio. She looked backward across the arid desert of her five years of society under Disbrowe influences, five years of life that seemed worthless and joyless compared with that year of a happiness she had almost forgotten, till her husband's death carried all her thoughts back to the past: to the time when she had given him love for love; to the days that she could think of without remorse.

"Oh, God, if I had died at the end of that year, what a happy life mine would have been!"

She thought of the tomb on the Campagna, the splendid monument of a husband's love, near which she had sat in her carriage with Mario to watch the gathering of a gay crowd, and the flash of red coats against the clear blue of a December day, the hounds trotting lightly in front of huntsman and whip, the women in their short habits, patent-leather boots flashing against new saddles; men on well-bred hunters; the whole picture so modern and so trivial against the fortress tomb with its mystery of a distant past—only a name to suggest the story of two lives.

"If I had only died then," she thought.

To have ended her life in that year of gladness, innocent, beloved, while all her world was lovely in the freshness of life's morning. To have died then, before the blight of disillusion or the taint of sinful thought had touched her, to have passed out of the world, beloved and worthy of love, and to have been laid to rest in the cemetery at San Marco, beside her girl friend. Ah, what a happy destiny! And now what was to be her doom? A cold breath touched her as she leaned over the balustrade, with her hands clasped over her eyes, a cold breath that thrilled her and made her tremble. It was only the cooler wind of evening, breathing across the gathering shadows, but it startled her by the suggestion of a human presence.

She rose from the marble bench where she had been sitting since the sun began to sink behind the umbrella pines on a hill in the distance, and while the far-reaching level of the Campagna began to look like the blue waters of a sea in the lessening light, and walked slowly back to the villa, by the long terrace, and under a pergola where the last roses showered their petals upon her as she passed.

The lamps were lighted in the saloon, and logs were burning in the vast fireplace at the end of the room, a distant glow and brightness, a pleasing spot of colour in a melancholy picture, but of not much avail for warmth in a room of fifty feet by twenty-five, with a ceiling twenty feet high. But the comfort of the villa was not dependent upon smouldering olive logs or spluttering pine-cones. There was a hot-water system, the most expensive and the best, for supplying all those palatial rooms with an equable and enervating atmosphere.

There was a letter lying on Vera's book-table, a table that always stood by her armchair at one side of the monumental chimneypiece. This spot was her own, her island in that ocean of space. This chair was large enough to absorb her, and when she was sitting in it, the room looked empty, and a servant had to come near her table before he could be sure she was there.

She took up the letter, and looked at the address wonderingly. It had not come by post. There was something familiar in the writing. It reminded her of Claude's; and then, in a moment, she remembered. The letter was from Mrs. Rutherford. Little notes had been exchanged between them in past years, notes of invitation from Vera, replies, mostly courteous refusals, from the elder lady.

Mrs. Rutherford must be in Rome. Strange! Had she, too, come to winter there?

"MY DEAR VERA,

"I hear you are at your villa, living in seclusion and refusing all visits; but I think you will make an exception for me, as it is vital for me to see you. I am in great trouble, and I want your help—badly. I shall call on you at noon to-morrow. Pray do not shut your door against me.

"Yours affectionately,
"MAGDALEN RUTHERFORD."

The address was of one of the smaller and quieter hotels in the great city, a house unknown to the tourist, English or American: a house patronised only by what are called "nice people."

Trouble! What could be Mrs. Rutherford's trouble? Had she anything in this world to be glad or sorry about, except her son?

The letter gave Vera a night of agitation and feverish dreams, and she spent the hour before noon pacing up and down the great room, deadly pale in the dense blackness of her long crape gown.

It was not five minutes past the hour when Mrs. Rutherford was announced. She, too, was pale, and she, too, wore black, but not mourning.

"You are kind to let me see you," she said, clasping Vera's hand.

"How could I refuse? I am so sorry you are in trouble. Is it—" her voice became tremulous, "is it anything about Claude? Is he ill?"

"No, he is not ill, unless it is in mind. But the trouble is about him, a new and unexpected trouble. A thunderbolt!"

The terror in Vera's face startled her. She thought the frail figure would drop at her feet in a dead faint, and she caught her by the arm.

"I think you may help me. You and he were great friends, pals, Susan Amphlett called you."

"Yes, we were pals. He was so good to me at Disbrowe, years and years ago."

"Yes, I know. He has often talked of that time. Well, you were great friends; and a young man will sometimes open his mind more to a woman friend than he will to his mother. Did Claude ever talk to you of his Church, of his remorse for his neglect of his religion, of his wanting to give up the world, to end a useless life in a monastery?"

"Never."

"I thought not. It is a sudden caprice; there is no real strength of purpose in it. He is disgusted and disappointed. He has made a failure of his life, and he is angry with, himself, and sick to death of Society. Such a man cannot go on being trivial for ever. A life without purpose can but end in disgust. My poor child, you are shivering, and can hardly stand. Let us go nearer the fire. Sit down, and let us talk quietly—and be kind, and bear with a foolish old woman, who sees the joy of her life slipping away from her."

The visitor's quick eye had noticed the great armchair and book-table by the hearth, and knew that it was Vera's place. She led her there, made her sit down, and took a chair by her side.

"Now we shall be warm and comfortable, and can look my trouble in the face."

"Tell me all about it," Vera said quietly, with her hand in Mrs. Rutherford's.

The wave of agitation had passed. She spoke slowly, but her voice was no longer tremulous.

"I dare say, if you have ever thought of me in the past, you have given me credit for being a strong-minded woman."

"Claude has told me of your strength of will—the right kind of strength."

"And now I have to confess myself to you, as weak, unstable, inconsistent; caring for my son's love for me more than I care for his eternal welfare."

"No, no, I can never believe that."

"But you will believe it when I tell you that he has taken the first step towards separating himself for ever from this sinful world, and giving the rest of his life to God; and that I am here in this city, here pleading with you, to try to change his purpose and win him back to the world."

"Oh!" said Vera, with a faint cry. "Has he made up his mind?"

"He thinks he has. But oh, what shall I do without him? It is horrible, selfish, unworthy; but I can only think of myself and my own desolate old age. Only a few years more, perhaps, only a few years of solitude and mourning; but my mind and heart rise in rebellion against Fate. I cannot bear my life without him. Again and again I have urged him to remember the faith in which he was reared; I have tried to awaken him to the call of the Church; I have begged Father Hammond to use his influence to rekindle the fervour of religion that made my son's boyish mind so lovely: and now when he has gone beyond my prayers, and wants to renounce this sinful world, I am a weak, miserable woman, and my despairing cry is to call him back to the life he has grown weary of. Do you not despise me, Vera?"

"No, no. I can understand. It is natural for a mother to feel as you feel; but, all the same, I think if he has made up his mind to retire into a monastery, it is your duty to let him go. Think what it is for a man to spend his last years in reconciling himself with God. Think of the peace that may come with self-sacrifice. Think what it is to escape out of this sinful world—into a place of silence and prayer, and to know that one's sins are forgiven."

"He has no sins that need the sacrifice of half a life. He has been the dearest of sons, the kindest of friends, honourable, generous, straightforward. Why should he shut himself in a monastery to find forgiveness for trivial sins, and neglect of religious forms? He can lead a new and better life in the world of action, where he can be of use to his fellow-men. Even Father Hammond has never advised him to turn monk. He can worship God, and lead the Christian life, without renouncing all that is lovely in the world God made for us."

Vera listened with a steadfast face, and her tones were calm and decided when she replied.

"Dear Mrs. Rutherford, the heart knoweth its own bitterness. I think, the better you love your son the less you should come between him and a resolve that must give him peace, if it can never give him happiness."

For the first time since Mrs. Rutherford had been with her, Vera's eyes filled with tears, tears that overflowed and streamed down the colourless cheeks, and that it needed all her strength to check.

"You surprise me," the elder woman cried passionately, flinging away the hand that she had been holding. "You surprise me. I came to you for sympathy, sure that I should find it, believing that you cared for my son almost as much as I care for him. You were his chosen friend—he devoted half his days to you. The closeness of your friendship made malicious people say shameful things, and has given me many an unhappy hour; and now, at this crisis of his life, when he is bent upon burying himself alive in a monastery—entering some severe order, for whose rule of hardship and deprivation he is utterly unfit, a kind of life that will break his heart and bring him to an early grave—you preach to me of his finding peace in those dreary walls—peace—as if he were the worst of sinners."

"No, no, you don't understand me. Father Hammond has told me about the monastic life—the Benedictines, La Trappe. He has told me what happiness has been found in that life of solitude and prayer by those who have renounced the world."

"Was it you who inspired this extraordinary resolve?"

"I? No, indeed. I knew nothing of it till you told me."

"What? He could take such a step without consulting you, without confiding in you—his closest friend?"

"Was it likely that he would tell me, if he did not tell his mother?"

"He told me nothing till he had come here; to make a retreat in a monastery; to give himself time for meditation and thought, before he took any decisive step. He is here in Rome, and has been here for some time. My first knowledge of his decision was a letter he sent me from here. Such an unsatisfactory letter, giving no adequate reason for his resolve, only vague words about his weariness of life and the world."

"What else could he say? That must always be the reason. One gets tired of everything—and then one turns to God—and a life of prayer seems best. It is death in life; but it may mean peace."

"Vera, I was never more shocked and disappointed. I thought you loved him when love was sin. I thought you loved him at the peril of your soul; and now, when a terrible calamity has left you free to do what you like with the rest of your life, now, when however deeply you may mourn for your husband's awful death, and grieve over any sins of omission in your married life, yet there must needs be the far-off thought of years to come, when without self-reproach, you may give yourself to a lover who in years and temperament would be your natural companion—"

"There has been no such thought in my mind," Vera said coldly. "I shall never cease to mourn for Mario Provana's death. I have nothing else in the world to live for."

"My poor girl. It is only natural that you should feel like that. I did wrong to speak of the future. You have passed through a horrible ordeal, and it may be long before you can forget. But you are too kind not to be sorry for a mother who is threatened with the loss of all that she has of joy and comfort in this world."

"I am very sorry for you," Vera said, with a mechanical air, as if her thoughts were far away.

"Then you will help me?" Mrs. Rutherford cried eagerly.

"How can I help you?"

"You can appeal to my son. You may have more influence over him than I. I believe you have more influence," with a touch of bitterness. "However indifferent you may be, and may have always been to him, I know that he was devoted to you, that you could have led him, if you had cared to lead him. And he will listen to you now, he will have pity upon me, if you plead for me, if you tell him what it is for a mother to part with the son of nearly forty years' cherishing, who represents all her life on earth, past, present, and to come. I cannot live without him, Vera. I thought that I was strong in faith, and patience, and resignation, till this trouble came upon me. I thought that I was a religious woman; but now I know that the God I worshipped was of clay, and that when I prayed and tried to lift my thoughts to Heaven it was only of my son that I thought, only for his welfare that I prayed. Help me, Vera, if you have a heart that can love and sympathise with another's love. Plead with him, tell him how few the years are for a woman of my age; and that there will be time enough for him to bury himself alive in a monastery when I am at rest. His dedication of those later years will not be less precious in the sight of God, because he has deferred the sacrifice for his mother's sake."

"I cannot think that he will listen to me, if he has not yielded to you; I know he loves you dearly."

"He did love me—never was there a better son. But he changed all at once. It was as if something had broken his life. But I think you can melt his heart. He will understand my grief better when it is brought home to him by another. I am to see him to-morrow afternoon, and I shall be allowed to take you with me. Will you come?"

The entreaty was so insistent, so agonising, that Vera could only bend her head in mute acquiescence.

Mrs. Rutherford threw her arms round the frail figure and strained it to her breast.

"My dearest girl, I knew you would have pity upon me. I will call for you to-morrow at half-past two. The house is on the hill, beyond the Medici Villa—a lovely spot—but to me, though it is only a place of probation, it seems like a grave. Vera!" with a sudden passion, "if I thought that this step were for his happiness, I believe I could submit; but when I parted with him last week his face was the face of despair. How changed, oh, my God, how changed!"

CHAPTER XIX

Mrs. Rutherford and Vera drove to the hill behind the Medici Villa in the golden light of a Roman November, when the gardens on the height were glowing with foliage that seemed made of fire, and only cypress and ilex showed dark against that splendour of red and amber; but to those two women all that beauty of autumn colour, and purple distances, of fairy-like gardens, and flashing fountains, was part of a world that was dead. The metaphysician's idea of the universe as an emanation of the individual mind is so far borne out by experience, that in a great grief the universe ceases to exist.

The room to which one of the brotherhood led them faced the western sky and was full of golden light when the two women entered.

It was a room that had once been splendid; but of all its splendour nothing was left but vast space, and the blurred and faded outlines of a fresco upon the ceiling.

The two women stood within the doorway looking to the other end of the room, where a solitary figure was sitting, huddled in a large armchair, in front of a fireplace that looked like an open tomb, where a little heap of smouldering logs upon a spacious hearth seemed a hollow mockery of a fire meant for warmth. That crouching form with contracted shoulders, and wasted hands stretched above the feeble fire-glow—could that be Claude Rutherford?

Vera shivered in the chillness of the dismal scene, where even the vast window, and the golden west, could not relieve the sense of cold and gloom.

Yes, it was Claude! He started to his feet as Mrs. Rutherford moved slowly along the intervening space. He looked beyond her, surprised at the second figure, and then, with one brief word to his mother, hurried past her and came to Vera.

He clasped her hands, he drew her towards the window, drew her into the golden light, where she stood transfigured, like the Madonna in a picture by Fra Angelico, glorious and all gold.

He looked at her as a traveller who had been dying of thirst in a desert might look at a fountain of clear water.

It was a long, long look, in which it seemed as if he were drinking the beauty of the face he looked at, as if, in those moments, he tried to satisfy the yearning of days and nights of severance. It seemed as if he could never cease to look; as if he could never let her go. Then suddenly he dropped her hand, and turned from her to his mother, who was standing a little way off.

"Why have you done this?" he asked vehemently.

"Because you would not listen to me. No prayers, no tears of mine would move you. I was breaking my heart, and I thought she might prevail when I failed; I knew her influence over you, and that she might move you."

"It was a cruel thing to do. I knew she was in Rome, that we were breathing the same air. The thought of her was with me by day and night. Yet I was rock. I made myself iron, I clung to the cross, like the saints of old time, who had all been sinners. Vera, why have you come between me and my God?"

"I could not see your mother so unhappy and refuse to do what she asked. Oh, Claude, forget that I came here. Forget that we have ever clasped hands since—since you resolve to separate yourself from the world. I will not come between you and the saving of your soul."

"Vera," Mrs. Rutherford cried passionately, "have you no compassion for me? Is this how you help me?"

"You know that I refused, that I did not want to see him. I ought never to have come. But it is over. We shall never meet again, Claude. This is the last—the very last."

"Heartless girl. Have you no thought of my grief?" urged the mother.

"No, not when I think of him. If you can come between him and his hope of heaven—I cannot." She turned and walked quickly to the door without another word. Mrs. Rutherford cast one despairing look at her son, before she followed the vanishing figure, muttering, "Cruel, cruel, a heart of stone!"

No words were exchanged between the two women as they left the monastery, conducted by the monk, who had waited for them in the stony corridor at the top of the broad marble stairs. He let them out of the heavy iron-lined door, into the neglected garden, where a long row of cypresses showed dark against a saffron sky. The greater part of the garden had been utilised for growing vegetables, upon which the brotherhood for the most part subsisted. Huge orange-red pumpkins sprawled among beds of kale, and patches of Indian corn were golden amidst the rusty green of artichokes gone to seed.

It was a melancholy place, and the aspect of it sent an icy chill through Mrs. Rutherford's heart as she thought of that light, airy temperament which had been her son's most delightful gift, the gay insouciance, the joyous outlook that had made him everybody's favourite. He the jester, the trifler, for whom life was always play-time, he to be shut within those frozen walls, immured in a living grave! It was maddening even to think of it. She had talked to him of his religious duties. Oh, God, was it her old woman's preaching that had brought him to this living death?

Vera bade her good-bye at the gate, saying that she would rather walk than drive, and left Mrs. Rutherford to return to her hotel alone.

"I wonder which of us two is the more unhappy?" she thought. "Why do I wonder? What is her misery measured against mine?"

For Claude a night of fever followed that impassioned meeting, a night of sleeplessness and semi-delirium. For the first time since he had been a visitor in that house of gloom he got up at two o'clock and went to the chapel, where the monks met for prayer and meditation at that hour. As a probationer making his retreat he was not subject to the severe rules of the order, and he need not leave his bed till four o'clock unless he chose. This night he went to the dimly-lighted chapel, and knelt on the chill stone, for respite from agonising thoughts, from the insidious whispers of the tempter. This night he went into the House of God to escape from the dominion of Satan.

Hitherto he had borne his time of probation with a stoical submission. He had sought no relaxation of the rule for penitents on the threshold. He had lain upon the narrow bed and shivered in the chilly room, and risen in the winter dark, to lie down again sleepless, at an hour when a little while ago his night of pleasure would have been still at full tide. He had submitted to the repellent fare, the vegetables cooked in half rancid oil, coarse bread and gritty coffee. He, who had been always a creature of delicate habits, accustomed to the uttermost refinement in every detail of daily life—his food, his toilet, his surroundings.

He had shrunk from no burden that was laid upon him, earnestly intent upon keeping his promise to Father Hammond. He was to spend six weeks in this place of silence and prayer, and at the end of that time he was to make his confession to the Superior, and to make his communion. Then would follow the slow stages of preparation for the final act, which would admit him to the brotherhood, and shut the door of the world upon all the rest of his life. He had learnt to think of that awful change with a stoic's resignation. He had brought himself to a Roman temper. He thought with indifference of the world which he was to renounce. He had done with it. This had been the state of his mind as he shivered over the smouldering olive logs. This iron calm, and his stony contempt for life, had been his till that moment of ecstasy when the woman he loved stood before him, a vision of ethereal beauty in the light of the setting sun.

Why had she come there? Why? The penitential days and nights, the stoic's iron resolve, all were gone in one breath from those sweet lips, faint and pale, but ineffably beautiful.

CHAPTER XX

It was a little less than three weeks after the meeting in the house of silence; but to Vera the interval seemed an endless procession of slow, grey days and fevered nights—nights of intolerable length, in which she listened to the beating of the blood against her skull, now slow and rhythmical, now tempestuous and irregular—endless nights in which sleep seemed the most unlikely thing that could happen, a miracle for which she had left off hoping. In all that time she had heard no more of Mrs. Rutherford, though the daily chronicle that kept note of every stranger in Rome still printed her name among the inmates of the Hotel Marguerita.

She was angry and unforgiving. Unhappy mother! Unhappy son!

Two pairs of horses had to be exercised daily, but Vera had no orders for the stables. That monotonous parade in the Pincio, which every other woman of means in Rome made a part of her daily life, had no attraction for Signor Provana's widow. The villa gardens, funereal in their winter foliage of ilex and arbutus, sufficed for relief from the long hours within four walls. Wrapped in her sable coat, with the wind blowing upon her uncovered head, she paced the long terraces for hours on end, or sat like a statue on the marble bench that had been dug out of the ruins of imperial baths. But though she spent half her days in the gardens she took no interest in them. She never stopped to watch the gardeners at work upon the flower-beds, never questioned them about their preparations for the spring. Thousands of bulbs were being planted daily, but she never wanted to learn what resurrection of vivid colour would come from those brown balls which the men were dropping into the earth. She walked about like a corpse alive! The men almost shrank from her as she passed them, as if they had seen a ghost.

She could never forget that last meeting with her lover. The last—the very last. She sat with her arms folded on the marble balustrade, and her head resting on the folded arms, with her face hidden from the clear, cold light of a December afternoon.

Her gaze was turned inward; and it was only with that inward gaze that she saw things distinctly. The outside world was blurred and dim, but the pictures memory made were vivid.

She saw Claude's agonised look, saw the melancholy eyes gazing at her: the yearning love, the despairing renunciation.

Mrs. Rutherford had called her cruel, but was not the cruelty far greater that submitted her to that heart-rending ordeal?

To sit brooding thus, with her arms upon the cold marble, had been so much a habit with her of late, that in these melancholy reveries she had often lost count of time, till the sound of some convent bell startled her as it told the lateness of the hour, or till the creeping cold of sundown awoke her with a shiver. In that city of the Church there were many bells—all with their particular call to prayer, and she could have told the progress of the day and night without the help of a clock. Now it was the bell of the Trinità del Monte, for the office of Benediction, distant and silvery sweet in the clear air. It was a warning to go back to the house—yet she did not stir. Solitude here, with the cold wind blowing upon her, and the twitter of birds among the branches, was better than the atmosphere of those silent rooms.

She raised her head at the sound of a footstep, not the leisurely tread of one of the gardeners, heavy and slow. This step was light and rapid, so rapid that before she had time to wonder, it had stopped close beside her, and two strong arms were holding her, and quick, sobbing breath was fluttering her hair.

"Don't be frightened! Vera, my angel, my beloved!"

She tried to release herself, tried to stand upright, but the passionate arms held her to the passionate heart.

"Claude, are you mad?"

"No. Madness is over. Sanity has come back. I am yours again, my beloved, yours as I was that night—before a great horror parted us. I am all your own—your lover—your husband, whatever you will. The miserable slave you saw in the monastery is dead. I am yours, and only yours. I have no separate existence. I want no other heaven! Heaven is here, in your arms. Nothing else matters."

"My God! Have you left the monastery!"

"For ever. I bore it till last night—but that was a night of hell. I told the Superior this morning that I was not of the stuff that makes a martyr or a monk. He was horrified. To him I seemed a son of the devil. Well, I will worship Satan sooner than lose you. I am your lover, Vera—nothing else in this sublunary world. 'We'll jump the life to come.'"

She clung to him in the ecstasy of reunion, and their lips met in a kiss more tragic than Francesca's and Paolo's, for their guilt was yet to come; while with Vera and her lover guilt had been consummated.

Presently, with a sudden revulsion, she snatched herself from his arms, and stood looking at him reproachfully.

"Oh, my dearest, why did you not stand firm? Think how little this poor life of ours means compared with that which comes after."

"I leave the after-life to the illuminated—to Symeon and his following. I want nothing but the woman I love. Here or hereafter, for me there is nothing else. Vera, forget that I ever tried to forsake you—that I ever set my soul's ransom above my thoughts of you. It was a short madness, a cowardly endeavour. Forget it all, as I shall from this hour. Here are you and I—in this little world which is the only one we know—with just a few more years of youth and love. Let us make the most of them; and when the fire of life dies down, when these fierce heart-throbs are over, we will give our fading years to penitence and prayer."

This is what happens when a man of Claude Rutherford's temperament puts his hand to the plough.

CHAPTER XXI

Just two years after the sudden close of Mr. Rutherford's retreat there was a quiet wedding in Father Hammond's chapel—a bride without bridesmaids, a marriage without music, a bride in a pale grey gown and a black hat, with just a sprinkling of the Disbrowe clan to keep her in countenance. Three stately aunts, Lady Okehampton being by far the most human of the three, and their three noble husbands, with Lady Susan Amphlett, vivacious as ever, and immensely pleased with her friend.

From a conversational point of view she had been living upon this marriage all through the little season of November fog and small dinner-parties at restaurants or at home. She knew so much more than anybody else, and what she knew was what everybody wanted to know. She discussed the subject at Ritz's, at Claridge's, at the Savoy, at the Carlton, and seemed to have something fresh to say at each place of entertainment. There was more variety in her information than even in the hors d'oeuvres, which rise in a crescendo of novelty in unison with the newness of the hotel.

People wondered they had not married sooner, since, of course, everybody knew it must end in marriage.

Susie shrugged her pretty shoulders, and flashed her diamond necklace at the company.

"The sweet thing is exaltée. She is one of Francis Symeon's flock; and she thought respect for her husband obliged her to wait two years. She only left off her mourning last week."

"But considering that she was carrying on with Rutherford years before Provana's death?"

"You none of you understand her. Their friendship was purely platonic. She and I were like sisters, and I was in and out of her house just as Claude was. There never was a more innocent attachment. I used to call them Paul and Virginia."

"I should think Paolo and Francesca would be more like it," murmured one of the company.

Susie shook her fan at him.

"You men will never believe in a virtuous friendship. However, there they are—absolutely devoted to each other. They will be the happiest couple in London, and they mean to entertain a great deal."

"Then I hope they are on the look-out for a pearl among chefs. People won't go to Portland Place to eat second-rate dinners."

"Provana's dinners were admirable, and his wines the finest in London."

Then there came the question of settlements. How much of her millions had Mrs. Provana settled upon Rutherford?

"I don't think there has been any settlement."

"The more fool he," muttered a matter-of-fact guardsman. "What's the use of marrying a rich woman if you don't get some of the stuff?"

"Don't I tell you they are like Paul and Virginia?" said Susie.

The Provana murder had died out long before this as a source of interest and wonder. It had flourished and faded like a successful novel, or a play that takes the town by storm one year and is forgotten the year after. The Provana mystery had gone to the dust-heap of old things. Slowly and gradually people had resigned themselves to the knowledge that this murder must take its place among the long list of crimes that are never to be punished by the law.

Romantic people clung to their private solutions of the tragical enigma. These were as sure of the identity of the murderer as if they had seen him red-handed. The quiet marriage in the Roman Catholic chapel revived the interest in the half-forgotten crime, and Lady Susan had the additional kudos of a close association with the event.

"Vera and I were together at Lady Fulham's ball within two or three hours of that poor fellow's death," she told her friends at a Savoy supper-table. "I never saw her look so lovely, in one of her mermaid frocks, and a necklace and girdle of single diamonds that flashed like water-drops. Other people's jewels looked vulgar compared with hers. She was in wonderful spirits, stayed late, and danced all the after supper waltzes. She was fey."

"Rutherford was there, of course?" said someone.

"Of course," echoed Susan; "why shouldn't he be there? Everybody was there."

"But everybody couldn't waltz or sit out with Madame Provana all the evening, as I heard he did," remarked a middle-aged matron, fixing Susan with her long-handled eyeglass.

"Why shouldn't they waltz? They are cousins, and have always been pals, and they waltz divinely. To watch them is to understand what Shakespeare meant by the poetry of motion. Everything Vera does is a poem. Every frock she wears shows that she is a poet's daughter. And now they are married, and are going to be utterly happy," concluded Susie with conviction.

The world in general does not relish that idea of idyllic happiness—especially in the case of multi-millionaires. It is consoling—when one is not a millionaire—to think of some small counterbalance to that overweening good luck, some little rift within the lute.

A cynic, as cold and sour as the aspic he was eating, shrugged his shoulders.

"If I had a daughter I was fond of, I don't think I would trust the chances of her happiness to Claude Rutherford," he said quietly.

"Claude is quite adorable," said a fourteen-stone widow, whose opulent shoulders and triple necklaces had been the central point of the public gaze at the theatre that evening.

"Much too adorable to make one woman happy. A man of that kind has to spread himself. It must be diffused light, not the concentrated glow of the domestic hearth," said the cynic, smiling at the bubbles in his glass.

Everybody found something to say about Vera and her husband. Certainly their behaviour since Provana's death had been exemplary. They had never been seen about together, at home or abroad. The house in Portland Place had been closed, and the widow had lived in Italy, a recluse, seeing no one. Half the time had been spent by Claude Rutherford in Africa, hunting big game with a famous sportsman. The other half in well-known studios in Antwerp and Paris. He had thrown off his lazy, dilettante habits, and had gone in for art with a curious renewal of energy. The man was altered somehow. His old acquaintance discovered a change in him: a change for the better, most likely, though they did not all think so.

And now he had attained the summit of mortal bliss, as possible to a man of nine-and-thirty, who had wasted the morning of life. He had won a lovely woman whom he was supposed to adore, and whose wealth ought to be inexhaustible.

"However hard he tries, I don't see how he can run through such a fortune as that," his friends said.

"That kind of quiet, unpretentious man has often a marvellous faculty for getting rid of money," said another; "it oozes out of his pockets without the labour of spending. Rutherford is sure to gamble. A man of that temperament is too idle to find excitement for himself. He wants it ready-made—at the baccarat table, or on the turf."

"Well, it will last him a few years, at the worst, and then he can go into the Charter-house."

The idea of Claude Rutherford going to bed at ten o'clock in the Charter-house made everybody laugh.

The long interval of mourning and probation, of melancholy solitude on Vera's part, and of forced occupation on Claude's, was over: and they two, who in thought and feeling had been long one, were now united in that closer bond which only death or sin can sever. In the intensity of that union it seemed to them as if they had never lived asunder, as if all of their existence that had gone before were no more than a long, dull dream, the grey monotony of life that was less than life, hard and mechanical even in its so-called pleasures.

"I never lived till now," she told him, when she was folded to his heart, in their sumptuous alcove in the great room in Venice, in an hotel that had been a palace, an alcove surrounded with a balustrade, a bed that had been made for a king. "I never lived till now—for now I know that nothing can part us. We belong to each other till death."

"If it were now to die 'twere now to be most happy," he murmured in a low, impassioned voice that soothed her like music.

"And the past is dead," she whispered.

"The past is dead."

The voice that echoed her words had changed.

The winter moonlight sent a flood of cold light across the shining floor, and the glow of burning logs on the hearth glimmered redly under the sculptured arch of the Byzantine fireplace. It was a wonderful room in a wonderful city. Vera had never been in Venice till this night, when she stepped from the station quay into the black boat that was to bring them to the hotel, man and maid and luggage following in a second gondola. To most travellers so arriving, Venice must needs seem a dream city; but to Vera all life had been a dream since she had stood before the altar and heard Father Hammond's grave voice pronounce the words that made her Claude's wife.

She had chosen Venice for their honeymoon, because it was the one famous city in her beloved Italy in which she had never been with Provana.

"It will be all new and strange," she told Claude, and then came the unspoken thought. "He will not be there."

He had been with her in Rome, almost an inseparable companion, until she had grown accustomed to the thought that he must be with her always, wherever she went, an inseparable shadow; but with her marriage the bond that held her to the past was broken, the shadow was lifted. She was young again; young and thoughtless, living in the exquisite hour, almost as happy as she had been when she was an impulsive, light-hearted child of eleven, leaping on to her cousin's knee, and nestling with her arms round his neck, while they watched the waves racing towards the rock where they were sitting, she rather hoping that the waters would rise round them and swallow them. That blue brightness could hardly mean death. They would only become part of the sea—merman and mermaid, children of the ocean. How much better than to return to the dull lodgings, and Lidcott's harsh dominion!

That solitude of two in the loveliest city in Europe seemed altogether of the stuff that dreams are made of. They kept no count of the days and hours. They made no plan for to-morrow. They wandered along the calle, and in and out of the churches, in a desultory and casual way, looking at pictures and statues without any precise knowledge of what they were seeing—only a dreamy delight in things that were beautiful themselves, and which awakened ideas of beauty. They spent idle days in their gondola going from island to island, musing among the historic arches of Torcello, or sauntering along the sands of the Lido. The winter was mild even in England, and here soft air and sunshine suggested April rather than December. It was a delicious world, and in the seclusion of a gondola, or in the half-light of a church, they seemed to have this lovely world all to themselves. There were very few strangers in Venice at this season, and the residents had something more to do than to wander about the narrow calle, or loiter and look at things in the churches, or the Doge's Palace. These two were learning Venice by heart in those leisurely saunterings, a little listless sometimes, as of people whose lives had come to a dead stop.

They never talked of the past, or only of that remote past when Vera was a child, the time of childish happiness by the blue waves and dark cliffs of North Devon. They talked very little of the future. Their talk was of themselves, and of their love. They read Byron and Shelley and Browning, and De Musset. They drank deep of the poetry that Venice had inspired, until every stone in the City of Dreams seemed enchanted, and every noble old mansion, given over perhaps now to commerce, glass-blowers, and dealers in bric-à-brac, seemed a fairy palace.

They drained the cup of life and love. Claude forgot that he had ever thought of the woollen gown and the hempen girdle; Vera forgot that she had ever seen him, haggard and hollow-eyed, crouching over the smouldering olive logs in the monastery on the Roman hill.

Early on their wedding journey, leaning against the side of the boat, hand locked in hand, they had sworn to each other that all the past should be forgotten. Come what, come might, in unknown Fate, they would never remember.

And now they were going back to London in the gay spring season, and Lady Susan Amphlett had another innings. It was delicious to be moving about in a world where everybody wanted to know things that only she could tell them.

"And are they really going to live in the house in Portland Place?"

"Really, really. Where could they get such rooms, such air and space? And that old Italian furniture is priceless. There is nothing better in the Doria Palace. It took the Provana family more than a century to collect it—even with their wealth."

"Well, when I saw the painters at work outside I thought the house must have been sold. This world seems full of strange people. How Vera can reconcile herself to life in that house passes my comprehension. I could understand her keeping the furniture; but to live inside those four walls. I should fancy they were closing in upon me, like a mediæval torture chamber."

"Vera is all poetry and imagination, but she is not morbid."

"Vera knows that we are in the midst of the unseen, and that our dead are always near us," said a thrilling voice, and Lady Fanny Ransom's dark eyes flashed across the table. "The house can make no difference to her. If she loved her first husband she has not lost him."

"Nice for her, but not so pleasant for her second," murmured a matter-of-fact K.C.

"She was utterly devoted to poor Provana," protested Susie, "but it was the reverent looking-up kind of love that an innocent girl feels for a man old enough to be her father. She has told me the story of their courtship—so sweet—like Paul and Virginia."

"A middle-aged Paul! I thought Rutherford was the hero of the Paul and Virginia chapter of her history."

"Oh, well, they were little lovers as children, and Vera and Claude are the most ideal couple that ever the world has seen. They are going to entertain in a sumptuous style. Their house will be the most popular in London."

"In spite of its being the scene of an unsolved mystery and undiscovered crime. That's the worst of it," said sour middle-age in a garnet necklace. "For my part, I could never sleep a wink in that awful house."

"Ah, but you'll be able to eat and drink in it," remarked Mr. Hortentius, K.C., dryly. "We shall all dine there, if the dinners are as good as they were in poor Provana's time."

Poor Provana! That was his epitaph in the world. On the marble tomb at San Marco, to which the dead man had been carried—in remembrance of a desire expressed in those distant days when he and Vera wandered in the olive woods—there was nothing but his name, and one word: "Re-united."

Vera had been too ill and too much under the dominion of Lady Okehampton to make the dismal journey with her dead; but she had gone from Rome to San Marco, and had spent a melancholy hour in the secluded corner where the cypress cast its long shadow on Guilia's tomb.

She had stood by the tomb in a kind of stupor, hardly conscious of the present, lost in a long dream of the past, living again through those bright April days, with father and daughter, and hearing again the ineffable tenderness in Mario Provana's voice, as he talked to his dying child. What an abyss of time since those sad, sweet days! And now there was nothing left but a name—

MARIO PROVANA

—here, and in certain hospitals in London and Rome, where there were wards or beds established in memory of Mario Provana.

CHAPTER XXII

Mrs. Rutherford was the fashion in that first year of her second marriage, just as she had been in her London début as Madame Provana. It seemed as if one of the fairies at her christening had given her that inexpressible charm which captivates the crowd, that elusive, indescribable attractiveness which for want of a better name people have agreed to call magnetism. Vera Rutherford was a magnetic woman. Mr. Symeon went about telling people that she had psychic attributes which removed her worlds away from the normal woman, and Miranda, the only, the inimitable dressmaker, told her patronesses that it was a delight to work for Mrs. Rutherford, not because she was rich enough to pay for the wildest flights in millinery, but because her pale, ethereal beauty lent itself to all that was daring and original in the dress-designer's art. "People preach to me about Mrs. Montressor's lovely colouring, and what a joy it must be to invent frocks for her; but those pink and white beauties are difficult," said the dressmaker. "They require much study. A nuance, just the faintest nuance on the wrong side, and your pink and white woman looks vulgar. A wrong shade of blue and the peach complexion becomes purple, but with Mrs. Rutherford's alabaster skin every scheme of colour is possible."

Mrs. Rutherford was a social success, just as Madame Provana had been. Her entertainments were as frequent and as sumptuous as in the old days, when Mario Provana stalked like a stranger through crowded rooms where hardly one face in twenty afforded him a moment's interest. The entertainments were as sumptuous, but they were more original. The tone was lighter, and gilded youth from the Embassies found the house more amusing.

"Vera is ten years younger since her second marriage," Lady Susie told people; "Claude aids and abets her in everything frivolous. She used to be just a little too dreamy—Oh, you may call it 'side,' but that it never was. But she is certainly more sociable now; more eagerly interested in the things that interest other people. Claude has made her forget that she is a poet's daughter. She is as keen as mustard about their house and racing stables at Newmarket. She goes to all the big cricket matches with him, things she never thought of in Provana's time. They are not like commonplace husband and wife, but like boy and girl lovers, pleased with everything. I don't wonder Mr. Symeon thinks she has degenerated. He says she is losing her other-world look, and is fast becoming a mere mortal."

"And as a mere mortal I hope she won't allow Rutherford to spend all her money," said Susie's confidant, an iron-grey bachelor of fifty, who spent the greater part of his life sitting in pretty women's pockets. "A racing stud is a pretty deep pit for gold at the best; but a man who has married a triple millionaire's widow may safely allow himself one hobby. Rutherford goes in for too many things: his dirigible balloons and his aeroplane, his racing cars and his motor launches: his Ostend holiday, where people say he is hardly ever out of the gambling rooms. Your friend had better keep an eye on her pass-book."

"Vera!" cried Susie, with uplifted eyebrows. "Vera look at a pass-book!"

"As a banker's widow she might be supposed to know that there are such financial thermometers. She must have learnt something of business from Provana."

"She never took the slightest interest in his business, and he was far too noble to degrade her by talking of money."

"A pity," said the bachelor; "when a woman's husband is a great financier he may want to talk about money; and his wife ought to be interested in things that are of vital concern for him."

"That's a counsel of perfection," said Susie, "and very few women rise to it. All I have ever known about my husband is that he is interested in railways and insurance companies and things, and that when any of them are going wrong I'd better not talk of my dressmaker's bills, or let him see my pass-book."

"Then you know what a pass-book is."

"I have to," sighed Susie, "for my normal state is an overdrawn account. I think the letters n.e. and n.s. are quite the horridest in the alphabet."

"Yet you never ask a friend to help you out of a fix?"

"Not much; when it comes to that I shall make a mistake in measuring my dose of chloral, and it will be 'poor Susan Amphlett, death by misadventure'!"

Susan, who had never had adventures or "affairs" of her own, was a kind of modern representative of the chorus in a Greek play, and was always explaining people, more especially her bosom friends, of whom Vera was the dearest. She was really fond of Vera, and there was no arrière pensée of envy and malice in her explanations. Her intense interest in other people may perhaps be attributed to the fact that she hardly ever opened a book—not even the novel of the season—and that her knowledge of public events was derived solely from the talk at luncheon tables.

Certainly it might be admitted, even by the malicious, that Claude and Vera were an ideal couple. They outraged all modern custom in spending the greater part of their lives in close companionship; he originating all their amusements, and she keenly interested in everything he originated.

They were happy, and they were continually telling each other how happy. They always went back to the childish days at Disbrowe.

"I feel as if all that ever happened after that was blotted out," Vera whispered, one sunlit afternoon, as they sat side by side among silken cushions on the motor launch, while all the glory of the upper Thames moved past them; "all between those summer days and these seems vague and dim: even the long years with poor Grannie. The wailing about want of money, the moaning over the things we had to do without, the people she hated because they were rich; all those years and the years that came after have gone down into the gulf of forgotten things. A dark curtain, like a pall, has fallen upon the past; and we are living in the present. We love each other, and we are together. That is enough, Claude, is it not? That is enough."

"That is enough," he echoed, smiling up at her from his lower level among the pillows. That heap of down pillows and his lounging attitude among them seemed to epitomise the man and his life. "All the same, I want Sinbad the Second to win the Leger."

"Ah, you always laugh at me," she cried, with a vexed air. "You can never be serious."

"No, I can't," he answered, with a darkening brow, and a voice that was as heavy as lead.

They were living upon the rapture of a consummated love: which is something like a rich man living upon his capital. There comes a time when he begins to ask himself how long it will last.

They had loved each other for years; first unconsciously, with a divine innocence, at least on the woman's part, then consciously, and with a vague sense of sin; and then, all obstacles being removed, triumphantly; assured of the long future, in which nothing could part them.

She repeated this often—in impassioned moments. "Nothing can part us. Whatever Fate may bring we shall be together. There can be no more parting."

He was not given to serious thoughts. He never had been. His one irresistible charm had been his careless enjoyment of the present hour, and indifference to all that might come after. He had never considered the ultimate result of any action in his life. He left the Army with no more thought than he left off a soiled glove! He threw up a painter's art, and all its chances of delight and fame, the moment he found discouragement and difficulty. He hated difficult things; he hated hard work; he hated giving up anything he liked. His haunting idea of evil was the dread of being bored.

Once Vera found herself making an involuntary comparison between the dead man and the living.

If Claude had had a dying daughter whom he loved, could he have watched her sink into her grave, and kept the secret of his sorrow, and smiled at her while his heart was breaking? She knew he could not. He was a creature of light and variable moods, of sunshine and fine weather. She had loved him for his lightness. He had brought her relief from ennui whenever he crossed her threshold; he had brought her gladness and gay thoughts, as a man brings a bunch of June roses to his sweetheart. And now that the past was done with, and that she was his for ever, they were to be always glad and gay. There was to be no gloom in their atmosphere, no long, dull pause in life to give time for dark thoughts.

"Everybody has something to be sorry for," Vera told Susan Amphlett; "that's why people's existence is a perpetual rush. Niagara can have no time to think—but imagine, if nature were alive, what long aching thoughts there might be under the bosom of a great, smooth lake."

"You know, my darling Vera, I generally think everything you do is perfect," Susan answered, more sensibly than her wont, "but, I sometimes fear that you and Claude are burning the candle at both ends. You are too much alive. You seem to be running a race with time. Neither your health nor your beauty can last at the pace you are going."

"I'll take my chance of that. There is one thing that I dread more than being ill and growing ugly."

"What is that?"

"Living to be old."

"What, you've caught my fear?"

"I dread the long, slow years—the long, slow days and sleepless nights—old people sleep very little—in which there is nothing but thought, an endless-web of miserable thoughts, going slowly round and round, never stopping, never changing. That's what I am afraid of, Susie."

"Strange for you to be afraid of anything," her friend said thoughtfully. "I think you are the most courageous woman I ever heard of—as brave as Joan of Arc, or Charlotte Corday."

"Why?"

"Because you are not afraid to live in this house."

"Why not? What does the house matter?"

"It must make you think sometimes," faltered Susan.

"I won't think! But if I were to think of the past, the house would make no difference. My thoughts would be the same in Mexico—or at the North Pole. I have heard of people who go to the end of the earth to forget things, but I should never do that. I should know that memory would go with me."

For three seasons in London, for three winters in Rome, the pace went on, and was accelerated rather than slackened with the passing of the years. Claude Rutherford won the Blue Ribbon of the turf, with Sinbad the Second, and was equally fortunate with his boat at Cowes. If he did not cross the Channel or fly from London to Liverpool, he did at least make sundry costly excursions in the air, which kept his name in the daily papers, and made his wife miserable, till, aviation having resulted in boredom, he promised to content himself with the substantial earth. After those three years this boy and girl couple began to discover that they had done everything brilliant and exciting that there was to be done; and the fever called living began to pall.

And now Susan Amphlett told people that Vera was killing herself, and that her husband, though as passionately in love with her as ever he had been, was selfish and thoughtless, and was spending her money, and ruining her health, with the extravagances and agitations of a racing stable that was on a scale he ought never to have allowed himself.

"After all, it is her money," said Susan, "and it's bad form on his part to be so reckless."

"But as she has only a life interest in Provana's millions, and as her trustees are some of the sharpest business men in London, Rutherford can't do her much harm," said masculine common-sense, while feminine malice was lifting its shoulders and eyebrows with doleful prognostics.

"Well, I suppose the money is all right," said Chorus, still inclined to be tragic; "it's her health I'm afraid of. She's losing her high spirits, her joy in everything, and she is getting out of touch with her husband. She could hardly give him a smile when Blue Rose won the Oaks. She sat in a corner of her box, looking the other way, while that lovely animal was coming down the hill neck and neck with the favourite, at a moment when any other woman would have been simply frantic."

"She is not of the stuff that racing men's wives are made of," said Eustace Lyon, the poet. "No doubt she was worlds away—in dreamland—and did not even know whose mare the bookies and the mob were cheering."

"She was not like that two years ago," said Chorus. "She and Claude were in such perfect sympathy that it was impossible for either of them to have a joy that the other did not share. It was a case of two souls with but a single thought."

"I can quite believe that, for I never gave C. R. credit for thinking," replied the poet.

Satiety had come. It came in a day. The fatal day that comes to all the favoured and the fortunate, and which never comes to the poor and the unlucky. That evil at least is spared to Nature's stepchildren. They never have too much of anything, except debt and difficulty. They never yawn in each other's faces, and ask themselves where they can go for the summer. They never turn over the leaves of a Continental Bradshaw and complain that they are tired of everywhere.

It is the people who can go everywhere and have everything who find the wide earth a garden run to seed, and feel the dust of the desert in their mouths as they talk of the pleasure places that the herd long for. This time had come for Vera, at the end of her third season as Claude Rutherford's wife. He, the gay and the insouciant, was careless still, but it was a new kind of carelessness: the carelessness that comes from hating everything that an exhausted life can give.

They had fallen into the fashion of their friends of late, and were more like the normal semi-detached couple than the boy and girl lovers upon whose bliss Lady Susan had loved to expatiate.

When the Goodwood week came round in this third year with the inexorable regularity that one finds in the events of the season, Vera declared that she had had enough of Goodwood and would never go there again.

"Of course, that won't prevent your being there," she said.

"Well, not exactly, when I have Iseult of Ireland in two races."

"Yes, of course, you must be there. I forgot."

"You seem always to forget my horses nowadays. Yet you were once so keen about them."

"They were very interesting at first, poor, sweet things, but the fonder I was of them, the more cruel it seemed to race them."

"You'd like them kept to look at, eh?"

"I should like to sit with them in their boxes, and feed them with sugar, and make them lie down with their heads in my lap."

"A Lady Rarey!"

"I sometimes long for a paradise of animals, some lovely pastoral valley with a silver stream winding through the deep grass, where I might live among beautiful innocent creatures—sheep, and deer, and Jersey cows, and great calm, cream-coloured oxen from the Campagna. Creatures that can lie in the sun and bask, knowing nothing of the past, feeling nothing but the warmth and beauty of the world; and where I myself should have lost the faculty of thought."

"That's a queer fancy."

"I have many queer fancies. They come to me in my dreams."

"You'd much better come to Goodwood. All the world will be there, and you'd like to see Iseult win. Haven't you enough frocks? Is that the reason for not coming?"

"I have too many frocks, some that I have never worn."

"Hansel them at Lady Waterbury's. You'll be the prettiest woman there."

"It's dear of you to say that"—her eyes clouded as she spoke—"but I can't go. I'm so tired of it all, Claude, so tired!"

"Do you suppose I am never tired of things? Sick, sick to death! but I know that to be happy one must keep moving. That's a law of human life. You'd better come, Vera. You'll be moped to extinction alone."

"I don't mind loneliness, and I shall have Susan part of the time, and there will be a meeting in the Albany."

"De gustibus? Well, if you prefer Symeon and his spooks to a racecourse in an old English park, there's nothing more to be said." He stooped to kiss the pale forehead before he sauntered out of the room, yawning as he went. He had always a tired air; but it had verily become a law of his being to keep moving.

"Nemesis is like the policeman on night duty," he used to say. "She won't let us lie in the dust and sleep. We must trudge on."

Trudging from one costly pleasure to another might not suggest hardship to the loafer on the Embankment, but to a self-indulgent worldling who has drained the cup of life to the dregs, that necessity of going on drinking when there are only dregs to drink may seem hard to bear.

CHAPTER XXIII

Vera told her husband that she did not mind solitude; yet it was a face of ashen whiteness that he left behind when he shut the door of her dressing-room, after his hurried and cheerful good-bye on the first day of the Goodwood meeting.

He was driving his sixty horse-power Daimler to Goodwood, steering for himself, while the chauffeur sat behind ready for road repairs, or to give a hand in carrying a corpse to the nearest hospital.

The speed limit was naturally disregarded, as the thing that Claude wanted was excitement, the hazards of the road as they sped past hamlet and farm, followed by the long, white dust-cloud that flashed across the landscape like the fiery tail of a comet, while startled villagers gaped, and wondered if a car had passed. Peril was the zest that made the journey worth doing: to feel that his hand upon the wheel held life at his disposal, and that any awkward turn in the road might bring him sudden death.

He was gone, and Vera was alone in the gloomy London house—so much more gloomy than the vast halls and galleries of the Roman villa, where colossal windows let in vast spaces of blue sky. Here the heavily-draped sashes admitted only a slit of sunshine, tempered by London smoke.

She was alone, but she told herself that solitude did not matter. It was not solitude that weighed upon her spirits as she roamed from room to room in the emptiness and silence. It was the sense of not being alone that weighed upon her. It was the consciousness of a silent presence—the invisible third who had come between her and her husband of late—who had come back into her life. In the noontide of her love, while passion reigned supreme, and the man she loved filled her world, the shadow had been lifted from her path. She had seen all old things dimly—dazzled by the glory of her life's sun. She had remembered nothing, except her childish bliss with the boy who was to be her fate. Her life began and ended in her husband; as it had begun and ended in Claude Rutherford when he was only her friend and companion, the light-hearted companion, whose presence meant happiness.

In the first two years of her second marriage she had been completely absorbed in that transcendent love, and in the ceaseless round of pleasures and excitements that her husband contrived for her, filling her days and nights with emotional moments, with little social triumphs and trivial ambitions.

Satiety came in an hour—or it may be that it came so slowly and so gradually that there was an hour when Vera awoke to the consciousness that she was tired of everything, that the earth with all its changing loveliness, its surprises of mountain and lake, wood and river, was but a sterile promontory, and the blue vault above Como only a pestilent congregation of vapours. The suddenness of the revelation was startling; but the not uncommon malady that afflicted the Prince of Denmark had been eating her heart for a long time before she was aware of its hold upon her. And with the coming of satiety, the distaste for amusement, the distrust of love, came the shadow. Memory that had been lulled asleep by the magic philtre of passion, awakened and was alive again. She roamed the great, silent house, haunting with a morbid preference those rooms that were particularly associated with the dead man, that range of spacious rooms on the ground floor where nothing had been altered since Mario Provana lived in them: his library, and the severe, official-looking sitting-room adjoining, where he was often closeted with his partners and allies, his head clerks and managers, his business visitors from Vienna, Rome, Berlin, Madrid, New York.

When the drawing-rooms had been transformed by a gayer style of decoration, more in harmony with Vera's frivolous entertainments, Claude had been urgent that these ground-floor rooms should be refurnished, and every trace of their severe, business-like aspect done away with and even certain priceless old masters that Provana had been proud of despatched with ruthless haste to Christie's sale room; but to his astonishment Vera had told him that nothing was to be changed in the rooms her husband had occupied—that all things touched or valued by him were to be sacred.

For this reason, while approving Claude's plan of colour for the walls and draperies and carpets in the drawing-rooms, she had insisted upon retaining the Italian cabinets of ebony and ivory, and the Florentine mosaic tables, the things that had been collected all over Italy a century ago, in the beginning of the Provana riches.

And now, solitary and dejected, she moved restlessly from room to room. Sometimes standing before one of the bookcases in the library, looking along the titles of books that she had learnt to love, in those far-off days before she had been launched by the Disbrowes—a frail cockle-shell, spinning round and round in the Society whirlpool—while she and her husband were still unfashionable enough to sit together in the autumn twilight, or to spend tête-à-tête evenings in this solemn-looking room. His mind was with her there to-day, in the July sunshine, as it had been in those evenings of the past, while he was a living man. His remembered speech was in her ears to-day, grave and earnest, telling her the things she loved to hear, widening her view of life, opening the gate to new knowledge, the knowledge of authors she had never heard of, the story of heroes and statesmen, philosophers and poets, whose names had been only names till he made them living people, people to be admired and loved. He had taught her to comprehend and love Dante to appreciate the verse of Carducci, the prose of Manzoni. He had taught her to revere Cavour, to adore St. Francis of Assisi, to weep for Savonarola and Giordano Bruno. He had made Italy a land of genius and valour, a land alive from the Alps to the Adriatic with heroic memories. He had made her know and love the history of his country, almost as he himself loved it.

And now his spirit filled the room in which the man had lived. His shadow had come into the house that had been his, and had taken possession of the place and of the atmosphere. Whatever might still remain of the undisciplined love, the passion of unreasoning youth, that she had given to her second husband, she could never again release herself from that first marriage tie. It was the bond of death.

She went into the dining-room when luncheon was announced, carrying a volume of Browning, and made some pretence of eating, with the book open by the side of her plate, a proceeding upon which the butler expatiated somewhat severely that afternoon as he lingered over tea in the housekeeper's comfortable parlour.

"I don't know what's come over the Missus," he said, as he took an unwelcome "stranger" out of his second cup, and parenthetically, "This tea isn't what it was, Mrs. Manby. She don't eat enough for a tomtit, let alone a sparrow—and she's falling back into that dreamy way she was in when Provana was in America, and for a long time before that, as you may remember; that time when it was always not at home to Mr. Rutherford."

"She was trying to break with him," said Mrs. Manby. "I give her credit for that."

"So you may, but that kind of trying was never known to answer, when once they've begun to carry on," remarked Mr. Sedgewick; "I've watched too many such cases not to know the inevitability of them," he added, having picked up the modern jargon, more or less incorrectly.

The long day wore on to the melancholy twilight, and Vera was dreading the appearance of her maid to remind her that it was time to dress for her solitary dinner. She had talked lightly of having Lady Susan at her disposal, but she knew that her friend was at that very hour contributing to the vivacity of one of the smartest of the Goodwood house-parties, and would be so engaged till the end of the week. She had thought, in her weariness of the mill-round, that solitude would be better than the Society that had long become distasteful; but she found that, in the melancholy hour between dog and wolf, the shadows in a London house were full of fear, vague and shapeless fear, an oppression that had neither form nor name, and that was infinitely worse than any materialisation. She was standing by the window in her morning-room looking down into the grey emptiness of the wide carriage way, where no carriages were passing, and on pavements where unfashionable pedestrians were moving quickly through a drizzling rain, when a servant announced Father Hammond.

"Can you forgive me for calling at such an unorthodox time? I happened to be passing your door, and as I have called several times at the right hour and not found you, I thought I would try the wrong hour."

"No hour can be wrong that brings you," she said in a low voice, as she gave him her hand; and the words sounded more sincere than such speeches usually are.

"I am glad to hear you say as much, and I believe you. In the whirlpool of frivolity a few serious moments may have the charm of contrast."

"I have done with the whirlpool."

"Tired of it? After only three years? There are some of my flock who have been going round in the same witches' dance for a quarter of a century, and are still in the crowd on the Brocken. I can but think you have made the pace too fast since your second marriage, or perhaps it is your husband who has made the pace."

"You must not think that. We both like the same things. We are companions now as we were when I was a child at Disbrowe Park, and when we were so happy together."

Her eyes filled with tears. Oh, how far away that time of innocent gladness seemed, as she looked back! What an abyss yawned between then and now.

"I have distressed you," the priest said gently, taking her hand.

"No, no, but it is always painful to look back."

Father Hammond drew her towards the sofa by the open window, and seated himself at her side.

"Let us have a real friendly talk now I have been so lucky as to find you alone," he said. "I am glad—very glad—that you are tired of the whirlpool, for to be tired of a bad kind of life is the beginning of a better kind of life. You know what I think of modern Society, especially in its feminine aspect, and how I have grieved over the women who were made for better things than the witches' dance. We have talked of these things in your first husband's lifetime, but then I thought you were taking your frivolous pleasures with a careless indifference that showed your heart was not engaged in them, and that you had a mind for higher things. Even your dabbling with Mr. Symeon's quasi-supernatural philosophy was a sign of superiority. His disciples are not the basest or most empty-headed among worldlings, though they keep touch with the world. In those days you know I had hopes of you, but since you have been Claude Rutherford's wife, I have seen you given up to an insatiate love of pleasure, a headlong pursuit of every new thing, the more extravagant and the more dangerous the more hotly pursued by you and your husband; so that it has become a byword, 'If the thing is to cost a fortune, and to risk a life, the Rutherfords will be in it.'"

"Claude is impetuous, easily caught by novelty," she said deprecatingly, with lowered eyelids.

"He was not always so impetuous, rather a loiterer, indifferent to all strenuous pleasures, delighting in all that is best in literature, and worshipping all that is best in art, though too idle to achieve excellence even in the art he loved. But since his marriage—and forgive me if I say since his command of your wealth—he has changed and degenerated."

"You are not complimentary to his wife," Vera said, with a faint laugh.

"I am too much in earnest to be polite, but it is not your influence that has done harm, it is your money—that fatal gold which has changed the whole aspect of Society within the last thirty years, a change that will continue from bad to worse as long as diamond mines and gold mines are productive, and the inheritors of great names can smile at the vulgarity of millionaires who 'do them well' and will give the open hand of friendship to a host who to-morrow may be branded as a thief What does it matter, if the thief has bought Lord Somebody's estate, and shooting that is among the best in England?"

"Well, it is all done with now, as far as I am concerned," Vera said wearily. "I used to go everywhere Claude liked to go. People laughed at us for being inseparable; but I am sick to death of it all, and now he must go to the fine houses alone. No doubt he will be all the more welcome."

"Perhaps; but I did not come to talk of trivialities or to echo hackneyed diatribes against a state of things so corrupt and evil that its vices have become the staple of every preacher's discourses, cleric or layman. I want to talk about you and your husband, not about the world you live in. Since you have done with the whirlpool, there is nothing to keep you from better influences. Will you let mine be the hand to lead you along the passive way of light and love, the way that leads to pardon and peace?"

Vera turned from him, trying to hide her agitation, but the feelings he had awakened were too strong, and she let her head fall upon the arm of the sofa, and gave herself up to a passion of tears.

"Pardon?" she gasped, amidst her sobs; "you know I need pardon?"

"We all need pity and pardon. No man's life is spotless, and the life you and Claude have been living is a life of sin—aimless, sensual, godless. I have had a wide experience of men, I have known the best and the worst, and have seen the strange transmutations that may take place in a man, under certain influences—how the sinner may become a saint, and the saint fall into an abyss of sin—but I have never seen changes so sudden and so inexplicable as those I have seen in your husband, whom I have known, and I think I may say I have loved, from the time when he began to have a will and a mind."

"I hope you do not blame me for his having left the monastery and come back to the world."

"How can I blame you when his mother was the active agent? She is a good woman, though a weak one, where her affections are engaged. She was perfectly frank with me. She told me how you had refused to use your influence to keep her son in the world, and she loved you because she thought it was his love for you that made him abandon his purpose. She rejoiced in his marriage, but I doubt if she has been any more edified than I have been in watching the life you and her son have been leading since then. No, I do not blame you for Claude's sudden breakdown, but I deeply deplore that he should have turned back, since I know that his resolution to have done with the world was a right one—astounding as it seemed to me when I first heard of it. I urged him against a step for which I thought him utterly unprepared. I did not believe in his vocation, but after-consideration made me take a different view of his case. I knew that such a man would never have contemplated such a renunciation without so strong a reason that it was my duty to encourage him in his sacrifice of the world rather than to hold him back. I will say something more than this, Mrs. Rutherford, I will tell you that if it was to make his peace with God that your husband entered the Roman monastery, he lost all hope of peace when he left it, and he will never know rest for his heart and his conscience until he returns to the path that leads to the cloister."

"Claude is happy enough," Vera answered lightly. "He has so many occupations and interests. He is not as tired of things as I am. But no doubt I shall have to go on giving parties now and then, on Claude's account. He is not tired of the maelstrom, and it would not please him for me to drop out altogether, and to be talked about as eccentric, or 'not quite right.'"

She spoke with a weariness that moved the priest to pity. And then he spoke to her—as he had sometimes spoken in the past—words that were profoundly earnest, even eloquent, for what highly-educated man, or even what uneducated man, can miss being eloquent when his faith is deeply rooted and sincere, and his feelings are strongly moved?

He offered her the shelter of the Church, the only armour of defence against the weariness and wickedness of life. He would have led her in the passive way of light and love. He offered her the only certain cure for that Welt-Schmerz of which her husband had complained when he wanted to end his life in a cloister. He had pleaded with her before to-day, had tried to win her, years ago, when the pleasures of life had still something of their first freshness. He had tried vainly then, and his efforts were as vain now. She answered him coldly, almost mechanically. Yes; it was true that she was tired of everything, as Claude had been years ago, before their marriage, as he would be again perhaps by and by. But the Church could not help her. If she were to become a Roman Catholic it would only be in order to escape from the world—to do as Claude had wished to do, and make an end of a life that had lost all savour. But until she was prepared to take the veil she would remain as she was—a believer, but not in formulas—a believer, in the after-life and in the influencing minds, the purified souls that had crossed the river.

"I see you prefer Mr. Symeon's religion of the day before yesterday to that of the saints and martyrs of two thousand years," Cyprian Hammond said in his coldest tones, as he rose to leave her. "You are as dark a mystery as your husband is. God help you both, for I fear I cannot."

The grey darkness of a wet summer night was in the room as Vera rose to ring the bell and switch on the lamps. The clear white light showed her face drawn and pale, but very calm.

She held out both her hands to the priest.

"Forgive me," she said; "the day may come when I shall ask you to open the convent door for me; but I am not ready yet."

CHAPTER XXIV

The Goodwood of that year was a brilliant meeting. The winners were the horses that all the smart people wanted to win. The weather, with the exception of that first rainy twilight, was perfect, and all the smart frocks and hats spread themselves and unfolded their beauty to the sun, like flowers in a garden by the Lake of Como.

Among the owners of winning horses Mr. Rutherford was conspicuous.

"You rich people are always lucky," said his friends. "You never buy duffers, and you can afford to pay for talent. I don't suppose you make much by your luck, but you have the glory of it."

The house in which Claude Rutherford was staying was one of the smartest houses between Goodwood and Brighton, a house where there were always to be found clever men and handsome women—musical people and painting people, and even acting people—people who could sing and people who could talk; women who shone by the splendour of physical beauty, and women whose audacious wit made the delight of princes. It was a house in which cards were a secondary consideration, but where stakes were high and hours were late.

Lady Waterbury, the hostess, expressed poignant disappointment at Vera's non-arrival.

"My poor little wife is completely run down," Claude told her. "She was a rag this morning, and it would have been cruel to persuade her to come with me, though I hated leaving her in London at this dismal fag-end of the season. I thought her pal, Susan Amphlett, would have spent most of the week with her, but I hear Lady Susie is at the Saxemundhams'."

"Do you suppose Susie would miss a Goodwood—no, not for friendship," exclaimed Sir Joseph, the jovial host, one of the last of the private bankers of London, coming of a family so long established in wealth that he could look down upon new money. "Well, there is one of our beauties ruled out. I don't know what we should do if we hadn't secured Mrs. Bellenden."

"It was just as well to ask her this year," said his wife, with pinched lips, "though it was Sir Joseph's idea, not mine. I doubt if the best people will care about meeting her next season."

"What has Mrs. Bellenden done to risk her future status?" Claude asked, and then, with his cynical smile. "Certainly she has committed the unforgivable sin of being the handsomest woman in London, which is quite enough to set all the other women against her."

"It isn't her beauty that is the crime, but the use she makes of it. She has made more than one wife I know unhappy."

"And yet you ask her to your house?"

"Sir Joseph invites her. I only write the letter. So far she is just possible; but if I have any knowledge of character, she will be quite impossible before long."

"Let us make the most of her while her good days last," Claude said, laughing. "I should like to make a sketch of her before the brand of infamy is on her forehead. I have met her often, but my wife and she have not become allies; and if she is a snare for husbands and a peril for wives, it's rather lucky that Vera is not with me, for after a week in this delightful house they must have become pals."

"I don't think proximity would make two such women friends," Lady Waterbury replied severely. "Again, if I am any judge of character, I should say that Vera and Mrs. Bellenden must be utterly unsympathetic."

"My wife and I have a friendly compact," said Sir Joseph. "She may invite as many dowdy nieces and boring aunts as she likes, provided she asks no troublesome questions about the pretty women I want her to ask, and gives my nominees the best rooms."

"Poor Aunt Sophia had a mere dog-hole last Christmas," sighed Lady Waterbury.

"Well, didn't she bring her dog?"

"Poor darling; she never goes anywhere without Ponto: and, of course, she is a shade tiresome, and it is rather sweet of Joe to put up with her. Mrs. Bellenden may pass this time."

"Did I hear somebody talking of me?" cried a crystal clear voice, and a woman as lovely as a midsummer dawn came with swift step across the velvet turf towards the stone bench where Claude Rutherford and his host and hostess were seated.

They had strolled into the Italian garden, after an abundant tea that had welcomed the first batch of guests, a meal at which Mrs. Bellenden had not appeared, preferring to take tea in her dressing-room, while she watched her maid unpack, and planned the week's campaign; the exact occasion for every frock and hat being thought out as carefully as the general in command of an army might consider the position of his forces. It was to be a visit of five days and evenings, and none of those expensive garments which the maid was shaking out and smoothing down with lightly caressing fingers, was to be worn twice. All those forces had to be reviewed. Not a silk stocking not a satin slipper must be reported missing. Silken petticoats that rustled aggressively; petticoats of muslin and lace that were as soft and noiseless as the snow whose whiteness they imitated; fans, jewels, everything must be put away in perfect condition, ready for a lady who sometimes left herself the shortest possible time for an elaborate toilette, and yet always contrived to appear with faultless finish.

And this evening, as she came sailing across the garden, having changed her travelling clothes for a mauve muslin frock of such adorable simplicity that a curate's wife might have tried to copy it with the aid of a seamstress at eighteenpence a day, she was a vision of beauty that any hostess might have been proud to number among her guests.

She took her seat between Sir Joseph and his wife with careless grace, and held out her hand to Claude Rutherford without looking at him.

"Lady Waterbury told me that you and Mrs. Rutherford were to be here," she said. "Is she resting after her journey?"

"I am sorry to say she was not able to come with me."

"Not ill, I hope?"

"Not well enough for another Goodwood."

"The race weeks come round so quickly as one gets old," sighed Mrs. Bellenden. "There seems hardly breathing time between the Two Thousand and the Leger—and while one is thinking about where to go for the winter, another year has begun and people are motoring to Newmarket for the Craven."

"The story of our lives from year to year is rather like a merry-go-round in a fair, but Mrs. Bellenden is too young to feel the rush."

"Too young! I feel old, ages old. As old as Rider Haggard's Ayesha when the spell was broken and the enchantress changed to a hag. But I am sadly disappointed at not meeting your wife," she went on, turning the wonderful eyes that people talked about with full power upon Claude. "I wanted to meet her in a nice friendly house. We have only met in crowds, and I believe she rather hates me."

"How can you imagine anything so impossible?"

"At any rate, she has given me no sign of liking, while I admire her intensely. Francis Symeon has talked to me about her. I have had so much of the world, the flesh, and the devil, that I want to know something of a lady whom he calls one of his beautiful souls."

Upon this Mr. Rutherford had to say something polite, a something which implied that his wife would be charmed to see more of the lovely Mrs. Bellenden.

People talked of Mrs. Bellenden's beauty to her face. It was one of the things which her own sex registered against her as a mark of bad style. She might be ever so handsome, other women admitted, but she was the worst possible style. A circus rider, promoted from the sawdust to a Mayfair drawing-room, could hardly have been worse.

It was not long since this woman had burst upon the world of London—a revelation of physical loveliness.

Then felt they, like some watcher of the skies,
When a new planet swims into his ken.

There are planets and planets, as there are skies and skies. Assuredly neither Uranus nor Neptune created a greater ferment in the world of the wise than was made by Mrs. Bellenden's first season in the world of the foolish.

The phrase "professional beauty" had been exploded, as vulgar and stale, but the type remained under new names.

Mrs. Bellenden was simply the new beauty; invited everywhere; the star of every fashionable week-end party, every smart dance or dinner. Afternoon or evening—to hear divine music or to play ridiculous games; to be instructed about radium, or to lose money and temper at bridge, there could be no party really successful without Mrs. Bellenden.

Men looked round the flower-garden of picture hats with a disappointed air if her eyes did not flash lovely lightning from under one of them. Impetuous youths made a bee-line for her, and threaded the crowd with relentless elbows, calmly ignoring their loves of last season and the season before last.

"Men are absolute idiots about that woman," the last seasons told each other. "No one has a look in where she is."

Mrs. Bellenden was a young widow, a widow of two years' widowhood, the first of which it was whispered she had spent in a private lunatic asylum.

"That's where she got her complexion," said Malice. "It was just as good as a year's rest in a nursing home."

"And a strait-waistcoat. That's where she got her figure," said Envy.

She was now six-and-twenty, a widow, living in a small house in a narrow street like the neck of a bottle, between Park Lane and South Audley Street, with an income of two thousand a year, but popularly reputed to be spending at least five thousand. Her reputation in her first season had been unassailed, but she was rather taken upon trust, on the strength of the houses where she was met, than by reason of any exact knowledge that people had of her character and environment. Good-natured friends declared that she was thoroughbred. A creature with such exquisite hands and feet, and such a patrician turn of the swan-like throat, could hardly have come out of the gutter; and her husband had belonged to one of the oldest families in Wessex. So in that first season, except among her rivals in the beauty show, the general tone about her was approval.

Then, in her second year as the lovely widow, things began to leak out, unpleasant things—as to the men she knew, and the money she spent, the hours she kept in that snug little house in Brown Street; the places at which she was seen in London and Paris, chiefly in Paris, where people pretended that she had a pied-à-terre in the new quarter beyond St. Geneviève. People talked, but nothing was positively stated, except that she did curious things, and was beginning to be regarded somewhat shyly by prudish hostesses. She still went to a great many houses—smart houses and rich houses; but not quite the best houses, not the houses that can give a cachet, and stop the mouth of slander.

She gave little luncheons, little dinners, little suppers, in the little street out of Park Lane, and her lamp-lit drawing-room used to shine across the street in the small hours, as a token that there were talk and laughter and cards and music in the gay little room for tout le monde, or at least for her particular monde. She had a fine contralto voice, and sang French and Spanish ballads delightfully, could breathe such fire and passion into a song that the merest doggerel seemed inspired.

But before this second season was over there were a few people in London who had dreadful things to say about Mrs. Bellenden, and who said them with infinite cruelty; people for whose belongings—son or daughter, foolish youth or confiding young wife—this lovely widow had been a scourge.

Looking at the radiant being people did not always remember, and some people did not know, the tragedy of her youth. She had been a good woman once, quite good, a model wife. She had married, before her eighteenth birthday, a husband she adored. A creature of intense vitality, made of fire and light, sense and not mind, love with her had been a flame; unwise, unreasoning, exacting; love without thought; wildly adoring, wildly jealous. A word, a look given to another woman set her raging; and it was after one of the fierce quarrels that her jealous temper made only too frequent that her husband— handsome, gay, in the flower of his youth—left her without the goodbye kiss, for his last ride. He was brought back to her in the winter twilight, without a word of warning, killed at the last ditch in a point-to-point race, a race that was always remembered as the finest of many seasons; perhaps all the more vividly remembered because of that tragedy just before the finish, when Jim Bellenden broke his neck.

For some time after that dreadful night Kate Bellenden was under restraint; and then, after nearly a year, in which none but near relations had seen her or had even known where she was, she came back to the world; not quite sane, and desperately wicked. That small brain of hers had not been large enough to hold a great grief. Satan had taken possession of a mind that had never been rightly balanced.

"I have done with love," she told her âme damnée. She had always her shadow and confidante, upon whom she lavished gifts and indulgences. "I can never love anybody after him: but I like to be loved, and I like to make it hard for my lovers."

And then, in still wickeder moods, she would say, "I like to steal a woman's husband, or to cut in between an engaged girl and the man she is to marry. I like to make another woman as desolate as I was after Jim was killed, but I can't make her quite as miserable. I am not Death. But," with a little exulting laugh, "I am almost as bad."

There were people—a mother, a sister, or a wife—here and there in the crowd we call Society, who thought Mrs. Bellenden worse than Death; people who knew the fortunes she had wasted, the houses she had ruined, the hearts she had broken, the careers she had blighted, and the souls that had been lost for her.

CHAPTER XXV

Finding Claude Rutherford the most agreeable person in a house full of people, Mrs. Bellenden took possession of him on the first evening—not with any obvious devices or allurements, but coolly and calmly, just as she possessed herself of the most becoming arm-chair in the drawing-room, with such an air of distinct appropriation that other women avoided it.

"You seem to be the only amusing person here," she said, as he came to her side after dinner. "Isn't it strange that in so small a party there should be such a prodigious amount of dullness?"

"Have you sampled all the people? There is Mr. Fitzallan over there, talking to Lady Waterbury, a musical genius, who sets Shakespeare's sonnets and Heine's ballads deliciously, and sings them delightfully. You can't call him dull."

"Not while he is singing—but I have heard all his songs."

"Ask him to sing presently, and you will find he has brought a new batch. Then there is Eustace Lyon, the poet."

Mrs. Bellenden smiled.

"Do you know what they say of him?" she asked.

"Who can remember half the things people say of a genius who lays himself out to be talked about?"

"People are impertinent enough to say that he invented me."

"That is to make him equal to Jove, nay, superior, for it was only incarnate wisdom—not surpassing beauty—that came from the brain of the Thunderer."

"I believe he did rave about me the year before last, when I set up house in London—went about talking idiotically—called me 'a soothing gem,' and a hundred other ridiculous names."

"But you didn't mind? You bear no malice."

"No, he and I are always chums. I rather liked being advertised."

"Gratis?"

"Of course. I treat him rather worse than my butler, but I admire his genius, and I let him sit on the carpet and read his poems to me, before they go to the printer."

The poet joined them presently, stalking across the room, a tall, slim figure, with a pale, lank face and long hair.

The composer joined the group five minutes afterwards, and Mrs. Bellenden, having appropriated the only interesting men in the party, sank farther back in her deep chair, slowly fanning herself with her large white ostrich fan, and, as it were, withdrawing her beauty from circulation.

Other women might affect a little fan, but Kate Bellenden knew the value of a large one, when there is a perfect arm with a hoop of Brazilian diamonds to be displayed.

"I am only one of three," Claude said later in the week, when one of the men chaffed him about Mrs. Bellenden's favours. "She is a tête de linotte, and at her best in a quartette. One would soon come to the end of one's resources as an amusing person in a tête-à-tête."

He told himself that this peerless beauty might soon become a bore; and he thought how much peerless loveliness there must have been in the Royal Preacher's palace at the very time he was writing Ecclesiastes: but all the same he found that Mrs. Bellenden's conversation—empty-headed as it might be—gave a gusto to his days and nights during that Goodwood week. Their trivial talk was pleasant from its very foolishness. It was conversation without disturbing thought. There were no flashlights of memory to bring sudden sadness. A good deal of their talk was sheer nonsense—of no more value than the dialogue in a musical comedy—but it was a relief to talk nonsense, to laugh at bad puns, and to ridicule the serious side of life. Claude gave himself up to the mood of the moment, and was at his best: the irresponsible trifler, the mocker at solemn things, who had once been the desire of every hostess; the light, airy jester, to keep the table in a roar, the insidious flirt and flatterer, to amuse women after dinner.

People told each other that Rutherford was quite in his old form. He had become horribly blasé and distrait of late, as if all the sparkle had gone out of him under the weight of his wife's gold.

"I don't believe a millionaire can be happy," said the poet. "Rutherford has been deteriorating ever since his marriage. He rushes about doing things; racing, ballooning, flying, acting, hunting, shooting; perpetual motion without gaiety. He was twice the man when he was loafing about the world on fifteen hundred a year."

"He is one of those men whom marriage always spoils," replied the painter. "A chameleon soul that ought never to have worn fetters. To chain such a creature to a wife is as bad as caging a skylark. If he can't soar, he can't sing."

"I take it he will soon be out of the cage. He has done two years of the married lover's business, and we shall see him presently as the emancipated husband."

CHAPTER XXVI

Mr. and Mrs. Rutherford were to winter in Rome, but there was the autumn still to be disposed of. Neither of them wanted Marienbad. They knew the place inside out, and hated it; and after wasting half an hour at the breakfast-table turning over a Continental Bradshaw, they had only arrived more certainly at the conviction that they were tired of everywhere.

The whole system of continental travelling was weariness and monotony: the race to Dover through the freshness of morning, the race across sunlit waves to Calais, the hurried luncheon in the station, and the three hours' run to Paris, the huge Gare du Nord, with its turmoil of blue blouses and loaded barrows; the long drive to the hotel, and the early start in the Rapide for the South: or the Engadine express, with the night journey through pine woods, and the rather weary awakening at Lucerne, and then on to Locarno and the great lake. It had been delicious while it was new, and while it was new for these two to be together, wedded and inseparable for evermore. But all the tracks that had been new were old now; and though they were lovers still, something had come between them that darkened love.

"Tyrol, Engadine, Courmayeur? No," said Vera, throwing Bradshaw aside. "No, no, no. The hotels are all alike, and they make the scenery seem the same. If one could be adventurous, if one could stop at strange inns, where one need never hear an English voice, it would be better. But it is always the same hotel, the same rooms, and the same waiters, and the same food."

"A little better or a little worse; generally worse," assented Claude.

"I have had a letter from Aunt Mildred this morning. She wants us to spend August at Disbrowe."

"Would you like it?" he asked.

"Like it?" she echoed, with her eyes clouding, and a catch in her voice; and then she started up from her seat and came to her husband, and put her hand upon his shoulder.

"I think we have been getting rather modern of late, Claude," she said in a low voice, "rather semi-detached. Disbrowe would bring us nearer together again. We should remember the old days."

"Disbrowe, by all means, then," he answered gaily.

"We must never drift apart, Claude," she went on earnestly, with something of tragedy in her voice, which trembled a little as she crept closer to him. "Remember, we have nothing but our love, nothing else between us and despair."

"Don't be tragic, Vera," he said quickly. "Disbrowe, by all means. Let us play at being boy and girl again. Let us do daring things on Okehampton's twopenny-halfpenny yacht, and ride horses that other people are afraid to handle. Let us put fire into the embers of the past. I suppose your aunt will have a few amusing people. It won't be the vicar and his wife and sister-in-law every night, and the curate at luncheon every other day."

"She will have all sorts and conditions, but that doesn't matter. I want to be with you in the place where we were so happy."

"You want to fall in love with me again? Well, it was time," he said, half gaily and half sadly; but with always the air of a man who means to take life easily.

August was August that year, and Disbrowe was at its best. The great red cliffs, the azure and emerald sea had the colour and the glory that had made North Devon fairyland for the child Vera in her one blissful summer.

Other children, as they grew up, had a succession of delicious summers to look back upon, and could make comparisons, and wonder which was happiest; but Vera had only one season of surpassing joy to remember. She remembered it now, and contrived to draw a thick curtain over all other memories.

Aunt Mildred was full of compliments.

"This air evidently suits you, child," she said, when her niece had been with her a week. "You look ten years younger than when I saw you last in London."

These two who had begun to be tired of each other were lovers again—and even memory was kind— even memory, the slow torture of thoughtful minds. They recalled the joys of fifteen years ago; and the joys of to-day were almost the same. Instead of the thirteen two barb there were half a dozen hunters— thoroughbreds of fine quality, the disappointments of Claude's racing stud—instead of the dinghy there was Okehampton's forty-ton cutter, a rakish craft that had begun life at Cowes, another disappointment. There was the sea, and there was the moorland, and there were the patches of wood on the skirts of the park, that had seemed boundless forests to Vera in her twelfth year. Her twelfth year? She remembered Claude's affected contempt for her youth.

"Why, you are only a dozen—and not a round dozen, only eleven and a half. No wonder your cousins in the school-room look down upon you. If there were still a nursery, you would be there, sitting on a high chair at tea, your cheeks smeared with jam, and a bib tied under your chin."

She remembered all his foolish speeches now, and what serious insults they had seemed to her, or to the child that she had once been—that innocent child whose identity with herself was so hard to believe.

They were happy again, they were lovers again. Here they could say to each other, "Do you remember?" Here memory was a gentle nymph, and not an avenging fury.

For Vera, who had hunted with her husband every year since their marriage, a season at Grantham, a season in the Shires, and two winters in the Campagna, it might seem a small thing to ride with Claude and a handful of squireens and farmers rattling up the cubs in the woods, yet she found it pleasant to rise before the dawn, and creep through the silent house and out into the crisp morning air, and to spring on to a horse that seemed to skim the ground in an ecstasy of motion. Flying could hardly be better than to sit on this light, leaping creature, and see the dewy wood rush by, and the startled rabbits flash across the path; or to be lifted into the air as the thoroughbred stood on end at the whirr and rush of a pheasant.

A discarded racer was scarcely the best mount for pottering about after the cubs; but the pursuit of pleasure, that was always a synonym for excitement, had made Vera a fine horsewoman, and she loved the surprises that a light-hearted four-year-old can give his rider; and when the last cub had been slaughtered, to gratify Mr. Somebody's hounds, Claude and Vera had to ride to please their horses, and there was a spice of danger in the tearing gallop across great stretches of pasture, where the green sward sloped upward or downward to the crumbling edge of the red cliffs, and where they saw the wide, blue floor of the sea, and the dim outline of the Welsh coast.

One morning, when they were riding shoulder to shoulder, at a wilder pace than usual, and when Vera's horse was doing his best to get absolute possession of his bridle, she turned with a light laugh to her husband.

"Isn't this delicious?" she asked breathlessly, thrilled by the freshness of the air and the rapture of the pace. "Would you mind if we were not able to stop them on this side of the sea?"

"Would I mind?" he echoed, looking at her with his careless smile, the smile in which there was often a touch of mockery. "Not I, my love. It wouldn't be half a bad end, to finish one's last ride in a headlong plunge over the cliff—to know none of the gruesome details of dissolution—nothing but a sense of being hurled through bright air, forty fathoms deep into bright water. All the same, I don't mean these brutes to have their own way," he concluded in his most matter-of-fact tone, with his hand upon Ganymede's bridle.

They turned their horses, and trotted quietly home, Vera pale and somewhat shaken by the excitement of the long gallop. They were near the end of their country holiday, and they were to part at the end of the week, Claude to spend a fortnight at Newmarket, Vera to start alone for Italy, stopping here and there for a few days, on her way to her Roman villa, where Claude was to join her, bringing his hunters with him, not these light thoroughbreds, but horses of coarser quality and more experience, fitter for the rough work of the Campagna.

It had been Vera's own fancy to revisit familiar places in Italy. Claude had been urgent with her to abandon the idea, but she would not listen to him.

"I want to see San Marco, where I lived so long with Grannie; when we were poor and shabby—such a humdrum life. I sometimes wonder how I could bear it?"

"Poor child! It was hard lines for you. But why conjure up the memory of things that were sad? Looking back is always a mistake. Looking back at the old worn-out things, going back to long-trodden paths! Nobody can afford to do that. Plus ultra is my motto. In Rome there will be plenty for us to do. We must make our third winter more astounding than either of the other two. I know lots of people who are to be there, all sorts of big pots, pretty women, scribblers, painters, soldiers. You will have to invent new features for your evenings, new combinations of all kinds, and you must cultivate the new lights. When the season is over people must go about saying that Mrs. Rutherford has made Rome."

Vera looked at her husband curiously. How shallow he was, after all, how trivial! There were moments when her heart felt frozen, dreadful moments of disenchantment in which the man she had loved seemed to change and become a stranger; moments when she asked herself with a sudden wonder why she had ever loved him.

These were but flashes of disillusion. A touch of tenderness, a thought of all they had been to each other, and her bitter need of his love, made her again his slave. From the hour when he surrendered his chance of redemption, and came to her in her Roman garden, came to claim her with passionate words of love, he had been something more than her lover and her husband. He had been her master, ruling her life even in its trivialities, with a mind so shallow that it could find delight in details, leading and directing her in an existence where there was to be no room for thought.

He had planned their days at Disbrowe so that there should be no margin for ennui. When they were not riding they were on the yacht racing round the coast to Boscastle or Padstow: or they were playing tennis or croquet with the house-party, creating an atmosphere of excitement.

They parted at Disbrowe, Claude leaving for Newmarket; and they were not to meet till November, when he was to find Vera established in the Roman villa. All gaiety and excitement seemed to have left her with him, and Aunt Mildred remarked the change.

"You ought to have gone to Newmarket with your husband," she said, "though I have always thought it a horrid place for women, a place where they think of nothing but horses, and talk nothing but racing slang, and are as full of their bets as professional book-makers. I hate horsey women; but you and Claude are such a romantic couple, that it seems a pity you should ever be separated."

"Romance cannot last for ever, my dear aunt. We have been married nearly three years. It is time we became like other people. I have just your feeling about Newmarket. I was keen about the stud for the first year or two, petting the horses, and watching their gallops in the early mornings; and then it began to seem childish to care so much about them; and whether they won or lost it was the same thing over and over again. The trainer and his boys said just the same things about every success and every defeat. The crack jockeys were all the same, and I hardly knew one from another. I still love the horses for their own sake; and I am miserable if any of them are sold into bondage. But I am sick to death of the whole business."

There was a fortnight to spare before Vera was to start for Italy, and Lady Okehampton wanted her to stay at Disbrowe till a day or two before she left England.

"Portland Place will be awfully triste," she said; "I cannot see why you should go and bury yourself alive there for a fortnight."

Vera pleaded preparations—clothes to order for the winter.

"Surely not in London, when you can stop in Paris and get all you want."

There were other things to be done, arrangements to be made, Vera told her aunt. A certain portion of the staff was to start for Rome, by direct and rapid journeying, while she, with only her maid and a footman, was to travel by easy stages along the Riviera.

Lady Okehampton was rather melancholy in the last hour she and her niece spent together in her morning-room.

"I'm afraid the pace at which you and Claude are taking life must wear you out before long," she said. "You are never quiet; always rushing from one thing to another; even here, where I wanted you to come for absolute rest, just to dawdle about the gardens, and doze in a hammock all the afternoon, with a quiet evening's bridge. But you have given yourself no more rest here than in London. Okehampton told me the way you tore about on those ungovernable horses, miles and miles away over the moor, while other people were jogging after the hounds, or waiting about in the lanes. He said it was not cubbing, but skylarking; and the skipper complained that Mr. Rutherford insisted on sailing the yacht in the teeth of a dangerous gale. 'He's the generousest gentleman I've ever been out with,' old Peter said, 'but he's the recklessest; and I wouldn't give twopence for his chance of making old bones.'"

"Poor old Peter," sighed Vera. "We often had a squabble with him—what he called a stand-further. He's a conscientious old dear, and a fine sailor; but he would never have found the shortest way to India."

"You wanted rest, Vera; but instead of resting, you have done all the most tiring things you could invent for yourself."

"Claude is the inventor, not I. And it is good for me to be tired; to lie down with weary limbs and fall into a dreamless sleep or into a sleep where the dreams are sweet, and bring back lost things."

"I should not say all this, if I were not anxious about your health," Aunt Mildred continued gravely. "You look well and brilliant at night, but your morning face sometimes frightens me; and you are woefully thin, a mere shadow. It is all very well for people to call you ethereal, but I don't want to see you wasting away."

"There is nothing the matter. I was always thin. I have a little cough that sometimes worries me at night, but that has been much better since I came here."

"You ought to take care of your health, Vera. You have a great responsibility."

"How do you mean?"

"Have you ever thought of those who have to come after you? Do you ever consider that your splendid fortune dies with you, and that your power to help those members of our family who need help—alas, too many of them—depends upon your enjoying a long life."

"My dear aunt, I cannot promise to spin out a tedious existence in order to find money for poor relations."

"That remark is not quite nice from you, Vera. You yourself began life as a poor relation."

"I have not forgotten, and I have given my needy cousins a good deal of money since I have been rich; and, of course, I shall go on doing so."

"As your aunt, and the most attached of all your own people, I must ask a delicate question, Vera. Have you made your will?"

Lady Okehampton asked this question with such a thrilling awfulness, that it sounded like a sentence of death.

"No, aunt. Why should I make a will? I have nothing to leave. You know I have only a life interest in the Provana estate."

"Nothing to leave! But your accumulations? Your surplus income?"

"I don't think I can have any surplus. Claude and I have spent money freely, at home and abroad; and I have given large sums for the foundation of a hospital in Rome, in memory of Mario and his daughter. Claude manages everything for me. I have never asked him whether there was any money left at the end of the year."

"And of that colossal income—which you have enjoyed for five years—you have nothing left? It is horrible to think of. What mad waste, what incredible extravagance there must have been. You ought not to have left everything in Claude's hands. Such a careless, happy-go-lucky fellow ought never to have had the sole management of your immense income. It would make Signor Provana turn in his grave to know that his wealth has been wasted."

"He would not care. We never cared for money."

"Nothing left at the year's end, nothing of that stupendous wealth! It is monstrous!"

"Don't agitate yourself, dear Aunt Mildred. There may have been a surplus every year. I never asked Claude whether there was or not. But I shall always be rich enough to help my poor relations."

There was no time for further remonstrance. Aunt Mildred parted from her niece with more sighs than kisses, though those were many.

She perused the sweet, pale face with earnest scrutiny, for she thought she saw the mark of doom on the forehead where the lines were deeper than they should have been on the sunny side of thirty. She remembered the short-lived mother, the consumptive father.

Vera sat in a corner of the reserved compartment and read Browning's "Christmas Eve" all though the swift journey from the red cliffs of North Devon and the wide, blue sky to the grey dullness of a London twilight. It was a poem which she read again and again, which she knew by heart. It lifted her out of herself. She felt as if she were out in the winter darkness on the wind-swept common, as if her hands were clutching the edge of the Divine raiment. Was not that sublime vision something more than a dream in a stuffy Methodist chapel?

Were there not moments in life when earth touched heaven, when Divine compassion was something more real than the words in a book; when Christ the Redeemer came within reach of the sinner, and when Faith became certainty? Nothing less than this, nothing but the assurance of a Living God, could lift the despairing soul out of the abyss.

The house to which she was returning was a house of fear, and in spite of all she had said to her aunt, she knew that there was no necessity for her return. The rich man's widow had nothing to do that a telegram to her housekeeper would not have done for her. But the house drew her somehow. She had a morbid longing to be there, alone in the silence and emptiness of unused rooms, without Claude, whose presence jarred in rooms where another figure was still master.

She found all things in perfect order, no speck of dust in the rooms on the ground floor, her morning-room brilliant with Japanese chrysanthemums. She went to the library after her solitary dinner. The evening was cold, and fires were burning in all the rooms. She drew a low chair to the hearth, and sat brooding over the smouldering cedar logs, perhaps one of the loneliest women in London; and yet not quite alone, since nothing that had happened in her futile life of the last years had shaken her belief in Mr. Symeon's creed, and she felt that the dead were near her.

Giulia, who had loved her, Giulia, the happy soul who had known neither sin nor sorrow, the yearning of unsatisfied love, or the seething fires of guilty passion. Giulia's gentle spirit had been with her of late, the spirit of her only girl friend, and she had lived over again the tranquil hours at San Marco, the talk of books that had opened a new world to her, Giulia having read so much and she so little. Father and daughter had opened the gates of that new world for her. It was from them that the poet's daughter had learnt to understand and love all that is highest in the poetry of the world.

"If Giulia had lived," she thought to-night, as she crouched over the lonely hearth, sitting in that low chair in which she used to sit, as it were, at her husband's feet, sometimes in the dreamy twilight letting her drooping head rest upon his knee, while his hand hovered caressingly over the blonde hair.

Had Giulia lived, would everything have been different? Would Mario have loved and married her, and would they three have lived in a trinity of love? It seemed to her that Giulia would have been a hallowing influence. They two would have been like sisters, loving and understanding the man who loved them both. No cloud of jealousy could have come between them; all would have been sympathy and understanding. That wall of separation which had risen up between her and her husband would never have been. Neither pride on her part nor distrust upon his part would have killed love. Giulia would have sympathised with both; and her love would have kept them united.

She mused long upon the life that might have been, the life without a cloud. She thought with longing of the girl who had died sinless, in the morning of an unsullied life. Was not such a life, wrapped round with love, and free from the shadow of sin—such a death, before satiety had come to change the gold to dross—the happiest fate that God could give to His chosen?

"And to think that I was sorry for her, that I pitied her for being taken from such a beautiful world, from such a devoted father. How could I know that Death was the only security from sin?"

She sat long in that melancholy reverie, only rousing herself and taking up a book from the table at her side, when she heard the door opening, and a servant came in to put fresh logs on the fire.

She told the man that her maid, Louison, was not to sit up for her. Nobody was to sit up. She would not be going upstairs for some time. She wanted nothing, and she would switch off the lights.

In a house lighted by electricity the lights were of very little consequence. The footman took elaborate pains with the fire, piling up the logs, and arranging the large brass guard that fenced the hearth, and then retired with ghostly step to remote regions, where his fellows were lingering over the supper-table, some of them talking of the journey to Rome, and those who were to remain in charge of the house complaining of the dullness of a long winter, and the low figure of board wages, which had remained more or less stationary, while everything else was going up by leaps and bounds.

"I'd leap and bound you, if I had my way," said Mr. Sedgewick; "a pack of lazy trash. If I were Mr. Rutherford, I should put a policeman and a bull dog into the house, and lock it up till next May. You that are left have a deal too soft a time, while we that go have to work like galley slaves. Three parties a week, and a pack of Italian savages to keep up to the mark; fellows who are more used to daggers and stilettos than to soap and water, better for a brigand's cave than a high-class pantry, and who think nothing of quarrelling and threatening to murder each other in the middle of a dinner-party. There's no sense in a mixed staff. My pantry was a regular pandemonium last Christmas, and I wished myself back in sooty old London."

Mrs. Manby was to stay in Portland Place, mistress of the silent house, with one footman, two housemaids to sweep and dust, and a kitchen wench to cook for her. She had saved money, and was independent and even haughty.

"When I go to Italy it will be to the Riviera, for my health, and I shall go as a lady," she told Sedgewick, who, notwithstanding his abhorrence of Roman footmen, liked his winter in Rome, as a period that afforded better pickings than even a London season, Italian tradesmen being more amenable than London purveyors, who had been harassed and bound of late by grandmotherly legislation.

Supper had been finished in "hall" and housekeeper's parlour long before Vera left the library. It was after midnight when a sudden shivering, a vague horror of the silence came upon her, and she rose from her low chair in front of the dying fire and began to wander from room to room. The last of the logs had dropped into grey ashes in the library, and all other fires had gone out. The formal room, with large, official-looking chairs and severe office desk, where Mario Provana had received formal visitors, was the abode of gloom in this dead hour of the night: and yet it was not empty. The sound of the dead man's voice was in the room, the voice of command—so strong, so stern in those grave discussions which Vera had often overheard through the half-open door of the library, in the days when she had shared her husband's life—before fashion and Disbrowes had parted them.

His image was in the room, the massive figure, the commanding height, the broad shoulders, a little bent, as if with the weight of the noble head they had to carry. He was standing in front of his desk, facing those other men with the grave look she knew so well—courteous, serious, resolute—and then slowly, with a movement of weariness at the conclusion of an interview, he sank into the spacious arm-chair. She saw him to-night as she had seen him often, watching through the open door, while she was waiting for the business people to go, and for him to join her for their afternoon drive.

What ages ago—those tranquil days in which they had driven together in the summer afternoons—not the dull circuit of the Park, but to Hampton Court, or Wimbledon, or Richmond, or Esher, escaping from the suburban flower-gardens to green fields and rural commons, glimpses of woodland even, in the country about Claremont. Their airings were no swift rushes in thirty horse-power car, but a leisurely progress behind a pair of priceless horses, with time for seeing wild roses and honeysuckle in the hedges, the dogs and children on rustic paths, and the peace of cottage gardens.

She remembered how those tranquil afternoons had become impossible, by reason of her perpetual engagements; and how quietly Mario Provana had submitted to the change in her way of life, the succession of futile pleasures, the hurry and excitement.

"I want you to be happy," he told her, when she made a feeble apology for not having an afternoon at his service.

"You are young, and you must enjoy your youth. Things that seem trivial and joyless to me are new and sweet to you. Be happy, love. I have plenty of use for my time."

That was in the beginning of their drifting apart. Looking back to-night she could but wonder as she remembered how gradually, how imperceptibly that drifting apart had gone on; until she awoke one day to find that she and her husband were estranged. He was kind, had only an indulgent smile for the folly of her life, but the happy union of their first wedded years was over and done with. In Lady Susan's brief phrase, "They had become like other people."

And now she and Claude Rutherford had drifted apart, and were like other people. The reunion of a few weeks at Disbrowe was but a flash of summer across the gathering gloom of their lives.

"He can be happy," she thought, brooding in the night silence. "He cares for so many things. I care for nothing but the things that are gone."

And then, while the clock of All Souls struck that solemn single stroke which has even a more awful note than the twelve strokes of midnight, she thought of her dead—all her dead. Her poets, Tennyson, Browning, Swinburne—men who had lived while she was living, and one by one had vanished—of the great tragic actor whose genius had thrilled her childish heart—of all that company of the great who had died long before she was born—and it seemed to her in her dejection as if the earth were an empty desert, in which nothing great or beautiful was left. They had all gone through the dark gates of death— across the wild that no man knows. Her poet father, her lovely young mother, phantoms of beauty, distant and dim, evanescent shadows in the memory of a child. Yet, if Francis Symeon's creed were true, they were not gone for ever. They had not gone across the wild to dark distances beyond the reach of human thought. They were only emancipated. The worm had cast its earthly husk, and the spirit had spread its wings. Released from the laws of space and time, the all-understanding mind of the dead could be in sympathy with the elect among the living.

With Us, the elect, who have renounced the joys of sense, and lived only to cultivate the pleasures of the mind: for us the poets we worship still live, the minds that have been the light and leading of our minds are our companions and friends. We need no salaried medium's abracadabra to summon them, no weary waiting round a table in a darkened room, disturbed by suspicions of trickery. They come to us uncalled, as we sit alone in the gloaming, or wander alone over the desolate down, or by the long sea-shore. The poem we read is suddenly illuminated with the soul of the poet: the printed page becomes a message from the immortal mind.

To-night, in that silent hour, it was only of the dead Vera thought, as she wandered from room to room in the house of fear, shrinking from the prospect of the long, sleepless hours, weary yet restless. Restlessness made her wander into regions that were almost strange.

She drew aside a heavy curtain, and pushed open a crimson cloth door that led from the hall of ceremony to those inferior regions common to servants and tradesmen—the long stone passage, with doors right and left, the passage that ended at the door into the stable-yard, the door by which Mario Provana had entered on the night of his death.

Rarely had her foot trodden the stone pavement, yet every detail of the place—the form of the doors, the white ceiling, the unlovely drab walls had been burnt into her brain.

A single electric lamp gave the kind of light that is more awful than darkness. She heard clocks ticking: one that sounded solemn and slow, as if it were some awful mechanism that was measuring the fate of men; one with a thin and hurried beat, like the pulse of fever; she heard the heavy breathing of more than one sleeper; and presently, in front of the yard door, she came upon the watch dog, the Irish terrier, Boroo.

He was lying asleep on a rug in front of the door, and her light step upon the stone had not roused him. It was only when she was close to his rug that he started up and gave a low, muffled bark, and sniffed at the skirt of her dress, and being assured that she was to be trusted, sprang up with his fore-feet upon her hip and licked her hands.

She stooped over him and stroked his rough head, and let him nestle close against her, and then she knelt down beside him and put her arms round him and fondled him as he had never been fondled before by so beautiful and delicate a creature. From those long thoughts of a world peopled by the dead, the spontaneous love of this warm, living creature touched her curiously. There was comfort in contact with anything so full of life; and she laid her cold cheek against the dog's black nose, called him by his name, and made him her friend for ever.

"Poor old dog, all alone in this cold place. Come upstairs with me; come, Boroo."

The house dog needed no second invitation. He kept close to her trailing silken skirt as she moved slowly through the hall, switching off lights as she went, and so by the stately staircase to the second floor.

The fire in her morning-room had been made up at a late hour by Louison, who was now accustomed to her mistress's nocturnal habits; and the logs were bright on the hearth, and brightly reflected on the hedge-sparrow-egg blue of the tiled fireplace.

The terrier looked round the room with approval. Till this night he had seen nothing finer than Mrs. Manby's parlour, where—when occasionally suffered to lie in front of the fire—he had always to be on his best behaviour. But in Vera's room he made himself at once at home, jumped on and off the prettiest chairs, rioted among the silken pillows on the sofa, looking at her with questioning eyes all the time, to see what liberties he might take, and finally stretched his yellow-red body at full length in the glow and warmth of the hearth, wagging a lazy tail with ineffable bliss.

Vera seated herself in a low chair near him, and stooped now and then to pat the broad, flat head. He was a big dog of his kind; and though intended only for the humblest service, to rank with kitchen and scullery-maids and under-footmen, he was naturally, in that opulent household, a well-bred animal of an unimpeachable pedigree. His parents and grandparents had been prize-winners, and his blood might have entitled him to a higher place than the run of the servants' hall and stables and a mat in a stone passage. But whatever his inherited merits or personal charms, Vera's sudden liking for him had nothing to do with his race or character. It was the chill desolation of the silent hour, the freezing horror of the empty house, that had made her heart soften, and her tears fall, at the contact of this warm, living creature in the world of the dead. It was almost as if she had lost her way in one of the Roman catacombs, and had met this friendly animal among the dead of a thousand years, and in the horror of impenetrable darkness.

"You are my dog now, Boroo," she told the terrier, and the small, bright, dark eyes looked up at her with a light that expressed perfect understanding, while the pointed ears quivered with delight. He followed her to the threshold of her bedroom, where she showed him a White, fleecy rug on which he was to sleep, outside her door. He threw himself upon his back, with his four legs in the air, protesting himself her slave; and from that hour he worshipped her, and followed her about her house in abject devotion.

He went with her to Italy. Of course, there would be difficulties about his return to England; but canine quarantine might be ameliorated for a rich man's dog. He became her companion and friend; and it was strange how much he meant in her life. Strange, very strange; for in all the years of folly and self-indulgence she had never given herself a canine favourite. She had seen almost every one of her friends more or less absurdly devoted to some small creature—Griffon, Manchester terrier, Pekinese, Japanese, King Charles, Pomeranian—dogs whose merits seemed in an inverse ratio to their size—or the slaves to some more dignified animal, poodle or chow. She had seen this canine slavery, and had wondered, with a touch of scorn; and now, in the stately spaciousness of the Roman villa, she found herself listening for the patter of the Irish terrier's feet upon the marble floors, and rejoicing when he came bounding across the room, to lay his head upon her knee and express unutterable affection with the exuberance of a rough, hairy tail.

The clue to the mystery came to her suddenly as she sat musing in the firelight, with Boroo stretched at her feet.

She had wanted this dog. She had wanted some warm-hearted creature to love her, and to be loved by her. It had been the vacant house of her life that called for an inhabitant. She had awakened from her fever-dream of happiness, to find herself alone, utterly alone, in a world of which she was weary. Claude Rutherford was of no more account to her. The thing that had happened was something worse than drifting apart. Gradually and imperceptibly the distance between them had widened, until she had begun to ask herself if she had ever loved him.

Boroo went with his mistress on the long journey to San Marco, and behaved with an admirable discretion at the big hotel at Marseilles, where, though he would have liked to try conclusions with a stalwart dogue de Bordeaux that he met in one of the long corridors, he contented himself with a passing growl as he crept after Vera to his post outside her room. All things were strange to him in these first continental experiences; but he bore all things with sublime restraint, concentrating all his brain-power and all his emotional force on the one supreme duty of guarding the lovely lady who had adopted him.

At the Hôtel des Anglais Mrs. Rutherford was received with rapture, and the spacious suite on the first floor was, as it were, laid at her feet. She would, of course, occupy those rooms, and no other; the rooms where Signor Provana and his sweet young daughter had lived. Signor Canincio ignored the fact that the sweet young daughter had also died there.

No. Mrs. Rutherford would have the rooms in which she had lived with her grandmother.

"I want our old rooms, please," she said.

"The rooms in which you were so happy—where you spent two winters with the illustrious Lady Felicia."

Signor Canincio at once perceived how natural it was for Madame to prefer those rooms. Everything should be made ready immediately. His season had not yet begun; but his hotel would be full to overflowing in December, when he expected many of Madame's old friends to settle down for the winter. Vera smiled as she remembered those "old friends" with whom she had never been friendly; the sour spinsters and widows who had always resented Lady Felicia's determination to deny herself the advantage of their society.

It was the dead season of the year. The late lingering roses on the walls had a sodden look, the pepper trees drooped disconsolately, and a curtain of grey mist hung over the parade, where Vera had walked, alone and dejected, before the coming of Giulia and her father. The hills where they had driven looked farther away in the shadowy atmosphere. There was no gleaming whiteness on the distant mountains. All was grey and melancholy—and in unison with her thoughts of the dead. She had come there to look upon her husband's grave. She had been prostrate and helpless at the time of his burial, and had only just been capable of arousing herself from a state of apathy, to insist that he should be carried back to the country of his birth, and should lie beside his daughter in the shadow of the cypresses, between the sea and the olive woods.

Even in that agonising time the picture of that familiar spot had been in her mind as she gave her instructions; and she had seen the marble tomb in its green enclosure, and the tall trees standing deeply black against the pale gold of the sky, as on that evening when Mario Provana had found her sitting by his daughter's tomb. He must lie there, she told his partner, nowhere else; no, not even in Rome, where his family had their stately sepulchre. It was under the marble tomb he had made for his idolised child that he must rest.

And now, in the dull grey November, she stood once more beside the marble and read the lines that had been graven under Giulia's brief epitaph. "Also in memory of Mario Provana, her father, who died in London, on July the thirteenth, 19—, in the fifty-seventh year of his age." And below this one word— "Re-united."

She stayed long in the green enclosure, her dog coming back to her after much exploration of the wood above, where he had startled and scattered any animal life that he could find there, and the seashore below, where he stirred the tideless waves by the vehemence of his plunges; and then she went for a long ramble in the familiar paths where she had walked with Provana in those sunny afternoons, before the ride to the chocolate mills. She stayed nearly a week at San Marco, repeating the same process every day; first a lingering visit to the grave, and then a long, lonely walk in the paths she had trodden with the man whom she had thought of only as her friend's father, until by an imperceptible progress he had made himself the one close friend of her life. She took pains to find the very paths they had trodden together, the humble shrines or chapels they had looked at, the rocks where they had sat down to rest.

When she had first spoken of revisiting San Marco Claude had done his uttermost to dissuade her. "Don't be morbid," he had said more than once. "Your mind has a fatal leaning that way. You ought to fight against it."

Yes, she knew that she was morbid, that she had taken to brooding upon melancholy memories, that she was cultivating sadness. Alone in the olive wood, watching the evening light change and fade, and the shadows steal slowly from the valley and the sea, while memory recalled words that had been spoken in that narrow pathway, among those grey old trees in the light and shade of evenings that seemed ages ago, she had a feeling that was almost happiness. It was a memory of happiness so vivid that it seemed the thing itself.

She had been very happy in those tranquil evenings. She knew now that she had begun to love Mario Provana many days before his impassioned avowal had taken her by storm. His eloquence, his power of thought and feeling, had made life and the world new. She "saw Othello's visage in his mind." His rugged features and his eight-and-forty years were forgotten in the charm of his conversation and the rare music of his voice. The world of the scholar, of the thinker, and the poet, had been an unknown world to the girl of eighteen, whose poor little bit of flimsy education had been limited to the morning hours of a Miss Greenhow at a guinea a week. He opened the gate of that divine world and led her in, and they walked there together; he charmed by her freshness and naïveté, she dazzled by his wealth of knowledge and his power of imagination. Not even her poet father could have had a wider knowledge of books, or a greater power of thought, she told herself; which was a concession to friendship, as she had hitherto put her father in the front rank of those who know.

She looked back at those innocent hours, when he who was so soon to be her husband was only thought of as her first friend.

She looked back to hours that seemed to her to have been the happiest in all her life. Yes, the happiest; for happiness is sunshine and calm weather, not fever and storm. There were other hours more romantic and more thrilling, but agonising to remember—sensual, devilish. Those hours in the woods had been serene and pure, and she had walked there with the heart of a child.

How kind he had been, how kind! It was the kindness in the low, grave voice that had made its music: only the kindness of a friend of mature years interested in her youth and ignorance, only a grave and thoughtful friend, liking her because she had been loved by his dead daughter. That is what she had thought of him for the greater part of those quiet hours. Yet now and then she had been startled by a sudden suggestion. She did not know, but she felt that he was her lover.

It was in vain that Signor Canincio pressed her to occupy his piano nobile as the only part of his hostel worthy of her. She insisted on the old rooms, the salon that had been growing shabbier and shabbier in the years of her absence, and which had never been redecorated. There were the same faded cupids flying about the ceiling, where many a crack in the plaster testified to an occasional earthquake; and there was the same shabby paper on the walls. Nothing had been altered, nothing had been removed. Vera went out upon the balcony and looked down at the little town, and the distant ridge where the walls of a monastery rose white against the grey November sky. Everything was the same. She had wanted to come back. It was a morbid fancy, perhaps, like many of her fancies. She knew that she was morbid. She wanted to steep herself in the memories of the time before she was Mario Provana's wife; the time when she knew that he loved her, and was proud of his love.

She walked up and down the room, touching things gently as she passed them, as if those poor old pieces of furniture, with their white paint and worn gilding, were a part of her history. This was the table where she had sat making tea, a slow process, while Mario stood beside her, watching her, as she watched the blue flame under Granny's old silver kettle, the George-the-Second silver that gave a grace to the cheap salon. Lady Felicia had kept her old silver—light and thin with much use—as resolutely as she had kept her diamonds.

"If ever I were forced to part with those poor things of mine I should feel myself no better than the charwoman who comes here to scrub floors," she told Lady Okehampton, and that kind lady, who was taking tea with "poor Lady Felicia," in her London lodgings, had approved a sentiment so worthy of a Disbrowe.

Vera paced the room slowly in the thickening light: sometimes standing by the open window, listening to footsteps on the parade, and the talk of the women from the olive woods, tramping bravely homeward with heavy baskets on their heads, baskets of little black olives for the oil mills that dotted the steep sides of the gorge through which the tempestuous little river went brawling down to the sluggish sea.

And then she went back into the shadows, and slowly, slowly, paced all the length of the room, thinking of those evenings when she had made tea for the Roman financier.

The shadows gathered momentarily and the shapes of all things became vague and dim. There was Granny's sofa, and Granny was sitting there among her silken pillows. She could see the pale, thin face, and the frail figure wrapped in a China crape shawl. The white shawl had always had a ghostly look in a dimly lighted room.

She went over to the sofa and felt the empty corner where Granny used to sit. No, she was not there. The sofa was a bare, hard object, with nothing phantasmal about it. There were no silken cushions. Those amenities had been Lady Felicia's private property, travelling to and fro by petite vitesse. There was no one on the sofa, and that dark form, the tall figure near the tea-table, was nothing but shadow. It vanished as she came near and there was only empty space, with the white table shining in the faint light from the open window.

"Nothing but shadow," she thought, "like my life. There is nothing left of that but shadow."

"How happy I must have been, when I lived in this room, how happy! But I did not know it. How sweetly I used to sleep, and what dear dreams I dreamt. I was only seventeen in our first winter, and I was a good girl. Looking back I cannot remember that I had ever done wrong. I was always obedient to Granny, and I tried hard to please her, and to care for her when she was ill. I always spoke the truth. The truth? Why should I have been afraid of truth in those days? There was no merit in fearless truth. But the difference, the difference!"

It seemed so strange now that she had not been happier. To be young and without sin: to believe in God and to love Christ. Was not that enough for happiness?

The room was almost dark before she rang for lamps. In that southern paradise the shutting of windows must precede the entrance of lighted lamps; and one is apt to prolong the time entre chien et loup.

The darkness fostered those morbid feelings that she had indulged of late. She thought of Francis Symeon, and his belief in the communion of the living and the dead.

Her husband might be near her as she crept about in the darkness. She might know that he was there; but she was not to hope for any visible sign of his presence.

To see was reserved for the elect; and for them only when the earthly tabernacle was near its end, when the veil between life and death had worn thin. Then only, and for the choicest spirits only, would that thin veil be rent asunder and the dead reveal themselves to the living, in a divine anticipation of immortality.

"Not for all, not for those who have loved earthly things and lived the sensual life, not for them the afterlife of reunion and felicity."

"Not for me—never for me." She fell on her knees by Granny's sofa, and bowed her head upon her folded arms and prayed—a wild and fervent prayer—a distracted appeal for mercy to One Who knew, and could pity. Such a prayer as might have trembled on the Magdalen's pale lips while, with bent head and hidden countenance, she washed the Redeemer's feet with her tears.

The spell that was woven of silence and shadow was broken suddenly by the opening of the door and the tumultuous entrance of the Irish terrier, followed by Louison, who saw only darkness and an empty room.

"Mais où donc est Madame?" she exclaimed.

Boroo had found his mistress by something keener than the sense of sight, and had pushed his cold, black nose against her cheek, despite of the bowed head, and leapt about her as she rose to her feet, just in time to hide all signs of agitation as Signor Canincio's odd man, in a loose red jacket, looking like a reformed bandit, brought in a pair of lamps and flooded the room with light.

Louison rushed to shut the windows and exclude cette affreuse bête le moustique, from whose attentions she herself had suffered.

"Mais, madame, pourquoi ne pas sonner? Vous voilà sans lumière, sans feu, et les fenêtres grandes ouvertes. Accendere, donc," to the odd man, "apportez legno, molto legno, et faire un bon fuoco, presto, subito, tout de suite."

It may be that this noisy solicitude was meant to cover a certain want of attention to her mistress; Ma'mselle having lingered over the tea-table in the couriers' room, where a dearth of couriers at this dead season was atoned for by the presence of Signor Canincio and his English wife, she dispensing the weakest possible tea, with condescending kindness, and wife and husband both alert to hear anything that Louison would tell them about her mistress, while the animated gestures and expressive eyes of the host testified to his admiration for la belle Française, an admiration that was made more agreeable to Louison from the consuming jealousy which she saw depicted in the countenance of the travelling footman, whose inferior status ought to have excluded him from that table. But Louison knew that Canincio's hotel had always been what Mr. Sedgewick called une affaire d'un seul cheval.

CHAPTER XXVII

The Roman villa was a fairy palace of light and flowers, and its long range of windows flashed across the blue vapours of the December night, and might have been noticed as a golden glory in the far distance by solitary watchers in the monasteries on the Aventine hill.

It was Vera's first reception; and all that there was of Roman rank and beauty, all that there was of transatlantic wealth and cosmopolitan talent in the most wonderful city in the world had assembled in prompt response to her card of invitation.

"Mrs. Claude Rutherford, at home, 9 to 12. Music.

"The Villa Provana."

The financier's palace still bore the stamp of mercantile riches. Claude had urged his wife to give the splendid house a splendid name; so that, in the ever-changing society of the Italian capital, the source of all that splendour might be forgotten; but he had urged in vain.

"It was his father's house, and it was my home with him," she said, with a strange look—the look that Claude feared. "While I live it shall never have any other name."

"You are the first woman I ever knew with such a cult of the dismal," he said. "Most widows wish to forget."

"Most widows can forget," she answered.

He turned and left her at the word; and she heard him singing sotto voce as he went along the corridor, "La donna e mobile."

"At least I do not change," she thought.

This had happened in their first winter in Rome—a mere flash of melancholy—soon forgotten in those wild days when the pace was fastest, and when life went by in a hurricane of fashionable pleasures. Visiting and entertaining, opera and theatre and race-course; a rush to Naples to hear a wonderful tenor; to Milan to see the new dancer at the Scala; something new and fatiguing for every week and every day. They were both calmer now, and it may be that both were tired, though it was only Vera who talked openly of weariness.

To-night she was looking lovely; but a Russian savant, who was among the most illustrious of her guests, whispered to his neighbour as she passed them, "She will not live her hundred and forty years."

"I am afraid it is a question of months rather than years," replied his friend, a famous Roman doctor.

Something there was in the radiant face, pale, but full of light and life, in which the eye of an expert read auguries of evil; but to the elegant mob circulating through those sumptuous rooms Mrs. Rutherford was still beautiful with the bloom of health. Her pallor was of a transparent fairness, more brilliant than other women's carnations. The popular American painter had made one of his most startling hits, two years before, by his exquisite rendering of that rare beauty, the alabaster pallor, the dreaming eyes, blue-grey, or blue with a touch of green. He had caught her "mermaid look"; and his most fervent admirers, looking at the portrait in the Academy crowd, declared that the colour in those mysterious eyes changed as they looked. The portrait was the sensation of the year. Her eyes changed, and she seemed to be moving out of the canvas, said the superior critics; and the herd went about parroting them. She had her far-away look to-night, as she stood near the doorway in the Rubens room, the first of the long suite; and though she had a gracious greeting for everybody, those who admired her most had a strange fancy that she was only the lovely semblance or outer shell of a woman, whose actual self was worlds away.

There was nothing dreamy or far-away about Claude Rutherford to-night. He was a man whose nature it was to live only in the present, and to live every moment of his life. To-night, in these splendid surroundings, in this crowd of the noble and the celebrated, he felt as one who has conquered Fate, and has the world at his feet. He was a universal favourite. The hearts of women softened at his smile; and even men liked him for his careless gaiety.

"Always jolly and friendly, and without a scrap of side."

That was what they said of him. To have the spending of the Provana millions and to be without side, seemed a virtue above all praise. People liked him better than his ethereal wife. She was charming, but elusive. That other-world look of hers repelled would-be admirers, and even chilled her friends.

The Amphletts had arrived at the villa on a long visit, just in time for Vera's first party; and Lady Susan was floating about the rooms in an ecstasy of admiration. She had never seen them in Mario Provana's time, and though she had been invited by Vera more than once in the last three years, this was her first visit.

Her tiresome husband had preferred Northamptonshire, and she had not been modern enough to leave him; and now he had been only lured a thousand miles from the Pytchley by the promise of hunting on the Campagna.

"At last Vera is in her proper environment," Lady Susan told a young attache, who had been among the intimates in London. "She was out of her proper setting in Portland Place. Nothing less beautiful than this palace is in harmony with her irresistible charm. Other women have beauty, don't you know; Mrs. Bellenden, par exemple."

"Mrs. Bellenden is an eye-opener," murmured the diplomat.

"Yes, I know what you are thinking, the handsomest woman in Europe, and all that kind of thing; but utterly without charm. Even we women admire her, just as we admire a huge La France rose, or a golden pheasant, or a bunch of grapes as big as plovers' eggs, with the purple bloom upon them; the perfection of physical beauty. But the light behind the painted window, the secret, the charm is not in it. Beauty and to spare, but nothing more."

Mrs. Bellenden sailed past them on the arm of the English Ambassador while Susie expatiated.

It was her first appearance in Roman society, and she was the sensation of the evening.

A form as perfect as the Venus of the Capitol, a face of commanding beauty, a toilette of studied simplicity, a gown of dark green velvet, without a vestige of trimming, the décolletage audacious, and for ornament an emerald necklace in a Tiffany setting, which even among hereditary jewels challenged admiration, just a row of single emeralds clasping a throat of Parian marble.

Mrs. Bellenden had the men at her feet; from Ambassadors to callow striplings, new to Rome and to diplomacy, sprigs of good family, who were hardly allowed to do more than seal letters, or index a letter-book. All these courted her as if she had been royal; but the women who had known her in London kept themselves aloof somehow, except the American women, who praised and patronised her, or would have patronised, but for something in those dark violet eyes that stopped them.

"It isn't safe to say sarcastic things to a woman with eyes like hers," they told each other. "It would be as safe to try to take a rise out of a crouching tiger, or to put a cobra's back up, for larks."

Lady Susan was about the only woman of position who talked to Mrs. Bellenden; but Susie loved notorieties of all kinds, and had never kept aloof from speckled peaches, if the peaches were otherwise interesting.

"I call Bellenden a remarkable personality," she told Claude, whom she contrived to buttonhole for five minutes in the corridor after supper. "A rural parson's daughter, brought up on cabbages and the tithe pig. A woman who has spent a year in a lunatic asylum, and yet has brains enough to set the world at defiance. You will see she'll be a duchess—a pucker English duchess—before she has finished."

"She is more than worthy of the strawberry leaves; but I don't see where the pucker duke is to come from. Her only chance would be a fledgling, who had never crossed the Atlantic."

If her own sex persisted in a certain aloofness, Mrs. Bellenden had her court, and could afford to do without them. In the picture gallery, after supper, she was the centre of a circle, and her rich voice and joyous laughter sounded above all other voices in the after-midnight hour, when the crowd had thinned and most of the great ladies had gone away.

Susie watched that group from a distance, and wondered when Mrs. Bellenden was going to break through the ring of her worshippers and make her way to the Rubens room, where the mistress of the house was waiting to bid the last of her guests good-night.

The first hour after midnight was wearing on, and Susan Amphlett, who had eaten two suppers, each with an amusing escort, was beginning to feel that she had had enough of the party and would like to be having her hair brushed in the solitude of her palatial bedroom. But she wanted to see the last of Mrs. Bellenden, if not the last of the party; and she kept her cicisbeo hanging on, and pretended to be interested in the pictures, while she furtively observed the proceedings of the notorious beauty. She was making the men laugh. That was the spell she was weaving over the group who stood entranced around her. Light talk that raised lighter laughter: that was her after-midnight glamour. She had been grave and dignified as she moved through the rooms by the side of the Ambassador. But now, encircled by a ring of "nice boys," she was frankly Bohemian, and amused herself by amusing them, with splendid disregard of conventionalities. Reckless mirth sparkled in her eyes; uproarious laughter followed upon her speech. Whatever she was saying, however foolish, however outrageous, it was simply enchanting to the men who heard her; and in the heart of the ring Claude Rutherford was standing close beside the lovely freelance, hanging upon her words, joyous, irresponsible as herself. The spell was broken at last, or the fairy laid down her wand, and allowed Claude to escort her to her hostess, who just touched her offered hand with light finger-tips; and thence to the outer vestibule, an octagon room where the white marble faces of Olympian deities, who were immortal because they had never lived, looked with calm scorn upon the flushed cheeks and haggard eyes of men and women too eager to drain the cup of sensuous life. Claude and Mrs. Bellenden stood side by side in the winter moonlight while they waited for carriage after carriage to roll away, before a miniature brougham of neatest build came to the edge of the crimson carpet. They had had plenty of time for whispered talk while they waited, but there had been no more laughter, rather a subdued and almost whispered interchange of confidential speech; and the last word as he stood by the brougham door was "to-morrow."

Lady Susan and Vera went up the great staircase together, Susie with her usual demonstrative affection, her arm interwoven with her friend's.

"Your party has been glorious, darling!" she began. "I see now that it is the house that makes the glory and the dream. Your parties in Portland Place were just as good, as parties, but oh, the difference! Instead of the vulgar crush upon the staircase, and the three overcrowded drawing-rooms, immense for London—this luxury of space, this gorgeous succession of rooms, so numerous that it makes one giddy to count them. Vera, I see now that it is only vast space that can give grandeur. The bricks and stone in your London house would have made a street in Mayfair; but it is a hovel compared with this. And to think of that good-for-nothing cousin of mine leaving a bachelor's diggings in St. James's to be lord of this palace. There never was such luck!"

"I don't think Claude cares very much for the villa, or for Rome," Vera answered coldly. "He prefers London and Newmarket."

"That's what men are made of. They don't care for houses or for furniture. They only care for horses and dogs, and other women," assented Susan lightly.

They were at the door of Vera's rooms by this time, but Susie's entwining arms still held her.

"Do let me come in for a cause."

"I'm very tired."

"Only five minutes."

"Oh, as long as you like. I may as well sit up and talk as lie down, and think."

"What, are you as bad a sleeper as ever?"

"I have lost the knack of sleep. But I suppose I sleep enough, as I am alive. Some people talk as if three or four sleepless nights would kill them; but Sir Andrew Clarke let Gladstone lie awake seven nights before he would give him an opiate."

"But you will lose your beauty—worse than losing your life. You looked lovely to-night—too lovely, too much like an exquisite phantom. And now, my sweet Vera, don't be angry if I touch upon a delicate—no, an indelicate subject. You must never let Mrs. Bellenden enter your house again."

"Indeed, Susie! But why?"

"Because she is simply too outrageous!"

"Do you mean too handsome, too attractive?"

"I mean she is absolutely disreputable. If you had seen her in the picture gallery, with a crowd of men round her—your husband among them—laughing immoderately, as men only laugh when outrageous things are being said!"

"And was she saying the outrageous things?"

"Undoubtedly. I watched her from a distance, while I pretended to be looking at the pictures. Vera, I don't want to worry you, but that woman is dangerous!"

"Dangerous?"

"Yes, like the Lurlei and people of that class. She is the very woman Solomon described in Proverbs—and he knew. She is a danger for you, Vera, a danger for your peace of mind. She is a wicked enchantress, an enemy to all happy wives; and she is trying to steal your husband."

"I am not afraid.".

"But you ought to be afraid. Roger and I are not a romantic couple; but if I saw him too attentive to such a woman as Mrs. B. I should—well, Vera, I should take measures. Remember, the woman is the danger. It doesn't matter how much a man flirts, as long as he flirts with the harmless woman. You really should take measures."

"That is not in my line, Susie. When my husband has left off caring for me I shall know it, and that will be the end."

Susan looked at her with anxious scrutiny.

"I'm afraid you are leaving off caring for him," she said rather sadly.

"Never mind, dear. The sands are running through the glass, whether we are glad or sorry, and the end of the hour will come."

"Don't!" cried Susie, wincing as if she had been hit.

"Good night, dear, I am very tired."

"Yes, that's what it means!" Susie kissed her effusively. "Your nerves are worn to snapping point, you poor, pale thing. Good night."

Vera was on the Palatine Hill next morning before Lady Susan had left her sumptuous bed, a vast expanse of embroidered linen and down pillows, under a canopy of satin and gold. Painted cherubim looked down upon her from the white satin dome, cherubs or cupids, she was not sure to which order the rosy cheeks and winged shoulders belonged.

"They must be cupids," she decided at last. "They have too many legs for cherubim."

Vera was wandering among the vestiges of Imperial Rome with the dog Boroo for company. She liked to roam about these weedy pathways, among the dust of a hundred palaces, in the clear, sunlit morning, at an hour when no tourist's foot had passed the gate.

The custodians knew her as a frequent visitor, and left her free to wander among the ruins as she pleased, without guidance or interference. They had been inclined at first to question the Irish terrier's right to the same licence, but a sweet smile and a ten-lire note made them oblivious of his existence. He might have been some phantom hound of mediæval legend, passing the gate unseen. Simply clad in black cloth, a skirt short enough for easy walking, a loose coat that left her figure undefined, and a neat little hat muffled in a grey gauze veil through which her face showed vaguely, Vera was able to walk about the great city in the morning hours without attracting much notice. Among some few of the shopkeepers and fly drivers who had observed her repeated passage along particular streets, she was known as the lady with the dog. In her wanderings beyond the gates, in places where there were still rural lanes and cottagers' gardens, she would sometimes stop to talk to the children who clustered round her and received the shower of baiocchi which she scattered among them with tumultuous gratitude, kissing the hem of her gown, and calling down the blessings of the Holy Mother on "la bella Signora, e il caro cane," Boroo coming in for his share of blessings.

They were lovely children some of them, with their great Italian eyes, and they would be sunning themselves on the steps of the Trinità del Monte by and by, when the spring came, waiting to attract the attention of a painter on the look-out for ideal infancy; wicked little wretches, as keen for coin as any Hebrew babe of old in the long-vanished Ghetto, dirty, and free, and happy; but they struck a sad note in Vera's memory, recalling her honeymoon year in Rome, and how fondly Mario Provana had hoped for a child to sanctify the bond of marriage, and to fill the empty place that Giulia's death had left in his heart. A year ago Vera had been killing thought in ceaseless movement, in ephemeral pleasures that left no time for memory or regret, but since the coming of satiety she had found that to think or to regret was less intolerable than to live a life of spurious gaiety, to laugh with a leaden heart, and to pretend to be amused by pleasures that sickened her. Here she found a better cure for painful thought, in a city whose abiding beauty was interwoven with associations that appealed to her imagination, and lifted her out of the petty life of to-day into the life of the heroic past. In Rome she could forget herself, and all that made the sum of her existence. She wandered in a world of beautiful dreams. The dust she trod upon was mingled with the blood of heroes and of saints.

She had seen all that was noblest in the city with Mario Provana for her guide, he for whom every street and every church was peopled with the spirits of the mighty dead, from the colossal dome that roofed the tomb of the warrior king who made modern Italy, to the vault where St. Peter and St. Paul had lain in darkness and in chains.

She had seen and understood all these things with Mario at her side, enchanted by her keen interest in his beloved city, and delighted to point out and explain every detail.

For Mario every out-of-the-way corner of Rome had its charm—for Claude Rome meant nothing but the afternoon drive along the Corso, and the bi-weekly meet of hounds on the Appian Way. Everything else was a bore. It was the Palatine where she and Mario had returned oftenest and lingered longest, for it seemed the sum of all that was grandest in the story of Rome, or, rather, it was Rome. How often she had stood by her husband's side on this noble terrace, gazing at the circle of hills, and recalling an age when this spot was the centre of the civilised earth! Here were the ruins of a forgotten world; and the palaces of Caligula and Nero seemed to belong to modern history, as compared with the rude remains of a city that had perished before the War-God's twins had hung at their fierce foster-mother's breast. Every foot of ground had its traditions of ineffable grandeur, and was peopled with ghosts. They stood upon the ashes of palaces more splendid and more costly than the mind of the multi-millionaire of to-day had ever conceived—the palaces of poets and statesmen, of Rome's greatest orators, and of her most successful generals; of Emperors whose brief reign made but half a page of history, ending in the inevitable murder; of beautiful women with whom poison was the natural resource in a difficulty; of gladiators elevated into demi-gods; of mothers who killed their sons, and sons who killed their mothers;

and of all those hundred palaces, and that strange dream of glory and of crime there was nothing left but ruined walls, and the dust in which the fool's parsley and the wild parsnip grew rank and high.

Amidst those memories of two thousand years ago, Vera felt as if life were so brief and petty a thing, such a mere moment in the infinity of time, that no individual story, no single existence, with its single grief, no wrong done, could be a thing to lament or to brood over. Nothing seemed to matter, when one remembered how all this greatness had come and gone like a ray of sunshine on a wall, the light and the glory of a moment.

And what of those grander lives, the Christian martyrs, the men who fought with beasts, and gave their bodies to be burned, the women who went with tranquil brow and steadfast eyes to meet a death of horror, rather than deny the new truth that had come into their lives?

There were other, darker memories in her solitary wanderings. She returned sometimes to the hill behind the Villa Medici. She lingered in the dusty road outside the Benedictine monastery, and peered through the iron gate, gazing into the desolate garden, where only the utilitarian portion was cared for, and where shrubs, grass, and the sparse winter flowers languished in neglect, where the gloomy cypresses stood darkly out against the mouldering plaster on the wall; the prison gate, within which she had seen her lover sitting by the dying fire, a melancholy figure, with brooding eyes that refused to look at her.

"It would have been better for us both if he had stayed there," she thought. "If we had been true to ourselves we should have parted at the door of his prison for ever. It would have been better for us both—better and happier. The cloister for him and for me. A few years of silence and solitude. A few years of penitential pain; and then the open gate, and the Good Shepherd's welcome to the lost sheep."

Yes, it would have been better. No pure and abiding joy had come to her from her union with her lover. They had loved each other with a love that had filled the cup of life in the first years of their marriage; they had loved each other, but it had been with a passion that needed the stimulus of an unceasing change of pleasures to keep it alive; and when the pleasures grew stale, and there were no more new things or new places left in the world, their love had languished in the grey atmosphere of thought.

She knew that her love for Claude Rutherford was dead. The third year of wedlock had killed it. She looked back and remembered what he had once been to her. She saw the picture of her past go by, a vivid panorama lit by a lurid light—from the July midnight in the rose garden by the river, to the November evening in Rome, when he had come back to her from his living grave—and she had fallen upon his breast, and let him set the seal of a fatal love upon her lips—the seal that had made her his in the rose garden, and had fixed her fate for ever. This later kiss was more fatal; for it meant the hope of heaven renounced, and a soul abandoned to the sinner's doom. For her part, at least, love had died. Slowly, imperceptibly, from day to day, from hour to hour, the glamour had faded, the light had gone. Slowly and reluctantly she had awakened to the knowledge of her husband's shallow nature, and had found how little there was for her to love and honour below that airy pleasantness which had exercised so potent a charm, from the hour when she met and remembered the friend of her childhood, until the night of the ball, when he had whispered his plan for their future as they spun round in their last waltz. All had shown the lightness of the sunny nature that charmed her. Even in talking of the desperate step they were going to take he had seemed hardly serious. His confidence was so strong in the future. Just one resolute act—a little unpleasantness, perhaps; and then emancipation, and a life of unalloyed happiness—"the world forgetting, by the world forgot"—themselves the only world that was worth thinking about.

And it was to this shallow nature that she had given her love and her life; for she could see nothing in life outside that fatal love. As that perished, she felt that she must die with it. There was nothing left— no child—no "forward looking hopes."

But there was the memory of the past! In her lonely walks about the environs of Rome, the past was with her. She was always looking back. She could not tread those paths without remembering who had trodden them with her when the wonder of Rome was new. The man who was her companion, then the strong man, the man of high thoughts and decisive action, the thinker and the worker. The man of grave and quiet manners, who could yet be terrible when the fire below that calm surface was kindled. She had seen that he could be terrible. One episode in their happy honeymoon life had always remained in her memory, when at a crowded railway station he had been separated from her for a few moments in the throng and had found her shrinking in terror from the insolence of a vulgar dandy. She had never forgotten the white anger in Mario Provana's face as he took the scared wretch by the collar and flung him towards the edge of the platform. She never could forget the rage in that dark face, and it had come back to her in after years in visions of unspeakable horror. He who was so kind could be so terrible. So kind! Now in her lonely wanderings it was of his kindness she thought most, his fond indulgence in those days when he had made the world new for her, days when she had looked back at her long apprenticeship to poverty—the daily lesson in the noble art of keeping up appearances, and Grannie's monotonous wailings over cruel destiny—and wondered if this idolised wife could be the same creature as the penniless girl in the shabby lodgings. She knew now that the devoted husband of that happy year was the man who was worthy of something more than gratitude and obedience, something more than duty, worthy of the best and truest love that a good woman could feel for a good man. This was the noble lover. Wherever she went in that city of great memories the shadow of the past went with her. He was always there—she heard his voice, and the thoughts and feelings of years ago were more real than the consciousness of to-day. Forgotten things had come back. The fever-dream had ended: and in the cold light of an awakened conscience she knew and understood the noble friend and companion she had slighted and lost.

Lady Susan was a somewhat exacting visitor; but it was years since she had seen the inside of a dining-room before luncheon, so Vera's mornings were her own. The half-past twelve o'clock déjeuner even appeared painfully early to Susie, though she contrived to be present at that luxurious meal, where there were often amusing droppers-in, lads from the embassies, soldiers in picturesque uniforms, literary people and artistic people, mostly Americans, people whom Susie could not afford to miss.

Vera's mornings were her own, but she was obliged to do the afternoon drive in the Pincio gardens and along the Corso with Lady Susan, and after the drive she could creep away for an hour to her too-spacious saloon where all the gods and goddesses of Olympus looked down upon her from the tapestry, and sit and dream in the gloaming—or brood over a new novel by Matilda Seraio, her reading-lamp making a speck of light in a world of shadows.

Here, by the red log-fire, where the pine-cones hissed and sputtered, the Irish terrier was her happy companion, laying his head upon her knee, or thrusting his black nose into her hand, now and then, to show her that there was somebody who loved her, and only refraining from leaping on her lap by the good manners inculcated in his puppyhood by an accomplished canine educator.

Sometimes she would throw down her book, snatch up a fur coat from the sofa where it lay, and go out through the glass door that opened into the gardens; and then, with Boroo bounding and leaping round her, letting off volleys of joyful barks, she would run to the lonely garden at the back of the villa, where there was a long terrace on a ridge of high ground shaded with umbrella pines, and with a statue here and there in a niche cut in the wall of century-old ilex.

The solitary walk with her dog in a dark garden always had a quieting effect upon her nerves—like the morning ramble in the outskirts of Rome. To be alone, to be able to think, soothed her. The life without thought was done with. Now to think was to be consoled. Even memories that brought tears had comfort in them.

"What can I do for him but remember him and regret him?" she thought. "It is my only atonement. If what Francis Symeon told me is true and the dead are near us, he knows and understands. He knows, and he forgives."

Sad, sweet thoughts, that came with a rush of tears!

These quiet hours helped her to bear the evening gaieties, the evening splendours. She went everywhere that Claude wanted her to go, gave as many parties as he liked, déjeuners, dinners, suppers after opera or theatre, anything. Her gold was poured out like water. The Newmarket horses were running in the Roman races; the Leicestershire hunters were ridden to death on the Campagna. Claude Rutherford was more talked about, and more admired, than any young man in Rome. He laughed sometimes, remembering the old books, and told them he was like Julius Cæsar in his adolescence, a "harmless trifler." Claude Rutherford was happy; and he thought that his wife was happy also. Certainly she had been happy at Disbrowe less than half a year ago; and there had been nothing since then to distress her. The long rambles of which Susan told him, the evening seclusion, meant nothing. No doubt she was morbid; she had always been morbid. If she had a grief of any kind she loved to brood upon it.

"What grief can she have?" Susan asked. "There never was such a perfect life. She has everything."

"I don't know. We have no children. She may long for a child."

"Do you feel the want of children?" Susan asked bluntly.

"Yes. I should have liked a child. Our houses are silent—infernally silent. A house without children seems under a curse, somehow."

Susan looked at him with open-eyed wonder. This trivial cousin of hers, who seemed to live only for ephemeral delights, this man to sigh for offspring, to want his futile career echoed by a son. He who was neither soldier nor senator, who had no rag of reputation to bequeath: what should he want with an heir? And to want childish voices in his home—to complain of loneliness! He who was never alone!

Mrs. Bellenden had not been invited to the Villa Provana after the night when Susie had made her protest, nor had Claude urged his wife to invite her. Mrs. Bellenden had begun to be talked about in Rome very much as she had been talked about in London. The noblest of the Roman palaces had not opened their Cyclopean doors to her. There were certain afternoons when all that was most distinguished in Roman Society crossed those noble thresholds, as by right—went in and came out again, not much happier or richer in ideas, perhaps, for the visit, but just a shade more conscious of superiority.

Mrs. Bellenden, driving up and down the Corso, saw the carriages waiting, and scowled at them as she went by. Mrs. Bellenden was not bien vue in Rome. The painters and sculptors raved about her, and she had to give sittings—for head and bust—to several of them. She was one man's Juno, and another man's Helen of Troy. Her portrait, by a famous American painter, was to be the rage at next year's picture show. If to be worshipped for her beauty could satisfy a woman, Mrs. Bellenden might have been content; but she was not.

Her exclusion from those three or four monumental palaces made her feel herself an outsider; and she bristled with fury when no more cards of invitation came from the Villa Provana.

"I suppose that white rag of a woman is jealous," she thought; but she had just so much womanly pride left in her as to refrain from asking Claude Rutherford why his wife ignored her.

Lady Susan had not even spoken of Mrs. Bellenden after the night when she had delivered herself of a friendly warning. But although she did not talk to Vera of the siren, she had plenty to say to other people about her, and plenty to hear.

"I hope that foolish cousin of mine is not carrying on with that odious woman," she had said tentatively to more than one great lady.

"Why, my dear creature, everybody knows that he is making an idiot of himself about her. She is riding his hunters to death; and she made an exhibition of herself at the races last Sunday when one of Rutherford's horses won by half a length, putting her arms round the winner's neck and shaking hands with the jockey. The King and Queen and all the Quirinal party were looking at her. She is the kind of woman who always advertises an intrigue. After all, I believe she is not half so bad as people think her; only she can't keep an affair quiet. She must always play to the gallery."

Susie shook her head, with a sigh that was almost a groan.

"Oh, my poor Vera, so sweet, so pure, so ethereal."

"That's where it is, my dear," said her friend. "Men don't care for those ethereal women—long. Women hold men by their vices, not by their virtues."

CHAPTER XXVIII

It was the end of February, and the Roman villa was soon to be left to cobwebs and custodians. The Piazza d'Ispagnia and the broad steps of the Trinità were alive with spring flowers, and the air had the soft sweetness of an English April on the verge of May. White lilac and Maréchal Niel roses were in all the shops; bright yellow jonquils, and red and blue anemones, filled the baskets of rustic hawkers at the street corners. Rome's innumerable fountains plashed and sparkled in the sun; and Rome's delicious atmosphere, at once soft, caressing, and inspiriting, made the heart glad.

The carnival was over, and the season was waning. Lady Susan Amphlett was never tired of telling people that she had had the best time she had ever had in her life—excursions to Naples, Florence, and all the cities of Tuscany; motor drives to every place worth seeing within fifty miles of Rome; a midnight party with fireworks in the Baths of Caracalla; a dance by torchlight, and a champagne supper, in the Colosseum. In this latter festivity the strangeness of the scene had been too exciting, and the revel had almost degenerated into an orgy.

"My cousin is simply wonderful at inventing things," Susie, playing her accustomed part of chorus, told people, "and he gets permissions and privileges that no one else would dare ask for."

The end had come. To-morrow's meet at the tomb of Cecilia Metella was the last of the season; and Mr. and Mrs. Rutherford were to start for London on the following day—a long journey in a lit-salon, with the monotony of dinner-wagon meals to make the journey odious.

"If one could only take a box of bath buns and foie-gras sandwiches!" sighed Susie. "With those and my tea basket I should be utterly happy; but the same insipid omelette, and the same tough chicken and endive salad, for eight and forty hours! Quelle corvée!"

It was the last morning, a lovely morning. Sunshine was flooding the great rooms, and making even the tapestried walls look gay. Susan, for once in her life, came down to breakfast, in a black satin négligé, with a valenciennes cap that made her look enchanting.

"I wanted to see Claude in pink—Roman pink," she said, looking at the slim, tall figure in Leicestershire clothes. "You ought always to wear those clothes," said Susie, clapping her hands, as at the reception of a favourite actor. "They make you bewilderingly beautiful. Now I know why you are so keen on hunting."

"Do you think any man cares how his coat is cut, or who made his boots, when he may be dead at the bottom of a ditch before the end of the run?" Claude said, laughing. "Some of the best days I have had have been in rat-catcher clothes."

He was radiant with pleasant expectations. He could do without Leicestershire hedges, and hundred-acre fields, and all the perfection of English fox-hunting. To-day the Campagna would be good enough—with its rough ground and yawning chasms, wider and deeper than the worst of the Somersetshire rhines. The Campagna would be good enough. He was in high spirits, and he was singing a wicked little French song as his man buckled on his spurs, a little song that Gavroche and his companions of the Paris gutters had been singing all the winter.

Lady Susan drove to the meet in one of the Provana carriages, picking up a couple of lively American friends on her way. Vera excused herself from going with her friend, and went off for a ramble with the Irish terrier, much to Susie's disgust.

"You like that rough-haired beast's company better than mine," she complained.

"Only when I want to be alone with memories and dreams."

"You are growing too horridly morbid, Vera. I am afraid you have taken up religion. It's very sweet of you, darling, but it's the way to lose your husband. Religion is the one thing a husband won't put up with. He hates it worse than a bad cook."

"No, I have not taken up religion."

"Then it's spiritualism, which is just as bad. It is all Mr. Symeon's doing. You live in a world of ghosts."

"There are ghosts that one loves. But there will be no ghosts where I shall be walking to-day. Only wild flowers and spring sunshine."

She watched Susan take her seat in the carriage—a vision of coquettish prettiness and expensive clothes. Susan's husband had gone back to London and Newmarket some time since, not being able to "stick" Rome after the Craven meeting. He had enjoyed some good runs with the Roman pack, and he had been shown St. Peter's and the Colosseum, and had played bridge with famous American players at Claude Rutherford's club; so what more was there for him to do?

Vera and her dog went to the Campagna by a roundabout way that avoided that noble road between the tombs of the mighty, by which the hunting men and their followers would go. She roamed in rural lanes, where violets and wild hyacinths were scenting the warm air, and sat in a solitary nook, musing over a volume of Carducci, while Boroo hunted the hedge and scratched the bank, in a wild quest of the rats that haunted his dreams as he sprawled on the Persian prayer-rug before the fire.

It was late afternoon when Vera left the quiet lane and turned into the dusty road that led to the tomb of Cecilia Metella; lingering on her way to admire a team of those magnificent fawn-coloured and cream-white oxen, whose beauty always went to her heart. She recalled Carducci's lovely sonnet, "Il Bove," those exquisite lines which Giulia Provana had repeated to her as they drove along the rural roads near San Marco, and which she learned from her friend's lips before she had ever seen a printed page of the Italian's verse.

All signs of horse and hound had disappeared before she came to Cecilia's tomb; there were no people in carriages, no loitering peasants or British bicyclists, waiting about on the chance of a ringing run, which would bring pack and field sweeping round the wide plain in sight of the starting-point. There was no one—only the vast expanse of greyish-green herbage, with here and there a heap of ruins that had been a palace or a tomb, and here and there a red-capped shepherd and his flock. Vera strolled along the grass, taking no heed of vehicles or foot-passengers on the higher level of the Appian Way. She had her time chiefly engaged in keeping Boroo to heel, where only duty could keep him, instinct and a passionate inclination urging him to make a raid on the sheep. Distance would have been as nothing. He would have crossed the expanse of rugged ground in a flash, if Vera's frown and Vera's threatening voice had not subjugated that which, next to fighting, was a master passion.

She was absorbed in her endeavour to keep the faithful beast under control, when the sound of laughter on the road above made her come to a sudden stop, and look, and listen.

She knew the laugh. It had once been music in her ears. That frank, joyous laugh, the ripple of gladness that defied the Fates, had once been an element in the glamour that cast its spell over her life. But now the laugh jarred: there was a false note in the music.

A woman was riding at Claude's bridle-hand; their horses walking slowly, close together; and he was leaning over her to listen and to talk; his hand was on her saddle, and their heads were very near, as he bent to speak and to listen. Vera could hear their voices in the clear air of a Roman sundown; but not the words that they were speaking. One thing only was plain, that after each scrap of talk there came that ripple of joyous laughter from the man; and then, after a little more talk, with heads still closer, the boisterous mirth of a reckless woman.

The woman was Mrs. Bellenden. What other rider after those Roman hounds had a figure like hers, the exquisite lines, the curves of bust and throat that the sculptors were talking about?

The woman was Mrs. Bellenden, in one of her amusing moods. That was her charm, as Susan Amphlett had explained it to Vera. She made men laugh.

"That is her secret," said Susan; "she remembers all the stories her madcap husband told her when she was young and they shocked her. She dishes them up with a spice of her own, and she makes men laugh. She can keep them dangling for a year and hold them at arm's length; while a mere beauty would bore them after a month, unless she came to terms. That's her secret. But, of course, it comes to the same in the end. Such a woman's affairs must have the inevitable conclusion. Her pigeons last longer in the plucking, and she gets more feathers out of them. You had better look after your husband before he goes too far!"

Nothing had moved Vera from her placid acceptance of fate. "I suppose my husband must amuse himself with a flirtation now and then, when his racing stable begins to pall," she said.

"Vera, you and Claude are drifting apart," exclaimed Susie, with a horrified air.

It was a gruesome discovery for Chorus, who had gone about the world singing the praises of this ideal couple—these exquisite married lovers—and talking about Eden and Arcadia.

Vera smiled an enigmatic smile.

Drifting apart! No, it was not drifting apart. It was a cleft as wide and deep as one of those yawning chasms on the Campagna, that the sportsmen boasted of jumping with their Northamptonshire hunters.

This was Vera's last day in Rome. They started on the homeward journey next morning, but instead of travelling with her husband by the Paris express, she took it into her head to linger on the way. She stopped at Pisa, she stopped at Porto Fino, she stopped at Genoa; and last of all, she stopped at San Marco to look at Mario Provana's grave.

"I may never see Italy again," she said, when Susan tried to dissuade her. "I have a presentiment that I shall never see this dear land any more."

"For my part I should not be sorry if I knew I was never coming back to the villa," her husband answered. "It is too big for a house to live in. It must soon fall to the fate of other Roman palaces, and become one of the sights of the city; to be shown for two lire a head to Dr. Lunn and his fellow-travellers."

Vera had her way. In this respect she and her husband were essentially modern. They never interfered with each other's caprices. He travelled by the Paris express, and stayed at the Ritz just long enough to see the latest impropriety at the Palais Royal, and it happened curiously that Mrs. Bellenden was travelling by the same train on the same day, stopping at the same hotel, attended by a young lady who would have been faultless as a dame de compagnie except for a chronic neuralgia, which often compelled her to isolate herself in her hotel bedroom. Vera went along the lovely coast with Susie, who declared herself delighted to escape the monotony of the dinner-wagon, and to see some of the most delicious spots in Italy with her dearest Vee, to which monosyllable friendship had reduced Vera's name. In an age that has substituted the telegraph and the telephone for the art of letter-writing, it is well that names should be reduced to the minimum, and that our favourite politician should be "Joe," our greatest general "Bobs," and our dearest friend M. or N. rather than Margherita or Naomi.

Vera showed Lady Susan all the things that were best worth seeing in Genoa and the neighbourhood, and they lingered at Porto Fino, and other lovely nooks along that undulating coastline; garden villages dipping their edges into the blue water, and flushed with the pink glory of blossoming peach trees, raining light petals upon the young grass. It was the loveliest season of the Italian spring; and all along their way the world was glad with flowers. They missed nothing but the birds that were making grey old England glad before the flowers, but which here had been sacrificed to the young Italian's idea of sport.

There was only one spot to which Vera went alone, and that was Mario Provana's grave. Happily, Susan had forgotten that he was buried at San Marco; and she wondered that Vera should have arranged to break the journey and stop a night at a place where there was absolutely nothing to see.

Certainly it was not very far from Genoa; but a slow train and a headache made the journey seem an eternity to the impatient Susan, and when San Marco came she was very glad of her dinner and bed, and to have her hair taken down, after it had been hurting her all the way, and to no end, as she was utterly indifferent to the opinion of a couple of natives, the provincial Italian being no more to her than a red-skinned son of the Five Nations or a New Zealander.

Vera was able to spend an hour in the yew tree enclosure in the morning freshness, between six and seven. She had telegraphed her order for a hundred white roses to the San Marco florist the day before, and the flowers were ready for her in a light, spacious basket, in the hall of the hotel, when she came downstairs in the dim sunrise.

"It is the last time," she said to herself, as she covered the great marble slab with her roses, and stooped to lay cold lips on the cold stone. "Giulia—Mario," she murmured tenderly, with lingering lips.

"I am not afraid," she said to herself. "I know that he has forgiven me."

Maid and footman and luggage went by the morning train; and half an hour after Vera and her friend left San Marco, in a carriage that was to take them to Ventimiglia. By this means they had the drive in the morning sunshine, and escaped the long wait at the frontier, only entering the dismal station five minutes before their train left Italy.

They spent that night in Marseilles, where Susan Amphlett insisted upon seeing the Cannebière by lamplight; and they were in Paris on the following evening, and in London the next day.

"And now you are going to begin a splendid season," said Susie, "in this dear old house. The rooms look mere pigeon-holes after your Roman villa; but there's no place like London. And I really think Claude is right. The Villa Provana is much too big, and just a wee bit eerie. It suggests ghosts, if one does not see them. One of those sweet young Bersaglieri told me that your husband's father made a man fight a duel to the death with him in one of those weird upper rooms; and that the stamping of their feet and the rattle of their rapiers is heard at a quarter past two on every fifteenth of November. When I heard the story I felt rather glad I did not come to you till December. Aren't you pleased to be home, Vera, in these cosy drawing-rooms?"

Everything in life is a question of contrast, and after the Villa Provana the drawing-room in Portland Place, with its five long windows and perspective of other drawing-rooms through a curtained archway, looked as snug as a suburban parlour.

"Aren't you glad to be home?" persisted Susan.

"No, Susie. I would rather have spent the rest of my life in Italy."

"Oh, I suppose you prefer the climate. You are one of those people who care about the state of the sky. I don't. I like people, and shops, and theatres, and the opera at Covent Garden. Milan or Naples may be the proper place for music; but we get all the best singers. Don't think me ungrateful, Vera. I revelled in Rome. A place where one can go, from buying gloves and fans in the Corso, to gloating over the circus where the Christian martyrs fought with lions, must be full of charm for anybody with a mind. Rome made a student of me. I read two historical primers, and a novel of Marion Crawford's; besides dipping into Augustus Hare's delightful books. I haven't been so studious since I attended the Cambridge extension lectures, with my poor old governess, who used to amuse us by going to sleep, and giving herself away by nodding. Her poor old bonnet used to waggle till it made even the lecturer laugh."

Susie went off to join Mr. Amphlett in Northamptonshire; but she was to establish herself at the little house in Green Street directly after Easter, and then she and her dearest Vee must spend their lives together.

Vera was not sorry to speed the parting guest. She had had rather too much of Susie in that month of Rome; for though she had lived her own life, in a great measure, there was always the sense that Susie was there, and that she ought to give more of her time to her friend.

She had suffered one grief in coming to London, for on landing at Dover she had to part with the Irish terrier, who was led off by a famous dog-doctor's subordinate, to spend six months in isolation, which was to be made as pleasant to him as such imprisonment could be made to an intelligent dog, warmly attached to a mistress who had raised him from the canine to the human by her companionship. Boroo was to pass six months in quarantine before he could stretch himself on the prayer-rug at his mistress's feet, and roll upon his back in an ecstasy of contentment. Boroo might be made comfortable in the retreat, as one of the favourites of fortune; but Boroo would not be happy without his mistress, and the first telephonic communication from the canine hotel informed Mrs. Rutherford that her faithful friend had refused food and was very restless. The functionary who gave this information assured her that this was only a passing phase in dog-life, and that the terrier would be happier next day. And the account next day was comparatively cheerful; the terrier had eaten a little sheep's head and was livelier. Vera hated the law which deprived her of the only friend who had comforted her in hours of deepest dejection. The dog's welcome after every parting, the dog's abounding love, had given a new zest to life. Was there any other love left her now quite as real as this? Her husband, her enthusiastic friend Susan, all the train of affectionate aunts and cousins—the girl cousins who came to her to relate their love affairs; the baby cousins who kissed her when their nurses told them, holding up cherry lips, and smiling with sweet blue eyes—three generations of Disbrowes! Was there one among them all whose love she could believe in as she could in her Irish terrier?

Six months without Boroo! It was a dreary time to think of. Boroo was the only creature who could take her mind away from herself and her life's history. He had given her the beatitude of loving and being loved, without romance—without passion—without looking before or after: and, realising the difference this dumb creature made, she could but think with melancholy longing of what a child would have meant in her life.

And now began the familiar round in the familiar house, with the Disbrowes gathering strong as of old to help and to suggest—to bring to Vera's parties the few great people who had not yet discovered that a Mrs. Rutherford whose wealth had come out of the City could be so particularly attractive, or could give parties that had always a touch of originality that made them worth one's while. These mighty ones told each other that it was the absence of conventionality that made Vera's house so agreeable; while Lady Susan, still playing her part of Chorus, told the mighty ones that it was because her cousin was a poet's daughter, and made an atmosphere of poetry round her.

"Vera lives in a world of dreams," she said, "and we are all dreamers, though the horrid everyday world comes between us and our fairest visions. I think that's why we love her."

A Princess of the blood royal happened to meet Vera at this time, and became one of her most ardent admirers, lunching or dining in Portland Place at least once a week, and visiting Mrs. Rutherford in her opera box. She had heard of the Roman villa and the Roman parties.

"I shall spend next January in Rome on purpose to see more of you," she said, upon which Claude, who was present, begged that her Royal Highness would make the Villa Provana her home whenever she came to the Eternal City; an invitation which her Royal Highness graciously promised to remember.

"My sweet girl, you are on the crest of the wave," Lady Okehampton told her niece. "You were never so much the fashion as this year. You ought to be proud of your social success."

"I wish I had my dog out of quarantine," was all Vera said.

"Get another dog—a Pekinese lion; ever so much smarter than your rough brute."

The season wore through somehow in perpetual gaieties which the wife hated, but which were essential to the husband's well-being. He had all the racing world, and never missed an important meeting; but when there was no racing he wanted dinner-parties, or crowded evenings, abroad or at home. Later there would be Cowes, where he had a new yacht just out of the builder's yard, waiting to beat every boat in the Channel.

He did not often look at his wife's visiting list, being content to give her the names of the men who were to be asked to her dinners, taking it for granted that they would be asked. Every evening party was more or less an omnium gatherum; and about these he asked no questions—but more than once, between March and June, he had suggested that Mrs. Bellenden should be invited to dinner—to some smallish semi-literary and artistic dinner—and this suggestion being ignored, he had advised her being included in one of the big dinner-parties, where the mighty ones had been bidden to meet the royal Princess.

"I don't think that would do," Vera answered coldly.

"You forget that Mrs. Bellenden is one of the handsomest women in London," Claude answered with some touch of temper, "and that people like to meet a well-known beauty."

"I'm afraid Mrs. Bellenden is rather too well known. You had better give a dinner at 'Claridge's' or the 'Ritz,' Claude, and let Susan do hostess for you. Susie would enjoy it."

"I suppose it will come to that," said Claude. "I'll take one of your Wagner nights—when I know you'll be happy."

Lady Susan having warned her friend against the siren, was not so disloyal as to play hostess at a Bohemian dinner.

"No, Claude," she said when the idea was mooted. "I have never been prudish, but I draw the line at Mrs. Bellenden."

Her cousin shrugged his shoulders, and left the room with a snatch of a French chanson, which was his most forcible expression of temper. The light tenor voice, the gay French verse, harmonised with the nature in which there were no depths.

Goodwood was once more imminent, and Cowes was in the near future, when Vera sent out cards for her last evening party, which would be one of the last of the season, on the eve of the exodus of smart London. The Princess Hermione was to be at the party—and this royal lady was like that more famous heroine of the nursery, who rode her white horse to Banbury Cross in a musical ride; for, like that famous lady, the Princess expected to have music wherever she went, music, and of the best, for the royal Hermione was a connoisseur, and herself no mean performer on the violoncello. A famous baritone and an equally famous mezzo-soprano were to sing during the evening, in the inner drawing-room, not in a formal way with programmes and rout seats, for people to be packed in rows, to sit there from start to finish till, in our elegant twentieth-century English, they were "fed up" with squalling.

Everything was to be informal; and the people who did not want music would have space enough in the larger rooms and on the staircase to babble and to flirt as they chose; while that inner drawing-room would be, as it were, a sanctuary for the elect, a temple of the god of harmony.

Vera stood at the door of the larger drawing-room receiving her guests, from ten to half-past, when the Princess Hermione, who had just arrived, put her arm through her hostess's and asked eagerly:

"Did you get him?" Signor Pergolesi, the baritone, understood.

"Yes, ma'am, he is in the little drawing-room with Madame Rondolana, waiting to sing to you!"

"Take me there this moment, Vera!" and hooked by the royal arm in a crumpled glove, Vera led the Princess and her lady-in-waiting through the babbling crowd to the sanctuary where the elect were beginning to bore each other while they waited for the first song.

Herr Mainz was at the piano ready to accompany the two singers whose engagement he had negotiated. At all concerts of this clever gentleman's arranging it seemed to some people as if the artists were puppets, and that he pulled the string that set them going all through the performance. To-night, however, there was to be less string-pulling and more sans façon, or rather it was Princess Hermione who was to pull the string.

She certainly lost no time in telling Madame Rondolana what she wanted her to sing, and she kept that brilliant vocalist rolling out song after song in the rich abundance of a mezzo-soprano that nothing could tire. She sang song after song, at the Princess's nod; Italian, German, Swedish, nay, even English, with an ease that testified to power without limit. The baritone looked and listened with languid interest, not offended, for he knew that his turn would come, and that when once the Princess started him she would never let him leave off. He sat near the piano in an easy attitude; not listening, but turning his thoughts inward, and making up his mind as to what songs he would sing. Wagner? Yes. Bizet? Yes, but in any case "Die beiden Grenadiere" as a finish—and then those massive folding doors, that were shutting out the babblers, should be flung wide open, and he would sing to the whole of the company. He could stop their talking—those two grenadiers were infallible.

"Viz dat song I alvays knock zaim in ze Ole Ken' Road," he used to tell his friends.

At eleven o'clock there came a kind of subtle sense of something wanting, even beyond that exquisite music; and Lady Okehampton whispered to her niece that it was time the Princess went to supper, and that Claude must take her downstairs. Vera went in search of him. The crowd in the biggest drawing-room had thinned, and she was able to look for her husband—but without success; and she went through the other rooms to the spacious landing, in which direction most people were drifting, and there she met a perturbed spirit in the form of Susan Amphlett.

"What's the matter, Susie? Is there anything wrong?"

"Wrong!" cried Susie. "I call it simply disgusting. How could you be such a fool?"

"What have I done?"

"To ask that horrid woman, and with your Princess for the guest of the evening! She ain't prudish; but I fancy she'll think it a bit steep to find herself rubbing shoulders with Mrs. Bellenden."

"I have not invited Mrs. Bellenden."

"Someone else has, then. Or else she has come like the lady at Cannes, invitée ou non."

"Is Mrs. Bellenden here?"

"Yes, in the supper-room, in a mob of admirers. Claude took her down to supper."

"That's rather tiresome," Vera answered quietly, "for he ought to take the Princess, and I can't keep her waiting. Do be kind, Susie, and go and tell him he must come to the music-room this minute. The Princess ought to have gone down before anybody, and now you say there's a mob."

"A perfect bear-garden of greedy beasts. I don't believe there'll be an ortolan left by the time she comes. Anyhow, I'll make it hot for Claude!" and Susie hurried off, elbowing a desperate way through the crowd on the stairs. "Mon dieu, quel four!" she muttered.

Vera went back to the sanctuary, impounding her uncle Okehampton on the way, in case she found the friendly Hermione indisposed to wait for her host.

She found her Princess with a dark and angry brow, standing near the door, whispering to her attendant lady. She had the look of a Princess who had been "almost waiting," and who did not like the sensation. She heard that Mr. Rutherford was making his way through the crowd to attend upon her, with an air of supreme indifference.

"Lord Okehampton is one of my old friends," she said, and took his offered arm without looking at Vera. "Mr. Rutherford can bring Pauline," she said, as they moved away.

Pauline was the lady-in-waiting, a colourless spinster of seven-and-thirty, who loved everything the Princess loved, and hated everything she hated, and who dressed like the Princess, only much worse.

Lord Okehampton made himself vastly agreeable, and the mob, seeing the royal brow under the tiara, made way for the couple, and there was a table found for the royal lady in an agreeable position, and there were ortolans and peaches without stint; but when Claude came presently with the Honourable Pauline he received a snub so unmistakable that he was glad to carry his Honourable companion to the remotest corner of the room, where he gave her a sumptuous supper, and had the consolation of her sympathy.

"The Princess has a heart of gold," she told him, "but her temper is dreadful sometimes, and life is rather difficult with her."

"Not quite a bed of roses," said Claude.

"It would be ungrateful of me to call it a bed of stinging-nettles," said Pauline, "because as there are five of us at home, all unmarried, I have to do something; and the Princess is wonderfully kind, and then she is so clever and accomplished. She does everything well; but music is her passion."

"That's how I made my mistake," said Claude. "I thought her enjoyment of her own particular baritone would have lasted longer, and that I should have been in attendance before she was inclined to move."

"The Princess has a good appetite," said Pauline, discussing her fourth ortolan, "and one really does get very hungry at an evening party. Music is so exhausting. I hope that dear Pergolesi and Madame Rondolana are having something."

"Our good friend Mainz will take care of that."

"Apropos," said Pauline. "There is a lady here I am rather curious about. We passed her on the stairs. Mrs. Bellenden. Gloriously handsome, and all that; but frankly, Mr. Rutherford, I was just a wee, wee bit surprised to see her in your wife's house, especially to meet the Princess. I hardly like to speak of such things; but has she not been just a little talked about lately? Of course, I know she went everywhere two years ago; but just lately people have said things; and one has not run against her at the best houses."

"Of course she has been talked about," answered Claude, with his frank laugh. "Meteors are talked about. A woman so exceptionally beautiful is like Halley's Comet. People are sure to talk about her; and the ill-natured talkers will make scandal about her. Poor Mrs. Bellenden! Quite a harmless person, I assure you; open-hearted, generous, impulsive—a trifle imprudent, perhaps, as these impulsive women always are."

The lady-in-waiting had supped too well to be ill-natured.

"I am so glad you have told me. I shall tell the Princess that there is no foundation for any of the stories we have heard about poor Mrs. Bellenden," she said, as they left the supper-room.

The sanctuary was full of people when Lord Okehampton took the Princess back, after a leisurely supper, during which they had talked over old friends and things that had happened a dozen years ago, when Okehampton was Master of the Horse. The Princess had recovered her temper, and was ready to enjoy her favourite Pergolesi; but Vera, who had not left the music-room, looked white and weary; and the kindly Hermione chid her for not having followed her to the supper-room. All the best people were now gathered in the inner drawing-room; some for the Princess, and some for the baritone; and only the royal chair was vacant when the royal lady reappeared. Pergolesi chuckled at the thought that Rondolana had lavished her octave and a half of perfection on the chosen few; while he had all the finest tiaras, and the largest display of shoulders and diamonds for his audience.

Hermione beckoned him to her side, and they discussed what songs he should sing; she ordering, but he making her order what he wanted and had made up his mind about.

"I should like to finish viz 'Die beiden Grenadiere,'" he said in his broken English. "I think it is one of your favourites, ma'am?"

"Je l'adore."

Song after song was received with enthusiasm. Herr Mainz played a brilliant "Mazourka de Salon," while the baritone rested and whispered with the Princess, and when the silvery chimes of an Italian eight-day clock announced midnight, the great doors were thrown open and Pergolesi hurled his splendid voice upon the crowd in the outer room.

A phrase or two, and the babble of three hundred voices had become silence; and when the song was done the crowd melted away, still in comparative stillness, while Vera stood on the landing to see them pass, as if she were holding a review. No one wanted to begin talking after that stupendous song. People had stayed later than they intended, till it was too late to go on to other, and perhaps better, houses. The Princess had gone out by a second staircase, which had been kept clear for her, with Pergolesi and Okehampton to escort her downstairs, and Claude Rutherford to put her into her carriage. She went off in a charming mood, but could not refrain from a stab at the last.

"Your wife's party has been perfect," she said, "but the company just a little mixed. I suspect you of having introduced the Bohemian element, in the shape of that handsome lady whom everybody has been talking about."

There were lingerers after that, and the party was not over till one o'clock. The last guest strolled into the pale grey night as Big Ben tolled the first hour of day. Claude followed his wife up the broad staircase, where the heated atmosphere was heavy with the scent of arum lilies, and the daturas that hung their white bells in all the corners. She was moving slowly, tired and languid after the long evening, and she never looked back. He followed her to the door of her room; but she stopped upon the threshold, turned and faced him, ashy pale in her white gown, like a ghost.

"Good-bye," she said, with a face of stone.

"Vera, for God's sake! What's the matter?"

"Good-bye," she repeated, and, as he moved towards her, she drew back suddenly, so quickly that he was unprepared for the movement, and shut the door in his face.

He heard the key turning in the lock, shrugged his shoulders, and walked slowly along the gallery to his own room, not the room that had been Mario Provana's dressing-room.

"Some ass has been telling her things," he muttered to himself.

And then he thought of Mrs. Bellenden's appearance that night, in a gown of gold tissue, and a diamond tiara. She had been too insolently splendid in her overweening beauty, too tremendous, too suggestive of Cleopatra at Actium, a woman who lived upon the ruin of men.

What wife, who cared for her husband, could help being angry if she saw him near such a creature?

And he had been near her all the night. He had whispered with her in corners, hung over her perfumed shoulders, followed her close as her shadow, sat with her in a nest of tropical flowers in the balcony, instead of moving about among his guests.

He had taken her down to the supper-room, first among the first, neglecting duchesses and a princess of the blood royal for her sake. No doubt that malicious little wretch Susan Amphlett had been watching him, and had reported all his misdoings to Vera.

"What does it matter?" he said to himself. "My life was growing unbearable. The gloom was closing round me like a funeral pall. Kate was my only refuge. I have never been in love with her; but she stops me from thinking."

That was the secret. Mrs. Bellenden had been his Nepenthe, when the common round of pleasures had lost their power to make him forget.

Mrs. Bellenden was like strong drink, like opium or hashish. She killed thought. She filled the vacant spaces in his life—the Stygian swamps where black thoughts wandered in space, like angry devils. Her exactions, her quarrels, their partings and reunions, the agitations and turmoil of her existence, had filled his life. When he banged the hall door of the bijou house in Brown Street behind him after one of their stormy farewells he knew that he would go back to her in a week. He tramped the adjacent Park across and across, along and along, in a fury, and thanked God that he had done with "that harpy"; but he knew that he would have to go back to the harpy, to be reconciled again, with oaths and kisses and tears, and to quarrel again, and to obey her orders, and go here or there as she made him. The most degrading slavery to a wicked woman was better than the great silent house and the horror that inhabited it.

His wife had her consolations, nay, even her hysterical delights. She could shut herself in her white temple with the spirits of her worshipped dead. She heard voices. Death now hardly counted with her, neither Death nor Time. Saint Francis of Assisi was as near her as Robert Browning. Shakespeare was no more remote than Henry Irving. She was mad.

The emptiness, the silence, the gloom, were killing him. If there had been children, all might have been different. The past would have been forgotten in those new and forward-looking lives. His sons and daughters would not have let him remember past things. And Vera would not have had time for morbid thoughts, for nursing dark memories. Her children would have made her forget.

He had some kind of explanation with her on the day after the party, and made some feeble kind of apology. But she was cold and dumb; she expressed no anger, neither complained nor reproached him; she shed no tears. She stood before him in her white silence, still beautiful, but with a pale, unearthly beauty that chilled his heart. All the force of the old love swept back upon him; and his heart ached with a passion of pity and regret. He seized her by the shoulders—so frail, so wasted, since last year—and looked at her with despairing eyes. "Vera, you are killing yourself by inches. What can I do? What can I do for you? Shall we go away? Ever so far away? to new worlds—to places where the stupendous phenomena of Nature, and the things that men have made, will take us out of ourselves? There are things in this world so tremendous that they can kill thought. The Zambesi, the Aztec cities of Mexico, the great Wall of China."

"You are very good," she answered, coldly but not unkindly—rather with a weary indifference, as of a soul too tired to feel or think. "I am quite contented here. My life in this house suits me as well as any life could."

"In this house?" he cried.

"Yes, in this house. I am not alone here. But I don't want to keep you here if the house makes you unhappy. You had better go away, Claude; go anywhere you like, as you like. I shall not complain."

"Are you giving me a letter of license?" he asked, with a harsh laugh. "Is your love quite dead?"

"Everything is dead," she answered.

He could get no more from her, and he left her in anger.

"You had better divorce me and marry Francis Symeon," he said, "and cultivate spookism together."

The natural sequel to a scene like that was a little dinner at Claridge's with Mrs. Bellenden, and an evening at the silliest musical comedy to be seen and heard in London.

His wife had given him a letter of license. She had ceased to love him. He made himself so disagreeable to Mrs. Bellenden by dinner-time that the meal was eaten in sullen silence; and the Magnum of Veuve Pommeroy was hardly enough for two, for when Mrs. Bellenden was in a rage her glass had to be filled very often, and the waiters at the smart hotels knew her ways. The waiters worshipped her. "She tips as handsome as she tipples," had been said of her by one of them.

CHAPTER XXIX

Everything was dead. That had been Vera's answer when Claude asked despairingly if love was dead. The words were in her mind now as she stood alone in the room where her poets, and her actors, and her philosophers, looked at her from the white walls, and where the sound of the great hall door closing heavily as her husband shut it behind him was still in her ears.

Had he gone for ever? Was it indeed the end? Could love that had begun in ecstasy close in this grey calm? She felt neither sorrow nor anger. Everything was dead. She stood among the ruins of her life, feeling as a child might feel when the house she has built of cards shatters suddenly and falls at her feet. Everything was over. She had no thought of building another house; no desire to patch up a broken life and begin again. Perhaps her husband loved her still, and it was the gloom of this haunted house that had driven him to seek distraction in a baser love. It was her fault, perhaps, and she ought to be sorry for him. Poor Claude! She remembered his gaiety. The airy mockery that had enchanted her, the quick wit that had struck fire and light out of dull things. She remembered the joyous nature, the light laughter, the inexhaustible energy which made difficult things—in the way of sport—seem easy. Yes, they had been happy, utterly happy in the life of the moment, shutting out every thought that was irksome, every memory that hurt. And it was all over and dead, and she had nothing left but the shadows in this room, the dead faces, the words of those who were not. That scriptural phrase had always moved her. "He was not."

Her afternoons in Mr. Symeon's library had been all she had cared for in the season that was ending. She had gone wherever her husband asked her to go, and had given the entertainments he wanted her to give; but through all that brilliant summer she had gone about like "a corpse alive." That dreary simile had been in her mind sometimes when she thought of herself, sitting in her victoria, dressed as only the well-bred English woman with unlimited money can be dressed, lovely in her fragile fairness, admired and talked about. She had gone about, and held her own, in a quiet way, among crowds of clever men and women, and her life had seemed to her like the end of a long dream. Her only vital interest had been in the voices she heard in Francis Symeon's shadowy room. Those voices were of living men and women; but the words were the words of the dead.

She was not utterly unhappy. The past was past, and she had left off grieving over it, for now she had a transcendent hope in the near future—the hope of death. She would soon have passed the river that they had passed, Giulia and her father. The gate through which they had gone to a higher stage in the upward path of life would open for her; and no matter by what slow ascent, no matter with what feeble steps, she would climb the mountain up which they had gone, those emancipated spirits.

She had known for a long time that she was marked for death. She had no specific ailment, but in this last season she had felt her vanishing life, felt the painless ebb of vitality, and had measured, by a flight of stairs, by a pathway in the Park, where she walked sometimes in the early morning, the waning strength of limbs and heart. The dreadful sleeplessness of the first year of her widowhood had returned; and her nights were almost entirely spent in thought and reading, her brain never resting, her heart seldom quiet.

Although she looked forward to death as release, she could not escape the boredom of medical treatment. Lady Okehampton, whose daughters were all married, and wanted nothing from parental affection—except to be allowed to go their own way, and not to be obliged to invite Mummy to their choicest parties—devoted herself more and more to her favourite niece, who wasn't actually her niece, but only a first cousin once removed. Since, in those last days at Disbrowe, she had seen the mark of death on Vera's pale forehead, Aunt Mildred, who was really a warm-hearted woman, had interested herself keenly in the vanishing life, and had made unremitting efforts to combat the enemy.

"She has simply wasted her life since her second marriage," she said. "She has wasted her life as recklessly as Claude has wasted her money; but she shan't die without my making an effort to save her, even if I have to take every specialist in London to Portland Place."

"You'd better take her to the specialists," said his lordship. "It would save your time and her money."

"As if money mattered!"

"You could telephone for appointments, and do the whole of Grosvenor Street and Savile Row in a morning, with a good taxi."

"A taxi—when my niece has two superb Daimlers—no. By the by, the last Claude showed me is an S.C.A.T."

"Poor Provana!" sighed Okehampton. "To think that nothing could induce him to buy a motor car, although he was a man to whom moments are money. It was one of his few eccentricities to worship his horses."

"He might have been here now if he had not been quite so fussy about his horses," sighed her ladyship.

"What do you mean?"

"He might not have used the door between the house and the stables—the door by which he and his murderer came into the house on that awful night."

"True," assented her husband, "it was an infernally unlucky door, and I suppose if poor little Vera dies they'll carry her out that way to be cremated."

"Okehampton, you are too bad! Whoever said she was to be cremated?"

"Nobody. But it's the modern way, isn't it? And, of course, everything would be up-to-date."

"How can you be so heartless, and how can you use that odious expression 'up-to-date'?"

"Well, I hope the poor girl will be warned in time, and live to make old bones; but she didn't look like it at her last party. You'd better give her husband a good wigging. It will be more useful than calling in the specialists."

"I am utterly disgusted with Claude. He is throwing her money out of windows, and behaving atrociously into the bargain."

"I suppose you mean Mrs. Bellenden. Well, my dear, that was bound to come. Vera has been too much in the clouds for the last year. From what Susan Amphlett told me of her way of life in Rome, she was bound to lose her husband. No man can stomach neglect from a wife; unless all the other women neglect him. And Claude Rutherford is not a negligible quantity."

Lady Okehampton had tried her hand upon her young kinsman before this colloquy with her lord, and had found him hopeless. He turned the point of her lectures with a jest. He was light as vanity. He protested that his wife was alone to blame. He adored her, and thought no other woman upon this planet her equal in charm and beauty; but since she had taken up with Symeon and his spooks, she had surrounded herself with an atmosphere of sadness that would send the most devoted husband to the primrose path, in sheer revolt against the gloom of his home.

"We are poor creatures," he said, "and we have to be amused."

Once only in the course of numerous "wiggings" did Claude show anything like strong feeling, and then emotion came in a tempest that scared his mild kinswoman.

She had talked to him about his wife's health.

"Vera is absolutely wasting away," she said. "Something must be done, or she will not live till the end of the year."

"No, no, no," he cried. "My God, what do you mean? Is that to be the end? Is death to take her from me and leave me in this black world alone? You have no right to say such a thing! By what authority? Who has told you that she is in failing health? I see her every day. She never complains."

"You must be blind if you don't see the change in her."

"I don't believe there is anything seriously wrong. She is as lovely as ever. No, I don't believe it. You are cruel to come here and frighten me. She is all I have in the world, all, all! Do you understand?" His head drooped suddenly upon the table by which he was sitting, and she heard his hoarse sobs tearing his throat and chest, and saw his long, thin fingers writhing among his hair, the boyish auburn hair with a glint of gold in it that foolish women had praised.

"There is no need for despair, Claude. I only wanted to awaken you to the seriousness of the case. We shall save her, in spite of herself. I see you are still fond of her, and yet—"

"And yet I have been a brute, a senseless, idiotic beast. But that's all over, Lady Okehampton. Love her! I would lie outside her door, like that dog of hers, all through the long night only to get a smile and a touch of her hand in the morning. Love her! I loved her for five patient years, loved her passionately, and kept myself in check, and behaved like an elder brother. I, the man no woman could trust. Love her! The picture of her childish prettiness at Disbrowe was in my memory when I was going to the devil at Simla. You don't know what men are made of. You only know the model English gentleman, like your husband."

"Okehampton has never given me any trouble, except in his young days, when he used to ride dangerous horses. I know I have been exceptionally fortunate in my husband; and, of course, I know that modern husbands and wives are utterly unlike us; but I must say that your behaviour at your wife's last party was inexcusable. The dear Princess was sadly huffed; and I doubt if Vera will ever get her to her house again."

"I don't think Vera will try."

"But she ought to try. The Princess Hermione has been perfectly sweet about her."

"Vera doesn't care. That's her worst symptom, that I know of. She has left off caring about things."

"And that is a very bad symptom," said Lady Okehampton. "When Chagford's wife showed signs of it, I bundled her off to a nursing home for six weeks, and she came out of it just in time for Ascot, and as keen as mustard, as Chagford said in his vulgar way. She had been dieted, and massaged, and not allowed to see anyone but her nurses; and she was quite cured of not caring. She romped with her children, and ate jam pudding like one of them."

"Ah, you see there were children," sighed Claude. "There was something for her to come back to."

"Vera and you ought to have had a family. It is very disappointing," said Aunt Mildred, and the tone implied that when she said "disappointing" she meant "reprehensible."

"Never mind," she went on presently, in a more hopeful tone, "don't be down-hearted, Claude. If doctors can cure her, she shall be another woman before the end of the year."

"You love doctors much better than I do," said Claude, grasping her hands. "Find the man who can cure her and I will worship him."

After this Vera entered upon a wide acquaintance with the fashionable specialists: the man who was invincible in treatment of lung trouble; the only authority upon cardiac disorders; the man who knew more about the nervous system than any other physician in Europe; the man who had given his life to the study of the digestive organs; the hypnotic doctor, and the mesmerist; and finally, as a condescension, the all-round or common-sense man who might be consulted about anything, and sometimes, as it were by rule of thumb, succeeded where the specialists had failed.

These gentlemen came to Portland Place at irregular intervals through the month of August, Vera resolutely refusing to leave London in that impossible month, and Lady Okehampton again sacrificing her annual cure to the care of her niece, as she had done in the year of Mario Provana's unhappy death.

Lady Okehampton having made this sacrifice, almost the greatest which a woman of her age and position could make, naturally allowed herself some slight compensation in fussiness. She talked about her niece's health to boring point with her familiar friends, with the result of booking the name and address of some infallible specialist, hitherto unknown to her; and this accounted for the spasmodic appearance of a new consultant once or twice a week, in Vera's morning-room, all through that impossible month, in which the doctors themselves were panting for escape from London, to shoot grouse in Scotland, or do their own cures in Bohemia, after a season of hard dining. Vera was curiously submissive to these frequent ordeals. She answered any questions that the great man asked her; but she never volunteered information about herself, and she always made light of her ailments. The admission of a little worrying cough that was at its worst at night, a slight palpitation of the heart after going upstairs, was all that could be obtained from her by the most subtle questionings; but lungs and heart told their own story, without words.

She smiled when the nerve specialist asked her if she slept well, and again when he suggested certain harmless opiates which would ensure beneficent slumber. She had taken them all. She had exhausted Susan Amphlett's pharmacopoeia, which contained all these specifics, and others not so harmless.

When one physician after another—for on this they were all agreed—told her that she ought not to be in London in this sultry, depressing weather, while each advised his pet health resort, she smiled sweetly, and said she meant to remain in London till November, when she would go back to Rome.

"I am fond of this house," she said, "and the London air suits me."

"London air is very good air," answered Dr. Selwyn Tower, who understood her better than the various new lights, "but not in August and September. If you are to be in Rome in November, why not spend the interval in Italy, at Varese, for instance, a charming spot, with every advantage?"

No. Vera was not to be persuaded.

"I like the quiet of this home after the season. All I want is rest and silence," she said, and Dr. Selwyn Tower shot a despairing glance at Lady Okehampton.

"Your niece is absolutely charming; but as obstinate as a mule," he told her, when they had their conference in one of the drawing-rooms. All the doors and portières were open, and the doctor looked at the long vista of splendid emptiness with a faint shudder.

"It is a fine house, but a little depressing," he murmured.

"I call it positively uncanny; but that is all in my niece's line. She is dreadfully morbid. I am glad there was no occultism or Christian Science when I was young."

At these words Christian Science the famous consultant shuddered worse than at sight of the empty rooms.

"If your sweet niece is that way inclined we can do nothing for her," he said.

"No, thank Heaven, that is not one of her fads."

And then the fashionable physician gave his opinion of the case, or just so much of his opinion as he thought it good to give to an affectionate but not over wise aunt.

He found that the patient's strength was at a very low ebb. She had been wasting her resources, living upon her capital, refusing herself the rest that was essential for so fragile a form, so sensitive a temperament, and so over-active a brain. Lady Okehampton had told him of the gaieties, the rush from place to place, from amusement to amusement, the everlasting entertaining and being entertained; and he talked as if he had been there, watching and taking notes, all through that wild career. He was not going to extinguish hope; so he kept up a cheerful tone throughout the conference. There was nothing heroic in the treatment required. Rest, and a soothing regimen. Not much walking, but a great deal of fresh air, Drives in her open carriage to rural suburbs, if she should insist on remaining in London; a little quiet society; the utmost care as to diet, and constant medical supervision. He would be glad to confer with Mrs. Rutherford's regular medical man before he left London; and he hoped, on his return in three or four weeks, to find a marked improvement.

This was all. When questioned as to lung trouble, he said that there was trouble, but he saw no fatal indications. Yes, there was heart weakness; but nothing that might not be modified by care.

Simple as she was, Lady Okehampton did not feel altogether assured by all this bland talk, and the sound of the doctor's carriage wheels, as they rolled away from the door, recalled the moaning of the winter waves under the red cliffs at Disbrowe.

She repeated the specialist's diplomatic utterances to Claude, who did not seem to attach much importance to medical opinion.

"All doctors talk alike," he said. "I don't think Vera's is a case for the faculty. You remember what Macbeth said to his physician?"

Lady Okehampton did not remember; but she gave a sigh of assent that answered as well.

"I'm afraid Vera's is a rooted sorrow, and, God help me! I cannot pluck it from her memory. We had better leave her alone. We can do nothing more for her. We can't make her happy."

"Claude, this is too dreadful. Are we to let her die?" cried Aunt Mildred, with something like an elderly shriek.

"Is death so great an evil? At least it means rest, and there are some of us who can get rest no other way."

"Claude, it is positively dreadful to hear you talk like that, as if you cared for nothing in this life."

"I don't."

And then Lady Okehampton took him in hand severely, and talked to him as a good woman, but as a Philistine of the Philistines, would naturally talk on such an occasion; and after remonstrating with him for his want of religious feeling, and even proper affection, went on to reproaching him for spending his wife's money, squandering her magnificent fortune with a reckless wastefulness that might end in reducing her to beggary.

"No fear of that, Aunt Mildred. No doubt I have thrown money out of windows. Money has never been a serious consideration with Vera and me. We should have been quite as happy when we started on our Venetian honeymoon if we had had only just enough to pay for our tourists' tickets and our gondola, just enough for the gondola and a cheap hotel. Money could buy us nothing that we cared for. Later, when I knew what her income was, I spent with a free hand; but there's a good deal of spending in a hundred thousand a year—"

Lady Okehampton shivered, and stirred in her seat uneasily. That colossal income, and nothing done for the needy members of her husband's illustrious house!

"I wanted to amuse myself and to amuse my wife, and amusements are costly nowadays; so the money has run out pretty fast, but there has always been a handsome surplus. I see Mr. Zabulon, the banker, one of my wife's trustees, two or three times a year, and he has never complained. Vera's charities are immense; so there is really nothing for you to moan about, Lady Okehampton."

"Nothing," cried Vera's aunt, with uplifted hands. "Was there ever anyone so feather-headed, so feckless? Can you forget that when your wife dies her fortune dies with her?"

"No. But when she dies, I shall have done with all that money can buy. I shall be able to pension the old stable hands, and provide for my dogs, out of my fifteen hundred a year; and I can give my trainer half a dozen cracks that will make him comfortable for life."

"You are very considerate about your stable and kennels. I wonder if you have ever considered Vera's obligations to those who come after her."

"If you mean the Roman cater-cousins I certainly have not."

"Provana's heirs? Why, of course not! They will be inordinately rich when that splendid fortune is chopped up among them. No, Claude, if you had a proper family feeling, which to my mind is an essential element in the Christian life, you would have thought of our herd of poor relations. Nicholas Disbrowe, dying by inches in an East Anglian Vicarage, and not daring to winter in the South, for want of means; or poor Lady Rosalba, who is no better off than Vera's grandmother, and doesn't make half as good a fight as poor Lady Felicia did; or Mary Disbrowe Jones, who married so wretchedly, and is selling blouses in a shabby street in Pimlico—"

"I think Vera has done a lot for all of 'em. I know she sent the Reverend Nicholas a thousand pounds last winter, when his wife wrote her a doleful letter; and she gave her blouse-making cousin two hundred and fifty pounds last week, to save her from bankruptcy. Consider them, forsooth! Do you suppose they don't ask to be considered? Every man jack of them, down to the remotest connection by marriage. They are as eloquent with the pen as professional begging-letter writers. They blister their papers with tears. And Vera never refuses. She does not know how."

"Oh, I know she is generous. A thousand to that worthy man in the Fens was handsome; but that kind of casual help won't provide for the future; and when our poor dear is gone there will be nothing. May that sad day be long, long off; but in the meantime she ought to invest her surplus income, and leave it to those who want it most and would use it best. You may be sure I have no personal feeling; but the best of us are not too well off, and if there should come the general election that we are threatened with, I doubt if Chagford will be able to stand for North Devon. The ballot has made bribery more audacious and more expensive than ever. I am told three half crowns is the least the wretches will take. They will ride a candidate's motor to death, and then go and vote for his opponent."

"Let Chagford talk to my wife, if there's a dissolution," said Claude, with a half-smothered yawn that expressed weariness and disgust.

"Vera is always kind," sighed Lady Okehampton dolefully; but she refrained from suggesting that, when the dissolution came, Vera might not be there.

This was Aunt Mildred's last attack upon Claude Rutherford. He took matters into his own hands after this, and no longer depended upon accounts of his wife's health at second hand. He took all information upon that subject from Dr. Selwyn Tower, who had a great reputation at that period, and whom he was inclined to trust.

The physician was more frank with the husband than he had been with the aunt, though even yet he said nothing to extinguish hope. He told Mr. Rutherford that it would have been better for his wife to winter in the South, or by way of experiment to try a short winter in the Engadine, coming down to Ragaz before the snow melted; but as the dear lady seemed strangely bent upon staying in her own house, it would be safer to indulge her fancy. Lungs and heart were only a question of weakness. The mind was of serious consequence; and everything must be done to check the tendency to melancholia.

"If we can make her happy, we shall be able to deal with the lung trouble," said the physician. "Open air and good spirits might work a miracle."

Dr. Tower naturally inquired as to parental history, and was somewhat disheartened on hearing that the dear lady's father and mother had died young, the former of galloping consumption, during an open-air cure; yet even this did not induce him to pronounce sentence of death. Nor did he allow Mrs. Rutherford to suppose herself a desperate case, though he insisted on having a trained nurse, and of the best, in attendance upon his patient, as well as the maid Louison.

The French girl might be all that Mrs. Rutherford could require, he admitted, when Vera told him she wanted no one else.

"But you must allow me what I want," pleaded Dr. Tower with his most ingratiating air. "My treatment is of the mildest—nothing heroic or troublesome about it—but I must be sure that it is followed. I must have someone about you who is responsible to me. My nurse shall not be allowed to bore you. If she is intrusive or disagreeable to you, you can telephone to me; and she shall be superseded within the hour."

Vera submitted. Her indifference to most things, even to those that concerned herself, was one of her symptoms which made Dr. Tower uneasy.

"This woman will never help to cure herself," he thought, as he drove away, with that far-off look in Vera's face impressed upon his mind. "She does not want to get well. She is not absolutely unhappy— only indifferent. Something must have gone wrong in her life. Yet her husband does not seem a bad sort."

She was not unhappy. She had been allowed to take her own way, and to live as she wished to live—in the silence and peace of the spacious house, where the business of entertaining seemed to be at an end for ever. Whatever had been amiss in the life that was ebbing away seemed hardly to matter, now that she was drawing near the other life. Her husband came and went, and spend a good deal of his time in her room, talking with her, or reading to her, when she was too tired to talk. There had been nothing said of his offence against her; no utterance of that other woman's name. They were friends again, and could talk of the things that they loved—literature, music, art; of Henry Irving's Hamlet; of Millais and Browning, both of whom she had seen at Aunt Mildred's house in her childhood, and whose faces she remembered; of books new and old. They were as friendly and sympathetic as they had been in Mario Provana's lifetime, before the dawn of love. It was as if they were still at the same platonic stage. All that had come after was like a lurid dream from which they had awakened. Tristram was again the true knight. Iseult was sinless.

All that was best in Claude Rutherford was in the ascendant during these long, slow weeks of silent sorrow, in which he knew that the man with the scythe was at the door, that nothing money could buy or love devise could save the woman he loved. He had broken finally with that other woman: finally, for the fiery cup had lost its intoxicating power, and the end had been a vulgar quarrel about money. Whatever was to happen to him, he was safe from that siren's spells.

All his natural sweetness, his sympathy and charm, were for Vera, in those quiet weeks of September and October, when there was nobody in London, and the chariot wheels rolled no more in the broad roadway. He was at his best in his wife's white morning-room, where the faces of the immortals looked down upon him, and where he was kind even to the dog she loved—the Irish terrier, brought home after his half-year's quarantine—who stretched his strong limbs and rough, red-brown body against her satin slippers, as she lay on her sofa, a fragile figure, shadowy in her loose white gown.

All that was best in this man, the tenderness, the sympathy, was in evidence now; a failure no doubt, trivial and shallow, incapable of deep feeling, perhaps, but a sweet, lovable nature; a nature that had made women love him whether he wanted their love or not.

"It is very good of you to give me so much of your time," Vera said one day, slipping her thin little hand into his, which was almost as thin. "Invalids are wretched company, and I don't want you to have too much of this dull room."

"I do not find it dull—and it is no duller for me than for you."

"It is never dull for me. I have my faces. They are always company."

"Your faces—You mean those portraits?"

"Byron, Scott, Browning. Yes, they are always company. I have looked at them till they are alive. I have read Walter Scott's journals and Byron's letters till I know them as well as if they had been my intimate friends when they were alive. I know Browning's letters by heart; those sweet letters to the sweet wife. Shakespeare is different. It is so sad that there are no familiar records. One can only think of him as the poet and the creator; genius that touches the supernatural."

"I don't think it matters how little you know of the man, his deer-stalking or his tardy marriage, as long as you don't think there was no Shakespeare, and that the noblest poetry this world ever saw was written by the skunk who gave away his friend," said her husband.

"Bacon! Horrible!"

On one quiet evening, when Claude had been with her since his solitary dinner, she said softly:

"I sometimes forget all the years, and think you are just the same Cousin Claude who took pity on me at Disbrowe, when I was so shy that other people's kindness only made me miserable. Till you came I used to creep into any corner with a book, rather than mix with my Disbrowe cousins, who were so dreadfully grand and clever."

"Precocious geniuses, Mrs. Somervilles in the bud, who matured into two of the most commonplace women I know, and almost as ignorant as Susan Amphlett," said Claude.

"But you must not give me so much of your time, Claude," she said gently.

"I love to be with you; but I may slip away for the Cambridgeshire?" he said, the trivial side of his character coming to the surface.

She did not even ask if he were personally interested in the race. There had been a time when she knew every horse he owned, and made most of them her friends, rejoicing in their beauty as creatures whom she would have liked to keep for pets, rather than to expose them to the ordeal of the turf; albeit she had followed their fortunes, and speculated upon their chances, almost as keenly interested as her husband. But now they had become things without shape or meaning, like all the rest of the outside world.

"You need not be afraid of leaving me," she said. "I have this good friend to keep me company," smoothing Boroo's rough coat with her soft hand.

"I wish my mother were still in town. She would come to you every day."

"She is very good, but she and I have never been really friends. I know she would be kind; but she would talk of painful things. I don't want to remember. I want to look forward."

"Yes," he answered in a low voice, bending over her, and pressing his lips on the pale brow. "There must be no looking back."

It was the first time he had kissed her since the night of the concert. She looked up at him with a sad, sweet smile, and held his hand in hers for a moment.

"Susan must come to you every day to keep you in good spirits," he said.

"No, Claude, Susie doesn't like sick people. She sits by my side and chatters and chatters, telling me all the scandals she thinks will interest me; but I can hear the effort she is making. Her tongue does not run on as it used before I was ill; and once when she saw a spot of blood on my handkerchief she nearly fainted. I don't want too much of Susie. Mr. Symeon will come and talk to me sometimes; and his talk always does me good."

"I wish I could think so. I hate leaving you in London. You ought to have gone to Disbrowe, as your aunt wished. You would have done better in that soft air."

"No. I should be better nowhere than in this silent house. If I cannot be in Rome there is nowhere else where I should like to be. I want space and silence, and no going and coming of people who mean to be kind and who bore me to death. I want no fussing and talking about me. I can put up with my nurse, because she is quiet and does her work like a machine."

Rome? Yes, in the November afternoons when the world outside her windows was hidden in grey fog, she longed for the beautiful city, the place of life and light, the city of fountains, full of the sound of rushing water. The dull greyness of London oppressed her, when she thought of the long garden walks in their solemn stillness, the cypress and ilex, the statues gleaming ghostly in the dusk against the dark walls of laurel and arbutus, the broad terrace with its massive marble balustrade, on which she had leant for hours in melancholy meditation, thinking, thinking, thinking, as the multitude of church towers and the great dome in the hollow below her changed from grey to purple, as the golden light died in the west and the young moon rose above the fading crimson of the afterglow.

It was sad to think that she would never see that divine city again, and all that she had loved in Italy: Cadenabbia, where her honeymoon had begun, to the sound of rippling water, as the boats crept by in the darkness, to the music of guitars and Italian voices, singing in the light of coloured lanterns, while the cosmopolitan crowd clustered in the narrow space between the hotel and the lake.

Susan Amphlett came nearly every day, and insisted upon being admitted. She had come to London for a week, just to buy frocks for a winter round of visits.

"But much more to see you, my dearest," she said, and then she recited the houses to which she was going, and her reason for going to them, which seemed to be anything rather than any regard for the people she was visiting. She talked of herself as if she had been a star actress.

"I am touring in the shires this winter," she said. "I did Hants and Dorset last year, and was bored to extinction. Roger is happy in any hole if he can be riding to hounds every day, and he had the Blackmoor Vale and the North Hants within his reach most of the time; while I was excruciated by a pack of women who talked of nothing but their good works or their bridge, and they were such poor players that the good works were less boring than the bridge talk. 'Dear Lady Sue, would you call no trumps if?'—and would you do this and t'other? questions that babies in the nursery might ask over their toy cards."

Then came a long account of the frocks that were being made for the shires, and the scarlet top-coat to be worn with a grey habit, which Roger hated.

"I think he would like me in an early-Victorian get up, with the edge of my habit touching my horse's fetlocks, a large white muslin collar, and a low beaver hat with a long feather. Those early-Victorian collars cost two or three pounds apiece, my Grannie told me, and those poor wretches who never changed their clothes till dinner, wore them all day long; and yet they talk of our extravagance; as if nobody paid anything for clothes in those days."

And then, when the houses to which she was going, and the clothes she was to wear, and her quarrels with her husband and her maid had been discussed at length, Susan began to talk about her friend.

"Lady O. told me how ill you had been, ma mie, and of your curious whim about this house. She says Selwyn Tower would have liked you to go to the Transvaal, and told her that two or three months in that delicious climate would make you a strong woman; but finding you set upon stopping in your own house he gave way, as your illness is chiefly a question of nerves. It is a comfort to know that, n'est-ce pas, mein Schatz?"

"Yes, of course it is a comfort. I suppose, with nothing amiss but one's nerves, one might live to be ninety."

"True, dearest, quite ninety," Susan answered, shuddering.

Susan Amphlett was out of her element in a sick room. The mere thought that the friend she was talking to was marked for death seemed to freeze her blood. Her own hand grew as cold as the cold hand she was holding. She could not be bright and pleasant with Death in sight.

As she sat with Vera in the library that had been Provana's favourite room she felt as if there were someone standing behind the door of that inner room, a door that had been left ajar. There was someone waiting there whose unseen presence made her dumb. Someone! Not Provana—but another and more terrible shape.

"Vera," she burst out at last, "why do you sit in this horrid room instead of in your sweet white den, with Byron and Browning and all your dear people?"

"I like this room better, now that my thoughts have gone backward."

"What can you mean by thoughts going backward?"

"Now that I know time is measured for me, so much and no more; I like to live over the days that are gone. It spins out my life to live the dead years over again. This is the room Mario loved. His books are on those shelves, the books that opened a new world for me: the Italian historians, the Italian poets. In the first year of our life in this house, before I was the fashion, we used to sit here of an evening, long evenings, from nine till midnight, talking, talking, talking, or Mario reading to me. He was a banker, and a dealer in money; but he read poetry exquisitely."

"Vera!" Susan ejaculated suddenly, and sat staring.

"What's the matter?"

"I believe you loved Provana better than ever you have loved Claude."

"I don't know," Vera said dreamily.

She had been talking in a dreamy way, as if she were hardly conscious that anyone was listening to her.

"Perhaps you never were really in love with your second husband?"

"Yes. I loved him too much—and," after a perceptible pause, "not enough."

"Darling, I can't make you out."

"I am not worth making out."

"One thing I must tell you, Vera, even at the risk of agitating you. It is all over with that woman."

"Which woman?"

"Which? Mrs. Bellenden. There has never been so much as a whisper about any other since your marriage."

"Oh, it is all over? I thought so."

"Vera, what indifference! You might be talking of somebody in Mars. Yes, dear, it is quite at an end. They had a desperate quarrel; quite the worst of many frightful rows. There was furniture smashed, I believe—Sèvres and things—and now she has consoled herself."

"Really?"

"A German Prince. One of the German attachés told me he would marry her if he dared. Well, sweet, I must be trudging. I'm dining out, one of those nice little winter dinners that I love. You must make haste and get quite, quite well."

This was what Susie always said to a sick friend, even when the friend was moribund. The "quite, quite" had such a cheering sound.

"By the by, Lady O. told me you have had the Princess Hermione?"

"Yes, she came to see me two or three times when she was passing through town."

"That must have cheered you immensely. She is devoted to you, quite raves about you, I hear, in the highest circles. Get well, dear, and give a party for her when she is next in town."

Susie kissed her and patted her hair, and suppressed a shiver at the cold brow that her lips touched. It felt like the brow of death. Yet Vera's eyes were bright, and there was a rosy bloom on the thin cheek. Susan was glad when she had got herself out of the house and was walking fast through the cheerful streets. But she was sincerely attached to her friend.

"I shall be fit for nothing this evening," she told herself sadly; but she was at least fit for her part of Chorus, and entertained the little dinner-party with a picturesque description of her fading friend, dying slowly in that house of measureless wealth.

"Her income dies with her," she explained, "and though I suppose a few pennies have been saved out of a hundred thousand a year, and my cousin will get all that's left, he will be a pauper in a year or two, I daresay."

On this the company speculated upon how much might be left; and all were agreed that there was a good deal of spending in a hundred thousand, while one of the middle-aged men went so far as to make a rough calculation of the Rutherfords' expenditure in those five years of expensive pleasures; but even after reckoning the dances and dinner-giving, the yachts and balloons, the racing stable, and a certain amount of losses on the turf and at cards, they did not bring the annual outlay above eighty thousand, whereupon a dowager looked round with a smile, and said:

"You haven't reckoned Mrs. Bellenden."

"True. Now you mention her, I take it there would be no surplus."

And then that remarkable lady and her German Prince were discussed at full length—dissected rather than discussed; for when a woman is remarkable for her beauty, and has spent three or four fortunes, and is in a fair way of spending another, there is a great deal of amusing talk to be got out of her.

CHAPTER XXX

After Susan Amphlett's disappearance the house in Portland Place was given over to silence and solitude. Lady Okehampton was at Disbrowe, where she was on duty as a model grandmother, her daughters liking their children to spend the early winter in the ancestral home, where there were Exmoor ponies in abundance, and plenty of clever grooms to teach the "dear kiddies" to ride, and a superannuated governess of the "good old soul" or "dear old thing" order, to keep their young minds from rusting and coach them for their next "exam.," whether in music or science.

Lady Okehampton was established in her country house till Christmas; and Claude had turf engagements and shooting engagements enough to occupy him nearly as long. He had been reluctant to leave his wife; but once away from the silent house, he had all manner of distractions to prolong his absence; and while Newmarket was full of life and anticipations for next year, the house in which he had left Vera was a place of gloom, that haunted him in troubled dreams and made the thought of return horrible.

He wrote to her more than once, entreating her to let him take her to Cannes or Nice. She could have nurses and invalid carriages to make the journey possible, and her health would be renewed in the sunshine. But his wife's answer was always to the same effect:

"I am at peace. Let me be."

And then he fell back upon his stables and his racing friends; or his shooting in Suffolk; or on cards: any thing to stop that horror of retrospective thought, which had been like a disease with him of late years.

Vera was at peace. She had no trivial visitors, was not obliged to listen to futile chatter about other people's affairs. Dr. Tower came three or four times a week, unwilling to confide so precious a life to his "watch-dog," the general practitioner, and was cheerful and sympathetic. She had two hospital nurses now—one always on guard, day and night. She could no longer maintain her struggle for independence, for she too often needed a helping arm to support her as she went up and down the long corridors, or toiled slowly up the spacious staircase that had once been alive with the finest people in London, but where now the slender figure in a soft silk gown and white fur boa, with the nurse in cap and uniform, moved in a ghostly silence.

Father Cyprian Hammond came to see her sometimes, and sat long and talked delightfully; but he, who was past master in the art of making proselytes, could get no nearer the mind of this woman than he had got a year before. Whatever her burden was, she would not open her heart to him. Whatever her sense of sin, she would not ask him for absolution. It was in vain that he told her what his Church could do for a penitent—the ineffable power possessed by that one Holy and Infallible Church to heal the wounded heart and to bring the strayed lamb back to the Shepherd's arms.

"Try to think of yourself in the wilderness and that divine Shepherd seeking for you," said the priest gently.

But Father Cyprian, with all his gifts, could not win her to confide in him. It was only to Francis Symeon, the spiritualist, that she ever spoke of the thoughts that filled her mind, as she sat alone in the room that had been her husband's, dreaming over one of the books he had loved. Her intimacy with Francis Symeon had grown closer since the world outside that quiet room had closed upon her for ever, since he knew and she knew that the transition from the known to the unknown life was very near. He had told her the story of his own sorrows, the tragedy of love and death that had made him a mystic and a dreamer, whose hopes and convictions the world scoffed at.

Life had given him all the things he desired, and last, best gift of all, the love of a perfect woman, who alone could make that life complete for himself and for others, lifting him for ever above the sphere of sensual joys and worthless ambitions. It was she who had taught him to look beyond the present life, and to consider the beauty of the world no more than a screen that concealed the glory of diviner worlds, hidden from them only while they were moving along their earthly pilgrimage, always looking beyond, always dreaming of something better.

The day came, without an hour's warning, when he was to be told that her pilgrimage was nearly done. The after-life was calling her. The divine companions were beckoning.

All that there had been of high enthusiasm and scorn of life left him in that moment. He was as weak and helpless as a mother with her only child, her infant child threatened by death. The dreamer was no more a dreamer; and only the earthly lover remained, he who was to have been her husband. He hung upon moments, he listened to every failing breath, he counted time by her ebbing strength and the opinions of doctors. He lived only to watch and to listen beside her sofa, or in the curtained twilight of her sick room, when the pretty garden-parlour was no longer possible. Wherever she was carried in the vain pursuit of life he went with her. The time of alternating hope and dread lasted nearly a year.

"It was our union," he told Vera. "It was my only marriage. As I sat day after day with her hand clasped in mine I knew that this was all I could ever know of marriage or of woman's love. From the day of her death I had done with the world; and all the rest of my days were given up to searching for those who had gone—for those who were in her world, not in mine. I have waited at the door, as your dog waits when he cannot see you, and as he believes that you are there, on the other side, so I believe and know that she is near me; and my days have known no other business or interest than my patient search into the books of all ages and nations that help the science of the future life, and the society of those people whom you have met in my rooms, and who think and feel as I do. I am a rich man, but I only use money for the relief of distress; and I have allowed myself no luxury or indulgence beyond my books, and the rooms that are large enough to hold them and me."

The hospital nurse sat in the adjoining room, with the door ajar. So far, and so far only, was the patient allowed the privilege of solitude. Someone must be always there, within hearing. When she had a visitor the door might be shut, but not otherwise.

"There must be something very dreadful the matter with me," she said when Dr. Tower insisted upon this point.

"No, my dear lady, there is nothing dreadful in a tired heart; but I don't want you to faint without anybody at hand to look after you."

Vera assured him that she was not likely to faint, and made mock of his care.

He had been very insistent upon certain points in his treatment, which he arranged with the general practitioner who had attended her for minor ailments in earlier days, when she was rarely in need of medical care. He would not allow her to go up and down stairs any longer. That ordeal must be at an end until she was stronger. He had the dining-room made into a bedroom for her use. All the gloomy old pictures and colossal furniture had been removed, and the walls were hung with delicate chintz, while the choicest things in her rooms upstairs had been brought down to make this ground-floor apartment pleasant for her—a room that smiled as it had never smiled before, even on those gala nights when a flood of light shone upon the splendour of Georgian silver, and Venetian glass, and diamonds, and fashionable women.

"You are taking far too much trouble about me," Vera said, when first she saw this transformation.

"We only want to save you trouble. The ascent to the second floor of this lofty house is almost Alpine. I wonder you never established an electric lift."

"I never minded running up and down stairs."

She remembered the first years after her second marriage, the years of trivial pleasures and hurry and excitement, and with how light a step she had gone up and down that stately staircase, to give herself over to her Parisian maid, and to have her smart toilet of the morning changed for the still smarter clothes of the afternoon, while she submitted impatiently, with a mind full of worthless things: the fashion of her gown, the shape of her last new hat. That rush from one amusement to another—endless hours without pause—had been like the morphia maniac's needle. It had killed thought.

All that was left of life now was thought, or rather memory; for of late thought and memory were one.

Her doctors might do what they liked with her, so long as they let her stay in the silent house, and did not take away her dog.

Since his return from captivity the terrier had hung about her with a love more devoted even than before their separation. He watched her as only a dog can watch the creature it loves. He would not let her out of his sight. He could not forget how he had been kept away from her; and he lived in fear of another parting. If he were not lying at her feet, or nestling against the soft folds of her gown, he was sitting at the door of her room, the door that hid her from him; the cruel door that kept him from her immediate presence. He lay at her bedroom door all night, and rushed in, with the first entrance of nurse or maid in the morning, to greet her with hairy paws upon her coverlet, and irresistible canine kisses upon her cheek. This was the best love that remained to her; the love that had no after-thought, and left no sting. She had provided a friend for him in days when she would be no longer there. Francis Symeon had promised to take him, and love him, and give him a happy old age and a gentle sleep when he was weary.

As the winter days shortened she grew perceptibly weaker, and the tired heart felt as if its work in this world must be nearly done.

Mr. Symeon came every day, and stayed for a long time, a quiet figure sitting in the low armchair by the wood fire, sometimes in silence that was restful for the invalid, though she loved to hear him talk; for his thoughts were not of this narrow life and its trumpery pleasures and eating cares, but of the land beyond the veil.

"Do you believe they think of us, sometimes, those who have gone beyond?" Vera asked in her low, sweet voice, as they sat in the winter gloaming.

"I believe they think of us often—always, if they have loved us much."

"I had a friend whom I offended, cruelly, dreadfully," she said slowly, as if with an effort, "and he died before I had even begun to be sorry. And when he was dead and I knew that his spirit was there, among the shadows, near me, I was afraid, horribly afraid. I could only think of his anger, never of the possibility of his forgiveness. For a long, long time I was afraid that I should see him. I could imagine the dreadful anger in his face. His face and form were always there, in the background of my life; and I was afraid of being alone, afraid of silence and darkness and all lonely places; so I gave myself up to society, and the amusements and distractions of brainless people, without ever really caring for them—only to escape thought. But I could not stop my brain from thinking. Thought went on like a relentless iron mill grinding, grinding, grinding the same dead husks by day and night; and the friend whose love I had wounded was always there. And then there came a time when I sickened of everything upon earth—society, splendour, music, pictures, even mountains and lakes and forests, and all the beauty of the world. All things had become loathsome, and I wandered about with a restless spirit in my brain that would not leave me in peace. Then, slowly, slowly, the faint, sweet sense of peace came back—the angry face was gone—and the face that looked at me out of the shadows was only sad—and then the time came when I felt that the dead had changed towards me in that dim world you have taught me to understand, and that there was pardon and pity in the great heart I had wounded; and one day the burden was lifted from my soul, and I knew that I was forgiven. Now tell me, my kind friend, was this hallucination, was it just the outcome of my brooding thoughts, dwelling perpetually upon the same subject, or was the spirit of my dead friend really in touch with mine? Was it by his strong will reaching across the barrier of death that the assurance of forgiveness had come to my soul, or was I the dupe of my own imagination, my own longing for pardon?"

"No, you were not deceived. It is for such as you that the veil is sometimes lifted, the creatures in whom mind is more than flesh, the elect of human clay. I told you as much as that years ago when you first talked to me of the world we all believe in, we who meet together and wait for the voices out of the shadows, the wisdom and the faith that cannot die, the voices of the influencing minds. No, my sweet friend, have neither fear nor doubt. The sense of pity and pardon that has come into your soul is a message from the friend you loved.

"Would the happy spirit descend
From the realms of light or song,
Should I fear to greet my friend
Or to say 'Forgive the wrong'?

Believe that you are forgiven; you can know no more than that until you have passed the river, until the gate of a happier world has been opened."

"And then I shall be with him again, where they neither marry nor are given in marriage, but where they are as the angels of God in heaven?"

"That is the reunion to which we all look forward; that is the faith that looks through death."

There was a long interval of silence, and then she said slowly:

"If I could see him with these bodily eyes, see him as I see you looking at me in the firelight, I should be sure that the dream is not a dream."

"You have been privileged to understand the mind of your dead friend; to know that he is near you. That should be enough. Only to the rarest natures is it given to see. You questioned me about this possibility of vision once before; and I told you that I had known of one instance when the eyes of the living beheld the dead, in the last moments of earthly life."

"I do not think those moments are far off for me, my friend," Vera said softly.

Francis Symeon, in whose philosophy death was emancipation, did not say the kind of thing that Susan Amphlett would have said in the circumstances. She no doubt would have told Vera that she was talking nonsense, and that she was "going to get quite, quite well, and live for years and years and years, and have a real good time."

Mr. Symeon took her attenuated hand in his friendly grasp, and sat by her for some time in silence before he bade her his calm adieu, patted the dog, nestling against her knees, and went quietly out of the room and out of the house. He did not think that he would ever again be sitting in the firelight in that room, hearing the low sad voice. He knew that he had shut the door upon a life that was measured by moments.

Three days after that Vera was unwontedly restless. There had been a long telegram from her husband in the morning, announcing his return for that night. He had finished all his business with his trainer, engaged the jockeys who were to ride for him next year, and he was coming back to London—he did not say "coming home"—heartily sick of Newmarket, and his Suffolk shooting, and the friends who had been with him.

"Why do we do these things and call them pleasures?" He ended the message with that question, as with a moral.

"Poor Claude!" sighed his wife, as she folded the thin slips of paper and laid them among her books; and then she thought:

"How much happier for him if he had stayed with the Benedictines!"

The days wore on, such slow days. The nurses were more and more attentive, horribly attentive. There were three of them now. Two were always about her, while the third slept. She had left off asking questions. Dr. Tower came every morning, and sat with her quietly for a quarter of an hour, and patted and praised her dog, and told her scraps of the day's news, and was kind; but she heard him without interest, as if without understanding. She had what Susie called her mermaid gaze, as one who saw only things far away, across a vast ocean. She never questioned him now, and made no allusion to the third young woman in uniform, who had come upon the scene so quietly that she looked like a double of one of the others, a trick of the optic nerves rather than another person.

She had the nurses almost always near her; and that other sentinel, the terrier, was there always. There was no "almost" where his affection was concerned. As she grew weaker and moved with feebler steps he moved nearer her. She talked to him sometimes, to the nurses never, though she was gracious to them in her mute fashion, and understood that they liked her and were sorry for her.

One quiet, grey evening, the closing in of a day that had been curiously mild for an English December—a day that brought back the still, sad atmosphere of mid-winter at San Marco—she had an unusual respite from her watchers. It was tea-time, and they were sitting longer than usual over the low fire in the room beyond the library, with the door ajar—no lights switched on, no sound of laughter or loud voices—just two well-behaved young women whispering together in the firelight.

She was alone, moving slowly along the corridor. She had been wandering about for some time, with a restlessness that had increased in a painful degree of late, the dog creeping close against her skirt, until, all in a moment, when she bent down to speak to him, he slunk away from her and crawled under the dark archway that opened into the deeper darkness of the hall, as Vera entered through the open door of the library.

At last it had come—the thing she had been waiting for. It was no surprise when the dream she had been dreaming night after night became a reality. A shiver ran through her, as if the warm blood in her veins had turned to ice-cold water; but it was awe, not horror, that thrilled her. Night after night she had awakened from a vision of Mario Provana, from the sound of his voice, the touch of his hand, the glad, vivid sense that all that was past was a dream, that he was alive, and that she belonged to him and him only, as before the coming of trouble. She had awakened night after night, in the faint flicker of the shrouded lamp, when the room was full of shadows. She had awakened to disappointment and desolation. That had been the surprise—not this. There was neither doubt nor wonder now, as she stood on the threshold of the dim room, and saw Provana sitting by the hearth in the chair where he used to sit, calm, motionless, like a statue of domestic peace, the creator and defender of the home, the master, sitting silent by the hearth-fire that wedded love had made sacred. The dull red of that fading fire, and the pale grey of evening outside the uncurtained windows, made the only light in the room; but there was light enough for her to see every line in the face, the face of power, where every line told of force, unalterable purpose, indomitable courage.

The grey eyes looked at her, steel bright under the projecting brow. Kind eyes, that told her of his love, a love that Fate could not change nor diminish. Not Death, not Sin!

For these first moments she believed he had come back to her, that he had escaped the bonds of Death. She did not ask what miracle had brought him there, but she believed in his miraculous return. The blood ran swift and warm in her veins again. Her heart beat with a passionate joy. She stretched out her arms to him, trying to speak fond words of welcome; but her tremulous lips could give no sound. The muscles of her throat seemed paralysed.

She was yearning to tell him of her love—that she had sinned and repented; that he was the first—must always be the first—in her affection.

Her limbs failed her with a sudden collapse, and she sank on her knees by a large, high-backed arm-chair that stood near the door, and clung to the arm of it, with both her hands, struggling against the numbness that was creeping over her senses. She kept her eyes upon the face—the face of all her dreams, of all her sorrow—the face she had loved and regretted. For moments her widely opened eyes gazed steadily—then cold drops broke out upon her forehead, her limbs shook, and her eyelids drooped—only for an instant.

She lifted them, and he was gone. There was nothing but the empty chair—his chair in the quiet domestic evenings, before Mario Provana's house became the fashion, before the Disbrowes gave the law to his wife's existence.

That was the last she saw before the lifting of the veil.

CHAPTER XXXI

Chorus was at work again; not at a London dinner-table this time, but in the easier atmosphere of a North Riding manor house, which men left in the morning to shoot grouse, and came back to in the evening to gossip with their womenkind, in the cheerful light of an oak-panelled dining-room.

Chorus was wearing black, quite the prettiest thing in complimentary mourning, which all her friends assured her suited her to perfection and took ten years off her age. Susan Amphlett had received that kind of compliment too often of late. She thought people were beginning to lay a disagreeable stress upon the passage of time in relation to her personal appearance.

"I doubt if I shall ever wear anything but black for the rest of my poor little life," she said tearfully. "That darling and I were like sisters. And that she should have died when I was in Scotland, hundreds of miles away from her!"

"It must have been sudden?"

"Heart failure. No one was with her. She had three hospital nurses to look after her, but she died alone in a dark room, while two of them were dawdling over their tea, and the third was in bed. The dog whined, and they went to look for her. She was lying in a huddled heap on the carpet, near the open door, and that poor, faithful beast was standing by her, whining piteously."

"Where was Rutherford?"

"At Newmarket, of course, the only place where he has been happy for a long time, settling up next year's campaign, who was to ride for him, and so on."

"What had become of the devoted husband you used to tell us about?"

"Does anything last in this decadent age? There never was a more romantic couple than that sweet creature and my cousin Claude three years ago. Their marriage was a poem, everything about their lives was full of poetry, their house was the most popular in London, their chef quite the best. They were all sweetness and light; the most brilliant example of what youth, and cleverness, and good looks, and unlimited money can do. But the Goodwood before last changed all that. Vera was ennuied and run down—the two things go together, don't you know—and broke her engagement to stay with the Waterburys for the race week. Claude went there without her. You all know the sequel, so why recapitulate? Nothing was ever the same after that."

"Was there an inquest?" asked the host.

"Thank Heaven that wasn't necessary. Her doctor had been seeing her every morning, and knew she might go off at any moment. Heart failure. She was buried in Italy, at a dull little place on the Riviera, in the grave with her first husband and his daughter. Her own wish. She was all poetry to the last, a poet's daughter."

From the tragedy of Mrs. Rutherford's early death, the conversation somehow took a retrospective cast, and people talked of the murder that had happened a long time before. It is curious how long the interest in a murder may survive if the murderer has not been discovered. There always remains something to wonder about. After nearly half a dozen years the Provana murder could still bear discussion. People's pet theories seemed as fresh as ever, and were discussed with as much animation; while those people who had theories which they would die rather than divulge, were the most interesting of all the theorists, for they could be driven to ground with close questioning, as in the familiar game of "clumps," until they made a resolute stand, and refused to say another word upon the subject.

"I dare say it is quite horrid of me to think what I think," said one vivacious lady, "and you would hate me if I were to tell you."

"Give us the chance at any rate. It will be a new sensation for you to be hated."

"One thing at least I may say. It has always been a mystery to me how those two people could bear to live in that house."

"Oh, but you cannot bar a fine house, and your own property, because your husband has been unlucky enough to get himself murdered in it."

Here Chorus, who had sat disapproving and even angry while her friends were discussing the murder, chipped in suddenly.

"You don't know Vera," she said. "Her memory of Provana was an absolute culte, and she loved the house for his sake."

"It's a pity she kept her worship for the husband's memory," said somebody. "For the state of things between her and Rutherford for some years was an open secret. Everybody knew all about it."

"Nobody knew Vera as I knew her. She had no more of common earth in her composition than if she had been a sylph. People might as well talk scandal about Undine."

The men of the world who were present, and the women who knew nearly as much of life, smiled and shrugged their shoulders.

"Well, it is all ancient history," said a bland worldling, with smooth, white hair and a smooth, elderly voice. "The romantic friendship, the murder, the marriage with the romantic friend. Tout lasse, tout casse, tout passe. Nothing can matter to anybody now."

"Nothing except who killed Signor Provana," said the lady who had declared she would sooner die than tell anybody her theory of the murder.

CHAPTER XXXII

Father Cyprian Hammond sat alone in the winter gloaming after a hard day's work in his parish, which was a large one, covering several of those obscure little slums that lie hidden behind handsome streets in north-western London. The table had been cleared after his short and simple dinner, and he was half reclining in his deep arm-chair while Sabatier's "Life of St. Francis of Assisi" lay open on the table under the candles that made only a spot of light in the lofty room. It was one of the books which he opened often on an evening of fatigue and depression. The "Life" or the "Fioretti" were books that rested his brain and soothed his spirits.

He lay back in his chair with his eyes closed, not asleep, but resting, and listening with a kind of sensuous pleasure to the light fall of wood ashes on the hearth. His winter fire of old ship logs was one of the few luxuries he allowed himself.

"I told you I would see no one to-night," he said, as his servant came into the room.

"It is Mr. Rutherford, Father, only just back from Italy. He said he was sure you would see him."

"Very good, I will see Mr. Rutherford. You can light the lamp. Come in, Claude," he called to the figure standing outside the door.

Claude came into the room, while the servant lighted a standard lamp of considerable power, that shone full upon a face from which all natural carnation had changed to an ashen greyness, the face of a man in the last stage of a bad illness.

"You look dead-beat," said the priest, as they clasped hands. "You have been travelling night and day, I suppose."

"I came straight from her grave, from their grave. She lies in the cemetery at San Marco, beside her husband and his daughter, the girl who loved her, and whose love brought those two together."

"It was her wish, I conclude."

"There was a letter found—a letter written half a year ago, at the beginning of her illness, in which she begged that I would lay her there—in his grave—nowhere else. It was he that she loved best, always, always. Her real, her only perfect love was for him."

"May that absolve her of her sins. I would have done much, striven long and late to bring her into the fold, if she would have let me, but she would not. Well, she shall not want for an intercessor while I live and pray."

And then, looking up at his visitor, who stood before him, a tragical figure in the bright, hard light of the lamp, his face haggard and wan against the rich darkness of his sable collar:

"Sit down, Claude," he said gently, in a tone of ineffable compassion, the voice that day by day had spoken to sorrow and to sin. "I see you have come to tell me your troubles. Take off that heavy coat and draw your chair to the fire, and open your heart to me, unless indeed you will come to my confessional to-morrow and let me hear you there. I would much rather you did that."

"Selon les règles. No! Be kind, Father, and let me talk to you here. I will keep nothing back this time. There shall be no more secrets—no surprises. I have come to the end of my book. She is dead, and I have nothing left to care about—nothing left to hide. There is not a joy this world can offer to man for which I would hold up a finger now she is gone."

"What do you want me to do for you?"

"What you did for me six years ago. Open the gate of a refuge where a sinner may hide the remnant of a worthless life, where I may spend the last dregs in the cup, drop by drop, where I may die day by day, on my knees, in penitential prayer."

"I opened that gate. You were safe in such a refuge; and you broke out again and came back to the world, twenty times worse than you were before. The life you have been leading since you married Provana's widow is about the most worthless, the most abject life that a reasonable being could lead, the life of empty pleasure, of sensuality and self-indulgence, a life that debases the man himself, and corrupts and ruins his associates."

"I had to forget. If all that the world calls pleasure could have been distilled into one little drug that would have blotted out remembrance, I should have wanted no more race-horses, no more racing yachts, no more flying-machines, no more cards or dice, only that one little drug. Father, when I stood before you six years ago in this room, a miserable wretch, I had to keep my secret for her sake. I have nothing to hide now. It was I who killed Mario Provana."

"I knew."

"You knew?"

"Yes, I knew that night as much as I know now. I knew the guilt you wanted to hide in a cloister. I knew your sin and your remorse; but I doubted your perseverance; a doubt that was too speedily justified by the event."

"It was the fatal course my mother took. She brought Vera to the place where I thought that I and my sin were buried. I did not yield without a struggle; in long days of depression, in long nights of fever, I wrestled with Satan for my soul. I called upon my manhood, my honour, my will-power, and I even thought that I had conquered; and then, in an instant, my passionate heart gave way, and I walked out of that house of rest, a fallen spirit. But, oh, the rapture of the moment when I held her in my arms, and told her that I renounced all—the hope of heaven, the certainty of peace—for her love."

"Oh, the pity of it, my unhappy Claude!"

"You ask me no questions, Father?"

"To what end? You are not in the confessional. There may be details that would in some degree mitigate your guilt; but murder is a heinous sin, and I fear in your case it had been led up to by guilt almost as dark, the spoiling of a pure woman's soul. If the murder was not deliberate you cannot urge the same excuse for the sin of seduction, that sin which includes every abomination—hypocrisy, the falsehood that betrays a trusting fellow-creature, the calculating cruelty that sets a man's strength of will against a woman's yielding love."

"No, no, no. Father, have you forgotten those two lost souls Dante saw, driven through the malignant air; they who had stained the earth with blood? Sorrow and sin had been theirs; but Francesca's lover was not a deliberate seducer, and even in that world of pain the love that linked those two who never could be parted more was no base or selfish passion. No man ever fought a harder battle than I fought for her sake. I loved her when we were boy and girl together, when she was a child, a lovely, innocent child, who gave me her heart in that happy morning of life, who had been shut out from all the affection that makes childhood beautiful, the caresses, the praise of an adoring mother, the love of father, brothers, sisters. She had known nothing better than the tepid kindness of a peevish old woman, and she gave her heart to me in the first joyous days of her life, I taught her what youth and happiness meant; and that spring-time of our lives was never forgotten. Vera was the romance of my boyhood. I carried her image in my heart for all the years in which we were strangers; and when Fate brought us together again our hearts went out to each other, as if the years had never parted us, as if she had been still as unconscious of passion as the child who clambered on my knee and flung her arms round my neck on the rocks at Disbrowe."

"But with a certain difference," said the priest. "She was Mario Provana's wife."

"I did not forget that. I told myself that I need never forget it. She was the centre of a selfish clan, who meant to run her for all she was worth. I knew to what account the Disbrowes would turn a millionaire cousin; and I took upon myself to stand between her and a herd of cold-hearted relations, who only valued her as a counter in the social game. Except Susan Amphlett, who is a fool, and Lady Okehampton, who is not much wiser, there was not one of the crew that had a spark of real regard for her."

"And you thought your affection was pure enough to save her from all the pitfalls of Society."

"I thought that I was strong enough to take a brother's place. I had lived my life; I had been a failure. I had sinned, and paid forfeit for my sin. I thought I had done with passionate feeling; and that I could trust myself as fully as Vera trusted me, in her absolute unconsciousness of danger. I was deceived. The fire still burned in the grey ashes of a wasted life, and the time came when it burst into flame and consumed us."

"You were with her that night when Provana came home unexpectedly?"

"I was with her. No matter how that came about. The die had been cast weeks before, when she and I were at the Okehamptons' river villa. We were alone there as if we had been in a wood, and our secret was told and our promise was exchanged. Nothing was to matter any more in our lives except our love. We were to go to the other side of the world and cruise about in the South Seas till we found an island, as Stevenson did, a paradise of love and peace, to end our days in. The yacht was waiting for us at Plymouth, manned and found for an ocean voyage—almost as fine a vessel as the Gloriana. We were to start by an early train that morning. I wrung a promise from her at Lady Fulham's ball; and we met a few hours earlier than we had intended."

"And he found you together, and you killed him?"

"It was her life or his. We faced each other at the door of his dressing-room. The other door was open and the lights were on. I saw death in his face as he stood for a moment looking into her room, the white, dumb rage that means bloodshed. He gave me only one contemptuous glance as he dashed past me to the desk where his pistol case was ready for him. He had the pistol in his hand and had cocked it in what had seemed an instant, and was on his way to her room while I snatched the second pistol from the case. For me he could bide his time. For her, doom was to be swift. I think I read him right even in those fierce moments. His fury was measured by the love he had given her. His foot was on the threshold when I fired. I could hear her stifled sobs as she lay on the floor, where she had fallen at the sound of his footsteps on the landing, half unconscious, in her agony of shame. She told me afterwards that strange lights were in her eyes, a roar of waters in her ears. She was lying in a world of red light."

"Well, what do you want of me now?"

"Open the door of my cell, the Benedictines, the Carthusians, La Trappe—in France or Spain, any order where the rule is iron, and where my days will be short. I have lived the sinner's life, and it has not brought me happiness. Let me live the saint's life, and see if it can bring me peace. I am not a much blacker sinner than some of the fathers of your Church who wear the aureole. Let the rest of my life be one long act of expiation, one dark night of penitential prayer."

"My dear Claude, my son, all shall be done for you. The path of peace shall be made smooth; but this time there must be no turning back."

"To what should I come back? The light of my life has gone out."

EPILOGUE

A month later, when Christmas was over, and the people who had done with their guns, and did not mean hunting, were making a little season in London on their way to Egypt or the Riviera, Lady Susan Amphlett as Chorus was in her best form at cosy dinners.

"Now will you believe that Claude Rutherford was a devoted husband, and that he broke his heart when his wife died?" she asked triumphantly.

"I believe that he was nearly as much of a crank as his pretty wife. She was a disciple of Francis Symeon, and he was under Father Hammond's thumb. The dark room in the Albany, or a cell in La Trappe! There's not much difference."

"From a racing stable to a cloister is a bit of a leap in the dark."

"Claude was always a bold rider. I've seen him skylarking over a hedge, on his way home, without knowing where he was to land."

"I think he is rather lucky to land in a cloister," said the lady who had refused to tell people her theory of the Provana murder. "But I wonder what they think of it all in Scotland Yard!"

Mary Elizabeth Braddon – A Concise Bibliography

The Trail of the Serpent (first published as Three Times Dead, 1860)
Garibaldi & Other Poems (1861)
The Octoroon or The Lily of Louisiana (1861)
The Black Band (1861)
Lady Audley's Secret (1862)
Ralph the Bailiff and Other Tales (1862)
Woman's Revenge or, The Captain of the Guard (1862)
The Lady Lisle (1862)
John Marchmont's Legacy (1862–63)
The White Phantom (1862-63)
The Captain of the Vulture (1863)
Aurora Floyd (1863)
The Factory Girl or, All Is not Gold That Glitters (1863)
Eleanor's Victory (1863)
Henry Dunbar: the story of an outcast (1864)
The Doctor's Wife (1864)
The Banker's Secret (1864-65 Later reprinted as Rupert Godwin)
Sir Jasper's Tenant (1865)
Only a Clod (1865)
The Lady's Mile (1866)
Daviola (1866-67)
Birds of Prey (1867)
Circe, (1867) (as Babington White)
Rupert Godwin (1867)
Run to Earth (1868)
Dead-Sea Fruit (1868)
Charlotte's Inheritance (1868)
Fenton's Quest (1871)
The Lovers of Arden (1871-72)
To the Bitter End (1872)
Robert Ainsleigh (1872)
Strangers and Pilgrims (1872-73)
Lucius Davoren; or, Publicans and Sinners (1873)
Milly Darrell, and Other Tales (1873)
Lost For Love (1874)
Taken at the Flood (1874)
A Strange World (1875)
Hostages to Fortune (1875)
Joshua Haggard's Daughter (1876)
Weavers and Weft, or, In Love's Nest (1876)
Dead Men's Shoes (1876)

An Open Verdict (1878)
The Cloven Foot (1879)
Her Splendid Misery (1879-80)
Vixen (1879)
Just as I am (1880)
Aladdin and Other Stories (1880)
Asphodel (1881)
Le Pasteur de Marston (1881)
Mount Royal (1882)
Phantom Fortune (1883)
The Golden Calf (1883)
Ishmael (1884)
Flower and Weed and Other Tales (1884)
Wyllard's Weird (1885)
Mohawks (1886)
One Thing Needful (1886)
Under the Red Flag and Other Tales (1886)
The Good Hermione: A Story for the Jubilee Year (1886, as Aunt Belinda)
Cut by the County (1887)
Like and Unlike (1887)
The Fatal Three (1888)
The Day Will Come (1889)
One Life, One Love (1890)
Whose Was the hand (1890)
The World, the Flesh and the Devil (1891)
The Venetians (1892)
All Along the River (1893)
The Christmas Hirelings (1894)
Thou Art The Man (1894)
Sons of Fire (1895)
London Pride; or, When the World was Younger (1896)
The Little Aunty (1896)
Rough Justice (1898)
In High Places (1898)
His Darling Sin (1899)
The Infidel (1900)
A Lost Eden (1904)
The Rose of Life (1905)
Alias Jane Brown (1906)
The White House (1906)
Her Convict (1907)
Dead Love Has Chains (1907)
During Her Majesty's Pleasure (1908)
Our Adversary (1909)
Beyond These Voices (1910)
The Green Curtain (1911)
Miranda (1913)
Mary (1916)

Plays

Loves of Arcadia (Comedietta), unpublished, 1860
The Model Husband, unpublished, (performed in 1868)
Griselda, unpublished, 1873
The Missing Witness, London: Maxwell, 1880 (performed in 1874)
Marjorie Daw, unpublished, 1881
Married Beneath Him, unpublished, 1882
The Dross; or, the Root of All Evil, unpublished, 1882
For Better or Worse, 1890
A Life Interest, unpublished, 1893

Single Short Stories published in Periodicals

Captain Thomas (Welcome Guest, 1st September 1860)
The Cold Embrace (Welcome Guest, 29th September 1860)
My Daughters (Welcome Guest, 20th October 1860)
My First Happy Christmas (Welcome Guest, 22nd January 1861)
Samuel Lowgood's Revenge (Welcome Guest, 23rd February 1861)
The Lawyer's Secret (Welcome Guest, 2, 9, 16th March 1861)
Ralph, the Bailiff (St. James's Magazine, April-June 1861)
The Mystery of Fernwood (Temple Bar, November-December 1861)
Lost and Found (London Journal, 12 September 1863-26 March 1864)
At Daggers Drawn (Belgravia, January 1867)
Eveline's Visitant: A Ghost Story (Belgravia, January 1867)
How I Heard My Own Will Read (Belgravia, February 1867)
Found in the Muniment Chest (Belgravia Christmas Annual, December 1867)
Dorothy's Rival (Belgravia Christmas Annual, December 1867)
A Great Ball and a Great Bear (Belgravia, January 1868)
The Mudie Classics, No 1. Sir Alk Meyonn, or the Seven against the Elector (Belgravia, March-April 1868)
Christmas in Possession (Belgravia Christmas Annual, December 1868)
My Wife's Promise (Belgravia Christmas Annual, December 1868)
The True Story of Don Juan (Belgravia Christmas Annual, December 1868)
My Unlucky Friend (Belgravia, November 1869)
A Very Narrow Escape (Belgravia, December 1869)
Sir Philip's Wooing (Belgravia Christmas Annual, December 1869)
The Scene Painter's Wife (Belgravia Christmas Annual, December 1869)
Levinson's Victim (Belgravia, January 1870)
Mr. And Mrs. De Fontenoy (Belgravia, February 1870)
The Splendid Stranger (Belgravia, March 1870)
On the Brink (Belgravia, September 1870)
The Sins of the Fathers (Belgravia, October 1870)
John Granger: A Ghost Story (Belgravia Christmas Annual, December 1870)
Too Bright to Last (Belgravia Christmas Annual, December 1870)
The Zoophyte's Revenge (The Summer Tourist, August 1871)
At Chrighton Abbey (Belgravia, May 1871)

Hugh Damer's Last Ledger (The Illustrated Newspaper, 17th June-1st July 1871)
In Great Waters (Belgravia, August 1871)
Old Rutherford Hall (Belgravia Christmas Annual, December 1871)
The Dreaded Guest (Belgravia Christmas Annual, December 1871)
Colonel Benyon's Entanglement (Belgravia, July-August 1872)
Three Times (Belgravia Christmas Annual, December 1872)
A Good Hater (Belgravia Christmas Annual, December 1872)
Prince Ramji Rowdedow (Belgravia Christmas Annual, December 1873)
Sir Hanbury's Bequest (Belgravia Christmas Annual, December 1874)
Sir Luke's Return (Belgravia Christmas Annual, December 1875)
Sebastian (Belgravia Holiday No, July 1876)
Weavers and Weft (Boston Weekly Journal and District News, 26 August-9 December 1876)
Her Last Appearance (Belgravia Christmas Annual, December 1876)
The Clown's Quest (Harper's Bazaar, 29 December 1877-5 January 1878)
Dr. Carrick (All the Year Round, 29th June 1878)
George Caulfield's Journey (Mistletoe Bough, 1879)
The Shadow in the Corner (All the Year Round, 22 November 1879)
If She Be Not Fair to Me (Mistletoe Bough, 1880)
His Secret (Mistletoe Bough, 1881)
Flower and Weed (Mistletoe Bough, 1882)
Under the Red Flag (Mistletoe Bough, 5 November 1883)
Thou Art the Man (Flower and Weed & Other Tales, 1884)
Across the Footlights (Mistletoe Bough, 1884)
The Little Woman in Black (Mistletoe Bough, 1885)
Stapylton's Plot (Mistletoe Bough, 1887)
It is Easier for a Camel (Mistletoe Bough, 1888)
One Fatal Moment (Mistletoe Bough, 1889)
My Dream (Mistletoe Bough, 1889)
"If There Be Any of You" (Mistletoe Bough, 1889)
His Oldest Friends (Mistletoe Bough, 1890)
The Ghost's Name (Mistletoe Bough, 1891)
The Island of Old Faces (Mistletoe Bough, 1892)
All Along to River (Manchester Times, 20 January-2 June 1893
Does Anything Matter (untraced, in her dairy as written 7th February 1893)
A Modern Confessor (Pall Mall Magazine, June 1893)
The Dulminster Dynamiter (Pall Mall Magazine, August 1893)
Drifting (To-Day A Weekly Magazine-Journal, 23 December 1893)
The Higher Life (Tales for the Homes, 1907 but written in 1894)
Sweet Simplicity (To-Day A Weekly Magazine-Journal, 24 March 1894)
His Good Fairy (The Illustrated London News, Summer Number, 28th May 1894)
Herself (Sheffield Weekly Telegraph Christmas No, 1894)
Where Many Footsteps Pass(Christmas No of the Lady's Pictorial, 5th December 1896)
The Honourable Jack (1895 untraced)
The Good Lady Ducayne (Strand Magazine, February 1896)
Poor Uncle Jacob (Bolton Journal and Guardian, 25th April 1896)
Wild Justice (Bolton Journal and Guardian, 8th August 1896)
Theodora's Temptation (The Englishwoman, October-November 1896)
The Winning Sequence (Lloyd's Weekly Newspaper, 27th December 1896)

In the Nick of Time (The Christmas Tree, Downey's Annual, December 1898)
As the Heart Knoweth (T.P's Weekly, 24th July 1903)
For His Son's Sake (Cassell's Magazine, December 1905)
The Cock of Bowkers (London Magazine, April-May 1906)

Miscellaneous Writings

London on Four Feet (Welcome Guest, 15th December 1860)
How the Romans Supped (Welcome Guest, 22nd December 1860)
Waking (Brighton Herald, 2nd February 1861)
In Memoriam (Temple Bar, January 1862)
Trontlemouth (Temple Bar, January 1866)
Sweet Violets (Belgravia, April 1867)
May (Belgravia, May 1867)
The Dinner at Richmond (Belgravia, May 1867)
French Novels (Belgravia, June 1867)
Lunch on the Hill (Belgravia, September 1867)
After the Battle (Belgravia, February 1868)
The Hawking Party (Belgravia, March 1868)
Glimpses at Foreign Literature (Belgravia, April 1868)
The Lady of the Land (Belgravia, July 1868)
In the Firelight (Belgravia, January 1869)
Whose Fault Is It? (Belgravia, August 1869)
Violets (Belgravia, April 1870)
Lord Lytton (Belgravia, March 1873)
In Memoriam (Belgravia, June 1873)
Ireland for Tourists: A Reminiscence of a Recent Excursion (Belgravia, July/August 1874)
Macbeth at the Lyceum Theatre (Belgravia, November 1875)
My Heart is Thine: A New Musical Valentine (Belgravia, February 1876)
Dinners at Elementary School (The Time, 30th April 1880)
Boscastle, Cornwall, and English Engladine (World, September 1880)
The Observant Child (World, 28th September 1881)
A Little Hunting (World, 5th October 1881)
The Children at Christmas (World, 21st December 1881)
People Who Write to the Times (Whitehall Review, 24th January 1884)
A Friendly Mount (World, 30th June 1886)
St. Ives (World, 18th August 1886)
The Queen of the West (World, 25th August1886)
Clovelly-Flamouth-Fowey (World, 15th September 1886)
Paramé, St. Malo (World, 22nd September 1886)
In the Olive Grove (World, 21st December 1887)
In Southern Latitudes (World, 22nd February 1888)
An East End Andromeda (World, 19th September 1888)
Jonnie (Punch, 29th November 1890)
Le Pètrolium; ou les Saloperies Parisiennes (Punch, 28th February 1891)
From Forest Depths (World, 9th March 1892)
Strawberries: A Lament (World, 10th August 1892)

On Cranbourne Chase (World, 21st September 1892)
Switzerland in Eight Hours (World, 28th September 1892)
A Lost Pleid (World, 23rd November 1892)
A Modern Confessor (Pall Mall Magazine, June 1893)
My First Novel (The Idler, June 1893)
Furniture in Fiction (Sala's Journal, 15th July 1893)
Herman Sudermann (National Review, 21st August 1893)
Time Was (World, 18th July 1894)
Holiday Island (World, 22nd August 1894)
In the Days of My Youth (The Theatre, September 1894)
In a Van in Wharfedale (World, 5th September 1894)
A Voice from Marienbad (World, 19th September 1894)
Honeymoon Land (World, 3rd October 1894)
Ã Mon Maître (World, 17th November 1894)
The German Play of the Hour (Theatre, 1895)
Cornubia (World, 5th June 1895)
Where Many Footsteps Pass (Lady's Pictorial, 5th December 1896)
Homburg Versus Marienbad (World, 22nd September 1897)
Pallanza (World, 29th September 1897)
Zinal (Valais) (World, 24th August 1898)
Saas Fee (Valais) (World, 31st August 1898)
North Cornwall (World, 31st August 1898)
Zermatt (World, 7th September 1898)
Cadanabbia, Lago Do Como (World, 14th September 1898)
Beaulieu (World, 28th December 1898)
Fifty Years at the Lyceum Theatre (Strand Magazine, January 1903)
I Remember, I Remember (Daily Mail, December 1903)
Little Books (Black and White, 7th January 1905)
My Best Story and Why I Think So (Grand Magazine, July 1905)
The Shrine of Jane Eyre (Pall Mall Magazine, February 1906)
The Life Beautiful (Chambers Journal, 10th November 1906)
The Woman I Remember (Press Album, 1909)
The Smart Sets in History (Strand Magazine, 11th October 1910)

www.ingramcontent.com/pod-product-compliance
Lightning Source LLC
Chambersburg PA
CBHW020112180626
46812CB00006B/2562